To Sylvia

A

NEW YEAR

FOR

EVE

Best wishes for your 80th
Birthday

DAWN BRAMWELL

Lots of love from
Dawn x.

ISBN: 978-1-326-82720-5

PublishNation
www.publishnation.co.uk

For Tony, Maggie and Guy,
my own wonderfully dysfunctional family.
You are amazing.

With thanks to my equally amazing friends,
without whom these last few years
would have been so much darker.

Finally, to my own Sam. Parting with you was
one of the hardest things I have ever done.
And I still miss you.

CHAPTER ONE

I slipped and fell into the pond.

Not the most drastic of occurrences. It could quite easily happen. Kneel just a little too close to the edge whilst weeding. Slip on a mossy paving stone. Or stumble drunkenly in haste and simply topple in. But whatever the circumstances, surely it must be preferable to take such a tumble maintaining at least the dignity of being dressed.

Don't get me wrong. I love my son and enjoy his company. I like his best friend Tim. Usually, I would greet them with a smile and ask them if they would like something to eat or drink, motherly instincts kicking in hard. I doubt any mother though, would like to present herself to her eighteen year old son and friend, whilst totally naked and thoroughly pissed. Hence the mad dash around the bushes. Ergo the disastrous splash!

"Aagh!" I couldn't stop the exclamation from bursting forth. Icy water and slimy pondweed is not pleasant. Neither is hitting your bottom on an ornamental rock. "Fuck that hurt!" I clamped my mouth shut, too late.

"What the hell was that?"

A gap appeared in the bushes and Tim poked his head through. He was the same age as my son, with a mop of dark curly hair, coal black eyes and gleaming white teeth which were displayed to perfection as he grinned broadly at me. I ducked down as far as I could under the murky water, clutching at my discarded clothes floating on the surface.

"Jake, you've got a pond nymph in your garden."

My son came round the other side of the bushes and nearly tumbled into the pond with me.

"Mum, what the bloody hell are you doing?"

1

"New Year's resolution," I said, with my teeth chattering fiercely. "I'm going green. I mean, why use all that electricity in the washing machine when I've got a perfectly good pond right here." I scooped up my clothes, which were now completely ruined with weed and slime and covering myself as much as I could with the soggy pile, I stood up. I stepped out of the pond, having to walk past Tim, whose grin was bigger than ever.

"I think you dropped these," he said with a wink.

"Thank you so much." I tried to be gracious as I retrieved my pink knickers which were dangling from his hand. What else could I do? I walked with as much dignity as I could muster up the garden path hoping that my naked bottom did not wobble too much.

"Happy New Year, Mrs A." Tim called after me.

"Happy New Year," I shouted back over my shoulder. Then unable to stop the habit of a lifetime, I added, "There's bacon in the fridge if you're hungry."

I was nearly at the back door when I heard Tim asking my son, "She do that often?"

Jake's reply was an explosive, "No!"

My hand on the back door, I then heard Tim say in a carrying voice, "She's got a great arse, your Mum."

My cheeks were already pink. Now they glowed with a touch of guilty pleasure. I had a stupid smile on my face as I fell drunkenly into my bed.

Despite having polished off half a bottle of ten year old Ardmore, I awoke with no hangover. Which was a real pity as it meant I had no way of blurring the edges around the reality that the first day in January brought with it. I quite envied those poor souls who would need at least until lunchtime to recover from the type of drinking session I had indulged in last night. They would have the perfect excuse to stay cocooned within their duvets as they slowly recovered from their excesses.

I on the other hand was wide awake and alert. I could recall perfectly the moments in which my twenty two year old marriage disintegrated before my eyes. I could picture as clearly as though he was standing in front of me, Andy's handsome face, ruffled dark brown hair, grey in places and summer sky blue eyes.

I could smell his aftershave, the favourite one I had bought him for Christmas, mingling with his own particular male scent. That lovely blend of man and fragrance that was unique to him. A scent that lingers on the pillows, making me hug them when he's not there. A scent that made me cry like a baby last night.

I could feel the tremors in his body, still lean and in good shape as he approaches fifty. My hands felt the coldness of his skin as though he was suffering from some kind of shock. He was. It just hadn't related to me yet. My lips tasted the salt of his tears that trailed down his face as he began to weep even before his mouth opened.

My ears tried to ignore the words he was telling me. Hours later I could hear perfectly well.

"It isn't that I don't love you anymore. I'll always love you. You've been the biggest part of my life. You're the mother of my children. Hell, Eve, how could I not love you? You're all any man could want?"

"But why then? I don't understand."

"I love someone else as well."

"More than me?"

"Differently."

"Is she younger than me, is that it?"

"No. In fact he's older than you. He's forty six."

"He? He? Andy, what the hell are you trying to tell me?"

That was he was gay of course. Always had been. Had known since he was a teenager. Tried to hide it. Suppress it. Fell in love with me, genuinely, and thought that with a normal life he would not have to battle with that other side of him. And then along came Jason and 'kerboom!'

I had cried. Yelled like a banshee out of control. Thrown a few pots and pans around the kitchen, too distraught to even care whether Megan and Jake were in the house or not. They weren't as it happened they were both out celebrating the New Year, Megan with her boyfriend Mark, and Jake with his best mate Tim.

In the end Andy had quietly packed an overnight bag and walked out, saying that he would leave me in peace for a little while.

My life as I knew it had just been royally pissed on and I was supposed to find some peace! I found instead, the bottle of Ardmore. By the time I had drunk half the contents I thought it would be a jolly good idea to strip off in my garden on the stroke of midnight. I sang and danced like a demented fairy under the light of the full moon. Until I heard Jake and Tim approaching the garden from the fields that were sandwiched between our house and the village a couple of miles away.

I don't embarrass easily. I am quite shameless at times. But there is a difference between causing yourself embarrassment and inflicting it upon your offspring. Any mother worth their salt would not willingly embarrass their son in front of his friend and that is exactly what I had done. Jake, my easy going, quick to smile, adorably huggable son, would have been mortified to find me off my head and cavorting naked with the garden gnomes.

It was going to take some explaining and I was just thankful that it had not been his elder sister Megan and her boyfriend who had discovered my lapse from respectability. Two years older than Jake, my daughter was frighteningly in control of her life. How had I possibly produced such an amazing person? And then I only had to look at her and see Andy reflected in her stunning good looks to know that she was all ours.

Back to Andy. Another spasm of pain and revulsion that had me sitting bolt upright, wondering if I was going to throw up. No. It was merely my stomach twisting itself into knots at the thought of my husband in bed with another man. For a second I flopped back onto the pillows, pulling the duvet over my head. Despair was ready to claim an overwhelming defeat.

"Come on girl, snap out of it!" This wasn't like me. I didn't do self-pity. I did stand and fight. Only this time I wasn't sure what weapons were at my disposal, if any. Throwing off the duvet, I got out of bed determined to repair the damage of trauma and too much alcohol. Not easy, when you're the wrong side of forty.

Thirty minutes later, I checked out my reflection in the mirror, hating what I saw. A tired old woman with empty eyes stared back at me. Where was the Eve that used to laugh and sing, and dance with such joy? Where was the girl who had a sparkle in her eyes and a dimple in her cheeks? It was another hammer blow to the heart when I sadly acknowledged what I had been ignoring for far too long. That girl had disappeared years ago.

I didn't like her replacement but for now I was stuck with her. I squirted some perfume liberally, as if that would magically transform me. It didn't. Tossing the bottle angrily back onto my dressing table, my eyes focused on the pile of clothes, still abandoned in a smelly heap.

"Oh hell!" I only then realised that in ditching my clothes into the pond, I had ruined the slinky new dress and shoes I had bought, solely with the intention of seducing Andy. It had been Megan's idea. I think she had suspected for a little while that things were not exactly as they should have been between her father and me. Oh we were friendly. Best of friends in fact. But no romance. No passion. No sex.

My daughter had taken me aside one day and warned me that I might need to spice things up a little. After all I didn't want Dad catching the eye of some younger woman did I? Ouch! That thought had hurt at the time. As I scooped up the remnants of my outfit and tossed them into the bin, along with the shattered fragments of my life, I winced with a pain that was almost physical.

I slammed the lid down with some force and then caught sight of one of the gnomes, peeking out from his hiding place in the bushes. It was smiling at me. More than usual that is, as my gnomes are always smiling.

I shook my head and rubbed my eyes. Maybe I was a little insane? Maybe last night had all been a weird hallucination. We had eaten wild mushrooms after all. What if they had been a little bit too wild? What if I had imagined the conversation with Andy? What if there had been magic in the moonlight that had made me behave so outlandishly?

Anything was better than facing the alternative.

That my husband was a cheating, gay, bastard, and I had humiliated myself in front of my son and his friend! I looked out of the window down to the bottom of the garden, to the cluster of bushes that hid both gnomes and pond. Had I really tossed my inhibitions along with my clothes into the moonlight? A snort of random laughter caught me by surprise. I really must be insane, if I could find it funny.

But you know what? I did. I shouldn't do. But I did.

With a glimmer of rebellion in the dark recesses of my soul, I took my cup of tea into the conservatory that was attached to the kitchen. It overlooked the garden and even now, on the first of January, it was bright and warm, absorbing all of the winter sun. I snuggled up on one of the sofas and tucked my feet underneath me, as I began to sip my tea and willed my mind to still.

It wouldn't.

From being a quiet and relatively content place, my mind had become a different country entirely. In response to my mood, my ten year old dog, Skip, jumped up next to me and pushed his cold wet nose into my hands. I stroked him, grateful for his unquestioning love and loyalty.

My phone beeped. Dozens of messages. Happy New Year and all that jazz.

"Sod off, sod off, sod off," I muttered to the senders, as one by one I deleted most of them. A couple were from Sally and Jenny, two of my closest friends, but I realised morosely that the rest were from the group of joint acquaintances that I had with Andy. I wondered if any of them knew his little secret. My mood worsened at this point and I threw the phone across the room.

Jake came in and caught me doing it. He walked slowly across the conservatory and picked it up, regarding me with a look I had never seen before in his eyes.

"Hi. Sorry about last night." I took the phone off him and placed it carefully back onto the table.

"Are you alright?" Jake sat down beside me, not in his usual carefree manner, openly ready to hug me, but with caution and a distance I hated.

"I'm fine," I lied, brightly.

He continued to look at me oddly.

"I really am sorry," I repeated.

"Just don't make a habit of it okay, Mum?" There was a question I couldn't answer in his voice.

"Promise." I diverted him then asking him how his latest song was going. Jake was an accomplished guitarist and together with Mark and Tim had a group going. Only three members but like The Jam and The Police, it really worked. I hoped one day they would have the same success. His talent for music came from me and it was partly why we had such a strong bond.

I watched as he relaxed into the conversation telling me that Megan had arranged with the landlord of the Maypoleton Arms for them to play a gig on a Friday night and, if it went well, to do a regular slot once a month. We were just settling back into our normal comfort zone, when I heard Andy's voice calling through from the kitchen.

"Where is everyone?"

Jake bounced up from the sofa, an eager puppy, ready to greet his pack leader. "Happy New Year, Dad. Where have you been?"

At once the nausea returned. Sheer force of will pushed it down. I composed an appropriate smile on my face and followed my son into the kitchen. My heart broke once more as I looked at father and son together. Both were tall, slim, with warm brown hair and blue eyes. I gritted my teeth painfully as I listened to their banter.

"I've just been playing a few rounds of golf now that the ground has thawed. I've missed quite a few matches recently."

"It's just not cool, Dad, all those gay sweaters and stupid trousers."

"Well it keeps me fit at least." Andy's eyes met mine as Jake turned away to root inside a cupboard for biscuits.

"You should come and play rugby with me and the lads some time, much more macho."

Oh that was sweet, I thought, as Andy's hand stilled in the act of filling the kettle. Bitter sweet it had to be said.

My errant husband said nothing until Jake had sauntered out of the room with a packet of biscuits in his hand.

"Brew?"

"I've just had one." Was that really my voice? Did I actually sound normal? The sky outside was rapidly heralding the end of the first day of the year and with it my marriage. How was it possible that I could be in the same room with him after what he had told me last night? How in God's name, could I even consider throwing myself into his arms, at the same time that I wanted to brain him with a frying pan? And how, for fuck's sake, could he possibly be standing there whistling as he made a cup of coffee.

Whistling!

Surely, a judge would accept a plea of temporary insanity if I killed him right now?

"Where's Meg?"

"Don't know. Out with Mark I suppose, visiting his family." Mark lived just ten minutes away but had jumped at the chance of moving in with us once his divorced mother had installed a new step-dad.

"Shall I light a fire in the lounge?" Andy asked softly, stirring the coffee.

I couldn't answer him. I was too dazed by his casual manner to do anything other than follow the habit of a lifetime and nod at his suggestion.

In the lounge I watched dumbly as Andy began to stack the logs in the fireplace. I knew this was the best part of the day for him. He took great satisfaction in coming home here, to his creation. Originally built in the eighteenth century, Cooper's Barn was one of half a dozen houses converted from farm buildings to executive homes. The whole project had been Andy's baby. Buying the plot of land ten years ago had been a smart move. When the time came to branch out on his own from the firm of architects he worked for, and move into property developing, he had been successful.

I knew we were lucky.

I had always known that.

That was why on so many lonely evenings, I had not nagged him for being late home from work, for never wanting to spend time with me. For being too tired for sex.

Naive bloody fool!

My eyes fell upon a log of wood. He was kneeling just in front of me, his head slightly bowed as he blew on the fire. My anger was urging me to pick up the log and wallop him hard with it, to crush the betrayal from him. To beat the deceit out of the man I had loved for over twenty years. I swear my fingers actually moved as though they were curling around the log.

Then he turned and smiled at me. The same blue eyes as Jake's only crinkled with laughter lines. The anger morphed cruelly into anguish. How could he not love me anymore?

He always could read my mind.

"I do still love you, you know." He reached out towards me and pulled me down onto the rug. I hated myself, even as I clung to him. I should be yelling and screaming at him.

Instead, what did I do?

I held him close as I wept and cursed myself for being such a coward.

CHAPTER TWO

After humiliating myself by sobbing into my husband's chest, I then had to listen to him explaining that, although he had felt incapable of keeping his alternative life a secret from me anymore, he saw no real reason for anything to actually change.

I am not the most intelligent female on the planet. However, even I was struggling with this concept. Okay, so the man is gay. He's shagging a bloke for Christ's sake. But he doesn't want to move out.

Because he still loves me.

At this point, fully aware that my eyes would be puffy and pink, and that my forty two year old complexion would be blotchy and creased, I could only stare at him in befuddled wonder.

And how unfair was it, I thought, that he should look so unfazed by it all? Actually that wasn't quite true. I could see the strain in his eyes, the slight twitch at the corner of his mouth. But other than that, he looked okay. He did not resemble someone who has just been run over by an emotional truck!

Not fair at all, I thought, with a shot of anger heating my blood.

"You haven't told anyone have you?" There was a note of urgency in his voice that dragged me out of my dazed state.

"Of course I haven't told anyone. I mean it's hardly the sort of thing you send round in a New Year's Day text is it? Happy New Year and guess what, my husband's been shagging a bloke all this time, aren't I thick for not noticing!"

He winced. Good! And then shot a hasty look at the lounge door. "Shh. That's not what I meant."

I understood. "No of course I haven't told the kids!" I couldn't bear his nearness then and I pushed away from him. I looked out onto the garden, cleverly lit by the lights that Andy had had installed. The glass was cool as I laid my aching head against it. What a mess. Jake and Megan were no idiots. They would know something was up, with or without my midnight splash! We had held on tight to family bonds throughout their growing up. Were those ties now about to be broken? I couldn't bear that.

Andy had come to stand behind me. His hands began to work in a familiar pattern on my shoulders, easing the painful knots of tension. I refused to let my body betray me, and fought against the longing to lean back against him, tensing my shoulders some more.

"How are we going to tell them?" It never crossed my mind that I should leave him to do this. They were my children. I had sheltered and protected them all their lives and I was not going to leave that task to Andy now. I didn't trust him not to make a hash of it.

"We aren't," he said quietly into my hair.

"Well they can't hear it from anyone else," I replied sharply. Living on the fringe of a large village, I knew very well how quickly gossip could travel. My head pounded harder at what the locals would say. Not that I cared. I didn't give a damn. But I cringed at what Megan and Jake would have to go through.

"We don't have to tell anyone."

About now, I remembered that I did actually have a temper. A devil of one. I guess that a lot of mothers do, and over years of practice, manage to control and damp down the fires inside them. I had been the peace keeper in my family for twenty years, determined that my children would grow up in a different environment to the one I had known. No cross words. No shouting matches. No violence. No hidden threats.

The stopper that held all that in, like a reluctant genie in a bottle, began to wobble, to clink against the sides of the glass.

"What do you mean we don't have to tell anyone?" I had never understood the term 'sheepish' before. Yet now, as Andy gazed at me with the most woolly headed of looks, I understood what it meant. "You aren't suggesting we keep this a secret are you? Carry on as if nothing has happened?"

Really, he would be baa-ing next. "Oh my God you are!" I hit him then. Well, not so much hit him, as slammed my hands palm down against his chest to shove him away from me. Hell I was mad. I stomped around the room looking for something I could throw at him without alerting Jake that we were rowing. There were plenty of cushions. Not very satisfying, I would far rather have hurled the heavy stone candle holders at his head, but it was better than nothing.

"Eve, calm down," he said, swatting the cushions away as if we were playing a new kind of game.

I reached for one of the candle holders then. "Don't, just don't tell me to calm down. I am calm, in case you haven't noticed." My teeth were gritted together in a savage grimace. "Have I thrown your suitcases out onto the lawn? Have I cut up your suits? Have I smashed the photo frames with you in them? Have I slashed your tires? Have I been anything other than calm?"

I could see the cogs working in his brain.

"I'm sorry, Eve." He ran his fingers through his thick brown hair, making it stick up in tufts, just the way Jake did. "I really am sorry. I never meant to hurt you, you know."

The trouble was I did know this. It would be so much easier for me if he was a bastard. But he wasn't. Apart from the agonising betrayal, he was one of the most decent blokes I have ever met. He remembered my birthday, and anniversaries. He bought me flowers when I was down, supported me in anything I wanted to do, always told me how much he loved me. And, the big one for me, he was absolutely the best Dad going.

My conflicting emotions defeated me. I dropped the candle holder back onto the table, heedless that it cracked the polished wood, and slumped onto the sofa. It just wasn't in me to make a fuss. Not at this point anyway. I was too numb. My first thought was, how was I going to keep the peace for everyone's sake?

"What do you want to do, Andy?"

And so I listened again, this time with more attention, to my husband explaining that he wanted to keep things the way they were. He loved me. He always would. But not in that way. It was something he could no longer hide from himself, or from me. Since meeting Jason his life would not be complete without him. Ouch. Big bloody ouch!

However, he could not see that having Jason meant that he could not have me as well. Oh really? I'd like Jeremy Kyle's take on that one! We were still good friends, we had this big lovely house to live in, and it wasn't as if I had another woman to be jealous of. Noooooooo!

11

So surely we could at least for the time being, say nothing and keep it a secret?

My finger nails had by this time dug into the palms of my hand so deeply, blood was about to spill. I opened my mouth to blast a missile of sarcasm at my husband, but before I could, voices called through the house.

"Anyone home? Happy New Year!"

I actually laughed then. Not with humour, but grim satisfaction. Andy's face was suddenly contorted with terror. The voice that was getting louder as footsteps drew nearer to the lounge, belonged to his mother.

Perfect!

"Don't worry," I hissed. "I won't say anything."

Watching Andy greet his parents, it struck me that he was exceptionally good at pretending things were absolutely fine. It helped that Sandra and Steven Armstrong were blessed with the remarkable ability to see only what they wanted to see and rarely noticed when things were amiss. I suppose there had been a pattern of this over the years.

They had had no idea that years ago, Andy had suffered a nervous breakdown, due to pressures of work, or that Megan had run away from home as a teenager, or that Jake had got into trouble with the police. Usual domestic grit and grind. All of which had been resolved and all of which had passed unobserved by Sandra and Steven.

It was something that I had often queried. Surely as their grandparents, they a) had a right to know what was really going on in our lives, and b) would be able to help? Andy would always suppress a shudder and reply with a firm no. His parents did not cope well with unpleasantness. Never having known my own parents, I couldn't really comment.

I wondered now, as more logs were thrown onto the fire and Andy went in search of a bottle of wine, what they would say if I told them what he had said to me last night? I really wanted to! Not in a sharing, needing to off load kind of way, in a spiteful, needing to hurt someone kind of way.

You couldn't blame me really. They had never liked me and had hated the thought that their precious son had actually married me.

The main issue was the fact that I had grown up in care, and had no idea who my biological parents were. I could have tainted blood for all they knew.

Andy looked at me, wine glass in hand, and warning light in his eyes.

I shook my head to the wine, and gave him a sickly grimace before excusing myself to make another herbal tea. When I came back into the room, Sandra had a pile of photographs out. I groaned inwardly. Andy's sister, Katy, who was ten years younger than him, had given birth to twins six months ago.

"And this is one of them sitting up together. Isn't it marvellous that they can do that at six months? I'm sure your two were older when they first sat up?" Sandra shoved a photograph under my nose.

I hoped my eyes did not reflect what I was seeing, because instead of my niece and nephew, all I could focus on was an image of Andy's naked body entangled with that of another man. I blinked rapidly and tried to think of something suitable to say. I must have taken too long, as Sandra nudged me sharply.

I scowled and in turn her well made up face frowned. She reached a perfectly manicured hand to her sculpted crop of cleverly dyed copper brown hair, astonishment in her chilly blue eyes.

Steven, who thank God showed marginally less enthusiasm for baby worship, coughed and made an effort to change the subject.

Unfortunately, it went along the lines of, "So you two any plans for this year?"

Even Sandra and Steven, however armour plated they were in their sensitivities, picked up on the immediate frost which settled into the room.

Steven, always as well turned out as his wife, wearing a suit for crying out loud on New Year's Day, raised his glass to Andy.

"Come on son, spit it out. I can see you've got something to tell us."

Andy's face froze but timing was on his side and he was saved from further probing by the arrival of Megan and Mark, back from their rounds of New Year's visits.

My relief at seeing my tall, gorgeous daughter, a female version of her father, stride into the room like a model, was short lived when I saw that Tim was with them. I could feel myself blushing straight away. Not helped by his wicked grin and the fact that as everyone else was saying hello, he winked at me. Actually winked!

"Happy New Year again, Mrs. A."

What I wouldn't have given at that moment for a complexion that never heated up. I smiled weakly at him and hoped that they would not be staying around for too long. No such luck. A few moments later, Jake appeared.

"Alright Tim, I thought you were going to Fee's for tea?"

"I was. But she decided at the last minute that her new boyfriend's children's need to go to the cinema was more urgent." Fee was Tim's rather slutty older sister.

"So we brought him back with us," said my daughter helpfully. "Thought we could have tea before they practise for the gig." Megan liked to think she was the manager of the group and to be honest without her pushing, they would probably never get further than playing at our house.

"Ooh, have you got a concert planned?" Sandra sat forward eagerly her hands smoothing the hem of her well cut tweed skirt.

"Just a gig, Gran," replied Jake somewhat dismissively.

I was too distracted at the way Tim had managed to shift positions, ending up sitting on the sofa next to me, to wonder at Jake's tone. The next twenty minutes or so passed in a peculiar blur. Andy, who must have been relieved to have the spot light turned onto Jake and his music, made sure that the conversation flowed along this vein. And all the time, I had Tim sitting next to me.

Normally not a problem. I liked Tim. He had been Jake's friend since starting college, and after the motley crew my son had hung around with in school, this young man was a welcome change. Not into drugs. Studying A levels like Jake and planning on going into the RAF, unless of course they both made it as rock stars.

As a friend for your son, what was there not to like?

As a young man who had seen you naked and commented on what a fine backside you had, it was impossible to think of him in such an easy way. Not helped, I have to add, by his physical assets. He was about six feet tall, with dark hair and eyes, and biceps that were always on display from the short sleeves of his tight t-shirts which he wore, even in the depths of winter. His legs, long, and lean, were equally well displayed in ridiculously skin hugging jeans. Nothing left to the imagination.

And right now, as his legs were dangerously close to mine my imagination was shooting off on a very strange planet. I thought my movement was so subtle as to be imperceptible but as my leg shifted, less than a hair's breadth, so did his. I could feel the heat of him coming through the denim to my thighs. It wasn't the only place heat was pooling.

"Eve, love, are you alright?" Sandra's voice cut into my dilemma. "You look awfully flushed."

You don't say! "I'm fine." I said with a stupid stutter which of course brought everyone's eyes towards me. Megan, with her piercing directness didn't help matters.

"Are you sure you're okay, Mum? You do look a little odd."

I didn't dare look at Tim, but I noticed how my son was sending a visual warning in his direction. Tim appeared immune to the eyeballed threats. The next moment I felt his arm snake around my shoulders, not at all the gesture of gentle comfort it looked on the surface. Not when his fingers brushed against me like that.

"Would you like me to get you a glass of water, Mrs. A?"

Feeling like a rabbit caught in headlights, I shot off the sofa and snapped at them all. "I'm fine, I really am. I suppose I ought to get on with supper if you're all staying."

I left the room and with indulgent purpose, slammed the door. Behind me I heard the vexed tones of Sandra twittering something about 'that time in life'.

Bloody cheek, I thought as I banged my pots and pans around in the kitchen. It wasn't me having a mid-life crisis, it was her precious son. My heart was pounding, which considering I had been stuck in a room with my gay husband, his parents and a randy eighteen year old, was not too surprising. I gave myself a pat on the back for keeping the lid on as well as I had done.

A drink would help though.

No more malt whisky so it would have to be vodka and coke.

Now all I needed was a little music. I trailed my fingers down the CD rack that hung on the wall. I was in the mood for a little dark Goth. Not literally of course. I wiped the dust off the CD case and inserted it into the machine. A short while later I had a large pan of

Bolognese on the go, merrily singing my head off. I had forgotten how wonderfully cathartic the Sisters of Mercy could be.

"Blimey, Mum, you're giving it some tonight," Megan turned down the music in a classic role reversal. "Don't you think that's a little loud?"

If it didn't drown out the unceasing questions in my head, it wasn't loud enough. Not something I could share with her though. Finishing my drink, I asked her if she would lay the table for me. Whilst she was busy with this task, I refilled my glass. If I was going to have to sit at a table with everyone present, I would need some liquid support.

"Can you drain the spaghetti?" I asked her when she had finished the table. "I need the loo."

Rosy coloured lighting in a bathroom was a bloody good idea, I thought, as I surveyed my reflection in the hope I didn't look too wrecked. I splashed some cold water on my face in an effort to cool my still burning cheeks (although the vodka could be to blame for the glow now) and reached for some anti-wrinkle cream. A sleepless night, too much whisky, and crying, did no woman any favours, least of all someone in their forties. My hand paused as it massaged in the cream.

Was it my fault that Andy had turned to someone else? Usually that was the case. The wife let herself go and a younger, sleeker, model came along. Then again, I thought angrily, how could I compete with another man? I dabbed on some lip gloss and reached for eye shadow.

I was smudging a soft green over my eyelids, muttering as I did so, "Bloody, bloody, two timing, lying, cheating, gay, bloody bastard," when there was a knock on the door.

"Cooee, are you alright in there? Are you going to be long?"

"Bloody, nosy, interfering old cow," I mouthed to my reflection. "Won't be long," I called out loud and started to muss up my hair. It was in short choppy layers which I liked because at times like this, I could just squirt some more mousse in the roots, tangle it with my fingers, and hey presto rock-chick look. I would never be smart or glamorous. I would never be beautiful like Megan. But sometimes, I could do sexy. The anger and alcohol lent my eyes a luminous glitter and turned my mouth into a sultry pout. Damn shame it would be wasted on Andy!

Sandra knocked again. I stuck my tongue out at the mirror, wishing I had the nerve to do it to my mother-in-law. Maybe one day. In the meantime, there was the ordeal of dinner to get through. A few minutes later, as everyone settled round our extravagantly large pine table, perfect for just such occasions, I made a promise to myself that I would behave, despite the presence of my in-laws, my husband, and Tim.

And I did behave.

Until it was time for everyone to go home.

Sandra and Steven were taking ages to collect their coats and photographs that they had left lying around everywhere, with Andy following them around like an obedient child. Jake and Mark had disappeared into the music room and Megan had gone to phone a friend. They had said goodbye to their grandparents and had shouted to Tim (on his way out in the hallway) to come round the following morning.

Which left me alone with Tim.

Who, ignoring the fact that he was my son's best friend, was looking rather bloody cute. I know, I should not even be thinking such things. But my world had been turned on its head and all sense of logic not to mention, morals, with it.

I needed fresh air. The vodka was hitting hard.

"I'll see you out," I said to him doing my best to sound motherly. "Are you sure you'll be alright to drive back?" His motor bike was parked in our driveway.

"I've not been drinking," he said with a cocky grin. "Don't need alcohol to have fun all the time, Mrs. A."

"Ooh I do wish you wouldn't call me that," I blurted out unable to stop myself. "It makes me sound like someone's Granny."

"Oh no," he drawled, pulling on his padded leather biker's jacket "You could never be mistaken for anyone's Gran. Hard enough to think of you as someone's mum, Eve."

All of a sudden I felt peculiar. It was the way he said my name. Such a little thing. Such a personal thing. I realised with some astonishment that Andy hardly called me by my name these days. It was usually, love, petal, sweetie-pie, or darling. Endearments, but all

17

uttered with a neutral tone that should have warned me ages ago. I wondered bitterly, how he said the name Jason. With passion? Lust?

Anger kindled and sparked in my belly. Then it turned into another kind of fire when he said my name again.

"Goodnight, Eve."

I opened my mouth to respond automatically, startled to find that he had stepped up close and was leaning in towards me.

"Good..." I got no further as he kissed me. Not a friendly peck on the cheek, but a cheeky peck on the lips.

Which was rather nice.

And no one was watching.

So I kissed him back and found myself locked in an embrace with a hungry teenager who had the body of a man. Nice, I thought, woozily as his tongue slipped into my mouth. Hell, very nice! God how long had it been since I had felt this kind of nice? Too bloody long by half! I stabbed back angrily at his tongue which encouraged him further, not that he needed much prompting. His hands were already tight on my bottom, pulling in firmly against his thighs, a perfect fit, his thrusting, mine ready to accept.

"Eve!"

"Mum, really!"

Shit! Caught mid grope, I jumped back to see Andy and his parents staring open-mouthed in horror and Megan leaning out of the bedroom window.

Megan was the quickest. "What the bloody hell are you doing snogging Tim?"

Right on cue, Mark and Jake appeared, passing across the hallway and spotting the commotion in the driveway.

"What do you mean, Mum's snogging Tim?" I winced at the tone of Jake's voice.

"Best be off then," said Tim straddling his bike and giving everyone an eyeful of an impressive erection against his jeans. I hoped he could ride in that condition. "No offence meant, mate," he addressed Andy with all the cockiness of an eighteen year old having just pulled a fast one. "Thanks for tea, Eve," he snapped down the visor of his helmet and disappeared in a roar of exhaust fumes and flying gravel.

Still reeling from the heat of Tim's kisses, I watched as Andy shoved his parents into their car as fast as he could. I saw Jake thumping Mark to stop him from laughing and did my best to avoid Megan's eyes as she continued to glare down from above.

"Mum, what the hell is going on, last night you were skinny dipping with gnomes, now you're snogging Jake's best mate?"

"Skinny dipping with gnomes?" Sandra shrieked loudly from the window of her car. She stuck her head out of the window and called to Andy. "Kissing an eighteen year old boy for heaven's sake! I think you need to get her some help. She's obviously going through the change."

That really pissed me off. "Oh chill out," I snapped back at them all. "It was just a kiss. I haven't fucked him!" And a wicked voice rang inside my head.

Yet.

CHAPTER THREE

Church was uncomfortable.

Well obviously, it is always uncomfortable, seventeenth century pews being what they are, and the draughty window frames letting in the cold January air. But church on the 4th January was more uncomfortable than usual. I was getting a numb bum and a crick in my neck from the cold. Little enough punishment, I suppose for my behaviour with Tim.

It was bloody annoying though that my husband seemed able to cope with the fact that he'd been screwing another bloke and yet all I had to do, was kiss a young man for a few minutes for me to feel like I had committed a mortal sin? But I was drunk at the time. So maybe that makes it less of a sin?

Apart from the fact that even though wildly intoxicated, it had not prevented me from thoroughly enjoying myself. It had not been just a little kiss, after all. It had been a full on, tongue twisting, body grappling snog. Just thinking about it made me fidget on the pew and utter a lusty sigh.

"Sorry," I hissed in response to Andy's hard stare and the turned heads of two old women sitting in front of me. I wished we could get on with singing a hymn because at least then I could stop thinking about Tim.

At last, time to stand and sing. Something I could do better than most here. When we had first moved to the village, the Women's Institute and the Vicar had made repeated attempts to entice me into the choir. It didn't work. I don't do ruffled smocks, thank you very much. Besides, I hated to keep to the right tunes.

I sang according to what mood I was in. Today my vocal talents were clearly more suited to the snarling tones of Johnny Rotten. I thought the sarcastic approach to the hymn sounded rather good, but by the second verse, I could see that my rendition was not gaining approval. Aware of Andy's stiff posture beside me, I clamped my lips shut. I stood in mute silence for the rest of the hymn, which was not very helpful for me. My mind kept wandering as it had done ever since New Year's Eve.

Andy and Tim.

I was lucky that the noises of everyone sitting down and shuffling through their prayer books covered another enormous sigh. I bowed my head with the others but instead of concentrating on the poor and afflicted, those in need and suffering, world peace and spiritual harmony, my thoughts flitted between the two men.

My husband. My son's best friend.

Lying, cheating, twisted bastard.

Cute, gorgeous, sexy boy. Boy for God's sake. Sorry God.

I forced myself not to think of how strong Tim's arms had felt around me, and how insistently his thighs had pressed against me. He had wanted me. Really wanted me! How long had it been since Andy had held me like that? Kissed me like that? Wanted me like that? Not since his break down. Ten long, lonely, dry years. I might as well have been a bloody nun, for Christ's sake! Sorry God. I raised my eyes to the vaulted ceiling, shame at my inappropriate thoughts.

And then a wave of anger washed that shame right out of me. What had I to be apologising for? I hadn't done anything wrong. I had kept my marriage vows. For better for worse, and all that crap. It had not been me who pulled the plug on the physical side of things and I had put up with it. Worse, I had not even noticed that my husband preferred men! What kind of an idiot was I?

I had devoted the last twenty two years to my marriage completely. Abandoned on the steps of a hospital, just as night was falling, hence my name, and shunted from foster home to foster home, nothing was more important to me than providing a stable background in which my own family could flourish.

I had known desertion, violence, loneliness and fear. And I was one of the lucky ones. I had escaped the system without any serious abuse, but it had been enough to make me determined that my children would not come from a broken home, nor would they ever be party to domestic strife and uncertainty.

Maybe that had been a mistake. Maybe I had tried too hard. Papered over cracks where I shouldn't have done. Ignored the tell-tale signs that Andy really wasn't interested in me, because if I did that, I would be stepping into dangerous territory. And look where it had landed me? Okay, I had managed to provide the type of home I wanted for my children, who were now adults. Mission accomplished.

But I was left with a life that was a lie.

I glanced sideways at Andy, who in his navy blue suit was looking totally gorgeous. Not fair! I still fancied him. Still could look at him and feel those twinges which I had got used to ignoring, telling myself that sex was for young people, not married folk in their thirties and beyond. And then I had a shattering image in my head of him grunting and thrusting with a faceless man.

I squeezed my eyes shut tightly to block out the picture. It refused to budge. I bowed my head low as everyone knelt to pray and butted the pew with my forehead in utter frustration and anger. It didn't help and only served to earn me another frosty look from those nearby, including Andy.

I bit my lip and thought back over the last couple of days, stifling a rebellious laugh at how I had completed the evening's entertainment on New Year's Day, by throwing up all over the tree that decorated the porch. Andy had hustled me upstairs to bed like a naughty child and ordered Jake to clean up the mess. Jake had then argued with him and refused to do it. He had thrown me such a dirty look as I staggered past him.

I think Mark had cleaned it up in the end. He had been living with us for six months, and not having known much domestic peace in his own home he was always quick to keep life flowing smoothly. Just like me, I suppose. I had made a point of thanking him the next day.

Megan, after the first initial, 'how could you Mum?' lecture, had taken the most unusual step of siding with her grandmother. Apparently Sandra had telephoned the morning after my second disgraceful incident in a row, to give her opinion that I was in need of HRT. Immediately!

Nice to know they all cared.

I had not seen anything of Tim. He had come round for a session on the guitars whilst I was still in bed and then spent the next couple of days at his girlfriend's parents in Manchester. So all quiet there.

As for Andy and his bombshell, well, he's a man isn't he? When I asked him, pointedly, if he wouldn't prefer to be spending time with Jason, he told me in a bumbling sort of way, that his lover was visiting his ageing parents in Bournemouth. He then found a large bucket of sand and stuck his head in it, pretending that nothing had happened.

It was even his suggestion that we came here today. Neither of us were huge church goers. I had done the usual cubs and brownie thing with Megan and Jake, but that was more for them really. Living in such a close knit community, church was hard to avoid, so we tried to make it about once a month or so, for appearances really.

I didn't even like the Vicar. I thought the Reverend Michael was a most ungodly person for a man of the cloth. Mean spirited and disapproving. All hell fire and damnation. He irked me now, as he launched into his sermon, badly chosen as far as I was concerned as it focused on the sanctity of marriage, and commitment to leading a moral way of life.

I hadn't realised my snort of disgust was quite so loud until he stopped and stared hard at me. It was like being back at school, when the head suddenly picks you out in assembly. Oops! I held his gaze. I can stare just as hard as the next person. Driven by a childish need to rebel at something, anything, I played chicken with him, just to see who would win.

I did. He looked away first.

Besides me, I heard Andy mutter crossly, "For goodness sake, Eve, behave yourself."

I shot him a look then and had the satisfaction of seeing him pale. One word from me, in front of all these people and his life would be a total nightmare. He knew it, I knew it. Don't push me, I warned him with my eyes. Just don't!

Finally it was time to step up towards the altar for communion. I cast my eyes around the congregation, wondering how many of them were harbouring dark secrets like my husband. Screw around, break hearts, then 'fess up to God and it would all be okay. What a load of bullshit!

I felt Andy nudge me as it was my turn to kneel at the altar rail. I watched him as he took the bread and wine as he had done so many times. I watched his lips move to say 'Amen'. Lips that had not kissed mine for such a long time. Lips that had kissed another man in passion. I watched as his hands cupped the chalice. Hands that had not cupped my breasts for such a long time. Hands that had instead, cupped a man's balls and...

"Sorry, not today, thank you." My voice rang as clear as a pealing bell in the heavenly silence of the church. I stood up abruptly, startling Andy and the person on the other side of me.

"Eve?" Andy looked at me in horror.

Reverend Michael was dithering with his chalice. "My child, are you not going to kneel and receive absolution for your sins?"

I shook my head. "I am not your child, and I haven't sinned enough. Not by a long way."

There was a rising crescendo of gasps and mutters as I marched down the aisle and out of the church. My legs were pumping hard with adrenaline and before I knew it I was over the stile at the far end of the church yard and half way across the fields that back onto Cooper's Fold. I didn't care that the bottom of my trousers were getting covered with mud, or that the wind was cold. I dug my hands into the warm pockets of my fake sheep skin jacket and strode on. To hell with the lot of them!

I loved this walk that lead from the village to the back of our house, and each time I came this way, I said a little thank you for the luck which had brought me to such a spot. A far cry from the shabby streets and crowded houses I had grown up around. The path leads across a winding brook, alders, bowing at its edges, and then on up a slight rise before dipping down again to slope into Cooper's Fold. At the top of the rise, there is a copse of trees, which the farmer, thankfully, has never cut down.

I always make for this group of trees, even though it means I have to walk a little further. There is something magical about the spot that draws me. Today was no different and I reached the mid- point between the church and my house in record time, heart racing with emotion and the effort of walking so quickly.

Leaning back against the broad trunk of the massive oak which stood in the middle of the copse I reached my hands out around the tree. My fingers drew up short as I tried to somehow cling on to the tree itself as if this could support me when everything around me was falling down.

24

Two hundred years or more of withstanding nature's storms. No doubt it would still be standing when all the inhabitants of Maypoleton were long gone. It would certainly outlive my marriage, I thought bitterly. A splinter from the bark went right under a nail. I snatched my hand to my mouth. Blood bubbled up from the tiny puncture wound. I tugged at the splinter with my other hand, but I struggled to see what I was doing. Tears were making my vision swim.

"Shit." I wiped my eyes with the back of my sleeve and clamping my teeth, pulled the splinter out. It made my finger bleed even more. I stuck it in my mouth and sucked on it, rooting in my pocket with my other hand for a tissue to wrap around it.

"'Ere you are Dearie, thee take that now. Better than a scrappy ol' tissue."

I jumped. I hadn't noticed the old woman appear from round the base of the tree. She was holding out a snowy white handkerchief, edged with lace. Without waiting for me to reply, she unbound the bloody tissue and neatly bandaged my finger.

"I can't let you do that," I protested. "It'll ruin it."

The old woman made a click with her tongue. "When thee gets to my age, Dearie, thee'll not be moidering about a wee scrap o'cheif." She had a curious way of talking and a lilt to her voice that I couldn't place.

"Thank you," I said, wondering where on earth she had come from. She was wearing an ankle length skirt with what looked like at least three old fashioned petticoats underneath, stout brown boots on her feet and a huge over- sized woollen cardigan that looked like it should belong to a man. Her hair was turbaned up in a colourful scarf and large gold ear-rings dangled from her lobes.

I realised at last that she was probably a traveller of sorts. From time to time caravans would park up on the outskirts of Maypoleton and scare the timid population in to thinking they were all going to be robbed blind and murdered in their beds. They never made me feel that way. And this old soul hardly looked capable of harming anyone.

She must have been ninety at least. Deep creases lined her weather beaten face, and there was an owl like wisdom shining out of her eyes. I felt so naive and innocent before that ancient gaze.

"What's troubling thee, me girl?" She asked as though she had known me a lifetime. "What woes drive thee to take comfort in t'arms of t'old uns?"

"I beg your pardon?"

The woman nodded at the tree. "Thee clung to t'sacred oak like it was a rock in a stormy sea, yet thee walked out o' church without t'blessing?"

I felt a prickle down my spine. How did she know that? "Have you been watching me?"

The woman smiled and revealed a mouth with missing teeth. "In a manner of speaking, child. I am right though, aren't I? The tree gives thee more solace than the chalice?"

Interesting notion. She was right though. This place under the oak, gave me the sort of peace that Reverend Michael preached should come from the altar. I smiled at her, thinking that I didn't mind her calling me 'child', yet it had grated so much when the Vicar had done so.

"Yes. Yes it does. I hadn't realised it was sacred though."

"All oaks are. All trees, all animals, all living things. It just depends how thee looks at them." The old woman walked around the base of the tree, her hands as gnarled and dark in colour as the bark itself. "This one is special. Druids used to pray here. Y'see how it stands apart from t'rest o't'rees? How they form a circle around it?"

I looked at the oak in the middle of the copse with fresh new eyes. I had never really noticed before but the woman was right. There was a cluster of rowan, birch and ash, which over the centuries had tangled their branches together, yet never intruding in the space of the oak around whose base their own roots spread.

I smiled at the old woman. "I never noticed until you pointed it out. I must have been blind." I laughed harshly. "But then I am blind." Anyone who could see with half an eye would have been able to spot the fault in my marriage years earlier.

The old woman startled me then by touching me gently on my forehead. Just the lightest of movements with two fingers of her left hand.

"Thee can see now, child. No more blindness for thee. Thee can see beyond what others may not."

It felt like a blessing, far more spiritual than anything Reverend Michael could have bestowed upon me. I caught hold of the woman's hands and gasped with shock.

"Oh you're so cold." She was like ice to touch. I started to take off my thick jacket. "Here, I don't really need this, you must take it."

The old woman laughed. "Bless thee, my dear child. I have no need of that. I feel no cold."

"Well at least come home with me for a hot cup of tea," I gestured over the fields towards my house. "I only live over there."

She shook her head, making the golden hoops jingle. "I must be on my way, child. I have lingered long enough."

I started to un-wrap the handkerchief from my finger. It was stained now with blood, but the flow had stopped.

"At least tell me where you are staying then I can wash this and return it."

Again, she shook her head. "Keep it, my Dearie. Now, off you go. I'll take a few moments rest here and be on my way."

I felt strangely reluctant to leave the old woman. I thanked her and tucked the handkerchief into my pocket before setting off across the fields. Half way, I turned to see if she was still there by the tree. She wasn't and a sudden sadness drenched my heart for no reason I could think of. By the time I had let myself in the back door of the kitchen, I had tears running down my cheeks like twin rivers.

Andy was waiting for me.

I had forgotten about him!

A look of grim fury was on his face as he turned round from the oven. I stopped in my tracks, uncaring that I was weeping silently, waiting for the attack. How dare I humiliate him in front of the Vicar and the congregation? That sort of thing.

I was so miserable, I really didn't care. What could he possibly say that could hurt me anymore? It must have shown in my face.

"The chicken's nearly ready." He said instead of bawling me out. "Do you want a glass of wine?"

I shook my head. "I think I should stay off alcohol for now. Maybe your Mum's right. Maybe I am going through the change."

"Why do you say that?" He watched as I hung my jacket up and took out the blood stained handkerchief.

I shrugged. "I don't know. Everything's gone weird. Not just you. Us. Other stuff." Like wanting to dance naked in the moonlight, and feeling as though I had just lost someone special after meeting an old woman for a few minutes.

"What's this?" Andy gently reached for the handkerchief. A gesture of truce maybe?

I told him briefly about my encounter. "Poor old woman, she looked as though she had hardly a penny in the world, yet she could give this to me."

Andy smoothed out the square of cotton. "Look, there's an initial embroidered in the corner, you don't see that these days." He held it out to me.

I felt a sharp pang of emotion when I saw the letter 'I', in faded lilac thread. "I never asked her name," I said sadly taking the handkerchief back and resolving to wash it carefully by hand, straight after lunch.

CHAPTER FOUR

I stared at the ceiling as though it would give me divine inspiration. It didn't. I was hit with the empty silence. Our bed now seemed ridiculously huge as there was only me in it. Oh and a big cuddly Tigger that Megan had bought for me as a joke the other Christmas. I wasn't laughing now.

I groaned and clung on tight to Tigger.

Who could have predicted when I finished work in December that I would be starting the next year like this?

The snooze button on my alarm went off, again.

"Tell it to sod off, Tigger," I used the cuddly toy to whack the alarm clock and ended up knocking it to the floor. "Oh well done." I had been awake most of the night talking to myself, and decided that Tigger was a better listener. I had told him all about how I had first met Andy.

I had been sharing a flat with the mates with whom I sang in a band and was getting by on a slap dash week by week existence. It suited me. As long as I had a roof over my head, food in my belly, and no one knocking me around, I was happy.

Then along came Andy. He was older than me by nearly ten years and already carving a niche for himself as an architect. Pretty impressive stuff for a girl like me. He was also good looking, charming, funny and kind.

But I wasn't ready to settle down. I was having too much fun touring round the country singing in pubs and clubs. Two years later though, back in Lancashire and with the band discarded it was time to grow up. Andy was still waiting for me. He had kept in touch all that time. Waiting for me.

That clinched it.

No one had ever wanted me before. Apart from sex that is. I was used to lads trying it on all the time. No big deal. Sex was sex. But Andy offered me something more.

Respect. Love. Security.

Of course his parents hated the idea of us getting married. I think it was the only time in his life that Andy went against them and because of that, I was determined to prove them wrong. He gave me the respect, love and security I craved and I vowed to give him loyalty and love in return. He gave me a lovely home, two beautiful children and I gave him a model wife and mother.

I thought it was a fair exchange. More than fair.

And if I sometimes felt like a bird whose wings had been clipped, I pushed it to the back of my mind. And if I sometimes felt lonely because he was so busy with work, I told myself not to be selfish. And if the thought crept into my mind, that he spent more time with the children than he did with me, I told myself I was lucky they had such a good father.

And if I went to bed, alone, needing the touch of a man and full of frustration, I got busy with my fingers and thought about film stars. It never crossed my mind that there was anything wrong. There were far too many ticks in the column to outweigh the crosses. Life was good. Good enough anyway. Too good to rock the boat.

Outside, I heard the slamming of two car doors, an unenthusiastic engine grinding into life, and then the churning up of gravel. Megan and Mark off to the university at Preston. Which meant I really was late for work! Unless they were going in early?

I leant out of bed and reached for the abandoned clock. Fuck! Skipping a shower I got ready as quickly as I could, glad that I had the sort of scruffy hair style that looked even better not washed. I dusted some bronzing powder over my tired looking skin, and slicked on some lip gloss, determined not to go to rack and ruin because of Andy.

Then I dressed in the hated uniform of baggy black trousers and a yellow spotty tunic. Childcare was not a glamorous profession and a hell of a long way from singing in a band. But it fitted in with bringing up my own two. I no longer needed to do that, but around here there were not many other options, so I remained working at Little Acorns Day Nursery, just on the outskirts of Maypoleton.

I normally walked to work unless it was absolutely chucking it down, but today I would have to take my car. Andy had already disappeared much earlier. I had heard him whistling across the landing in an outrageously carefree fashion. And then I tortured myself with the thought that he was probably going to see his lover sometime today. Bastard!

Jake was making his usual mess in the kitchen when I went in to grab a quick coffee. I was about to moan at him for the crumbs on the counter and the coffee spilt on the floor but he came over and gave me a squeeze of a hug. Irritation vanished in an instant. He always had that effect on me which probably meant I spoilt him. Andy and Megan would certainly say so. My next actions proved this point.

"Mum," he said, "can you run me round to Sam's? He's giving me a lift into college this morning."

"Why aren't you getting the bus?"

"Missed it."

"Come on then, but we have to go now, I'm running late as well."

"Cheers mum. Love you," a twinkle of his blue eyes and a flash of his dimple. I had been a sucker for both since the day he was born.

Altogether I was half an hour late for work when I parked my Suzuki Swift (twentieth anniversary present from Andy) at the back of Little Acorns. Marjorie was not going to be pleased with me.

"Ah, there you are, Mrs. Armstrong." Marjorie Burton, the nursery owner was waiting for me. Never a happy soul, she had a face on her like a shrivelled grape fruit this morning.

"Before you start, and I expect you to make up this time at the end of the day," she looked pointedly at her watch, "I would like a word with you." She turned her bony back on me and stalked poker-like down the corridor to her office.

God it was like being back at school! I had hated that as well. Thinking that a grown woman of forty two should not have to feel as though she is about to be scolded by the head mistress, even if she is wearing a bloody silly uniform, I trudged reluctantly after her.

As I sat in the chair opposite Marjorie's desk, my dislike for the woman mushroomed uncontrollably. She was a mean spirited bully, harsh with both children and staff alike, making personal preferences clear. I did my best to avoid her. No escape now though.

"I was in church on Sunday morning," she began frostily.

Oh bollocks. I had forgotten Marjorie sang in the choir. I composed my face into a suitably innocent expression and remained silent.

She looked disappointed that I was not going to be forthcoming on the matter and launched into her attack.

"I am rather concerned that perhaps you lack the moral standing which I feel is necessary for members of my staff. Not only did you make a scene in church, in front of some of our parents and their children, but it has come to my attention that you have been seen in a most compromising situation."

I felt my cheeks beginning to burn along with my temper.

"Do I have to expand?"

The thought of Marjorie expanding her stick-insect like body and her equally narrow mind, was highly unlikely.

"If you wish."

Her tight mouth compressed further. "You have been seen acting in a wholly unsuitable manner with a young man, young enough I may say to be your son."

Of course. The neighbourhood watch of Cooper's Fold. Two houses faced ours and I supposed it was likely that someone had seen what had happened on New Year's Eve.

"And your point is?" I regarded her coolly, satisfied in the certain knowledge that although Marjorie was about the same age as me, Tim would not have wanted to stick his tongue down her throat. I couldn't help it, I ending up smiling.

Marjorie huffed up her bony shoulders and glared disapprovingly. "Your attitude proves me right. You had better consider this a verbal warning, Eve. I will not have my nursery brought into disrepute because of the waywardness of its staff!"

"Then I can help you out," I said, standing up. "I'm leaving. I'll work my notice if you want but I warn you, I feel an acute attack of waywardness coming on, so maybe it would be better if I went now?" I looked at her as I had looked at my school teachers all those years ago, with a 'screw you' glint in my eyes and promise of bad behaviour.

"Go now. I'll send your P45 in the post."

I stopped off at the pre-school room to collect my own mug and a cardigan I had left behind, feeling a huge weight lifting from my shoulders. My mood rose higher when I told the girls I was leaving. Today.

One of them gave me a saucy wink. "Don't blame you, Eve. We overheard Mrs. Wetherby telling Marjorie all about it. I just hope I can manage a snog with someone as fit as Tim when I'm your age."

"Yeah, you go for it, girl," added Cheryl, another woman in her forties like me. "Get it while you can, and whilst you're at it, give him one for me!"

I left them with a smile on my face as their smutty conversation, completely unsuitable for the ears of three year olds, descended into verbal pornography as to what they would do with a body like Tim's given half the chance.

It was only a five minute drive from Little Acorns to our house, straight through the High Street. I usually walked this way enjoying casting my eye into the shop windows. Maypoleton was a little hidden gem, as charming in its own way as some of the pretty Cotswold villages, but without the crowds of people.

On the left hand side of the high street was the higgedly piggedly collection of older cottages which randomly surrounded the village green. They had low tiled roofs and deep set windows, brightly painted coloured doors and gardens full of flowers. The village green had the obligatory duck pond, complete with medieval stocks, and the May pole that gave the village its name.

It was a huge timber pole which had been sunk into the ground, centuries ago, before the church had been built a few hundred yards from it. Pagan in origin, dozens of ministers over the years, including the Reverend Michael, had tried to have the upright remains of the ancient tree removed. Strangely, it never worked. Wild weather would intervene, equipment would break, accidents would occur. Superstition took hold. The pole was there to stay.

On the opposite side of the high street, separated by a river which wound its way down from the fells, was the new part of the village. In actual fact many of the buildings here were a hundred years old, but that was still counted as modern. Newer still, was the housing estate which had sprouted over the last few years.

They had been built by my husband's firm, the one he had set up after his breakdown. Tasteful, in keeping with the local environment, they offered smart, affordable housing for the families who were finding themselves priced more and more out of their own local homes. Because of this we had been welcomed into the area, although it had taken some time to be considered true locals, even if we were both Lancashire born and bred.

It crossed my mind, as I drove slowly up the high street that living in such a small community was going to make it so much harder for us all, when Andy's 'coming out' became official. If we were still living in Preston, then the news would have been lost in the anonymity of the city. It also struck me, reverse parking neatly outside the bakery that I did not want to leave Maypoleton.

I liked the village. I enjoyed its quirkiness. I loved the countryside surrounding it, the fact that in pretty much every direction you could see hills and fells, fields and hedgerows. I understood why some families had generations buried here. Having no roots of my own I had come to see Maypoleton as my real home, and one I was not prepared to leave.

I pushed open the door to Mabel's bakery, feeling the need for a high sugar hit. As well as making the best pastries ever, Mabel Thorpe knew everything there was to know in the village. To her credit, she never made malicious use of it. She would have heard already about Tim and the episode in church, and I would have placed money on her even knowing about me leaving work, she was that close to being a witch!

"Morning love, not your usual time?" She greeted me with a smile blue eyes twinkling, plump cheeks as rosy as apples. Already her hand was sliding a pastry into a paper bag for me.

"I've just walked out of my job," I told her nodding at her to indicate that today would be a two pastry day.

"About time. You were miserable there with old sour sticks. What happened?"

"Walk or get sacked sooner or later. I've upset the apple cart."

Mabel grinned at me looking years younger than her sixty years. "So I heard." Then she winked. "Can't be doing with church myself. Much better ways to keep the faith if you know what I mean?"

It was rumoured that Mabel was the head of a coven, right here in Maypoleton. It wouldn't surprise me.

"Yes, well for now I shall be keeping away from the Reverend Michael. I've hit a turning point in my life, you could say."

"'Appens to us all, love. Kids grow up and you start thinking what on earth you are going to do with your life. Still, at least you've got a lovely bloke." She held her hands out for my money, shrewd eyes noting how my cheeks flushed.

"Ah. I also heard about Tim." She patted my hand as she gave me the change. "You want someone to talk to my love, old Mabel here has heard it all. Nothing you could tell me that would shock me."

"I'll bear that in mind," I said, wondering if she could see inside my head.

"You do. In the meantime, you let your hair down girl, and have a bit of fun. We're only here the once you know. Well, this is my third incarnation of course, I was a soldier in the Napoleonic wars last time, but you know what I mean."

I had to smile. "I think I do."

I took my pastries and went home, thinking about what both the girls at Little Acorns and Mabel had said to me. Maybe it was time for a little fun although I am not entirely sure that what Mabel had in mind would fit in with what happened next.

Back home I enjoyed a lazy cup of tea with one of the pastries, trying hard not to look at Skip as he eye-balled me throughout. Then after changing my horrible uniform into a pair of jeans and a sweater, I made the most of the nice morning by taking my dog for an extra-long brisk walk, to blow away the cobwebs and burn off the calories I had just eaten.

By the time I got back, I was revved up with energy and began a task I usually avoided at all costs. The housework. I managed to keep things tidy, for the most part, but I am the first to confess that I am a bit of a slut when it comes to the actual cleaning. Not so today.

I switched on some music, found some rubber gloves and got cracking on the kitchen cupboards. Two hours later and sweating somewhat from my efforts, I decided it was time for lunch, and perhaps the second pastry. I tossed my rubber gloves into the sink and peeled off my sweater, hot enough with just a cotton vest top on.

I had just put the kettle on, when Skip began to bark playfully. Someone he knew was coming in through the back door.

Grinning at me, as he stooped to make a fuss of Skip, was Tim. "Hi, Eve. Hope you don't mind me calling round the back. I did ring the doorbell, but you didn't answer and I knew you were in because of the music. By the way, that old witch from across the road, the one with purple hair, asked me if you would turn it down."

Crikey was it that loud? "You mean, Deirdre," I guessed, thinking of my lilac rinsed neighbour, who no doubt was the one who had reported me kissing Tim to Marjorie.

He shrugged and lounged against the counter as I went to turn down the music.

"What are you doing here?" I hoped my voice sounded normal because I was finding it hard to act that way. It didn't help that he was wearing a pristine white t shirt under his biker's jacket, moulded to his chest in the same way his ripped jeans were hugging his thighs. His hair was freshly washed and there was an attractive woody scent about him. He was, for God's sake, a walking advertisement for some kind of men's grooming product!

He produced a CD and handed it to me. "Jake asked me if I could drop this off for him. I was going to just drop it through the letter box but it seemed rude to do that if you were in." Again that smile. Full of youth, cheek, charm. And sex. Oh yes, definitely that.

"How come you're not at college yourself today?"

"I've just got back from Manchester and I've no lessons Monday afternoon."

"Oh yes," I said, wishing now that I had not stripped off my sweater. The way he was looking at my chest was rather unnerving. I should have been embarrassed. I wasn't. And that was perhaps what was unnerving. I was also conscious that I had sucked in my belly and had pulled my shoulders back a fraction. The kettle began to boil adding to the steam that was heating up the room.

"I'd love a cuppa," he said slipping off his jacket and putting it over the back of a chair. "I could do with a shoulder to cry on."

"Oh?" My hand reached automatically for two mugs as a voice inside my head held an argument. Tell him to go. Now! Ask him to stay. Go! Stay! "What have you got to cry about?"

"Stacey's finished with me."

36

"Your girlfriend in Manchester?"

"Yeah. She wants to go to Kenya to do charity work and I'm not part of the equation."

I had to smile then as I stirred three sugars into his tea, just like Jake had it. He sounded more offended than hurt.

"Somehow I don't think you'll be single for long," I pushed his brew along the counter towards him. "There are plenty of girls around here who will be celebrating that you're back on the market."

I blew on my own tea which was far too hot. As I did so he moved nearer and reached out a hand to touch a strand of hair that curled onto my neck. I nearly dropped my mug as his finger trailed along my collar bone.

"Not really interested in girls," he said slowly, his eyes boring into my back as I turned away a fraction. "Too shallow. Too inexperienced."

"Tim, I think I ought to tell you that we were seen. The other night, when you kissed me, I mean," I said firmly, daring to turn around and face him. It was a mistake. He had moved some more and now could place his hands either side of me to rest against the counter.

"So?"

"So it isn't really something you should be doing with a woman my age," I said aware all of a sudden that his hips had leant into mine and that he was already hard. The joys of youth, I thought half hysterically. One touch and ready to go.

"What has age got to do with it?" He asked me earnestly and there was a look of passion in his hot dark eyes that had me rapidly losing control of the situation. "You enjoyed it, didn't you, Eve?"

"That's beside the point," I squeaked as his mouth came down to nip the base of my throat, vampire like in its hunger. "Tim, stop."

He did for a second and I did my best to salvage the situation.

"I lost my job this morning because of you."

"No kidding? Shit I'm sorry, Eve." His hands were not resting on the counter now they were on my waist instead, fingers sliding absently between the cotton of my vest top and my jeans.

"It was a lousy job," I said weakly, wondering for one fatal second what it would feel like to have his hands all over my body.

He caught that moment of weakness, sensed the limpness in my body, not bracing against him, but melting in towards him.

"Might as well be hung for a sheep as a lamb then," he whispered softly in my ear, caressing my lobe with his tongue.

I groaned then and turned my head in for his kiss. I was sober this time. All the better to revel in the sensations of his mouth as his lips ground hard against mine and then opened up to search with his tongue. I clasped the back of his head pulling him down to me, greedy for more. Like a child deprived of sweets and then suddenly let lose in a Thornton's shop, I couldn't get enough of the taste of him.

Difficult to tell who was devouring who. We were both desperate and hungry. His hands had slid right under my vest top, snapping open my bra. He pulled away from me for a moment, just long enough to heave up my top over my head and tear my bra away. I gasped in shocked delight as his mouth clasped down hard on one nipple, his fingers toying with the other.

One small part of my brain told me that this should not be happening. I should not be pinned up against the kitchen counter having an eighteen year old feast upon my naked breasts as my clothes lay discarded on the floor. But the rest of my brain, and my body with it, screamed at me that it had been so long since I had felt like this, that I couldn't possibly let it stop. My knees were beginning to weaken and I was pulsing so hard with desire that it almost hurt. I needed more.

"Tim," I locked my fingers into his hair and tugged none too gently to bring his mouth back up to mine. Then with his lips fastened once more where I wanted them I reached for his own t-shirt. My turn. A strong, smooth back, lean belly and a smattering of hairs on his chest. The touch of skin against skin was my undoing. I pulled him in even closer, needing to feel my breasts crushed against his chest.

We paused for a moment. Breathing hard, lips bruised, faces flushed. Our legs were tangled together, already rocking and grinding. There was only denim and cotton in the way. We could have stopped then. Pulled apart, laughed a little, passed each other our tops. But he was a healthy eighteen year old with an erection straining to get out of his jeans, and I was a forty two year old woman who had not had sex in ten years.

I reached for his zip the same time he went for mine.

There was a fumble. There had to be. No way of doing this neatly. His hands were rough as he dragged my jeans and my briefs down past my hips, then tugged them off completely. My hands were shaking as I released him from his boxers and clasped him firmly for a moment. I had forgotten how smooth yet solid a man could be. Iron clad in silk. All I could think about was having the length of him inside me. Deep inside as far as it could possibly go.

He groaned and then lifted me up easily up so that my bottom was on the edge of the counter, hands digging into my buttocks, nails scraping pleasurably against my skin. I spread my legs to make it easy for him and locking my legs around his waist urged him on. I had to brace my hands against the counter as he pushed in hard. Unprepared for the suddenness of the thrust, I arched back my head and shouted in animal pleasure.

"Jesus Christ, Eve!" He groaned as he bit down hard on my neck and hammered into me again and again.

I tightened myself around him. Muscles I had thought dead, suddenly back to life. There was pain with the pleasure as he drove in so deep I could feel his balls bruising my flesh, unused to such an assault. And still I wanted it harder, deeper, faster. I drove him on with words and with the pumping action of my own hips, not giving him any chance to slacken his pace, or go softly.

I felt myself coming and began to pant and sob, terrified that the building pressure would disappear into nothing. It didn't. As he began to jerk uncontrollably, swearing wildly as he did so, my body went into melt down. I lifted my hands off the counter, slippery with sweat, and raked my nails into his back as I drew him in further than I thought possible, for the last few thrusts that were sending me over the edge, again, and again and again.

I felt like crying.

I felt like laughing.

I felt like a woman and I hadn't felt like that in such a long time.

I also felt rather sore.

"Wow," He said after breathing heavily onto my breasts for a few moments. "That was something else."

What could I say? I mean, literally what could I say? Thank you?

Well done Tim, jolly good show. Please can we do it again? Soon! No, no really I should not be saying that!

"Would you like another brew? I bet its gone cold by now."

He snorted with laughter and suddenly I was giggling hysterically with him. We clung together again, this time in shared mirth, knowing that we had done something really, really bad.

He was still inside me, and I didn't want to let him go. Already I could feel him hardening up and the light in his eyes told me he was game for more. I heaved a deep sigh.

"We'd really better not." I looked at the clock on the wall. Lunchtime had come and gone. There was always a chance that Megan, Jake, or Mark would be back early.

"Shame," he said, pulling out of me and hitching up his pants without a hint of embarrassment. For my part, sitting there naked, I was conscious of every sag and droopy bit of flesh now on show. I couldn't scramble back into my clothes quick enough.

"You might need to put another sweater on," he said with a smile and a gentle touch as he stoked my neck. "I got a bit carried away, sorry."

"You mean I've got a love bite?" I was actually quite thrilled at the idea. I hadn't had one of those since I was a teenager.

"I'd like to give you more," he said grabbing me for yet another lingering kiss. "But I suppose now is not the time."

"Now is most certainly not the time," I said, pushing him away with a laugh. "And I'm not sure there should even be another time. I'm old enough to be your mother for goodness sake! You're my son's best friend! What would Jake say?"

His eyes went round with horror. "Well, I'm not going to tell him. Are you?"

"No of course not!"

"Well then." Back came the cheeky grin. "Why don't you see it as you helping me with my education?"

He was like an irrepressible puppy. You just couldn't help but like him. "Out!" I shooed my hands at him. "Go on. I need to tidy myself up before anyone comes home. I must look a right state!"

"You look bloody gorgeous, and even better with no clothes on."

40

I pulled a face at him.

"Honestly, Eve. Age has nothing to do with it. You're a beautiful woman and as sexy as hell."

"Go!" I said, again, but with a wide smile on my face.

"Only if you promise I can see you again. Like this I mean. Otherwise I shall stay here 'til Jake comes home and tell him what we've been up to."

What was I getting myself into? "I promise," I said. "Lesson two will be scheduled for another day. Now hoppit."

"Yes teacher," he smirked and went out the back door.

I waited until I heard the sound of his motor bike pulling away from the house, before collapsing onto one of the kitchen chairs. Skip rose from his basket and came to put his head on my lap. He regarded me with curiosity in his faithful brown eyes. What, I wondered, had he made of the last half hour?

"Thank goodness you can't talk," I said to him and kissed his nose. Then abandoning the kitchen which still needed the cupboards re-stocking, I went upstairs to have a shower.

I didn't recognise the woman in the bathroom mirror. Her eyes were glowing, not a confused mix of blue-green and brown, but the colour of the sea. Her skin was blooming, wrinkles hardly visible. Her mouth was soft and sultry, a smile lingering. Her body was tingling, bitten, bruised, sore and wanton. I didn't want to wash away the traces of this woman. I liked her.

But I soaped away Tim's touch, mindful I had an act to perform now. Not only was I covering up my husband's deceit, I had my own lies to conceal. I winced a little at the soreness between my legs, and then froze at the thought that I had been totally irresponsible. I could have no more children, so that wasn't an issue. But how many times had I lectured my own kids on unprotected sex for other reasons.

As I smeared anti-aging body lotion all over myself, I wondered where the best place was to buy condoms.

CHAPTER FIVE

Is there in all of us, a capacity for hiding the truth? Was this how it was for Andy? Had it been as easy for him to get out of Jason's bed and then come home to me? Smile at the ready, old habits in place. Nothing to indicate a lie was being covered up?

Maybe it is part of human nature. Maybe we are designed that way. Survival instinct. As I listened to the competitive banter between Megan and Jake at the dinner table, I reckoned that it had to be the case. I would say that in essence, I am an honest person. Truth matters to me. I frequently get myself into bother because of my less than tactful nature.

Yet here I was, dishing up shepherd's pie, leaving Andy's covered on the side for later, as I always did, and asking Mark how his day at university had been, whilst my kids squabbled over who had the second helping. And all the time, my eyes seemed unable to stop looking over to the counter where I had screwed one of their friends like a complete slut.

And then I blamed Andy.

Because, I argued fiercely to myself, if he had not been so deceitful in the first place I would not have been put in this situation. If our marriage had been genuine, then I would not have spent the last ten years in an emotional and physical wilderness. I would not have erupted like Mount Etna at the first signs of passion.

Okay, shagging my son's best friend was perhaps not the best of options but I was definitely entitled to shag someone. Sex, after all is a basic human need and if my husband wasn't prepared to offer it, there was no more reason to stay faithful. It would perhaps have been more appropriate with someone my age.

But, not as wicked!

I heard the front door shutting and Skip shot off to welcome Andy home.

Knowing I couldn't let him see me with my ridiculous smile on my face, I pushed open the back door and wandered out into the cold evening air. There was no moon tonight, but the garden lights were on so I walked down the path to sit on the bench by my gnomes. I sat there chatting to them for some time, until it was too cold to linger any more.

I just couldn't face Andy. I had hardly been able to look at him, since New Year's Eve, and now I was even more muddled up. Thankfully, he was involved in a conversation with Megan in the lounge as I went back into the house. I gave them both a quick wave through the glass door and went upstairs.

The following morning, I awoke with the realisation that I didn't have a job.

I would need to find a replacement, although I had no idea what. The thought of staying in child care no longer appealed, but I wasn't really qualified for anything else. At the back of my confused mind, there was a persistently nagging thought that when Andy and I got round to sorting out the mess of our marriage, I may well have to earn more money than before, if I was going to be single.

It was not a concept that scared me. I had never been all that bothered about material things. If we had to sell the house and each of us buy something smaller, so be it. Luxuriating in having extra time in bed, I made myself a second cup of coffee and as everyone else went about their daily business, I picked up the local paper, intent on skimming through the property section.

Megan was running late herself and was berating Mark for not waking her when her she slept through her alarm clock. He had no lectures today so had no reason to get up, but Megan did not see that as an excuse. She huffed and puffed her way around the kitchen as I tiptoed past her with my newspaper.

Not quick enough.

"What's with you and Dad sleeping in separate bedrooms?"

The barn conversion had three bedrooms downstairs, one for Megan and Jake, and one used as their lounge. Upstairs, on the mezzanine level, there was our large en-suite room and a second office/ spare room. Since New Year, Andy had been sleeping in the spare room. I had hoped that this would go unnoticed. Like the love bite which I was hiding with the folds of my dressing gown collar.

My brain was trying to form an answer as she attacked a piece of toast, tearing it with her teeth. Megan seemed to do everything fiercely, even eating. She was glaring at me now, and I bristled in response. Some of her annoyance would be because she was late, none of which was my fault. And I didn't really see why I should have to explain my sleeping arrangements with anyone, daughter or not.

"Not really any of your business is it?"

"Have you two had a row?"

"Again, not really any of your business."

"Course it is. You're my parents."

"Do I poke my nose in when you and Mark have a tiff?"

"No."

"Well then."

"It's not the same. What have you done?"

That hurt. What have I done? Well alright, yesterday I had wild sex with one of her friends, but only because of what her father had done first. But I was never allowed to criticize Andy, not to Megan. Not in the mood for a full blown confrontation, I took the easy way out.

"If you must know, he's snoring a lot at the moment and it's doing my head in. There, happy now."

"Well why didn't you just say so?"

I arched my brows at her. "I shouldn't have to."

Back in bed I enjoyed my coffee and perused the for sale notices in the Mapoleton Mail. Then, having decided that I could be quite content in a much smaller cottage, perhaps on Cobblers Row, I got dressed, jeans shirt, v-neck sweater and a silk scarf around my bitten neck, and went back down stairs. Skip was looking at me impatiently. My normal routine was to take him out early before going to work. It was half past nine now, two hours late, his brown eyes reprimanded me as his tail swished against the flagged floor.

"Yes, I know," I kissed his soft black nose. "Don't worry I'll make it up to you. How about we go to Sally's hm? You can play with Bobby?" He understood me of course. A typical Border Collie Skip was a one woman dog, my faithful shadow.

44

I got my coat and boots out of the utility room. Then with Skip loose at my heels, I went down the garden path, through the gate and onto the fields. I had been this way every day since meeting the old woman who had given me her handkerchief but I had not seen her again. I had washed the small square of white cotton, rubbing my fingers more than once over the neatly embroidered 'I', wishing I knew what it stood for.

I paused up by the old oak tree and wondered if I could conjure her up simply by thinking of her. I couldn't of course, but at least the sun came out from behind a cloud, as if to say that I wasn't alone. I caressed the rough bark of the tree with my fingers and smiled. Perhaps the old gods who had once been worshipped here still lingered, if you listened hard enough.

I felt a surge of peace in my heart that had been missing for the last few days. The sharp stab of betrayal had dulled to a nagging ache, camouflaged no doubt by my own erratic and not to mention, erotic behaviour. Every time I thought of Tim, I caught myself smiling. And then I felt like crying. Because I still loved Andy.

And that was the crux of the matter.

You can't wipe out twenty two years in an instant.

You can't just stop loving someone. Or at least I couldn't.

"Any suggestions?" I spoke out loud to whatever spirits might hear me. No answer but I did feel a lifting of my soul as I continued on my way. It was such a beautiful day it was hard not to feel good about simply being alive. The cold snap which had made the air sharp and the ground hard before Christmas, was finally easing and by comparison the sun felt warm, the breeze gentle.

When I got to the gate at the far end of the field, I clipped Skip's lead back on. From here my walk would take me down the lane for ten minutes until I reached Maypoleton Lodge. Sally Farthing lived here as her family had done for generations. The old country house was now run as a riding school and livery yard, enabling Sally to combine her love of horses and pay the huge bills at the same time.

As well as being great friends with Sally, I got on well with Jenny, the on- site instructor and often stayed to help at weekends when they were short staffed, or simply busy with children's parties. Megan and Jake had not needed me as much at home, and Andy was forever golfing (or so he had said at the time) that I didn't feel guilty at the amount of time I spent there.

Sally also had two grown up children so naturally we had a lot in common and as girl- friends do, shared intimate gossip about our family lives. It was going to be very hard to not to tell her what was happening. But I had promised Andy I would not say a word, and as much as I loved and trusted Sally, it would be too easy for someone to overhear and spread the gossip.

I found her on the livery side of the yard, placating an angry owner.

"If you feel that strongly about it I'll have Henry section off a part of the field and Missy can be turned out by herself." She caught my eye and mimed the action of putting the kettle on.

I bumped into Jenny in the mammoth kitchen, cluttered as usual with horse magazines, bridles, and various other bits of tack. Jenny was in her mid-fifties, a no nonsense woman, with Scandinavian good looks and a reputation for saying what she thought. Like now.

"So what's it like to have your tonsils tickled by a randy eighteen year old then?"

I went scarlet, immediately thinking of yesterday and then realised that Jenny was referring just to the kiss. I told Skip to settle down in front of the fire and wondered what to say.

"His cousin was in my ten o'clock yesterday. Told me all about it. He's split up with his girlfriend as well I hear, so he may well be after more than a kiss." Jenny grinned at me.

"Now that would be daft," I croaked, anxious to make myself busy with the kettle so that I could avoid looking her straight in the eye. It was hard to fool Jenny.

"Daft," she said with a dirty laugh, "But not unimaginable. I certainly wouldn't say no. But then I'm not happily married."

Fortunately, she was called away by one of the grooms panicking over a colicky horse. Sally passed her on the way out and was instructed to get all the details before I went home.

"Right," said my friend, reaching for the biscuit tin which she kept hidden from the staff. "A couple of hobnobs and you can fill me in." Sally was forever on a diet, although I thought she was gorgeous just the way she was, curvy with a cleavage I would have killed for and pretty turquoise eyes.

46

I helped myself to the hobnobs and shrugged my shoulders. "Oh you know. It was just a kiss. I was drunk, Andy had pissed me off, and it just happened." How simple did that sound.

"Oh, is that all?" Her disappointment had her reaching for a third biscuit which I knew she would blame on me later. "I heard you got sacked for it though? The bible bashing mothers of Little Acorns didn't approve?"

"Bloody hell is there any gossip that doesn't go round at lightning speed?" I fidgeted on my chair, thinking what a field day would be had if people really knew what was going on.

"Sophie Tomson has a little sister at the nursery. Her mother was telling us yesterday whilst Sophie was waiting for her lesson."

"I wasn't sacked," I corrected the gossip. "I walked."

"Good for you. Ooh, yes, actually that is good. Perfect in fact." Sally looked positively thrilled.

"I aim to please," I said dryly.

"No, it's just that I could really do with some help here. I haven't seen you since New Year and it's been so hectic with pony club, I haven't even had chance to ring you. "

"What sort of help?"

"In the office mainly, answering the phone, dealing with the bookings, sorting out the supplies, that sort of thing."

"I thought that was Richard's job?"

Sally pulled a face. "It is, only my husband is having what can only be described as a mid- life crisis."

Oh God, not him as well. "What's he done?"

"He's decided he needs to go sailing with his Dad for one last time before he's too old, his Dad I mean."

Sounded reasonable. "That's fair enough. His Dad is nearly eighty after all."

"And that whilst he's away, his Mother should come and stay here."

"Aah." Sally's relationship with her mother-in-law was worse than that with mine. "Not good. How long is the trip for?"

"A year."

"A year! Where the bloody hell are they sailing? Around the world? Oh you're kidding me!"

"I'm not. Those two silly bastards are going round the world in a sailing boat and I have to look after Mary whilst they do it."

"Oh shit."

"Precisely. Which is why, Eve dearest, I shall be desperate for you to come and help me here, if only to stop me from murdering my mother-in-law. In fact, sod doing the office work, I can do that. I might just pay you to keep Mary company. You get on alright with her, don't you?"

"I think she's okay," I tried to be tactful. Mary was a handful but she didn't rub me up the same way she did to Sally, probably because I wasn't related to her. "But I tell you what, if you do murder her, I'll help you hide the body." I grinned at her. "We could always bury her in the muck heap!"

Sally laughed at the idea, but as I raised my mug of tea to my lips, I felt a chill run down my spine. Goose bumps prickled my flesh.

"You alright? You've gone awfully pale?"

I nodded, despite the urge to shiver. "I'm fine. Just tired. Didn't sleep too well last night." This was true and I tried to push away the horrible feeling that had crept over me.

CHAPTER SIX

I couldn't help it. My eyes strayed to the counter as soon as I set foot back in the kitchen. My thoughts of Tim were instantly banished by the sight of Andy's keys, taunting me by their presence. And then my heart gave that stupid little jump it always did at the thought that my husband had popped home during the day. Old habits die hard I guess. It was going to take more than a quick screw with a teenager to reboot the way my mind worked.

Just to confirm this, when Andy walked into the kitchen, his initial expression was one of surprise, then the old endearing love, before finally, that new look of his. Shifty guilt. I hated seeing that look on his face. It played havoc with my emotions. I still wanted him.

"Hi," I said with a smile, wondering how it was possible that I could contemplate throwing myself into his arms for a hug.

"You're not at work?"

We had avoided each other last night so he didn't know. "I'm not working at the nursery any more. As of yesterday." No need to tell him why. "I'm going to work for Sally instead."

"Oh well that's good. You weren't happy there anyway." He smiled and his eyes crinkled into the lines, developed over the years. "You never looked right in that uniform. A spotty top is not my Eve at all."

"I'm not though am I?" Could he hear the anguish in my voice? "I'm not your Eve anymore."

"Don't say that, Eve." He covered the distance between us, and pulled me close despite my attempts to remain rigid in his arms. "You'll always be my Eve."

I balled my fists up against his chest, frustration and anger building up dangerously. I really wanted to hit him. At the same

49

time, if he had kissed me, wanted me, I would have dissolved into his embrace willingly.

"We'll talk tonight," he said softly into my hair.

"No!" I pushed him away. "We'll talk now. I know what will happen, Andy. You'll be late, or Jake will want running somewhere, or Megan will need you for something, and you'll just sweep it under the carpet again! No, Andy, I'm not having it. I've kept my mouth shut since New Year and the least you can do is talk to me. Properly!"

At that moment his phone went off in his pocket. Automatically, he went to answer it. I glared at him. He was brief and to the point with his colleague and told him that he would be unavailable for the rest of the day. Well that was a first.

"Give me two minutes. I'm going to change."

"What for?" I was suspicious.

"I can't talk here, Eve. We'll go out somewhere. A drive and a walk maybe."

Skip pricked his ears up at that. At least someone was happy, I thought, watching my dog shake off his snooziness in an instant. Andy was as good as his word. Two minutes later he was back in the kitchen wearing jeans, the sweater I had bought him for Christmas, and thick woolly socks. We collected our walking boots from the utility room and set off.

Andy drove the car as if he was on auto pilot, taking us south east from Maypoleton towards the enigmatic outline of Pendle Hill. We hadn't been here in years. On the way we passed the pub where we had met, Andy leaning against the bar with his mates, as I sang in my band. I wondered if he remembered and if it was causing him the same stab of pain.

He slowed the car. "I'll never forget the first moment I saw you," he said, looking first at the pub and then at me. He wasn't lying. The look in his eyes was as clear and open as it had been on the night so many years ago. It made me want to cry and I turned my head away, not sure if I could bear this.

I heard him sigh and grate the gears clumsily as he sped away from the pub, up towards the winding road that would take us to the famous hill. We passed the ski club where we had both had our first lessons. Shuffling timidly up the slope sideways, laughing as we fell over, again and again. Hard not to think of all the skiing holidays we had taken with the children. Happy times. Shared moments. A lifetime together.

It mattered.

Just how much it mattered rocked me as though someone had punched me hard in the stomach, knocking the breath out of me. I gave a tiny gasp and hunched up in my seat.

"Are you alright?"

I nodded, feeling sick inside. I was glad when he stopped the car and I could get out. The wind was blowing cold up here, whipping my hair wildly around my face. We walked, absurdly, hand in hand, up the hill. Our feet taking the path they had done so many times before. No need to talk. Not just yet. It was enough for me, just to be there, to have my husband beside me, and I guessed that he felt the same. This had been our place when we were first together. He had asked me to marry me here. Right at the top.

"You are the only woman for me, Eve," he had said. "Now and always. There'll never be another woman in my life, I promise you that."

I had returned his kisses with passion and believed him.

Well he hadn't lied had he? Or broken his promise, exactly. There had not been any other women.

Did he remember, I wondered as we reached the top, cheeks burning now with the wind and the quick pace we had set? Was that why he had brought me here?

Of course. He had tears in his eyes as he came to a full stop, and I think he was for once, blind to the stunning view. The wind was blowing the clouds across the sky as though hurrying them along, and right now, a dark cluster of them had just cleared the sun, illuminating the valley below us. Timeless. A scene that would never change.

It made me think how small we were in comparison to Mother Nature. Yet how huge at times the burdens on our shoulders. Or maybe it was just the way we perceived them? Did it really matter if the man beside me wanted to share my bed, or that of another man? Did it really matter that I was so deeply miserable and lacking in self-esteem that I welcomed the attentions of a randy young man, barely a boy?

51

Yes. It did.

All of it mattered. Too fucking much and my head hurt because of it. Not to mention my heart. My pain deepened as Andy began to talk.

"I can't stop loving you, Eve. I've tried, but I can't. And I can't not love him either."

I resisted the urge to clamp my hands over my ears. It was me, after all, who insisted we talk. I just hadn't imagined we would end up doing so here. Andy carried on, his eyes focusing somewhere in the distance.

"His name is Jason Berry. I never meant anything to happen between us. It would have been impossible anyway when we first met."

"Why?"

"Because he was my therapist when I had my break down."

"Your therapist! But that was years ago. Don't tell me that this has been going on since then?"

"No! I couldn't lie to you all that time. I knew..." He stumbled a bit then. "When I met him I knew there was something and that he felt it too but of course nothing could come of it because of the situation. Ironic really." He gave a hard laugh, a sound I had never heard from him before. Dark and bitter.

"What do you mean, ironic?"

"My break down. It wasn't about work."

"Well what was it about then?" I heard the catch in my voice and hated my weakness. I was trying to be strong, but this was proving so much harder than I anticipated. I felt like Pandora with the lid off the box, desperately trying to ram it back down.

"It was about me. Who I am. What I am!" Andy shrugged his shoulders in a gesture of total frustration. "Don't you think I would change it if I could? Do you think I chose to be this way?"

It was a good job there was no one else about as he shouted into the wind.

"Gay, you mean?" I said flatly.

"Yeah. Gay, queer, a puff, shirt lifter, all those and more," he said with more of the bitterness coming to the fore. "Can you imagine what it was like for me growing up with my parents and thinking that I was different to all my mates, but not really understanding why? And then when I did, knowing that I would never be able to tell anyone?"

My tattered heart shed more blood for him at that moment. Yes. I could picture that all right. He would have suffered. Sandra and Steven

Armstrong would have put their son through hell if they had had any inkling of what had been in his mind. No wonder he had bottled it up. Tried to do the 'right thing.'

"Is that why you married me? As a cover?" I wouldn't condemn him if that was the case. But I needed to know.

For the first time, he turned and looked right at me. His blue eyes were so dark they looked nearly black, deep pools of swirling anguish.

"No!" He caught hold of my hands. "Eve, I married you because I loved you. I still do."

"As much as you can love any woman?"

"As much as I can love any woman." Honest at least.

I sighed and rested my head against his chest for a moment. How could I hate him for this? I couldn't. I hated what it did to me. I hated what it did to us. But I couldn't actually hate him.

We started to walk back down the hill, at a slower, less frantic pace than we had come up. Andy was talking more smoothly now, as if having started it was all beginning to flow in his head. I wish it was in mine.

"When did you realise properly? I mean that you were hiding what you felt?"

"When I saw Jason for the first time," he said with a smile that cut me right through to the bone He carried on, having no idea how much he was wounding me further with each word. "I was waiting in the reception area feeling a bag of nerves and wondering how I had got myself into such a state. I felt as if my life was over. Then I saw this man walking down the corridor and something burst inside me. I looked at this person and felt that I had known them all my life. Then he came over and introduced himself and that was that."

"Throughout the sessions Jason helped me to come to terms with who I really was, but of course he gave no inkling that he felt the same way. It was years later, last year in fact, when I bumped into him again, that things started to happen."

I might as well rub salt into the wounds. I never knew I was a masochist until now. "How exactly?"

"I was at the chemist getting some throat lozenges. He was there. He works one day a week now at the surgery at Maypoleton and the rest of the time he's based at the hospital in Lancaster, which is where I first saw him."

Great. Right on our doorstep. No wonder Andy wanted to keep it all quiet. "And?" I prompted, despite the agony. It was like waxing your own bikini line. Slowly.

"He asked me how I was doing and it just sort of took off from there."

Enough was enough. I couldn't cope with any more details. "I think I need a drink," I said as we neared the bottom of the hill. Something to numb the pain.

Andy was quiet as we drove back down the road to the pub we had passed earlier. The place we had first met. Appropriate maybe that it should mark the ending of our marriage as well? He was gentle with me, as we went inside and found a table next to the cosy log fire. He ordered a coke for himself and a half a Guinness for me.

I was tempted to get absolutely plastered but that would not solve anything and we still had much to discuss. Hungry all of a sudden, we both opted to order the steak and ale pie and ate it in a relatively companionable silence. Then it was time for me to talk.

I declined the offer of a second Guinness, needing to keep a clear head. "I think you are right that no-one should know," I began. "At least not for the time being. Jake does his A level's in six months' time and Megan has just about come to terms with her old school friend dying last year. Let them get this academic year out of the way, and then we get a divorce and you tell them, honestly, the reason why."

He regarded me then with such a look of relief that made me wonder what he had been expecting me to do. Shout it from the rooftops? Put an ad in the Maypoleton Mail? He was the father of my children, I could never do that. He coughed and asked if he could stay at the house.

I nodded. "God knows it's big enough. But when Jake's completed his exams, it gets sold and we split the difference. In the meantime, I promise to keep my mouth shut."

"And we stay friends?" He was looking at me so hopefully I nearly burst into tears. God this was so painful.

"And we stay friends," I said huskily, wondering how the hell I was going to stay sane in the interim.

As it turned out, I didn't do a very good job of it.

CHAPTER SEVEN

Confession may be very good for the soul, at least for the person off-loading. But for the recipient it is absolute agony. Andy was actually whistling by the time he changed back into his work clothes, ready to go back to the office to catch up on the work he had missed. He even went so far as to give me a peck on the cheek and a squeeze round my waist before saying a cheery goodbye.

Then he left me in the kitchen towelling Skip down from our walk, and feeling as though I had been flayed alive. How was that fair? I alternated between wanting to lay my head on the table and weep until there were no more tears left in me, and smashing up every breakable surface in the house. My chest was as tight as a drum and my breath was coming in short uncomfortable gasps.

I looked at the clock on the wall, thinking that this time yesterday I had been pinned up against the counter by Tim. An instant surge of lust gripped me at the same time anger flooded through my veins. He would be at college now, possibly even sitting next to Jake. Would he be thinking of me? I groaned out loud. My head was splitting with the turmoil inside.

By the time Megan and Mark arrived home, followed closely by Jake, I was in no better state. Maybe it had not been a good idea to have three successive cups of strong coffee, but it was either that or hit the booze again. I snarled and snapped my way through the evening, throwing pots and pans round the kitchen in a manner Gordon Ramsay would have been proud of.

I found fault with every little thing they did, including Mark which came as a shock to them as usually he was safe from my occasional blasts of temper. By the time it was eight o'clock, I had managed to insult them ten times over, giving rein to the bottled up feelings of frustration and generally acting like a total harpy.

Climbing the stairs, intent on drowning myself in the bath, I heard Jake grumble to his sister that if this was the start of me going through the change, then he would soon be moving out. Megan's reply was muffled, coming from inside her bedroom, but the tone was clear. She would sort things out. I stuck my tongue out childishly and slammed my own bedroom door behind me.

I hardly slept a wink that night. I went downstairs at three in the morning for a hot milk and whisky. Across the landing, I could hear Andy snoring his head off. Bastard! How dare he sleep like a baby? It was fortunate I had no job to go to, as I finally dropped into a thick and heavy slumber around half past four.

The house was quiet and empty when I woke much later. After a lazy breakfast, very late, as Jeremy Kyle was already on, I thought I might as well saunter over to Sally's and make a start finding my way round the office. I arrived to find Jenny and the other stable girls having their mid- morning break in the kitchen. They made a fuss of Skip who snaffled at least two biscuits before settling down beside Sally's dog, Bob.

"Where's Sally?" I asked, making myself a coffee. I really should cut down, but now was not the time.

"On the phone," replied Jenny somewhat unnecessarily as my friend burst through the door at that moment.

"Bloody, bloody, bloody, mother-in-laws!" Sally rarely exploded into temper but right now her pretty round face was nearly puce. Her hand was deep into the biscuit tin which made her swear again at the fact that she was been driven from her diet. "Bloody men and their stupid ideas. It's all Richard's fault!" She sat down grumpily at the table, munching crossly.

I was still hovering by the kettle so I made her a fresh brew, emptying the cold coffee which was in front it her.

"Get it off your chest," I encouraged, glad to be distracted by someone else's problems.

"I've just had her on the phone for an hour," she began, dunking her third biscuit into her coffee. "I won't bore you with the details but the upshot of it is her majesty is not content with coming to stay with us in the house, which as much as I am dreading the idea, is better than what she has in mind."

"Which is?" Jenny looked across at her before checking her watch for the time.

Sally ruffled up her feathered crop of light blonde hair which framed her bonny face softly. "She is insisting that she moves into the cottage."

"What cottage?" I asked the same time as Jenny who was now getting up from the table and nodding at the girls that they needed to be getting back on the yard.

"It's that tiny old cottage on the edge of the estate. Used to be home to the gamekeeper back in the day. It's perfectly habitable, the family have used it for generations, sometimes letting it out and other times using it ourselves."

"Well that's good, isn't it?" Jenny said what I was thinking as she chivvied the last stable girl along.

Sally shook her head. "You would think so wouldn't you? Not my mother-in-law. She's doing this to be as awkward as possible. On site but far enough away to be a damned nuisance. There's a telephone which connects the two properties and she'll be on that bloody line morning noon and night. I'll be tramping back and forth across the estate at her beck and call. At least if she was here, I would only have to dash down the hallway. I'd been planning on giving her the west wing all to herself. But no, that's not good enough for Richard's Mother! She's never forgiven me for keeping my name when we got married, but there have been Farthing's here since the Middle Ages."

I tried to calm her down. "At least I'll be here to share the load." I really didn't find Mary Smith quite so bad.

Sally harrumphed and had yet another biscuit, scowling as she did so. "Yes well I might just take you up on the idea of burying her in the muck heap. For the time being though," she found a smile at last, "you wouldn't mind helping me clear out the cottage, would you? It's been empty for a good couple of years and could do with a damn good sort out."

I relished the chance to get busy and have something else to occupy my mind. "Love to," I replied and jumped up, ready to get started.

"Oh God, not that quick, there's time for another brew surely?"

I shook my head. "No. That biscuit tin's half empty and you'll be moaning about your diet next."

"I thought I was the boss, not you," she muttered as I bundled her out of the kitchen.

The grounds of Maypoleton Lodge were mostly untamed woodlands apart from the managed paddocks that provided grazing for the horses. Gardening had never been a popular pastime amongst the Farthing family. Consequently, the surrounding acreage had been left to run wild. Hidden in the middle of a thick copse of trees and rhododendron bushes nestled the one and a half storey building. A fairy tale cottage in a wood.

"Like I said," Sally commented unnecessarily as we picked our way through the over grown path of wild weeds and brambles. "It's not been used in a long time."

"It's delightful," I fell in love at once with the white stone building. Two small windows were set deep either side of the low front door and in the eaves of the roof, perched an even smaller window, right in the centre. "The roses are beautiful," I added, catching the gentle scent of the flowers on the fresh winter breeze.

"What roses?" Sally paused with her hand on the door knob. "If you mean those brambles, then it's far too long since you've been bought any flowers."

I blinked and looked again. How silly. Of course there weren't roses round the door. And if there had been they would not have been in bloom in January. "I must have imagined them. Come on open up. I'm dying to see inside."

"There's not much to see," Sally said wryly. "I really can't understand why Mary wants to stay here instead of at the house. The plumbing's dreadful."

The cottage had two rooms downstairs, a small sitting room with an open fire, and a kitchen which had had a bathroom built onto the back at a later stage. Up the narrow staircase there was just the one bedroom. I thought it was magical.

"It's lovely," I said, blind to the cobwebs and dust, and the dark shadows as the dim winter light struggled to get through the dirty panes of glass. I saw instead, an oasis of calm from a bygone time.

Sally grunted. "It's cold and filthy."

"Yes but with the fire going and a bit of a clean it'll be perfect." I stood in the centre of the small sitting room, my hand on the stone mantel piece. I could feel the blaze of a fire warming my legs and smell the heady fragrance of wood smoke, mingled with rose blossom. I could hear laughter ringing in my ears, a joyful sound, rich and masculine. I turned with a start to see Sally tugging viciously at one of the curtain poles.

"Bugger!" It collapsed in a flurry of muck and dust. Sally sneezed. "I told you this was going to be more trouble than it's worth. I bet that chimney's blocked too." She nodded at where I was standing.

I looked into the blackened grate, cold and dark, with no signs of life. I sniffed the air sharply but instead of the scents of wood smoke and roses, I got a lung full of dust and dirt which made me cough harshly.

"Let's get these windows open, if we can," said Sally, bravely tugging at the other curtain. This one remained in place, but she screamed loudly as a huge spider ran down the edge of the fabric. "Jesus wept, look at the size of that!"

"It's a beauty." I laughed as Sally hopped around, frantically trying to avoid the long legged creature. I scooped it up in my hands and placed it outside.

"Ugh, I don't know how you could. Whole damn place is probably infested with them."

"Stop moaning. It's a wonderful place. I could live here." As I said the words I had a picture of myself sitting in the chair by the fire. Only it wasn't me. Not quite. Yet it felt so familiar, as if it was home. As if I belonged there. I gave myself a mental shake. It was just the cottage being so old. That was all. It had atmosphere.

Upstairs there was far more than that.

Sally insisted that I went up the wooden staircase first in case any more monster-sized creepy crawlies jumped out at her. Spiders never bothered me. I liked them. But as my hand reached for the door knob something did spook me. I heard again the laughter from downstairs. I stopped so suddenly that Sally bumped into me.

"Is it stuck?"

"No." I couldn't explain the sense of anticipation I felt at opening the door. That and a terrible feeling of dread. Gingerly, I stepped into the room. It was simply furnished with a metal framed bed in the centre, a narrow wardrobe and a chest of drawers under the window. Nothing to be afraid of. Yet as I walked across the wooden floor board, covered with a faded rug, I went icy cold.

"I really can't see Mary being happy here," said Sally with a shrug of her shoulders. "You watch, she'll have me sprucing it up, stay for a couple of weeks or so and then she'll be insisting that it was all my idea when she gets rheumatism from the damp. Then she'll blame me and say that I wanted to stick her out here by herself. Eve, are you alright?"

No I wasn't. I thought that I was going to pass out and had to stumble to the bed to sit down before I fell. I was aware of Sally hovering over me in concern but over-riding everything else, was the freezing sensation that was invading my mind and blocking out clear thought. When it finally began to thaw I was aware that I had tears in my eyes.

"Oh Sally, something really dreadful happened here. Can't you feel it?"

She looked at me in alarm. "No. Can you?"

"Yes. But it's going." I let out a long sigh and looked around the room once more. "And now it feels fine. Just my imagination. Forget it."

Sally gave a nervous laugh. "Are you sure? You freaked me out there, I thought you were going to faint. Maybe it is haunted, although no one in the family has ever said anything to that effect. But then none of us are psychic."

"Neither am I."

She looked at me.

"I'm not!" And then I had a sudden picture in my head of the old woman by the tree. What was it she had said? Something about no longer being blind, being able to see properly, beyond what others could not? I had thought at the time the woman meant it as a blessing but I wondered now if it had been a curse. "Come on," I said abruptly, "let's get back to work. You were right about there being loads to do."

We set to until eventually Sally went on strike, collapsing in one of the chairs.

"Good God, girl, I've not worked so hard in weeks. It's three o'clock! We've completely missed lunch and afternoon break!"

"Yes but doesn't it look better," I surveyed the tiny cottage with a satisfaction rare for someone who hated housework. We had swept, polished, scrubbed, vacuumed, we had even dared to shove a broom handle up the chimney, dislodging an old bird's nest. The curtains needed replacing and some new cushions would go down a treat, but other than that, it was ready to move in to. I was tired but happy. Apart from that spooky moment upstairs, I enjoyed being in the cottage and felt rather envious of Mary.

We made our way back to the main house, Sally grumbling with every step that she had muscles aching in places that muscles should not exist. I grabbed a quick cup of coffee and couple of biscuits before setting off back home with Skip at my heels.

It was going dark as I walked down the lane and back across the fields to Cooper's Barn but I was in no hurry to get back home. Part of me had wanted to stay in the cottage. It struck me as an ideal place to hibernate whilst the mess of my life crashed around me. I knew I had been a real pig to everyone last evening and was not looking forward to facing my family.

I was in for a surprise tonight though.

Megan and Mark were in the kitchen when I arrived home, just after four o'clock. Mark was busy laying the table, and Megan was standing at the oven, stirring something in my large pan. It smelt good.

"Mm, lovely." I went to my daughter and hugged her from behind aware that perhaps I had not done this too much of late. "Am I being pampered?"

"Well it's obvious you're really stressed about something at the moment," said Megan, flicking her hair back over her shoulders. "So we've had a little chat, and we've all agreed that you need a bit more help around the house. Jake included. I've sorted out everyone with a list of jobs which should give you a bit more time to yourself."

I smothered my smile. "Great."

"We know you got sacked from the nursery...."

"I walked," I had to interrupt.

"Oh. Well, anyway, we know you've lost your job because of that silly incident with Tim, which we know won't be repeated but was

61

obviously symptomatic of your state of mind at the moment, so to help get that sorted out, I've booked you an appointment with Doctor Jay tomorrow at 4 pm. I've not got any lectures then so I am coming with you."

It really was quite scary being organised by my daughter. I nodded and smiled, and beat down the treacherous stab of wicked glee that I had not only repeated 'my silly incident' with Tim, but had gone very much further. Still, if everyone wanted to think I was wildly hormonal, who was I to argue? Especially if it meant my lazy brood got off their arses long enough to clean up after themselves and make tea.

CHAPTER EIGHT

After yet another horrible night's sleep, plagued with disturbing and vividly lurid dreams, I decided that going to the doctors was a good idea after all and I probably would not have bothered making an appointment for myself. Not content with re-organising her day in order that she could shepherd me along to the surgery Megan had also decreed that we were going to go shopping first.

"You need some new clothes and make up," she told me with the air of one who must be obeyed. "You never spend any money on yourself."

I thought it wiser not to comment that the main reason for this was down to how much money Megan and her brother seemed to swallow up, despite their own part-time jobs. It was actually very nice spending half the day in my daughter's company as we mooched through the shops in Lancaster before stopping for a stupidly expensive coffee and a calorific slice of cake.

As I sat in the cafe feeling smug that I could indulge in my chocolate heaven and still get into a size eight pair of jeans, I regarded the mountain of bags at my feet.

"I really don't think I needed to buy so much."

"Nonsense. Besides, Mum, you've got a cracking figure for your age, you should show it off more. Those skinny jeans looked great and Dad will love you in those tops, especially the one with the scoop neck. You don't show your boobs off enough and you should, they're still quite perky after all."

Her voice was clear and cut across the crowded cafe, drawing eyes in my direction. I didn't know whether to thrust my chest out further, or shrink into my chair. As a well-dressed man at the counter gave me a flirtatious smile, I decided to go with the former. Fortunately Megan had her back to him. As I was wallowing in this little bit of attention, she continued talking.

"It's important at your time of life that you still make the effort. So many women let themselves go and then wonder why their husbands run off with a younger model. Not that you need to worry in that department of course, Dad would never do that. Still, you should keep him interested."

I wished then that I had not chosen the chocolate slice as my stomach seemed to erupt with bitter acid. The sad thing was, just over a week ago, I would have been able to sit here and nod smugly in agreement with my daughter. Now all I could think was that Andy had betrayed me and I had been driven into the arms of a teenager in a desperate bid for attention and revenge.

I pushed the last forkful of cake away. "I think I've have enough."

"You okay, you've gone a funny colour?"

"Just nervous about going to the doctor's I suppose. You know I hate going."

"You'll be fine," said Megan patting my hand and then wonder of wonders got up to pay the bill. "I'll come in with you if you like," she added as we walked out of the cafe, arms linked closely.

"No, honestly, that's sweet of you but I'll be okay. You've done more than enough for me today, it's been lovely, but there's no need for you to come with me at all. Why don't you drop me off in the village and go home. I can easily walk back from the surgery."

Megan gave me a cynical look which said that she didn't quite trust me to keep the appointment unless she actually saw me going into the doctor's room herself. Not wishing to spoil the mood I thanked her once more for her concern and said no more.

We were on time for my appointment but as per usual there was quite a wait. Megan flicked through the glossy magazines offering up her caustic opinions on the celebrities featured. I was happy to people watch especially when a completely gorgeous specimen of manhood walked into the waiting room.

I told myself it was healthy to look and appreciate aware that since the other day with Tim, my hormones seemed to have shot into overdrive. My body had remembered that I did actually have a libido after all. I scrutinised the man with the objective thought that at least he was in my age group.

Tall and slim, with thick toffee coloured hair, fantastic dark eyes, olive skin, and a bum that just made you want to grab hold of it. Yummy! I let my eyes feast upon this vision, as my mind wandered off into dark erotic places.

Then the receptionist called out to him as he started to walk past.

"Jason, would you be a love and take these through to Doctor Wensley as you're passing?"

Jason!

I shot to the edge of my chair startling Megan in to dropping her magazine.

"Bloody hell, Mum, you made me jump there. Are you alright?"

"Mm." Even to my ears I sounded like a strangled cat. I slid to the back of my chair whilst my eyes drilled into the back of the man who had picked up a set of papers from the receptionist and was now walking back towards the door, which lead to the consulting rooms. With perfect timing, the buzzer went to announce that a doctor was ready for their next patient and a light flashed up red on the wall mounted screen.

I ignored it, thinking savagely that it was so unfair. Did he have to be that bloody gorgeous!

Megan said crisply, "Mum, it's your turn, look up there. Eve Armstrong to see Doctor Jay."

Bollocks! I had no choice but to stand up and walk over to the door where the man was now looking behind him, a look of shock on that handsome face.

It was him. I wasn't just being paranoid. I knew as soon as I saw his eyes, treacly black and sexy as hell, flick to the screen where my name was still flashing. He covered the moment by opening the door and holding it for me.

"After you." His voice was deep and smooth, professionally neutral.

I gave the briefest nod of acknowledgement before sliding past him and scurrying down the corridor towards Doctor Jay's room. On the way, I noticed that one door (normally used for nurses) had a temporary name plate in the slot.

Jason Berry.

Counsellor.

My husband's lover.

I knocked on the door to Doctor Jay's room and entered, accepting her invitation to take a seat.

"So, Eve, what can I do for you?"

I rarely went to the doctors and then it was only when I was having problems with my periods. I just didn't know what to say. I looked at Doctor Jay, opening and shutting my mouth like a goldfish, no words coming out at all. If she had been impatient, I think I would have mumbled something about not sleeping. As it was, she sat back with the relaxed manner of someone who had all the time in the world to listen.

I was in shock I suppose. Coming face to face with Jason, especially after ogling him, was just too much. It all came out. I burst into tears and didn't stop for ten minutes during which time the whole sordid details of my marriage tumbled from my lips before I knew what I was doing.

"Oh I am sorry," I finally gasped, dropping the fourth soggy tissue that Doctor Jay had provided into the bin. "I didn't mean to say all that."

Doctor Jay was only in her thirties but she had the calm and compassionate manner of someone much older.

"I rather think you did," she said gently and pushed another box of tissues towards me. "Take your time. I can listen."

I snuffled miserably. "No, really, I don't want to waste your time. It was my daughter's idea to come in the first place. They all think I'm going through the change. I've been acting a little odd, you see."

"I'm not surprised. After the shock you've had, I think a little oddity could be allowed. You're being too hard on yourself, Eve. The sudden end of a marriage, especially one as long as yours, is like a bereavement, whatever the cause, be it death, divorce, or a situation like yours. You have to think about yourself. Stress like this can really eat away at you and before you know it, you will become ill."

"What do you suggest?"

"Well if you're adamant that you want to help your husband keep things quiet for the time being, then I suggest we look at how we can support you through what must be a very difficult time. I am going to suggest a mild sedative for a couple of weeks, just to help your sleep patterns get back to normal. After that, if you're still feeling on edge, we can think about the possibility of an anti-depressant." I pulled a face and she was quick to expand. "There are a lot of products on the market these days which don't have problems with side effects and addictiveness and they can really help level a person in time of acute and chronic imbalance."

"Oh I'm unbalanced alright," I laughed shakily. "I'm wobbling all over the place."

"You're bound to be, especially if you're not sleeping well. So let's get that problem sorted out first." She turned to her computer and tapped away at the keyboard. "I want to see you again in two weeks' time so we can see how these have affected you. Don't worry if you feel a little drowsy to begin with but watch the alcohol."

"Absolutely."

"Just one more thing," said Doctor Jay pressing the last button and sending the prescription automatically through to the on-site pharmacy. "It may help to talk to someone."

I shook my head. "I can't. I mean I have some great friends but you know what gossip is like in a place like this and the last thing I want is for Megan and Jake to find out from someone else."

"I wasn't suggesting a friend, although I can see your point on that score," she smiled "I have enough headaches with the gossips myself. I was meaning something a little more professional. We have a very good therapist who offers counselling sessions here on a weekly basis. He's here today in fact. I could put you on to his list?"

"No! Bad idea! Really bad idea." A bitter laugh tore from my throat, harsh and tinged with hysteria. Biting my lip, I said quickly. "I'm sorry it's not your fault. It's just, well believe me, it really wouldn't help."

"If you're sure? You can always change your mind. Make sure you book an appointment for two weeks' time."

"I will, and thank you."

I felt exhausted as I walked back down the corridor to the waiting room, my eyes on stalks in case Jason popped out from somewhere. His door was closed and for a mad second I considered barging in there and playing hell with him for wrecking my marriage. But a sliver of honesty stopped me. He hadn't wrecked my marriage. It had already been a farce, I just hadn't realised it.

Megan looked concerned as I pushed open the door to the waiting room. I had been rather a long time and it would have been obvious that I had been crying. Again!

"Bloody hell, Mum, are you alright?"

Teeth gritted firmly together in more of a grimace than a smile, I nodded. "I need to come back in two weeks," I said and went off to make the appointment.

"Has she prescribed you anything?" Megan asked when I had done that.

"Yeah."

"HRT?"

Sometimes I really wished she could talk a little quieter. The three people waiting to see the receptionist all stared pointedly at me. Bugger! One of them was a close friend of Deidre Brown from across the road. It would be all round the village that I was going through the change in a matter of hours.

Megan, mistaking the growl I appeared to be making, took my arm and said soothingly. "Don't worry Mum. It'll help I'm sure. You'll soon feel your old self again."

Somehow I doubted that. And besides, who exactly was my old self? A total doormat who had just given twenty of the best years of her life to a man who really didn't deserve them? Did I really want to be that person?

Hell no.

I sat in the pharmacy next to Megan, waiting for my prescription, resentment and anger bubbling up inside me once more. All the time my eyes kept sliding to the door. As if I had summoned a genie out of its lamp, or called up a demon from hell, he walked in and went to the counter to ask for some pain killers.

I hoped he could feel my eyes throwing thunder bolts of rage at him. I hoped his head was exploding behind that smooth, sleek, sexy exterior.

I hoped... Before I could curse him further one of the assistants called me over to collect my tablets. Just as he was turning to walk out. Brilliant. Here I go again. Face to face with my enemy.

His eyes met mine for a second. Held my gaze. Registered alarm. Looked away.

What would I have done if Megan had not been there? God only knows. As it was, motherly caution held sway and, curling my lip at him, I brushed past him to go to the counter. My mood was not helped when the assistant, a girl in her early twenties, sighed and watched him leave the pharmacy with a lust filled expression on her face.

"Just think," she said with a saucy smile in his direction, "some lucky woman is going home to him tonight."

"Don't you believe it pet," I muttered and snatched my prescription from her.

Fortunately, Megan thinking that I was in the grips of a tumultuous hormonal break down, meant that everyone in the house was ordered to give me a wide berth. Megan again offered to sort tea out and I was content to let her. I pleaded a loss of appetite and cloistered myself away in my bedroom for the early part of the evening as Andy and the lads came in from work and university.

I tried reading a book.

I channel hopped on the television.

I sent a couple of emails.

I phoned a friend.

I sent Tim a text.

Second lesson?

Within moments my phoned beeped. Message received. Show message. *When? Where?*

I replied. *Badgers Brock. Twenty mins.*

C U there.

Help. What was I doing? I bounced off the bed and tore round the room for two minutes in a mad panic. Was I completely insane? The wild eyed woman with the flushed cheeks and angry mouth who stared at me in the mirror, said yes. I was completely insane. Did I care? Not one jot.

I thought about changing my clothes, but that would have been far too obvious. So I stayed in the cherry red sweater and long suede effect skirt I was wearing with flat leather boots. But I brushed my teeth, squirted just a smidgeon of perfume in subtle places, and retouched my make-up. Then I sauntered downstairs to announce to everyone that Michelle, an old friend of mine, had called to ask if I

69

could baby sit for an hour or so at short notice. I was just putting on my brown leather jacket in the porch when Andy stopped me to ask if I was alright. By which I mean he looked at me as if he was feeling particularly guilty.

Swallowing my own guilt, I replied, "I'm fine, Megan's filled you in about the Doctor's I suppose?" God I was getting good at this innocent act.

"Yes, but she wouldn't have realised that you bumped into Jason there," he said with a shifty look over his shoulder.

I felt myself flushing and struggled to speak.

"He rang me," said Andy softly, his blue eyes full of concern. "He realised who you were and that you had obviously done the same."

"How astute." My voice amazingly was neutral.

"You're taking this very well," he said, brushing my cheek tenderly with one hand. "I don't think any other woman would cope like you are doing."

I smiled cat-like and positively purred at him. "Oh you know me darling I always find a way to cope." And right now it was going to be shagging the brains out of a randy teenager! I gave my husband a peck on the cheek, told him not to worry what time I would be back, and went.

Badgers Brock is a ten minute drive from our house. A wild stretch of moorland which had over the last ten years or so, been partly tamed by the forestry commission and laid out with walks, trails, and picnic spots. Heaving with people in the summer months, I could rely on it being deserted in the beginning of January. There was a lay by at the fork in the road which turned off up the hill towards the parkland.

I pulled in there and waited for Tim.

It was seven o'clock and completely dark. No road lights on this stretch of country lane. Anyone with a weaker heart would have been jumping at the shadows as they danced around, night birds calling, green eyes of foxes glinting in the distance. Not me. I was made of sterner stuff. Besides, I had other things on my mind.

Soon enough the single beam of a motor bike headlight came my way. I thrilled to the noise, body tingling in anticipation. The bike pulled up along- side my car and Tim pulled his helmet off. He leant in to my open window and planted a hungry kiss on my mouth. Oh yes, he was as eager as me.

"Follow me," I said when he pulled away. "There's a picnic spot just up the hill." Feeling very daring, I accelerated out of the lay by, Penelope Pit Stop at full throttle. I sped up the winding country road, safe in the knowledge that I was on a one way route now. Behind me Tim swerved in a show off manner. We both screeched to a halt, churning up gravel and mud in the sheltered parking area.

It was chilly in the evening air but I shrugged off my jacket and left it on my driver's seat. I wanted to feel Tim's hands on me. Besides, I was burning up already. He must have felt the same because as soon as his helmet was off, so was his own thick jacket, discarded on the seat of his bike.

"I've been waiting for this," he said with that lovely urgency in his voice. "Counting the hours, Eve."

"Well better make the most of it then," I said, leaning into his embrace. I was mixed up and angry. More than that. I was furious that I could find my own husband's lover so attractive. Jealous beyond words. I poured it all out into that kiss, biting at Tim's lips and tugging at the belt on his jeans with needy hands. He was already hard and I revelled in the knowledge that it was me who made him so. To be wanted so badly is a turn on in itself and I was driven by a need to send him further over the edge.

I broke away from his kisses, shushing his protests with a finger on his bottom lip. Then I let my knees fold and lowered myself down his body, heedless that my skirt would trail in the dirt as I placed myself before him.

"Oh, God, Eve," I heard the thrill of excitement, the barely contained lust in his voice as my hands, nimble now and certain in their movements, freed him from his jeans. My mouth curved in a smile before opening wide to take him in.

"Oh shit!" His body trembled and his hands clutched at my hair.

I felt good then. Powerful. To hold him in my mouth, caress him softly, tease him gently, then suck down hard, pull on him with my lips, grate with my teeth, devour his length until my throat was full of him, all the time knowing that the shaking of his limbs was because of me.

"Eve, I can't..."

His hips were beginning to judder and my mouth worked harder. Yes I would take him. I would take him all. I reached my hands round his buttocks pulling him in so that even if he wanted to pull out, he couldn't. I heard his sob of pleasure and relief as he filled my mouth. I gagged a little at the force thrust upon me suddenly, his orgasm wild and fierce, but I swallowed greedily, nipping him with my teeth, ever so gently, as I did so.

Worth it to hear the astonishment in his voice.

"Jesus Christ, Eve. That was....."

I clawed my way back up his body and silenced his comments with a kiss. My jaw was aching, my lips were swollen. The taste of him was on my tongue. He cradled my head gently between his hands and slowly now, our mouths began a new dance.

CHAPTER NINE

I had quite forgotten the pleasure that could be had in just kissing. Exploring the shape and textures of another person's mouth with one's own. Sliding back and forth in a relentlessly greedy fashion, selfish at all times, as I took what I wanted from Tim's lips and tongue. I drank him in with the thirst of one parched for too long, all the while letting my hands savour the hardness of his chest pressed against mine.

I felt small in his embrace, yet strong and powerful. Feminine and desirable. Warm and alive. My body was throbbing with my own unquenched needs but for now it was enough to mould my curves into his lean angles, to grasp tightly the energy and youth that was on offer before me.

We kissed and kissed. Bit and suckled at the flesh exposed by roaming hands. Kneaded muscles and traced curves and hollows. Explored what we could without stripping off completely, the thrill of touch, greater for being restricted. I had the advantage as his jeans were already slung around his knees and I let my fingers work where my mouth had already been. Cupping him, stroking, teasing him back into life.

I answered his groan with a throaty purr, dragging my lips from the crook of his collar bone, back up to his mouth, hands removed from where he was now aching with need. In answer his own hands reached down lower. Grabbed at the hem of my skirt and impatiently rucked it up around my thighs. At last I got the sensation of skin against skin as he pressed close to me. Thigh against thigh, his hardness now quivering against the thin silk of my pants.

My turn. I was starting to tremble with need. My belly was clenching in uncomfortable knots. My pelvis had begun to dance to its own tune. Taunting. Flaunting. Inviting. Demanding. His hands reached under the silk, one cupping me from behind, the other plunging into my depths. I gasped and ground upon him, shameless in my urgency for release. I would have let myself go right there and then, but he was not having it.

"Oh, no, Eve," he murmured against my breast, teeth biting my nipple through layers of cloth. "You're not coming like that. I want to be inside you." His fingers slid away and I moaned at the loss.

"Now then," I could not have offered myself more openly to him. Skirt hitched high, legs wide, my fingers tugging at the sides of my pants.

He had the control now. Covered my hands with his own and pulled until my knickers were on the floor, kicked aside by his feet or mine.

"Turn around," he said in a voice that held more demand than request.

Limp with desire I complied. He bent me over the bonnet of the car and folded his body close to mine, hands holding me by the hips. His breath was hot on the back of my neck. His movement was unsteady at first, positioning himself just right. Then in. One long driving thrust that would have sent me flying forward if he hadn't held me so tightly.

I placed my hands firmer on the bonnet, pushing back to meet his thrusts, inching my feet apart slightly to gain better balance. Anything to feel him more. I bent over further, lifting up my bottom meeting each pounding movement with a backwards jab of my own.

Settled into his pace, his balls brushing against the curve of my buttocks, he loosed his grasp on my hips and reached round to my front. One hand on my breast, the other on my pelvis and dipping lower. I was already melting into the hot fire of orgasm and when his fingers rubbed against me I was lost. I cried out in relief and pleasure, bucking wildly against his hand and hips that continued to hammer against me from behind.

But he wasn't ready to stop. It took him longer this time. Sodden with desire, replete for a second, I felt the flames begin to stoke up once more as he continued to pound. It was getting rougher. Hard, almost violent. The strength of a young man, not yet able to temper his power. I groaned, a little in pain, a lot in pleasure.

I was being taken so completely and thoroughly and was helpless to do anything other than lose myself in it. So I let myself ride the huge waves of sensation that rippled through me, again and again, sobbing each time one passed to build up higher the next time.

Dizzy now, with blood soaring through my veins like quick silver, I arched my throat back as my last tortured cry mingled with his. I collapsed limply onto the bonnet, his weight full on me for a long, hot moment, uneven breathing from two sets of exhausted lungs.

And that was when I heard the sound of an engine.

"Tim!" I hissed at him, unable to move a fraction.

"Oh God, Eve, I can't get enough of you." He groaned and let his hands wander down my back. He would, I was sure, have found the energy for a re-run. I had not mistaken though, the sound of a car coming up the single track road.

"There's someone coming." I shoved back at him, struggling to move with legs that were like jelly and arms shaking from the effort of supporting myself. I felt the wetness slide down my thighs as I twisted round to face him, and pulled my skirt down to cover myself. God knows where my knickers had gone.

Tim was tucking himself back into his jeans, taking his time with his belt. I threw his jacket at him and then held out his helmet.

"Go, before they get here."

"What? I can't leave you like that. Might be a mad axe man or something."

"You've been watching too many horror movies," I bundled him towards his bike, my eyes boring into the darkness towards the sound of the car. "Oh bollocks, it's the police. Look, quick, get on your bike and get going. I'll deal with it."

Bless him. He looked uncomfortable at the thought. "Not very manly."

"Never mind that, I don't want our local bobby finding us together. Now scram. And don't worry, I know you're all man."

He flashed me a grin then. Teeth white and even in the dark. "Just don't forget to book me in for lesson three. Soon."

I shooed him on and felt my heart rate rise as his bike powered into life, just in time. Tim's tail light had disappeared out of view when the police car came to a halt beside mine.

It was dark in the picnic area, thick evergreen trees crowding in and adding to the seclusion, with the moon, still full but beginning to

75

wane, shielded now and then by drifting clouds. Perfect really for illicit sex. A tad on the chilly side, but we had soon worked up a sweat. Not the sort of place though that people hang around on a January night, unless they are up to something dodgy. Not surprising, therefore, that PC. Plod, or to give him his proper name, Sergeant Hawthorne approached me with an attitude of dubious suspicion.

He had a torch with him, and was flashing it around the site.

"Good evening." His voice was deep and a shade gravelly with the flat vowels of a local voice tinged with another accent on top. I didn't trust his pleasant tone and felt distinctly uncomfortable that he could see me clearly, whilst he was just a shady outline. A large one at that.

"Evening officer. Is there a problem?"

"I hope not. Is there anyone with you?"

I shrugged my shoulders and looked around. "Does there look like it?"

"But there was. The man on the motor bike, who was he?"

I shrugged. "How should I know? He drove right past me."

"What are you doing here, by yourself?" Just a subtle pause but enough to tell me he didn't believe me.

"Getting some air."

"It's a cold night," he said. The moon lost its cloud and in the brilliance of its light I saw that his eyes, similar in luminosity were mocking me. Clear grey, cold as gunmetal.

I bristled instantly, folding my arms across my chest, thankful that Tim had not dragged my sweater and bra off me as well as my knickers. At least I looked presentable. Or that's what I told myself. Only when I got back home and looked in the porch mirror, did I realise that I had the sweat dampened hair, flushed cheeks, swollen lips and glittering eyes of a woman who has just been royally fucked.

So in my innocence, I gave him my best 'what the fuck has it to do with you' look, not practised since high school. I was, I thought with a suppressed giggle, rapidly descending in terms of age appropriate behaviour.

"I like the cold," I challenged him. "What are you doing here? It's not a crime to drive out and get some fresh air in an evening, is it?"

Sergeant Hawthorne had replaced our old timid bobby when he finally retired last year. I had not crossed paths with him until now, shunning the regular invites to neighbourhood watch meetings and the like. Mabel at the bakery had reliably informed me that Craig Hawthorne had been born and bred in Maypoleton and had come home after twenty years of service in Manchester. I had commented caustically that he couldn't be up to much if he was still a sergeant after such a long time. Mabel had shot me a dark look and told me that I shouldn't be too quick to judge.

I was wondering now, what kind of man he was under the surface. On the face of it, he was cold and rather brooding. A bit of a glum sort, I decided. No sense of humour.

"It is if you're buying drugs?"

"What?" I had been slow to think of that. "No drugs officer." I held my arms open wide in a taunting invitation. "You can search me if you like."

He flicked the torch up and down my body in a manner that was somehow insulting. Then the beam of light fell upon my discarded knickers, bright red against the dirt of the ground.

"I think someone's already done that." His voice dripped with disapproval. "Can't you find somewhere better to go?"

"And haven't you got anything better to be doing than playing at Peeping Tom? Or is that how you get your rocks off?" I moved round to the driver's door and started to get in. "Can I go now?"

He walked round to lean in, and I caught a whiff of something pleasant and woody. "I wasn't joking about the drugs. Someone is pushing them around the village and I will find out. In the meantime, don't let your husband catch you out," he dropped his harsh gaze to my wedding ring. "Or is he the sort to turn a blind eye?"

"None of your damn business," I spat at him, hating the choking sound of my voice. Hell he had touched a nerve. I revved the engine and grated the gears.

"No speeding mind," he cautioned as I turned my car around and set off.

My hands were trembling on the wheel and I wasn't ready to go home just yet. I couldn't risk Andy or the kids seeing me so frazzled. So I drove around for a while, a CD blasting out loud. Kings of Leon. Sex on Fire. Very appropriate. The sex with Tim had definitely been on fire. I squirmed a little on my seat, knowing I would be sore in the morning and revelled in the feeling.

By the time the CD had come to the end and I was drawing near to Cooper's Fold, I had shaken off the dark mood that Sergeant. Hawthorne had dumped upon me and could think only of the daring excitement the evening had held. It seemed a long time since that afternoon when I had howled my eyes out like a baby in the Doctor's surgery. I wondered if maybe I should call her and tell her the therapeutic effects of random wild sex. So much better than any pill.

And as for the seething jealousy that had bitten me to my core on bumping into Jason even that had been temporarily dampened down. With a bit of luck, I would get a decent night's sleep tonight. Whistling merrily to myself, I stopped with shock at my reflection in the porch mirror. Uh oh! Looking far too wild and happy for a session baby-sitting! And another bloody love bite. I was going to have to invest in a supply of polo necks at this rate.

I brushed down my hair, kept my jacket on and tiptoed in, managing to sneak upstairs without anyone noticing. Note to self, have ample supply of cover up make up in hand bag next time out screwing. Also body spray, face wipes, and emergency scarf if wearing low neck top. Second note to self, must buy more skirts. Easy access much appreciated.

I lounged in the bath for ages, scooting completely under the bubbles when Andy surprised me by knocking on the door.

"Thought I heard you coming in," he said, with a wine glass in hand. "Kids ok?"

Grateful for the steaminess of the bathroom, I nodded, reaching out a hand for the glass, whilst remaining submerged like a submarine.

"Mm, thanks," I took a glug, enjoying the crisp fruitiness as I swirled it around my mouth. "Did you want something?" I asked, aware that it had been months since he had joined me for a chat in the bathroom like this.

He flushed a little, but that could have been the heat from my bath water. "Something on my mind."

"Go on."

"I want to be fair to you."

"Mm?"

"Now you know about Jason, well it's not really right for me to expect you to not want somebody yourself."

"Mm?"

"I mean, it would have to be discreet. Because obviously for now we are pretending that everything's normal."

"Mm?" I was rather enjoying this.

"But I wanted you to know, that if you met someone, I would be okay with it."

I smiled at him sweetly. "How kind of you. I'll put an ad in the Maypoleton Mail tomorrow."

He gave a funny strangled laugh. "Of course you mustn't do that. But I just wanted to let you know. Fair's fair and all that."

"Oh yes," I drank deeply of my wine. "Fair's fair and all that." I shut my eyes and leant back against the bath, signalling that the conversation was over. When the door clicked behind him, I let out the breath I was holding and found to my surprise that a treacherous tear was sliding down my cheek. It wasn't fair at all, I thought drenched with sadness all of a sudden. Despite the steamy water, I felt chilled to my bones.

Later on in bed I crashed into a deep and dream-filled sleep that was not at all restful. Waking from a nightmare, which involved me being pulled limb from limb by a faceless beast, I staggered downstairs and made myself a hot milk and whisky. I couldn't face another early morning session of watching the clock going round. So I took another pill. Or it might have been two.

The next morning I felt sick and shaky, with a splitting headache and a tongue as rough as sandpaper. It was lunchtime before I was able to haul myself over to Sally's in an attempt to start work in her office. She took one look at me and put the kettle on.

"Are you alright? You look like you've got flu?"

"I'm fine. Bit groggy that's all. Sleeping pills." I didn't seem capable of managing longer sentences.

Sally brewed up a hellishly strong coffee and then shunted me through to the quiet of her office.

"Since when have you needed sleeping pills?" Sally's fabulous turquoise eyes probed sharply.

I slurped my coffee and then hissed at the scalding temperature.

"Come on out with it, Eve. You've been jumpy ever since New Year. What's going on?"

It was impossible to lie completely to her. "Me and Andy are in a mess."

"Oh?" Clearly she hadn't been expecting this. She pulled a face. "Mid-life crisis?"

"Something like that."

"Serious?"

"Yeah."

"Well I can see you don't really want to talk about it, and that's fine. But you know that for all that I love to gossip, you know you can tell me anything and it wouldn't go any further. I mean that." Then she patted my hand and said sweetly. "Don't worry. I'm sure it's a storm in a tea cup. He'll sort himself out. At least he's not beggaring off round the world and leaving you with Sandra and Steven."

I grunted. I could cope with the beggaring off bit certainly. Sandra and Steven? No I would probably kill them.

"Do you know yet when Richard is leaving?"

"At the end of next week can you believe it? Rotten swine's been planning this for months."

"So Mary will be in the cottage then?"

"Mm. Which brings me to ask, would you be able to take over the new curtains and hang them up? I was going to do it myself only I've got to wait in for a phone call. I need to speak to the vet. I think Jaspar's starting with navicular."

"Oh bloody hell that's a shame. Yes of course I'll do the curtains."

"You sure you'll be okay there by yourself?"

"Why wouldn't I?"

"The ghost?" She said with a giggle.

I waved a hand airily. "Trust me with what I've got going on in my life right now, I can handle a ghost."

Little did I know.

CHAPTER TEN

The phone rang just then and Sally picked it up, quickly telling me that the curtains were in the back sitting room. I told Skip, who had accompanied me down to the yard, to stay put and went to fetch them. Fortunately they were packaged in thick polythene bags with carry handles and I could manage them easily. I nodded at Sally on my way back through the office and with Skip at my heels set off across the yard.

Jenny was hosing down a sweating thoroughbred and called out to me. "Mind you don't get ghostified." She was grinning broadly. My spooky turn had obviously caused some entertainment. I replied that the vet was on the phone which wiped the smile off her face immediately. She swore and handed the hose to another girl. "See you later."

I wasn't sure if I would be able to find my way back to the cottage without Sally. The grounds were such a mass of wild shrubs and trees, all looking the same. Skip, though, found the way easily and darted off ahead, turning round every now and then to make sure I was following.

Virtually hidden, the cottage was as quaint as I remembered it. But cold and damp. There was a thick chill in the air that hung heavy as I let myself in to the tiny house.

"What about a fire?" I said to Skip who was now panting. As if to signal his agreement he lay down on the hearth rug. "It'll give me chance to see if I cleared the chimney out properly." There was no shortage of small twigs and branches for kindling and a stack of old newspapers were bundled at the side of the fireplace. I found some matches in the kitchen and soon had a small fire going in the grate. I took a few moments to enjoy the crackle and hiss of the flames, before getting started on the curtains.

Sally had chosen a lovely old fashioned print of small forget me not flowers on a creamy background, just perfect for the deeply mullioned windows. I quite envied Mary her chance of staying here. I hung up the curtains and pulled them together to check that they closed properly. Mary would notice such a thing immediately. As I shut out the soft winter light I was sure I could smell roses in the room.

My nose twitched. Definitely roses, mingling with the woody scent that was coming from the fire. It was a beautiful smell, soothing to my senses. I sat in one of the rocking chairs by the fire to enjoy the atmosphere of the cottage. Warm and cosy, smelling heavenly.

I let out a deep sigh and settled back further into the chair, allowing my muscles to relax completely. My head rested against the carved back and, for the first time since New Year's Eve, was no longer aching. I closed my eyes, so grateful to have the heavy feeling of pressure lifted from me.

On the arms of the chair, my hands were soft and fluid, fingers draping loosely over the edge. My feet, crossed at the ankles, felt as though they were sinking into the floor. The churning motion of my stomach slowed and stopped. The bitter acid in my gut disappeared. Tension and pain oozed out of me, drawn from each and every pore. I gave myself up to this sensuous feeling, letting the chair rock me gently, lulling me into the sweetest of dreams.

Sunshine was pouring into the cottage. I was arranging a vase of roses and soft ferns. I pricked my thumb on one of the thorns. Someone came up behind me. Strong arms caught me up and whirled me around. I laughed joyously. My heart was singing as the face in front of me smiled. Tender lips drew near to suck the blood from my thumb.

I felt my skin tingle and my blood heat up. Those loving lips moved to my mouth. A long tender hungry kiss. Deeply searching, intimately inviting. I felt the fire begin to kindle in my belly and kissing was no longer enough. I heard his laugh, low in his throat, sensual and knowing. I shivered with longing.

Felt his hand on mine as he took me to the foot of the stairs.

I woke with a start.

The room felt cold once more, the fire no longer burning in the grate. My eyes flew to the corner of the room, half expecting to see someone there. My heart was pounding and an irrational sense of fear made me want to flee the cottage. As previously, the sense of happiness was now tarnished by an under-current of bitterness, hatred even. Something very dramatic had happened here, I was sure of it, regardless of the scoffing from Jenny and the others.

No doubt they would laugh once more and tell me I was imagining things.

But there was no mistaking the blood that was welling up on my thumb.

I looked at it in astonishment. Deep and definite, a tiny hole, just right for the tip of a thorn, was oozing bright red blood. Automatically I stuck my thumb in my mouth and sucked hard. The feeling of the man in my dream doing this came back to me so strongly I felt a jolt in my stomach. I couldn't recall what he had looked like. But he had been real.

"Who was he? Did he live here?" I addressed the cottage as if it was a living breathing entity. No answer apart from the ticking of the clock and the soft hissing of the embers. I knew I was right though. The man I had dreamt about had once lived in this cottage. Did that mean he was a ghost? To be one implied that a spirit was restless.

I was reluctant to shake off the remnants of the dream. But the clock on the wall told me I had been asleep for at least an hour. The day was virtually over and all I had done was put up a couple of curtains. No sleeping pills for me tonight. It was probably down to them that I had experienced such an unearthly dream.

"Come on, get a grip," I admonished myself as I stood up. Skip jumped up at my movements and went straight to the front door, where he began to wag his tail, as if in greeting.

Still a little groggy, I was startled to see someone just outside the cottage. "Oh, I'm sorry, I didn't see you there." I smiled at the man as he was making such a fuss of Skip. My dog, an excellent judge of character, had flopped to the floor and rolled over for a belly rub. Anyone who liked my dog was instantly likable to me. "I'm Eve. I'm a friend of Sally's. I've been tidying the cottage."

He stood up, patting Skip who pawed eagerly at him for more attention and returned my smile. I felt my blood tingle with warmth.

He was about thirty, with a mop of chestnut brown hair and eyes the colour of polished pewter. He wasn't over tall, and had a wiry frame that hinted at a sinewy strength. The type of body that was used to physical work, I thought and realised that I was comparing him to Andy and Tim, whose bodies were kept in shape by regular work outs.

"I'm Jem. I've been asked to clear up the mess around here. Terrible overgrown it is."

"You're a gardener then?" It fitted somehow. He looked earthy and rugged. A man of the soil.

His smiled crinkled his eyes. "One of my jobs."

"It'll be nice to see the place properly cared for," I said, wanting to linger. "It must have been so pretty once."

"It was," he said softly. "Pretty as a picture, just like you."

Pleasure sprang up from a deep forgotten place in my soul. I knew I was blushing. "I must be going. Nice to have met you, Jem."

"I'll be seeing you, Miss."

My back was prickling as I walked away. I felt sure that his eyes were fixed upon me. I couldn't resist turning around to look. No sign of him. He must have gone round the back. I had a smile on my face all the way back to the yard.

Fortunately, Sally and the others were too wrapped up in the horse's tea time routine to wonder at the length of time I had been gone.

"Abscess." Sally said in greeting. "Not navicular."

I had forgotten about the lame horse. "Oh that's good. I got the curtains up alright. They look lovely." No need to mention falling asleep and dreaming. "I met your gardener as well."

"Oh yes, I've had to take someone on to make a start at clearing the grounds. Richard's Mum will make such a fuss if she has to tramp through that tangled mess. Honestly, the wretched woman is going to cost me a fortune. I could have bought another horse for the money I've spent so far."

I smiled. Sally saw everything in terms of horse pounds. Just then my phone beeped. It was a message from Megan reminding me that they were all going to be out that evening, so as it was Friday, why didn't I get a take away and have a quiet night in with her Dad as we would have the house to ourselves. I grunted and told Sally of my daughter's attempts to manage my life.

"God is it Friday already?" Sally never could keep track of time. But then horses were a twenty four seven business so it didn't really matter what day of the week it was. "Fancy that, first week in January over with."

"Mm, fancy that," I muttered, thinking that in one short week, I had discovered my husband was gay, met his lover, embarked on a torrid affair (if one could call it such) with my son's best friend, and was now having fanciful thoughts about a young gardener. I said goodbye to Sally, consoling myself with the thought that at least Jem was closer to my age than Tim, which alleviated some of the concern that I appeared to be turning into a bit of a nympho.

It was going dark again as I meandered down the country lane with Skip at my heels. I wasn't far off the gate which would lead me into the fields, when I heard the pleasant clip clopping of hooves on the tarmac. I turned to see an unusual sight these days, a traditional Romany wagon, being pulled by a horse. It was beautifully painted, and the horse looked well cared for, even in this dim light. There was a second one though, walking behind the wagon, patiently plodding attached by long reins, which didn't look quite as good.

I stopped to watch it go past, biting my lip a little at the state of the second horse, battling down an urge to call out and say something. I didn't have to though. Upon seeing me waiting on the grass verge, the driver of the caravan gave an easy tug on the reins and pulled up next to me.

"Evening, Lass. Is there anywhere near o'bout t'pull up 'n park? Light's caught me out."

He was old, about seventy I reckoned, with a deeply lined face and a shock of thick white hair. Thin too, I noticed, looking at the bones in his hands as they held the reins. His eyes, a funny mix of blue green and brown, light against his dark skin, were kind. Skip liked him, nosing forward for a friendly sniff.

I reached forward myself, patting the leading horse and admiring his condition, then letting my eyes flick pointedly to the horse at the back.

"This fellow looks well," I said, ignoring for now, his question.

"Aye. 'E would. 'E's mine. 'Ad him nigh on twenty five years. Foaled 'im I did."

I was impressed. For a horse that age he was looking very well. Again, I looked to the other one.

"Not my doin'," said the man. "Bought 'im off a rogue at Appelby. 'E'll be alright wi' a bit o' luv 'n care. 'E's tired though now, not as fit as Bracken 'ere."

Something in my face must have softened for he said once more. "So Lass, does thee know of a field I can rest a while. For 'orse's sake if nowt else?"

I went to stroke the horse at the rear. It was dark bay, the colour of Bourneville chocolate with a black mane and tail. Sad eyes regarded me soulfully. My heart melted. Decision made. The villagers and Andy would probably kick off, but hey, what could they do? It was half my field as well.

I grinned at him. "Actually if you want to follow me, there's a perfect place for you to put up camp." I lead the way down the lane for another five minutes, taking him past the road which turned into Cooper's Fold. Across from here was another piece of land that Andy owned. A large field which had a small brook running as one of its boundaries. Andy had been about to create another small development, when the recession hit hard. Wisely, he kept hold of the land, waiting until the market improved. It was well hedged by the roadside with one five bar gate as access. The horses would be safe there and there was fresh running water. Perfect.

I pushed open the gate and nodded at him to follow me through. He looked more than a little wary.

"Don't want to cause no trouble?"

"It's my field," I explained.

His face wrinkled into yet more lines as a smile flashed at me. "Then I thank thee kindly, Lass. An' what would thy name be?"

"Eve."

"Eve," he said softly. Then he followed this with a few words in a language foreign to me. Whatever it was sounded nice, so I smiled back at him. "I'm Seth," he said with a nod.

"I'd best be off," I patted both horses before calling Skip who had gone off after a rabbit.

From this point, it was only a minute's walk back down the lane to Cooper's Fold. I was about to turn into the cul-de-sac when a voice called me.

"You've a kind heart lass, but 'tis fair full 'o sadness, take care it don't lead you a stray."

I jumped. The old woman I had met at the oak tree had appeared out of nowhere. I was pleased to see her, my hand reaching into my jacket pocket where I had kept her handkerchief.

"Hello again, I washed this for you."

"Nay lass. 'Tis a gift." She stepped closer and touched my forehead as she had done before. "Thee has another gift now and it shows thee things others cannot see. Be careful where it takes thee lass. There is love and light around thee, but dark shadows also. Thee must not step into the shadows, for there will be no return."

I shivered. "Where do you live? Are you travelling?" I turned my head to look back at the field where I had left the old man. Was she connected to him in some way?

"No more travelling for me lass. I am at my journey's end. I just wanted to see you one more time. Heed what I said now. Don't step into the shadows."

She smiled and then she turned and walked away. A mist seemed to come from nowhere and I lost sight of her almost immediately.

I shook my head and rubbed my eyes. "Am I imagining things Skip?" Was the woman even real? My dog barked. What an odd day, I thought to myself, wondering if I was still under the influence of the tablets from the night before. I certainly would not be taking any more if that was the case. I turned into Cooper's Fold, glad of the bright street lamps which now lit the way.

But as I walked into the light, I heard the echo of the old woman's voice in my mind. Don't step into the shadows. It had been a warning. Well meant, but a warning nevertheless.

CHAPTER ELEVEN

Not surprisingly, my decision to let the old Romany stay in our field caused a few ripples in the smooth surface of life in Maypoleton. Our village just didn't go in for 'that sort of thing'. We repeatedly won the 'Best Kept Village' (large category) and we certainly had not achieved such status by inviting riff-raff of that ilk to take root upon our preciously guarded green belts.

Andy was the first person to question my decision which was fair enough as it was his field. He had also been prompted by our daughter that we would have the house to ourselves but instead of going down the route of snuggling in with the wife, had opted to spend the night with Jason instead. I could tell he was on the defensive about something by the way he launched straight into attacking me for allowing 'some random gyppo' to camp in our field.

I was curled up on the sofa in the lounge, having stoked up the fire, made myself a hot chocolate, and settled down with a good book. After the week I had had, I thought I deserved a bit of chilling out time. I was deeply engrossed in the third chapter of the latest J D Robb thriller when he came into the room, an air of suppressed agitation about him.

I kept my eyes glued to the page, and muttered an absent minded, "Hi."

He then went on for about five minutes as to the levels of my irresponsibility and careless actions. He had driven past the field on his way home. Slammed on the brakes at the sight of a camp fire and been astounded to find a Gypsy comfortably ensconced with apparently full permission to be there. I waited for the tirade to finish, thinking that he was being a little over the top, and not his usual amenable self, before closing my book with an exaggerated sigh.

"And your point is?"

"People will not like it."

"No they won't," I said in agreement. "But 'People' do not own that field. We do."

"You should not have made such a decision without asking me first."

"Would you have said yes?"

"No."

"There you are then."

"Well you'll just have to tell him to go. First thing tomorrow."

"He's an old man."

"He's a gypsy."

"Romany."

"Whatever. His sort always causes trouble."

I curled my lip at him. "His sort? Oh yes, he's the sort who are persecuted. Like Jews. And homosexuals."

His nostrils flared. "Don't, Eve."

"Don't what? Come close to the truth? I would have thought that you of all people would have some compassion and not give a stuff what people think. But then, no, of course you wouldn't. You're too much of a bloody coward for that, aren't you?" I couldn't stop the contempt from turning my voice into a razor.

"I want him to go," he said quietly. His face was flushed and there was a bitter glint in his eye. I think he hated me at that moment for speaking the truth.

"And I want him to stay. And unless you want me to blab about you, I get what I want. Is that clear?" I wasn't sure how we had descended onto such a petty level, but then I suppose it was unrealistic to think our civility and friendliness could be sustained for much longer.

"Bitch," he said coldly. "Is this the way it's going to be from now on, Eve? Every time you don't get what you want, you're going to throw that in my face?"

I smarted from the accusation. "When have I ever demanded anything from you? And maybe that's where I have been stupid. I've always said yes to everyone. I've always kept the peace. Well guess what, husband of mine, all that stopped on the night you decided to shatter my illusions and throw my life on to the scrap heap. So yeah, if that makes me a bitch, whatever! Seth stays."

He snorted then. "Seth! Jesus you're already on first name terms with him. You'll be inviting him round for supper next."

"Well he'd be more welcome than your bloody parents." I glared at him.

The atmosphere in the room crackled more fiercely than the fire. We had never rowed, never been nasty to each other. I hated it. But I was damned if I was going to back down. Neither apparently was he. He glared at me, foreign dislike scorching from his normally soft blue eyes.

Then he said abruptly. "I'm going to Jason's. I'll be staying the night. Tell the kids I'm over at Mick's. I'll be back on Sunday evening."

Mick was an old friend who lived in Liverpool. Two or three times a year, Andy did go over and spend the weekend with him so it would not seem out of place if he wasn't here.

"Megan will be disappointed," I said caustically. "She was hoping we would have a nice romantic time together."

He flinched and walked out of the room. When I heard the door slamming shut a short while later, it crossed my mind to text Tim. Then I realised he was probably with Megan and Jake. I reached for my book, thankful that J D Robb was such a good writer.

Over the course of the weekend I had more than a few villagers dropping by to let me know (in case I was unaware) that my field was occupied by a most unsuitable character. I gave them all the same reply. Yes I was aware. And then I gave my hard stare. I had spent hours practising it as a teenager in the care home. In my comfortable role as Andy's wife, I had had little need, or use for it. Now though I was remembering how handy it was. One by one they slunk away from my front door.

My offspring at least were on my side. Jake really couldn't care less who camped in the field and Megan thought it was very noble of me. She told me she had gone to introduce herself and I smiled, thinking that Seth would probably hurry to rush on if Megan decided he was a suitable 'project'.

Sometime around the middle of Sunday afternoon, no doubt as a result of the church going harpies ganging up on me, there was yet another interruption. The doorbell rang repeatedly and was ignored repeatedly. Megan was probably on the phone and Jake and Mark would be playing some infantile computer game. I huffed and puffed my way to the door and groaned to see Sergeant Hawthorne standing in our porch.

I was not a big fan of policemen. I liked even less the thought that one of them had virtually caught me, knickers round my ankles. I was preparing a beautiful scowl for him, when a sudden thought entered my head. What if something had happened to Andy? Instinctively my heart froze. Despite the harsh words between us, there were twenty years of history that couldn't be wiped out.

"There's no need to worry," he said quickly, "I'm not here with any bad news."

Okay, so he was a mind reader now. Or maybe it had been obvious what I was thinking. I stared at him blankly.

This didn't seem to offend him, and he went on smoothly, "I have received a number of complaints about a gypsy who has taken up residence in the field across the road, your field, I believe?"

"Romany," I corrected him. "Seth is Romany not a gypsy." I leant against the door frame and folded my arms, feeling the colour coming back into my face, now I knew nothing had happened to Andy.

His face remained like granite. He had a very strong face, all sharp angles and bones, with a jaw that looked as though it would crack a fist if on the end of punch. It did not look like a face that smiled much.

"Romany," he continued, "by the name of Seth Nightingale...."

"That's a nice name. Nightingale, I mean. I knew he was called Seth but he never mentioned his surname."

His eyes became flinty. "Does Mr. Nightingale have your permission to reside in the field?"

"Yes." My chin was small and elfin like, nevertheless I stuck it out in a determined fashion.

"And how long is he staying?"

"Is that police business?"

He held my gaze for a very long time. Actually it was probably only half a minute. But it felt longer. Credit to him, he was the only one so far who didn't drop his eyes. Then I got the vaguest impression there was the tiniest hint of a smile threatening to lurk around his mouth.

91

"Actually no it isn't. If the field is yours and he has your permission, it isn't anybody's business, providing of course that no trouble occurs as a result."

"I hardly think one old man is going to bring down a crime wave upon the population of Maypoleton, regardless of his race or origins. Do you?"

"No. No I don't. I had to follow it up though on behalf of the villagers who came to me." He gave me a brief nod, almost curt in its manner and turned to go.

Then he paused and said, "It's rather an unusual thing to do though, not many women would."

I snorted. "I am not many women."

"No. I rather got that impression the other night."

The swine left me unable to react to that one as he strode down the path before my mouth connected with my brain.

Not long afterwards, Andy returned home.

Complete with flowers and chocolates, a guilty conscience in full force. I battled down the urge to swipe him round the face with the bouquet, and feed the chocolates to a hopeful Skip, whilst I listened to his subdued apology. He had never meant to row over my decision. He admired me for putting an old man's needs before what others would think. He realised that I was under an immense pressure at the moment. He didn't want us to become enemies.

I was opening the box of chocolates in a somewhat mollified manner, when he let slip that Jason had talked him round to my way of thinking. Of course he would. He was a fucking therapist, who was fucking my husband. I nearly choked on a double nut praline, spitting it out to the delight of Skip who gobbled it up.

"I think you had better quit whilst you're ahead," I told him as calmly as I could. I wanted us to be enemies no more than he did. But it was salt in a bloody raw wound to think that his lover was the one who might have made him see sense.

Still, it moved us back into a state of truce, for which I was glad.

The next couple of weeks passed without incident. Unless of course you count the time that Tim had me in the garden shed, nearly skewering himself on a rusty rake, or the couple of hours we spent writing round his sister's bed whilst he was babysitting his niece and nephew, and I was 'helping Sally with some overdue invoices'.

Megan, and everyone else for that matter, seemed to think that my more 'normal' behaviour could be put down to the HRT tablets which they all thought I was on. As a result, they were less jumpy around me when Tim came to call. All of which proved delightfully entertaining as we did our best to sneak in the odd grope and furtive snog, whilst pretending that the New Year's kiss was a drunken, hormonal aberration.

I settled into a routine of going over to Sally's each day for a few hours work, although I did feel a shade guilty at getting paid for what she was asking me to do. Some of it was odd office stuff, but not in the least bit taxing, some of it revolved around the physical tasks necessary on the yard, and even standing in for Jenny the odd time with beginners lessons, but mostly, she kept telling me that she wanted me to be able to help her look after Mary when she arrived.

I slipped into the habit of calling by the field on the way home from the Lodge. Not every evening as I didn't want Seth to feel I was checking up on him. Having said that, he seemed to welcome my short visits and had the uncanny knack of knowing when I would be there. There was always a mug of strong sweet tea waiting for me. I would take a couple of carrots for the horses and spend most of my time talking about them so that he didn't feel I was being nosy.

He told me that Andy had called round one night and had been relatively friendly towards him, if not exactly gushing with enthusiasm. I was pleased to hear this. I hadn't liked to think of my husband as a bigot. That was something I reserved for his parents and in the third weekend in January, I got a taste of just how narrow-minded they could be, opening my eyes a little to the pressure Andy must have been under to hide his true nature.

It was Steven's birthday and I was still behaving in my programmed manner of playing at happy families, so I accompanied Andy along for the visit. It was the first time we had seen them since they had caught me kissing Tim and my reception from Sandra was frosty to say the least. Andy, with his typical ostrich behaviour, appeared not to notice. I just sat there with a dumb smile on my face and replayed in my mind the last time Tim had fucked me.

Fortunately for us, Andy's younger sister Katy and her husband Colin turned up with the two twins which took any attention away from us. I was busy wondering where and when I could next meet Tim again, when I received a poke in my ribs from Sandra.

"Of course I've told Katy you two will be happy to stand as god parents."

I must have been looking blank. I hoped I was looking blank and not lust filled.

She snapped at me. "The christening! Weren't you listening?"

"Yes of course I was," I smiled sweetly. "Are you sure you want us to be godparents?" I asked Katy in all seriousness. I mean it wasn't as if we saw a lot of them, or their children. With a ten year age gap between them, Andy and Katy had never really been close, and we had had our children young, so it wasn't as if we had anything in common with them now.

"Don't worry," said Katy, a pretty woman with Andy's pleasant manner and easy smile. "You don't have to if you don't want to."

"Of course they want to," intruded Sandra. She was not a regular church goer herself, but in line with being seen to 'do the right thing', used the services of their nearest church for events like baptisms, weddings and funerals.

Andy, ever the peace keeper with his mother, smiled and assured her that if Katy wanted us to be godparents, then we would be. At which point Katy reiterated that it really wasn't a problem either way. And then Colin decided it was time for his say.

"But it really is a serious matter," he said, sitting forward on the edge of his seat. "You have to promise to safe guard the children's souls and help to bring them up in the light of Christ." Colin genuinely was a church goer.

Not so Steven, who clapped him on the shoulder and said in a distinctly patronising manner, "Well as long as they turn up on the day and say the right thing, that's what counts isn't it?"

I saw Colin's mouth pinch together in a tight line. I felt sorry for him. Although I had fallen out with my own church, I respected anyone who had a strong belief in any faith.

"I agree with Colin," I said, much to everyone's surprise. "If you're going to do it, it should mean something." I had gone along with Sandra and Steven when my own children were young, having them baptised and later confirmed. I had wanted to please my husband and also to give them a sense of community and belonging that I had never experienced. Now though, I felt a bit of a hypocrite.

"I don't really believe in God. Or at least not in the way I'm supposed to."

Sandra had been carrying vegetables through to the dining area of their large all in one room when I said this and she nearly dropped the dish.

"What kind of a comment is that?"

"An honest one," said Colin ever so quietly.

"Well, do *you*?" I asked my mother-in-law, exposing her to one of my newly remembered hard stares. I heard a low groan which I think came from Andy. A snake of rebellion slithered in my belly. I had been the good wife and daughter-in-law for far too long. I shot him a look and saw his eyes widen in alarm. Was he starting to wonder at the monster he had created?

He should be, because I was wondering myself. I felt as though someone had cut loose the strings of respectability that had kept me dancing, puppet like, to everyone else's tune. Now it was time to march to my own beating drum.

I waited for an answer but Sandra chose to ignore my comment by making a huge fuss of seating the twins at the table in their matching high chairs.

"Shame Megan and Jake couldn't join us," said Steven and went on to grumble that he hardly saw his eldest grandchildren these days.

Andy tried to placate his father by saying that they were both hard at work studying for their exams which was true. And it wasn't as if they hadn't already rung to wish their grandfather happy birthday. Sandra then added that she hoped she would see more of Jeremy and Jemima as they grew up. This was totally unfair in my view as they had seen my children pretty much every week when they were smaller. They seemed to forget that Megan and Jake were adults now and living their own lives. I was about to snap out a reply, when Katy, catching my eye, smiled and dampened my fuse.

"I think it's great that they're so focused on their studies. Megan and Jake are lovely young people. I hope my two grow up as well adjusted."

95

I smiled at her in return and for while things settled down. Then, as dessert was being served, Steven suddenly racked up the volume on the television which had been kept on low throughout the meal, a habit I hated.

"Well that's just bloody ridiculous that is. I've never heard the like. Must be the newspapers making it up. Disgraceful that's what it is!"

"Whatever's the matter?" Sandra went to him and placed a soothing hand on his shoulder.

Steven pointed to the television screen as if it had become contaminated. "This story, that's the matter."

The presenter was calmly reporting that one of the most famous football players in the country had come back from a trip abroad to announce that he had had a civil marriage with his partner. There was nothing fantastic about that, apart from them both being male. The footballer had taken the brave decision to time his official 'coming out' with the news of his marriage.

"Well I never would have believed he was one of 'those'," said Sandra with pursed lips. "He looks normal to me."

"Shouldn't be allowed," said Steven, switching the television off and tossing the remote down in disgust. "If they have to be perverts they should keep quiet and not say anything. Load of nonsense this idea of men marrying each other. They're a bunch of self-indulgent pansies if you ask me. It's not all that long ago they would've been hung for such behaviour." It sounded as though he thought this should still happen.

I hardly dared look at Andy. When I did, I saw that his face was white and his mouth was compressed into a thin line. He sat there tightly for the next five minutes whilst his father ranted and raved about the whole sordid sickness that was polluting today's society. I winced with each word. There was such revulsion and loathing in Steven's voice, I couldn't even begin to contemplate what Andy must be feeling right now.

No wonder he had buried it deep within himself.

Finally, Steven asked Colin for his opinion. "Doesn't the bible say something about them?"

Colin, for all his staunch Christian values, appeared to hold a measure of compassion and reason within him.

"There are differing views," he said solemnly. "But the main thing surely, is whether or not a person is a decent human being, and not what sexual preferences they have."

"Absolutely, I agree." I wanted to stand up and cheer him. Instead I tried to convey a look of sympathy to Andy who was now a ghastly shade of grey.

Then his mother chirped up with, "I blame the parents."

"What?" I looked from Andy to her in horror. "How can you say that?"

"Well it has to be doesn't it? I mean this idea that people are born that way and can't help it. I think it's all down to upbringing. Surely you would see signs of them being different as a child if you were a good parent?"

"And then what would you do?" I challenged her, "beat it out of them? No. Don't answer that." I held up my hand to stop the words coming out of her mouth. "We're going now. Enjoy the rest of your day."

"Well there's no need to leave in such a hurry," said Steven in a miffed tone. And then his expression changed. He gave me a horrible look. "Oh don't tell me you've got friends like that. That's why you're all defensive. Well it wouldn't surprise me."

Quite how we managed to say goodbye to Katy and Colin and get in the car without either of us exploding, I'm not really sure. I took the car keys quietly off Andy who looked as though he might throw up at any minute.

"Are you alright?" I asked him once we were on the road.

"You mean apart from being a disgusting pervert who should have been beaten as a child and then hung as an adult? Yeah, I'm fine." His voice was loaded with painful bitterness. "Jesus, Eve, can you imagine what it's going to be like when I tell them, about me, about Jason?"

For the first time since he had told me, I felt more compassion for him than anger. "We'll cross that bridge when we come to it, and we'll do it together."

CHAPTER TWELVE

That week Sally's husband went off on his travels and Mary Smith moved into the cottage. Sally pleaded an emergency with one of the horses and had asked if I would stay with her mother-in-law to help her unpack. I jumped at the chance. I loved the little cottage, drawn to the atmosphere that wrapped itself around me whenever I was there which lulled me in to a dreamy state.

It must have been fairly apparent as Mary had to repeat what she was saying to me on more than one occasion. I would be moving something around, shifting a chair to the right, or a table lamp to the left, when I would hear from afar, that peal of laughter, girlish, rich with life and love. The scent of roses would tingle at my nostrils and I would sniff the air, eyes closed.

Mary, a handsome well-built woman in her middle seventies, with cropped white hair and stunningly smooth skin, would then probe me with her sharp brown eyes and ask me what on earth I was doing.

The third time she caught me at it, she gave a snort and demanded, "Are you away with the fairies, girl?"

"I do believe I am," I replied, "would you like me to say hello?" I grinned at her, unabashed at being caught out day dreaming in such a manner.

Mary snorted again. "Stuff and nonsense. Now pull yourself together and take my cases upstairs, they're far too heavy for me."

I dipped a fake curtsey at her. "Yes Ma'am, right away, Ma'am."

"Less of your cheek, my girl." She folded her arms under her impressive bosom, holding my gaze, but as I bent down for one of the cases, I caught the twitch of her mouth. I think she rather liked that I didn't pander to her all the time.

I started to lug the heavy cases up the stairs, one by one. I hadn't been in the tiny bedroom since that very first day and I pushed open the door cautiously. Sally had been very busy in here and the room was now charmingly finished off with a blue and yellow sprigged bed set and matching curtains and lamp shades. There was a new soft rug on the wooden floor boards, which were scrupulously clean, and a pretty vase of fresh flowers had been put on the dressing table.

Nothing to worry about at all.

I laid the suitcase on the bed and went back for the other two.

"Shall I unpack for you?" I called through to the kitchen, where I could hear the sound of a kettle whistling.

"I'm not completely infirm thank-you very much," came back the indignant reply.

"I'll take that as a no then?"

"You can take it how you like, my girl, as long as you don't go rooting through my belongings."

I grinned again, quite enjoying the verbal sparring and set to climbing the stairs once more. After my third trip with the last and heaviest of all the cases (what on earth did she have in them?) I sat on the end of the bed for a moment to catch my breath.

And jumped right up again!

Sat back down.

Bloody hell she was still there!

From my position at the foot of the bed, I could see into the oval mirror which sat on the dressing table. Only I couldn't see my face in the glass. Instead, as though I was looking at a portrait, not a mirror, I could see the face of a young girl. Very pretty, corn blonde hair dressed softly around a dimpling face, grey-blue eyes the colour of an April sky. She was smiling. I smiled back.

"Who are you?" She had to be the girl I had heard laughing.

"Are you talking to yourself now?" Mary's strident tones reached up from the bottom of the stairs.

"No, I'm talking to the girl in the mirror," I said in all honesty and then swore under my breath as she disappeared, her face now replaced with my own.

"Nutty as a fruitcake," tutted Mary as I came back down the stairs.

"Yes, but twice as sweet and speaking of cake, I think Sally brought one over this morning?" I plonked myself down in one of the rockers by the fire and smiled impishly at Mary. I was going to do no more work until I had been stocked up.

This seemed to suit her as well and we took a break for half an hour. When I left her later on, she was reaching for the phone that connected the cottage to the Lodge. I lingered on my way along the path that was slowly emerging through the wilderness of the grounds. Sally's gardener had clearly been hard at work these last couple of weeks but I hadn't seen anything of him. I knew I was being foolish. But something about Jem had settled in my mind the very first time I had met him and I couldn't shake it off.

Disappointed once more, I got back to the Lodge to have Sally greet me with a broad grin on her face. "She thinks you're barking mad."

I shrugged. "She's probably right."

"And she wants you to go round tomorrow to help her wind wool."

"Wind wool?"

"She knits," said Sally, cheerfully, "and she wants you to help her wind wool. Apparently I'm too clumsy to do this." She clapped me on the shoulder. "I knew it would be a good idea getting you two together."

There were worse ways of earning a living, I supposed, than keeping a lonely old woman company, and I went eagerly, in the hope that I would see either my ghostly girl or my gorgeous gardener. Sadly, I saw nothing of either of them during the rest of the week and by the time I had trekked home on the Friday evening, I was feeling rather glum. Then Megan burst into the room and chivvied me up.

"Come on, Mum, what are you doing sitting in the lounge with your feet up? You should be getting ready, they start playing in an hour."

I had completely forgotten that tonight, Jake and his band, including Tim, were playing their first gig at the Maypoleton Arms. I felt a frisson of naughty pleasure run through me at the thought of an evening legitimately watching my son's best friend, and wondered if there was any way I could get him alone.

That was enough to have me shooting upstairs and into the shower.

I had spent far more money and time on my appearance since New Year. Clothes, make-up, rich honey highlights in my dark blonde hair, the odd facial and a manicure, not to mention a small fortune in anti-wrinkle face and body creams. Tell-tale signs of course, but fortunately for me, Andy just thought it was my way of cheering myself up, and Megan thought I was doing it all for her Dad's benefit. I don't think it ever crossed their minds that it might all be for another man.

Let alone Tim.

The satisfaction of knowing three weeks into our affair, he was still as keen as ever, was a potent balm to my wounded pride. The urgency with which he shed my clothes, and then entered me, the raw power that his body used upon mine, the heat in his eyes and the moans that came from his throat, could not be faked. Nor were my screams of pleasure, my demands for more, always harder always faster always deeper.

Of course it was going nowhere. We both knew that. We were playing with fire, enjoying the flames, content to savour the heat, in the knowledge that it would one day sizzle out. I promised myself that I would recognise this day before Tim, and I would end it gracefully. For now though, there was an evening to look forward to, of twisted pleasure and pain. Watching my son and my lover whilst in the company of my husband and friends, definitely twisted.

The Mapoleton Arms was packed by the time we got there. I had dithered about wearing a daringly short skirt with flat boots and a lacy top, or skin tight jeans, heels and a top that exposed a newly discovered cleavage courtesy of an expensive lingerie shop. I went for the jeans, admiring the snug fit over my bum in my mirror. I had always kept in shape and it had paid off. I had the pert, curvy arse of a twenty year old, even if other bits needed more propping up.

Our friends, Carl and Bryony, seemed to think I looked more than okay. We hadn't seen them since Boxing Day. They had an apartment in Tenerife and always disappeared for a few weeks after Christmas. Sometimes we joined them, but not this year. I had been surprised when Andy had turned down the offer, but not later on when things became clear.

Bryony, a very attractive brunette with a voluptuous figure, was deeply tanned, green eyes standing out brightly in her bronzed skin. I would often feel insipid next to her with my fair colouring and mixed up coloured eyes. Tonight though, I felt I could hold my own. It helped that for once, I towered over her with my new four inch killer heels.

"Wow, you look good," she greeted me with a hug and kiss, careful not to smudge her berry coloured lips. "What have you been doing with yourself?"

Across the crowded pub I caught sight of a dark head, thick curls that I had run my fingers through in the grip of lust.

"Oh you know, bit more exercise, some new make-up. Nothing special." Sex. Illicit sex. With a teenager.

Carl was in agreement with his wife. "Well it's worked a treat," he said, rather tactlessly. "You look much better. Not that you didn't look good before, I mean you were always pretty, just sort of rough around the edges."

"Yeah thanks, Carl." I smiled at him, knowing that he couldn't help it.

We settled down with a round of drinks and began the usual catching up of gossip. Bryony had loads to tell us, mostly about their son Ricky. He was in the same year as Jake but went to the private sixth form not too far away, costing his parents a bomb. They thought he was worth it and he certainly seemed to shine at everything he did which I found ever so slightly nauseating.

He was sailing through his second year of A levels, and Bryony was keen to tell us what his tutors had thought of his progress recently. I zoned out a little at this stage. Jake had received an appalling report at parent's night just before Christmas and had been told if he didn't pull his socks up he would fail.

"It's so important that they get the grades this year," Bryony was saying earnestly, "the competition for places at university has never been higher."

Andy nodded in agreement. "I know. I keep telling Jake that he needs to knuckle down, but he thinks he can just cram it all in at the last minute."

"You can get away with that at O level or GCSE whatever it is these days," said Carl returning from the bar with a third round of drinks, "but A levels are a different story."

Personally, having left school, narrowly passing my Maths, English and very little else, I never pushed my son with his studies in the way that maybe another mother would have done. It was one area of parenting that Andy and I had not agreed on. I was happy that Jake was kind, sociable and in my eyes, a decent person. Not to mention a bloody good musician. I shushed them all now as he tapped on the mike to get everyone's attention.

They were good. More than good and Jake was by far the outstanding talent amongst them. He played the guitar from his soul, effortlessly and with passion. He was the singer as well as guitarist and when I heard his voice reaching into every corner of the pub, my heart melted with pride.

My son.

And then he filled my heart with love some more. In the quiet before starting the next song, one of my favourites which I was always singing around the house, he called me over.

"You have to sing this one," he said, passing me the mike stand.

"Me?" I had sung in church, hogged the karaoke machine whenever I could, was always singing at home, but I had not sung in a manner like this since marrying Andy.

"Yeah," said Jake. "It's written for a female anyway and you sing it better than I can."

Close by, I felt Tim's gaze, dark and hot upon me. How could I say no?

It was a lilting melody, a bitter sweet love song that Jake and Mark had written in half an hour one evening when I had told them about the cottage being haunted. It started off quietly and then gradually rose in tempo and beat until I was blasting out the lyrics full pelt. God I had missed doing this. Almost as good as sex, I thought as the last notes died away. And then I caught Tim's eye. No not quite.

It was a scramble then, to lose myself in the crowd of people who wanted to buy them a drink in the break, to head off towards the toilets, knowing that not far behind me, Tim would follow. Bryony was heading the same way.

She flashed me a smile. "Shame you're not twenty years younger. You could be a real singer with them."

"She is a real singer." Tim's voice was low and husky. "Age has nothing to do with it, does it, Eve?" As he brushed past Bryony to go into the gents, he gave me a wink.

"I'm just going out for some air," I said to Bryony but for Tim's benefit. "I won't be long."

"Mm, you do look a bit hot."

I had forgotten about the smoking ban in pubs. The area around the beer garden was clogged up with smokers. So much for grabbing a quick ten minutes with Tim. Still, I wasn't ready to go back in and I did need to cool off. I wandered around the side of the pub to the children's play area and sat on one of the swings.

A few minutes later Tim joined me.

"Ever done it on a swing?" He said, bending down and kissing me hard on the lips, tongue insistently probing. Red hot shivers went straight to my groin and I had to steady my legs as Tim pushed me back up, my bottom still perched on the swing.

I was becoming addicted to the taste and feel of him, happy to lose myself for a long hungry moment as my hands went into his hair and my mouth ground against him.

"I don't think, even with your agility, we could manage it," I said at last, casting a furtive eye over to the corner of the pub. There was no one around this side and hardly likely to be. The smokers would be huddled together by the heater the landlord thoughtfully provided. Still, we were far too exposed to try anything other than a few kisses.

That is until Tim clapped eyes on the Wendy house.

"Come on," he said, taking me by the hand.

"What? You're insane," I began to giggle as I lurched awkwardly in my high heels across the play area, covered in thick protective bark.

"I am," he replied. "Mad with lust, Eve, and I can't go back into the pub like this can I? So, you'll have to help me out." He placed my hand over his groin which was bulging hard against his jeans.

"Well if you will wear such tight jeans," I laughed, stroking him against the fabric.

He groaned and opening the door to the play house, put a hand on my head to duck me down and guide me in.

"I don't see how this is going to work," I said as he folded his own height into the cramped space.

His teeth flashed white in the dark. "Trust me I know what I'm doing."

And he did, credit to him for imagination. He wriggled around so that he was sitting against one of the walls, unzipped his jeans and shimmied out of them as much as was needed. My mouth went dry but already I could feel the wetness building between my legs. He was well built and so very eager for me.

"Straddle me, Eve," he urged with the impatience of youth.

How could I refuse? I kicked off my heels, dropped my own jeans and tugged them off as quickly as I could. I knelt across him, tempted to take him in my mouth first, to prolong his agony and build up the fire that was burning in my belly. But he caught the teasing glint in my eye and shook his head.

"I can't wait." He placed his hands on my waist, a strong grip, guiding with a sureness and certainty. Poised over him, I delayed the moment a second, to reach forward and bit upon his mouth. His hands drove me down, impaling me upon him, holding me there as he lifted his hips up to meet me.

"Oh God!" Insanity was a glorious place to be, I thought, as I felt him fill me completely. Lips locked together, we bucked and thrust wildly, hips grinding in an ever increasing pace. I pulled my mouth away from his, pushing back against his chest with my hands and began to arch my back as I took control. He was helpless beneath me now and I knew my mouth was curved in a siren like smile.

I went faster, working against him ruthlessly, savouring the way his eyes grew ever darker and his jaw clenched as I brought him closer and closer to the edge.

"Don't stop, Eve, Jesus, don't stop."

As if I could? God and all his angels could have walked in right then and I would have been powerless to stop. My own orgasm was racing towards me and nothing was going to get in the way of meeting it. My hips were slippery with sweat despite the cold air, skin slapping against skin as our breath grew louder and ragged, desperate for that final release. Which when it came was enough to have me throw my head back, curve my spine like a bow, and tear an animal cry from my throat.

Tim's fingers dug hard into my buttocks, scraping my flesh as his own hips jerked up in hard, repeated thrusts. Then the slow float back down to earth and the shared laughter.

It was wrong.

It was the best thing ever.

"Is that better?" I kissed him playfully on the top of his head as I wriggled off him and slithered back into my jeans.

"Oh yes," he sighed happily. "Much. Shit, I'd best get back in though, Jake and the others will be wondering where I've got to."

"Don't worry," I said. "We weren't exactly that long." It had been quick and frantic.

"Are you saying I can't last the distance?" He grumbled and then swore as he banged his head on the roof of the house.

"I know you can," I smiled in memory at a couple of times we had managed to spend in bed together at his sister's house. "But quick is good." I would not admit to him, that a five minutes' shag with Andy would have left me feeling very frustrated.

We crawled out of the play house and made our way back to the rear entrance of the pub. Just as we were reaching the corner, two figures came round bent close together and I wondered if someone else would end playing 'mummies and daddies' in the house.

They hadn't seen us yet and I whispered quickly to Tim. "I'll go in round the front, you go that way."

He nodded and walked away with a whistle, hands in jeans pockets. I heard him call out to one of the figures who were hugging the shadows by the wall.

"Alright, Ricky, have you got a light?"

It was Bryony's son then. I wondered who he was with but it was too dark to see.

I walked back into the pub via the front, as Tim joined Jake and Mark just in time to play the second set. Andy was scanning the pub with anxious eyes and a teeny, and I mean, absolutely teeny, dart of guilt stung me, but not for long.

"Hi," I said breezily, taking a grateful sip of the drink that was on the table in front of my space.

"Where have you been?" Andy and Bryony over-lapped as they spoke.

"Just outside," I said. "I needed to cool off."

"You took your time," said Bryony, raking her eyes over my face. Did I look like I had just had wild sex, or would it pass as a hot flush? I got away with the latter. "Andy said you hadn't been feeling so good recently. How's the HRT doing? Must be hell going through all that business. I've no signs yet thank God."

"Oh it's not too bad," I said, not minding for once that she was getting one up on me (or at least thinking she was). The idea of going through the menopause was at least giving me some cover for the odd irrational behaviour episodes. "I just have these hot and cold spells from time to time. I'm best just finding somewhere quiet to go until it settles down."

Bryony smirked. "It must feel terribly ageing for you. And you're three years younger than me!"

I shrugged. "Luck of the draw I suppose." I sipped my drink and let the rest of the evening wash over me, replete and satisfied. The only aspect of the night to irk me was the brooding presence of Sergeant Hawthorne who had walked in shortly after Jake had started playing again.

Bryony drew my attention to him with a sharp nudge. "Have you met our new bobby? I think he's a bit of a dish, don't you?"

The music was loud and she had to repeat herself. Carl tutted and rolled his eyes at Andy. "What are these women like, hey? Anything with a uniform on and they're after him."

"Well he is good looking, don't you think, Eve?"

I turned my head towards the bar where he was standing, orange juice at his side. His presence had gone unnoticed by my son who was still giving it his all but some of the locals had quietened down their response to the music. I scowled at him, annoyed that he should spoil things.

His eyes met and held mine over the heads of the crowd. He was tall, topping Andy by a good couple of inches and intimidating with his bulky form in black.

"No," I replied to Bryony. "I don't think he's at all good looking. He looks like a lump of granite."

"Well I wouldn't kick him out of bed," she said, prompting Carl to sigh in mock annoyance.

I said nothing, but was aware that the policeman's eyes seemed to be sharply assessing everyone in the pub that evening, more than once sliding over from our table to where Jake and the lads were playing. What, I wondered, was he looking for?

Then a horrible suspicion entered my head. Had Tim and I somehow been seen in the Wendy House? Was I going to get arrested for lewd and indecent behaviour in a child's playground? I imagined Jake and Megan's response and started to bite my nails anxiously.

CHAPTER THIRTEEN

As it turned out, Sergeant Hawthorne was not in the least bit interested in what had occurred in the Wendy House. Well, he very probably would have been, if he had known, but that was not the reason he had been casting his eagle eye over the proceedings on the Friday evening. By Saturday afternoon the gossip had gone all around the village. It was Mabel at the bakery who had told me what had happened.

I had called in to buy an apple pie for tea. Jake had announced that he was bringing a new girlfriend home that evening and I wanted to make a reasonable impression. It wasn't often Jake brought a girl home. He was fairly private about things like that. I had gathered from Megan that she was new to the area, having moved into one of the houses on the estate Andy's firm had built. Lexy, as she was called, had been in the pub on Friday, and had not taken her eyes off my son.

I did recall, in the moments that my own eyes were not fixed on Tim, that there had been a very pretty red haired girl at the front of the crowd all night. Jake had been as taken with her as she was with him, and had invited her round for tea. How sweet!

So I was determined to do my best motherly impression and produce a meal that was half way decent. Beef and ale stew with herb dumplings followed by apple pie. You couldn't go wrong with that. Unless of course she was a vegetarian in which case I was stuffed.

"Morning love." Mabel greeted me with a smile. I had been the last in a long queue and she looked like she was glad of the chance to catch her breath and have a little chat now the shop was empty, apart from me. "You're looking very well. Must agree with you, working for Sally. You're positively blooming." She grinned at me. "Or is it the HRT?"

"Bloody hell, is that all anyone talks about around here?" I said, and then asked for one of her large pies.

"Well if that's what HRT does for you, then I'd happily take it," she chuckled. "Mind you, I'm well past all that now. I heard your lad went down well last night? I caught a bit of it myself as I was walking past, catchy tune I thought. And I heard you sang one of them? Never can resist, can you?"

I smiled. "No. You know me and the karaoke. It made a change though to sing properly for once. I hadn't realised how much I had missed it. Singing in a band is not something you can really do when you're married and bringing kids up."

"Aye, there's always sacrifices," she said with a sigh. "I used to be a dancer myself."

Now there was an interesting image. I smiled at her and then saw her face turn cloudy. "Did you hear about Maisie?"

"No?" It can't have been good, judging from her face.

"In hospital."

"Hell what happened?"

"They think it was drugs," said Mabel, resting her bosom on the counter. "She collapsed in the toilets apparently and we all know she doesn't drink."

"Is she alright?" God it was every mother's nightmare.

"Yes. Her friend was with her and got her mum to call an ambulance straight away. It happened just after last orders."

"I remember hearing the sirens," I said with a shudder. "We had just got back home. Poor Maisie, and her parents, they must have been worried sick."

Maisie was the seventeen year old daughter of Terry and Beth who owned the Maypoleton Arms. They were responsible landlords and good parents. Having their own daughter taking drugs in their pub would come as a heck of a blow.

I hated drugs with a passion, having lost more than one of my own friends when I had been younger. Playing in pubs and clubs it had always been on offer. But not for me. I had never forgotten a friend in one of the care homes who had overdosed at the age of fourteen.

I had never really known if it had been an accident, a cry for help that had not been heard, or fully intentional. Either way it had been a

109

waste. As Megan and Jake had hit that age, I had told them repeatedly about Mandy. A talented artist who thought she'd had nothing to live for. I had even taken them to her grave, a lonely spot in a shabby city graveyard.

"Never be tempted," I told them again and again. "Once is one time too many. And no problem is ever that big that it can't be solved."

Back at the house I re-iterated this statement to them both. Megan and Mark were watching television and Jake was glued to Facebook. They were all still in dressing gowns even though it was nearly three in the afternoon but as I thought of poor Maisie lying in hospital having her stomach pumped, I hadn't the heart to nag them to get dressed.

"Honestly, Mum, do we look that stupid?" said Megan with a loud yawn and disinterested stare. She was catching up on the omnibus edition of her favourite programme. A bomb could go off and she wouldn't be interested.

"It's alright, Eve," said Mark, a shade more tuned in to my anxiety. "We know not to touch any of that crap, especially this Whizz stuff."

"Whizz?"

"It's the new thing," said Jake, swivelling round from the desk. "Lexy's just told me that's what they think Maisie had taken." He turned back to tap the keyboard rapidly. "It's a tablet," he added, as his fingers worked lightly. "Lexy says it's supposed to make you feel really alert, like you've suddenly got a really high IQ. It's not supposed to be dangerous."

"That's what they all say," I commented dryly, "Until you're hooked up to a life support machine." My lecture was stopped before it had even got started properly as the doorbell then rang.

"That'll be Tim," said Jake, jumping up from his seat. He was still keen to make sure that his friend and I didn't spend any time alone, even if Megan was now convinced I was back on the straight and narrow.

As a matter of fact it was Sergeant Hawthorne, looking grimmer than ever. Jake called to me from the hallway as I made my way into the kitchen preparing to do battle with the steak and dumplings.

"Mum, it's for you."

I groaned to see the police officer at my front door again. "What is it now?" I asked. "I'm about to make dumplings."

"Hardly had you down as the domestic sort," he said, stepping into the hallway. As he did so there was a familiar roar and Tim's bike swerved into the driveway, narrowly missing the Sergeant's car. I suppressed a grin.

Sergeant Hawthorne looked at the bike and then at me. Then Tim took his helmet off. Sergeant Hawthorne looked at him impassively and then returned his gaze to me. His eyes reflected an emotion I didn't care to put a name to. I felt heat stinging my cheeks.

"Hi Eve," Tim grinned at me. That wonderful, sexy cocky grin, that told me he really didn't care if the policeman had recognised his bike from the night at Badger's Brock. "Did you enjoy last night?" He stood close to me, the porch suddenly overcrowded with the two of them.

"Yeah, it was good," I said as nonchalantly as I could. My cheeks burnt hotter when Tim gave me one of his wicked winks in full view of the police man.

"Catch you later," he said and went through to Jake's lounge.

I turned my scarlet face to Sergeant Hawthorne, suddenly defensive. "Well what do you want?"

"A chat with all of you, if I may?"

"You'd best come through then." I lead the way and called to the others to join us in the kitchen. At least there I could keep myself busy making dumplings whilst we were interrogated. "Where's your Dad?" I asked Megan as they all trooped in and sat around the table.

"Playing golf," she said, offering to make Sergeant Hawthorne a cup of tea.

Screwing Jason more likely, I thought knowing his golf membership had been cancelled this year.

My face though must have betrayed some pain or twisted feelings as Sergeant Hawthorne addressed me directly.

"Are you alright, Mrs. Armstrong?"

"Eve," I said automatically. "Yes I'm fine. So why the inquisition, is it to do with Maisie?"

"She's not dead is she?" Megan blurted out, horror in her voice.

"No, no. Maisie is doing just fine," he reassured her quickly. "Hopefully she will consider it a lesson well learnt. But someone else

111

may not be so fortunate. Maisie was lucky in that her friend was with her when she collapsed and there were people around to get help. If she had been by herself the village would be preparing a funeral by now."

Mark whistled softly between his teeth. "That's bad. Was it Whizz?"

"So you all know about it then?"

"Just what everyone says, Sergeant," said Megan earnestly. "Nothing more than that."

"Craig," he said with a broad smile that was meant no doubt to lull the youngsters into a false sense of security. I had to admit it took me by surprise. A dimple appeared in his right cheek, lending a boyish hint to his otherwise rock like face.

"The kids at college have been saying stuff about it," put in Jake. "It's supposed to make you really smart."

Craig nodded. "In a way it does. It focuses the mind, brings everything into vivid clarity, makes reflexes sharper, speeds up the synapses in the brain. Allegedly. Not much more than a caffeine drink. Allegedly. Not as addictive as a caffeine drink. Allegedly."

"So where's the harm?" Jake wanted to know. "And why did it affect Maisie so badly?"

"It's a street drug," said Craig flatly. "It's not a known entity. It hasn't been tested in laboratories, it's been produced as a by-product from something else and at the moment it's doing the rounds as if it's as innocent as a bag of sweets. And for most people, it possibly is. But so far there have been three deaths connected with the drug in the North West alone. No-one is sure yet why."

"Shit!" I stopped playing with my dumplings and looked at my kids, all of them, including Tim. "Look you lot, if any of you know who's knocking this stuff out, spit it out now. This is serious." There was a hard edge to my voice. A picture of Mandy was clear in my mind.

Craig seemed surprised. "I have to say, I was concerned that perhaps one of you might know something."

"Why?" Megan was affronted.

"Stereo-typing of course. But with the band and the music scene, it kind of goes hand in hand."

I put the casserole dish, complete with dumplings, into the oven and slammed the door. I was too angry to speak. So I glared at him, floury hands on my hips.

"Not a chance," said Megan, only marginally less annoyed. "Mum would skin us alive if she thought any of us were mucking about like that."

Craig raised his eyebrows, dark over his light grey eyes, as if surprised. He obviously had not got me down as a respectable mother. I continued to glare, feeling no need to explain myself. I was not in the least bit intimidated by his presence, but my kids had not brushed against authority in the quite the same way I had, during their upbringing.

Jake stepped into the void. "Mum's best friend in the care home died from an overdose."

Craig kept his eyes on mine. I doubt if the others saw the tiny spark that flickered at Jake's words.

"She was only fourteen," he added. "Mum took us to her grave when we were her age. It isn't something you forget."

At last that steely probe changed direction. "No, I imagine it isn't," said Craig softly. He stood up and looked round the group. "Well you know where I am if you hear anything. And please, don't let any misguided loyalties stand in your way. Maisie could have died."

"Don't worry," said Megan with a little shiver. "We won't hide anyone from you."

"And for God's sake, don't be tempted to try it yourselves, no matter what anyone tells you. It isn't safe."

Whether it was his words, or simply his strong personality, I could see that all of them had taken it seriously. Remembering my dead friend, I was grateful to him, for that if nothing else.

"I'll see you out, Sergeant."

"Craig," he reminded me. "It's not so difficult."

"I'll let you know if I hear anything," I said once we got to the porch. And then I swore as I noticed Deidre from across the road coming over. She must have been waiting at her window to see when the police officer was about to leave.

"Is everything alright, Eve?" She cooed to me falsely as she edged her way onto our driveway.

I still hadn't forgiven her for grassing me up to Marjorie, even though it had been a blessing in disguise.

"Yeah, nothing to worry about, Deidre. Craig here was just giving me a warning not to make a habit of dancing round the Maypole stark naked at midnight. I've been frightening the bats off apparently."

She froze and looked from my innocent smile to the sudden grin that had split across Craig's face.

"She's joking, isn't she?"

Craig nodded in confirmation.

Deidre huffed and flicked her smoothly bobbed hair with an agitated hand. "I don't know how that lovely husband of yours puts up with you. You're enough to try the patience of a saint!" She stalked back to her lair, no doubt to pick up the phone and slander me some more.

"Interfering old gossip," I muttered as Craig made his way over to his car. He hesitated by Tim's bike.

"It's none of your business," I told him sharply, before he could begin to comment.

"You're right, it isn't. But still, be careful, Eve. You're playing with fire there."

"That's alright," I said breezily. "I'm an Aries. Fire sign." And I turned my back on him before I could admit to myself that the look in his eyes was making me feel very chilly deep inside.

The sombre mood that Craig's visit had cast over us lasted until the early evening when Jake's new girlfriend arrived. She was the red haired girl I had noticed the previous night. Bubbly and friendly, she appeared besotted already with my son. She was also a huge fan of steak and ale stew which ticked at least one box on my sheet. Megan put her through the usual grilling deemed necessary in her role as older sister and by the time Andy walked through the door, we knew everything there was to know about her.

Tim had stayed for tea as well, claiming the need to meet Jake's girlfriend properly, although he spent much more time sending me covert glances, than checking Lexy out. I was on edge for the rest of the evening, not liking the close proximity of everyone gathered around the table. As was often the case in our household, the kitchen became the social centre of the house for the night. Andy had called in at the off licence in the village on the way home from 'golf' and was generous in sharing round the beers and wine.

He had brought flowers too. Another guilty peace offering, misinterpreted by Megan who gushed to Lexy that it was so sweet how her parents were still dippy about each other after twenty odd years. Tim started choking on his beer at that point and I had to warn him with a stare when he recovered.

I watched as Andy charmed Lexy and joked with his son. It was weird, as if I was having an out of body experience. The falseness of it all, the hidden dramas and deceit suddenly made me feel sick. I couldn't get the expression on Craig Hawthorne's face out of my head. Contempt? Disgust? Curiosity? Sexual interest?

I was usually adapt at reading people, a skill learnt very early in life, moving from one foster home to another. But the granite faced police officer was equally skilled at keeping his feelings closed off. Whatever he thought, it had unsettled me. I pleaded a headache and called Skip from the table where he was sitting, ever hopeful, for scraps.

"I'll leave you to it," I said. "There's apple pie in the fridge with cream or ice cream which ever you prefer. I'm going to get a bit of fresh air."

Tim quirked his eyebrows and I gave him the slightest shake of my head. I really was going for some fresh air. It wasn't an excuse to get him alone. He answered with a tiny shrug and turned away. I went out the front as it was far too dark to go rambling over the fields. The full moon that had lit up the sky at the beginning of the month was barely visible now and what little light it gave off was shielded by thick clouds.

I took the footpath that lead out of the close to the lane, keeping Skip on his lead just in case any cars came racing along. Across the way I could see the light from Seth's camp fire, welcoming and cheerful. I headed towards it. The old man's company would do me good. The protests from the village seemed to have died down for the time being as the Romany was keeping quietly to himself. I had no idea how long he was planning on staying and for the time being I wasn't bothered.

Of course there was a mug of hot sweet tea waiting for me. There always was. And cake.

115

"Ooh this looks nice, Seth," I drooled my thanks and sat on the spare stool by the fire. Skip went immediately to his side and rested his chin on him adoringly. He had a way with animals, did Seth, which was the reason he had the cake apparently.

"Mabel from the bakery brought it over," he said stroking Skip's head.

"That was kind of her." I was pleased that at least someone in the village was making an effort to be friendly.

"I 'ealed 'er cat."

"Oh?"

"Arthritis."

I had got used to Seth's perfunctory way of talking. He needed quite a lot of prompting. "How did that come about, Seth?"

"'Appened to stop an' talk one mornin'. Said as 'ow 'er cat troubled wi' stiffness. Vitn'ry useless. Told 'er to bring it t'me. Not healed completely, can't do that. But 'elped wi' t'pain."

"How did you do that?" I finished off the carrot cake which was delicious and licked my fingers.

He held out his hands, bony and strong from years of hard work. "Tis all in t'touch. T'is a gift."

His words brought to mind the old woman I had met at New Year by the oak tree. I still carried her handkerchief in my coat pocket. Once or twice I had thought to ask Seth about her. Perhaps he knew her. But I refrained, anxious that he might think me too nosy. Telling me about Mabel's cat was about the chattiest I had known him so far. Encouraged by this, I dug my hand into my pocket.

"I was given a gift," I said tentatively. "I met an old woman at the beginning of the year. I think she was a traveller too." I stroked the square of cotton between my fingers. "She gave me a funny sort of blessing. Well I think it was a blessing. She touched me on the forehead and told me that I would be able to see properly. And then she gave me this." I held it out for him to see by the light of the fire.

His old hands caressed the material as if it was spun from gold. His head was bowed so I couldn't see his face. When he looked up his eyes were moist and shining. He had, I thought, lovely eyes, a curious mix of blue-green and brown that twinkled brightly against his dark weathered face.

"Isabella," He said at last, his fingers tracing the letter in the corner.

"You knew her then?"

"Aye, lass." He folded the square carefully and handed it back to me. I was reluctant to take it. The owner must have been someone he had known very well judging from his response. "When did thee say thee met 'er?"

"Just after New Year. The Sunday, so that would have been the fourth. Why don't you keep it, you obviously cared for her?"

"Nay lass. 'Twas given to thee, an' it's a gift rarer than thee can imagine."

"Who was she? Isabella?"

But Seth's eyes were lost in the flames of the fire and I had the feeling he was seeing things that were not mine to know. When he did raise his eyes to mine, it was not to comment on the handkerchief, or Isabella, whoever she may have been. It was to say this.

"Take care, lass. A storm is brewing."

He wouldn't say anymore but I had the distinct feeling he was not talking about the weather.

CHAPTER FOURTEEN

Or maybe he was.

February blew in with gale force winds and torrential rain. Working in the office at the Lodge, I was busy cancelling all the lessons that could not take place due to the treacherous conditions. A section of the indoor riding school roof had blown off and the outdoor arenas, not to mention the fields, were completely flooded.

"Bloody, bloody, British weather," grumbled Sally mid-morning on the Wednesday, the third day of rain. I bit my lip to stop from grinning. I had been snug in the office, heater blasting and regular cups of hot chocolate to keep me warm. Sally on the other hand had been out on the yard and was soaking wet. When she finally peeled off her soggy layers, she collapsed on a chair with the air of one refusing to move any more.

I put the kettle on and placed a chocolate brownie in front of her. I had braved the shops that morning before coming in, partly because I thought we could all do with a bit of cheering up, and partly because I had wanted to see how Mabel's cat was doing. Apparently Tiggles was acting like a four year old.

"Ooh, you angel," sighed Sally sinking her teeth into the oozing slice. "Have I told you how marvellous it is to have you working here?"

"Repeatedly, but don't stop. It's nice to be appreciated."

"Hm. Well I wish my bloody mother-in-law would appreciate that cottage," she said, slurping her tea.

"I thought she did?" I was surprised. Each day, after I had finished my jobs in the office, I would go over to the cottage and spend some time with Mary. I helped her to wind her wool for knitting, I played cards with her, I sorted out her embroidery threads, and sometimes I just listened to her. She seemed happy enough and I was equally happy to spend as much time there as possible.

The cottage still had an effect on me, although in Mary's company I was quick to hide the times when I heard the girl's laughter, or smelt the roses. And when she asked me to fetch something for her from upstairs, which was often, I would do so as swiftly as possible, confused by the desire to linger in the quaint little room, and flee from there as fast as I could.

Sally finished her chocolate brownie and pushed the plate away. "She does. She likes the place. What she is not happy with, is the cottage's behaviour." She arched her brows at me and waited for my reply.

"The cottage's behaviour?"

"She says it is trying to make her leave."

"Trying to make her leave?"

"Noises. Things that go bump in the night. Pictures falling off walls. Doors slamming. Creaking floorboards. Screaming."

"Bloody hell! I'd no idea. I mean, she's never said anything to me."

"No. She wouldn't. Apparently, the cottage only behaves itself when you are there, so she thinks you would think she was mad."

"Oh."

"So have you not heard or felt anything like that? I mean, since that first day we were there. You did say there had been something awful that had happened."

I shrugged, strangely reluctant to share my experiences of the cottage, even with her. "It was just one of those things. You know, old house and all that. I really like it there."

"Mm, well she spoke to me yesterday and said that if one more thing happened, then she would be moving in here with me."

Right on cue her mobile rang. She pulled a face as she checked the screen before answering it. The conversation was brief and one sided. All Sally got in was a 'Right, ok." She tossed the phone onto the table. "That's it then. Bloody ghost!"

I stared at her.

"She says something tried to push her down the stairs. She's not staying there a minute longer. She wants you to go and walk round with her and then pack up her things." Sally ragged her fingers through her hair and groaned. "Unbelievable. That cottage has been in my family for three hundred years and not once in all that time, have we had an inkling of a ghost. Now, the only time I need it for my mother-in-law, it suddenly becomes the Amityville Horror!"

I felt sorry for Sally but at the same time a twinge of excitement tugged at my stomach. Was the cottage really that haunted? And if so, why did I feel so happy there? I was already reaching for my coat, in eagerness to fetch Mary and take another look around.

"Are you sure you don't mind?" Sally decided she needed a second chocolate brownie to cope with the stress. "I hate to think of you as her dogsbody."

"Honestly, it's ok. I don't have a problem with Mary, or the cottage."

Truly I didn't. It wrapped its loving embrace around me as soon as I set foot through the front door. Mary was sitting in one of the rocking chairs by the fire, the one in which I had fallen asleep and dreamt so deeply. She was wearing her hat and coat and her face was as buttoned up as her clothing, lips pursed as though she had a lemon in her mouth. Her hands were clutching her bag so tightly that her knuckles were showing white.

I smiled warmly at her. This was not a cross old lady with a bee in her bonnet. This was a woman who had been scared out of her wits. Not that she was going to admit it to me, of course.

"Hello, Mary, I've come to walk you round to the Lodge and then Sally said you wanted me to pack up your things for you?"

"Indeed. I'm not setting foot upstairs again. Damp!" She insisted. "Terrible damp. Anyone would think my daughter-in-law was trying to kill me. I'll be lucky if I don't end up with pneumonia"

I escorted Mary out of the cottage and down the path that had now been cleared through the grounds. As the door shut behind us, slamming to quite of its own volition, I heard once more, the laughter that I knew had come from the girl in the mirror.

I found myself hurrying Mary along, impatient to get back into the cottage to collect her belongings. I wanted to see if the girl would show herself to me once more, now that Mary had left. I also was still hoping to catch a glimpse of Jem. I had seen him from time to time in the distance, a lean, lithe figure, always hard at work, always stopping to raise a hand and smile at me.

It seemed that the sun came out whenever he did and I would smile back in return often causing Mary to comment what a dopey expression I had on my face. Each time she had gone to the window to see what was making look me so happy, he had disappeared. I was glad. I didn't want Mary poking fun at my developing crush on Sally's gardener.

I left Mary in Sally's capable, if rather exasperated hands and went back to start packing up her belongings. I sang loudly to myself as I did this, quite happy to be alone in the cottage. I didn't want to leave but knew that Mary would be anxious to be settled in at the Lodge, so I packed up as quickly as I could. I had pinched a wheel barrow from the yard to transport her heavy luggage and was just balancing it all in together when I heard the sound of whistling nearby.

"She gone then?" Jem stood there, leaning on a long handled rake. He was tending the roses he had planted by the front door.

I stood transfixed. God he was beautiful. An angel walking the earth. Hair the colour of autumn chestnuts and silver eyes, luminous like the moon and just as magnetic. I couldn't look at those eyes without wanting to reach towards him. Spellbinding eyes.

"Yes. She wasn't comfortable here."

He smiled crookedly and my knees went weak. "No. She wouldn't be. You're happy here though?"

"I love the cottage. It feels like home."

"Aye. I'll be waiting for you. When you've taken her things back, I'll be here."

I could make no reply. My wits seemed to have deserted me. I pushed the barrow forwards, wondering what had just happened. Something had certainly. Without a shadow of a doubt, I was going to deliver Mary's belongings, and then rush back to the cottage. Drawn to a virtual stranger, I was unable to refuse the unspoken invitation.

It made no sense at all and yet my footsteps were light and quick as I returned down the path. He was still there, tending the roses. When he heard me coming he stopped and turned. The sunlight caught the top of his hair and it shimmered, coppery bronze. His hands, tanned and long fingered, snapped the head off a rose and held it out to me.

"You should have roses," he said with a smile that set a fire burning deep within me. "I always think of roses whenever I see you."

"But we've only spoken once."

"Once is enough. Once can last a lifetime."

As I cradled the fragile rose in my hand, he reached out his own to touch my face. His fingers were so cool against my skin, or maybe it was the heat in my cheeks that made it seem that way. His face came close to mine, those eyes blinding me to everything but him. Then his lips pressed down upon mine. Softly, tenderly, questioningly. I felt the tip of his tongue gently sliding along, seeking entrance and I willingly parted my own to draw him in. His hands cupped the back of my head, tilting me just so, until the angle was perfect. It was a long, slow, languorous kiss that melted every particle in my body and had me sinking weakly against him.

I slid my arms up around his back, needing to feel him closer, needing to hold onto him so I wouldn't dissolve into a puddle of molten lust on the floor. My head was beginning to swim. I had never been kissed like this. He was drinking from my mouth as if draining my very soul and I was glad to let him.

Just when I thought I would faint with desire, he took his mouth from mine, biting just once at my neck, before bending down and sweeping me up into his arms. He wasn't massively built, but he was strong and fit and he carried me as though I was a child. No man had ever held me like this before.

He was nimble up the narrow staircase, his feet steady and sure on the wooden treads that hardly creaked with his weight and mine combined. He wasn't tall, so had no need to duck his head under the low door which swung open easily at his kick, as if the room was expecting us. He laid me reverently on the bed and then eased his body on top of mine, hands roaming lazily from my throat to my hips. His touch set my skin on fire and I ached to feel his caress without my clothes as a barrier. My hands reached for the bottom of my sweater but he caught them.

"No rush, my sweet, we have all the time in the world."

I had grown used to my frantic fucking with Tim. Insane sessions of quick fire sex. This was different. Beyond different. Beyond anything I had ever felt before. As my body sank deeper and deeper into the mattress, my skin tingling, my nipples aching and my deepest parts throbbing for his touch, he made me wait.

Slowly, thoroughly, certainly, he uncovered my body, inch by inch and savoured every moment. My sweater first, then hands and mouth up my ribcage, into the valley between my breasts, along my collar bone. Hungry, sucking bites in the nape of my neck, clever fingers snaking beneath me and tracing my spine until shivers of lust had me arching up off the bed. Those same agile fingers made short work of my bra and then moulded and caressed my breasts, teasing my nipples that were already proud and tight.

I nearly sobbed when he took first one, then the other, into his mouth. His clever tongue stoking the fire that was raging below, greedy lips that sucked, sharp teeth that tugged and nipped. I rolled and writhed beneath him, my fingers tangling in his hair, pressing his head deeper against me. It was heaven and hell at the same time. I wanted him never to stop and yet I was desperate for him to take more of me.

His laughter rippled through his body as I bucked up against him, urging him to strip me of my jeans. After an agony of tortured pleasure, he lifted his mouth and hands from my breasts and moved lower. I rushed to help him but he brushed aside my hands, reaching back up to silence my protests with a hard and commanding kiss.

God I was helpless! Too weak and limp with lust to do anything other than to let him work his magic at his own pace. And it was magic, I thought hazily. This was out of the realms of reality. It had to be. This was the stuff of poetry and fiction. Utter fantasy.

Firm capable hands finally eased my jeans from me and my pants as well. I trembled as my body was exposed to his gaze, his eyes making love to me before he had even touched me. How was that possible? How could the simple act of looking deep into another person's eyes, bring you so dangerously close to the edge of oblivion?

"Jem, please," I begged, shamelessly. "I can't wait any longer." It was the truth. I think the moment he next touched me, I would come right there and then.

He smiled at me, knowingly, wickedly. And bent his head to my parted thighs. His tongue traced around the folds of my flesh, teasingly at first and then with an insistent probing that was more than I could bear. My head arched back, my spine curved, my hips juddered out of control, held firmly in place by his hands as his mouth took me to the precipice and then over.

I took a long time falling and I cried out in abandon all the way down. He caught me as I crashed to the bottom. Swept me up once more on a wave of passion as he shifted his body back up the length of mine, covered my mouth with his, and entered me now fully. No time to recover. Just more spiralling sensations that lifted me higher and higher onto a plain of ecstasy that made me want to weep.

He took me slowly at first, with an almost lazy movement of his hips that teased and beguiled. His body was light over mine his hands braced either side of my head. He kissed me deeply, softly, tenderly. He held his face so close to mine, his breath cool and sweet on my skin. I drowned in his eyes, sank into the sensations his body was causing in mine, felt my soul float right out of my body and lose itself somewhere completely out of time.

And then the fire between us grew hotter and the laziness vanished. Pressed tight against me now, mouth grinding against mine, hands sliding down beneath my buttocks to grip me harder, he drove me forward with a demanding urgency that I had to match. I came once, a shockingly sharp spasm that had me clutching my nails cruelly into his flesh, and then he carried me with him, further, higher, than I thought would be possible.

The room was spinning as he shuddered within me. My own body shook with a final, exquisite release that sent tremors rippling from head to toe. I lay beneath him, quivering and panting, for what seemed an eternity, cradling his damp head against my breast with more tenderness than I knew had within me.

I felt the hot sting of tears slide down my cheeks. I had heard people talk of weeping for joy, but never understood it. Not until now. If I died right there, if the blood stopped flowing through my veins, if my heart ceased to beat, I would be content.

Gentle fingers wiped away the tears.

"Do not weep, my love. Tears are not for us. Sleep now." He moved slightly, and kissed me on my lips, the lightest of touches, yet still it burnt. His eyes glittered into mine and I felt myself grow drowsy under his gaze. I closed my eyelids, aware of his smile as the room went dark.

It was cold when I woke. The winter sky was barely holding on to the last vestiges of light. The pillow beside me was empty, the bedroom silent.

"Jem?" I didn't know why I bothered to call out, I knew he wasn't there. I should have been cross that he had left me alone, crumpled on the bed like a discarded play thing. But I wasn't. For one thing, I knew this was no game. This was more than a casual afternoon screw. This was...

Well I wasn't entirely sure.

It was something special.

Something magical.

And if I had thought that I needed to keep Tim a secret, then I knew with even greater certainty, that what had happened with Jem, required deeper discretion. I stretched out on the bed, yawning like a cat who had dozed in the sun. As I sat up and reached for my clothes, I caught sight of her. The girl in the mirror.

She was smiling at me as if she knew me very well. Definitely a ghost, she had to be. But there was nothing about her that prompted fear within me. Maybe her spirit, or whose ever it was that had scared Mary away, was simply choosy about who stayed in her house?

"Who are you?" I asked her, but she laughed and I heard the sound echo round the room before it faded away, along with her image. She would tell me in time, if she wanted me to know. I dressed quickly, goose bumps from the cold air prickling my body. When I checked my watch I saw that I had been at the cottage for over two hours.

I didn't want to leave. I could have stayed there all night. I pictured myself tucked up in bed, waiting for Jem to return. Ridiculous! But I had a huge smile on my face as I shut the front door and started to walk home. I cut through the path that led from the cottage down to the lane, avoiding the Lodge. I had no wish to explain to Sally what I was still doing on her premises.

I must admit I was in a bit of a day dream when the car that came round the corner, nearly ran me over. My fault entirely, I had not heard it coming, and was slow to react. The brakes squealed and I smelt hot rubber as mud splashed up from the grass verge.

"What the bloody hell are you doing, walking like that, I could have killed you!"

It would have to be Craig Hawthorne in his police car. Anyone else and I would have started a fight, arguing just for the hell of it that they were in the wrong. Taking the corner too fast, not looking out for pedestrians, anything other than admitting I was totally to blame. But with him I couldn't.

"Don't you know better than to walk in the middle of the road at dusk with no torch or high viz on?" He had got out of his car, now parked neatly out of harm's way and towered over me, anger clear in his eyes. I couldn't help it. There was something about the uniform that just brought the worst out in me.

"Yes officer. Sorry officer. I won't do it again, officer. I promise I will buy a high viz tabard first thing tomorrow officer." I dimpled my cheeks at him and smiled meekly. I could almost hear him grinding his teeth.

"You wouldn't be so bloody flippant, madam, if you had scraped up the number of bodies from the tarmac that I have!"

Ice, so cold it burnt, blazed from his eyes. It scorched right into me and made me shiver. How had I ever thought that he was a man of no emotions? He just had a will of iron keeping them under control. I wondered, what would make him lose that control? For an idle second I found the thought intriguing, and then I rammed down tight the lid on my own rambling thoughts. Good God, girl! You've already got a teenager and a random gardener on the go. Don't start thinking about the local bobby as well.

Which of course, for that tiny, eeny, weeny, second, I did. Which made me giggle. So inappropriate.

"Sorry." I bit my lip as I withered under his scathing gaze. "I've had a bit of an odd day. I know it's not funny, and I know I have been daft. I'm not usually. Well, actually I am, very daft, I mean, but not on the road. I've just had a lot on my mind lately."

He snorted. "Like your son's best friend?"

Anger flared in my belly. "You don't know me so don't judge!"

"I know what I see, Eve. I see a very attractive woman, with a husband who clearly loves her, and a family who are close, playing the sort of game where someone ends up getting very hurt. As well as scraping body parts off roads, Eve, I've also picked up battered wives, and those poor souls who end up with getting knives in their hearts."

There was a harsh grit to his voice that stopped me from speaking out. That didn't happen often. I had got him pegged as a bit of a cop out (if you pardon the pun), a man who had got to his age and was happy to still be a plod on the beat. I remembered Mabel saying something to me in the shop. Funnily enough, she had almost echoed my own words. I didn't know him, so I shouldn't judge.

He had seen more of life than was clear on the surface. But then, of course, so had I.

"And your point is?" I regained my composure.

"Stop it whilst you still can. I don't want to be called to 3 Cooper's Fold because of a domestic incident turned nasty."

He turned away from me then before I could reply and wordlessly got back into his car to drive off. I glared after him for a few seconds and then made my way over to the gate that would take me into the fields. I was cross with him. He had spoilt my mood. The warm glow of euphoric joy that had been tingling inside me ever since Jem had kissed me had disappeared in a flash.

And the worst of it was I knew he was right.

What on earth was I playing at? In a matter of weeks I had turned from a respectably married woman, faithful even in celibacy, to a risk taking nymphomaniac, juggling her son's best friend, and her best friend's gardener.

It was a roller coaster ride, crazily thrilling and fraught with danger. I had no idea though just what would happen when it all finally did come crashing off the rails. And even Sergeant Hawthorne would not have been able to predict the outcome.

CHAPTER FIFTEEN

I tried to be a little more circumspect.

I was already entangled with Tim and I have to say he was showing no sign of losing interest. So did I really want to become embroiled in a second secretive affair? I felt I had to show some effort not to run head long back into Jem's arms, if only to disabuse myself of the notion that I was getting seriously out of control. When a very disturbing section of my brain turned a few random cogs and contemplated the possibility of separating Sergeant Hawthorne from his upstanding morals, I decided I was in danger of becoming seriously mentally ill.

No. One lover at a time was enough for any woman, and besides, I had no bloody idea who the hell Jem was, apart from Sally had hired him to sort out the grounds. At least with Tim there was the familiarity of knowing him, plus the added advantage that I knew it was not going to lead anywhere. Maybe that was the crux of the matter.

Tim was sex.

Glorious, hot, wicked, fun sex.

Jem could be something else.

My heart was not ready to consider what that might be. It was still battered and bruised from the pounding Andy had given it. It was easy to toss my body over to someone, quite another thing entirely to risk even thinking of lending my heart out again.

I would not think about Jem anymore.

I would continue to shag Tim whenever and however I felt like it. I would endeavour to support Andy in this transitional phase of his life. I would be the same reliably scatty mother my children had always known and I would enjoy my new occupation as office staff/ mother-in-law's companion for Sally.

It was, I thought, a simple plan. And for a while, things trundled along nicely.

Sally had found a way of keeping Mary entertained that involved me in a most enjoyable way. Her mother-in-law had been watching television one particularly foul, wet afternoon, which had given Sally a great idea. The programme had been one of those antique/what have you got hidden in your attic, type of thing, encouraging the great British public to venture into their lofts to root for treasure.

Sally Farthing had more than a loft. She had an attic that spanned the length and breadth of the house, stuffed to the very brim, she told us, of generations of bric a brac.

"There's probably a fortune waiting to be discovered," she said, no doubt costing out how many new horses she might be able to buy.

Mary, now channel hopping and tutting with disgust at what was on offer, tutted louder. "And it's just sat there rotting? What a waste. If I had an attic like yours, I'd know exactly what I had in it and where everything was."

"I can't imagine having generations of family belongings," I said wistfully. "I don't even know what my parents looked like, or what they were called."

"How do you not know that, girl?" Mary switched off the television and focused on me.

My precarious start in life was not something I often talked about. I just accepted it. "I was left on the steps of a hospital as a baby. My parents were never traced. I was adopted but taken into care when I was five because social services had overlooked the fact that my 'mum and dad' were drug addicts."

For once Mary had no caustic reply waiting on the tip of her razor sharp tongue. Instead, Sally jumped in brightly, clapping her hands at us, as if we were two toddlers who needed amusing.

"I know, why don't you two sort the attic out for me? You can go through everything and then maybe we can get an antiques dealer in to appraise the lot and sell it?"

"A proper one," said Mary quickly. "Not one of these fly by night sorts."

"A proper one," Sally promised. "And I'll even split the proceeds between us all, how does that sound?"

Money for nothing, I thought with a spark of interest adding to the flame of curiosity already burning. I looked at Mary who was doing her best to look thoroughly disinterested all of a sudden. Of course she would not want to be seen to be enthusing over an idea of Sally's.

"I'd really enjoy it," I said eyeballing her. "And it's not as if I'll ever have the chance to look through my own ancestor's belongings, not having any as it were."

Mary snorted and said in an off-hand way. "Well I suppose I could help out. I do have an eye for this kind of thing you know. Some folk can't tell tat from treasure."

Me being one of them, but I wasn't going to spoil her illusions. I was raring to get started straight away and even Mary looked like she was itching to get going, hiding her impatience behind an exterior of grumpiness. But before anything more could be said on the matter, one of the stable girls, Lucy, knocked on the door of the sitting room.

"Sorry to but in," she poked her head around the door. "But Seth's on the yard with one of his horses. Says he's come for Eve?"

Sally and Mary looked at me. I shrugged my shoulders. "I dunno."

I promised Mary I would return next morning to start in the attic and followed Sally out of the Lodge.

Standing in the middle of the yard, looking quite dapper, wearing a clean pair of corduroy trousers, a long woollen overcoat belted around his narrow waist with a length of rope, and a jaunty red and white checked scarf knotted around his neck, was Seth. His thick white hair had been newly brushed and he had obviously made an effort to clean up his well-worn boots.

Attached to him, via a tatty lead rope and head collar, was the dark bay horse I had grown used to seeing in the field with his other one. No longer looking quite so mangy and standing much better, he tossed his head upon seeing us and gave a cheeky sounding whinny. As if to say, hurry up, I've been waiting.

"Hello, Seth," I greeted both with a smile, and a friendly pat for the horse. "What can we do for you?"

Jenny and a couple of the other girls had come to take a look. A new horse on the yard always created interest and this one was bonny with a kind look in his eye. He nodded in acknowledgement at them now.

"I've brought thee a gift in return f' use o'field." He held out the lead rope to me.

"A gift? Your horse? I can't take your horse." Already I was holding the rope and feeling the animal's warm breath upon my cheek.

"'E's not my 'orse, never were. Just mindin' 'im 'till 'e found 'is owner. Now 'e 'as."

I stood there opening and shutting my mouth like a stupid goldfish.

Sally was perfectly able to talk. "Oh he's adorable, what is he, about fifteen hands? Just perfect for you, Eve. How old is he Seth?" Already she had his mouth open to check his teeth.

"Reckon mebbe fifteen?"

"Mm, I would agree with that," Sally looked across at Jenny who followed her actions and on surveying the state of the horse's teeth, nodded her head to confirm the age.

"Good feet," said Jenny, picking them up one by one, "I like them boxy, less danger of concussion, and he's got a good frog on them. Mud fever?" She asked Seth with a sharp eye.

"Aye. Just 'eeled it up now. Rogue I traded 'im off left 'im standin' on poached ground. Sore as 'ell 'e were when I took i'm."

Now, with Seth's care, he was a different animal. But still, that didn't mean he was mine. I let them all rabbit on for a few more minutes, discussing the horse's conformation and possible breeding (maybe Dales with a bit of Fell and Exmoor thrown in for good measure) and then coughed loudly.

"Yes this is all very well, he's a lovely horse but I can't just take him."

Three pairs of eyes surveyed me. One turquoise, one Scandinavian blue, and the other blue-green with a dash of brown swirled in the mix.

"Why not?" Sally was the spokesperson. "You can keep him here."

"Yes, but horses cost so much." And there was chance that I would not be enjoying my comfortable financial status at the end of this year once Andy and I parted company. More than a chance, a certainty.

"Put him on working livery," said Jenny. "He'd be perfect for the school and then we cover half the cost. You can't lose."

"I don't know," I said feeling the pull of the horse's liquid brown eyes. He was nuzzling into my shoulder and nibbling softly at the toggle on my hooded top. "I've got a lot on my plate at the moment."

"Aye lass, but sometimes the love of an animal can mend what is broken." Seth stepped a little closer and turned his body so that he could look directly into my eyes and speak without the others hearing him. "Besides lass, mebbe takin' care o'im will stop thee gettin' into other bother."

I swallowed hard. Looking into his eyes was like looking into a mirror. He nodded wisely and I had the feeling that he was pleased with himself.

"Alright," I said at last. "I'll take him. Just on a trial you understand, see how we get on."

And that was that. I ended up with a horse.

The combination of getting used to Sam (as the horse was called) and starting to clear the attic for Sally, not to mention seeing Tim whenever I could, meant that the days went quickly over the next couple of weeks with little time for day dreaming about Jem. I also found that each day, seeing Andy come home from work, or from seeing Jason, the pain of his betrayal seemed less intense. Frankly, I didn't have the time to brood.

My mind was occupied with rummaging through a plethora of antiques in the Aladdin's cave that was Sally's attic, and my body was well and truly exercised with horse and lover. It could be fair to say that for this short period, I actually felt pretty content. As long as I continued to ignore the realities of what I was actually doing, I could go around with a much happier heart.

And then Valentine's Day came along. Ouch! It was ironic really. All the years when I had been spoilt rotten by Andy, huge cards, expensive gifts, lavish meals out, I had never really given much thought to the occasion. It was just one of those days when there was an excuse for a bit of a treat and over the last few years I would gladly have traded them for more time and attention from my husband, not to mention an evening of passionate sex.

But this year, when there would be none of it, I was suddenly aware of every bloody red heart and ribbon that festooned the shops in Maypoleton and Lancaster. It was as if they were taunting me with their gaudy parade.

It wasn't helping matters either, that Megan and Lexy had arranged for the four of them to go to a Valentine's Night and between them were plotting to arrange a blind date so that Tim could go too and make it six. They caught me one evening, about three days before and sat me down in the kitchen with them to discuss it.

"We've narrowed it down to three," said Lexy, flicking her wavy red hair out of her eyes. She had quickly become a fixture around our house and I was glad. Her easy going nature was just right for Jake.

"Three what?" I said, reluctant to admit that I hadn't been listening to their earlier chatter. I had been watching the sky change colour, from black to pinky yellow. It looked as though snow was on its way.

"Options for Tim."

The mention of his name got my attention quickly enough. "What about Tim?" I left my sky watching and sat down with them at the table. They had the lap top in front of them and the page was full of photos of girls their age.

"Mum!" Megan gave me an exasperated look. "We're trying to sort out a blind date for Tim for Valentine's night."

"Oh."

"He's said he's happy for us to do it as long as we don't fix him up with a total dog."

"Oh." I felt as though a stone had fallen to the bottom of my stomach. "Is he looking for a new girlfriend?"

"Not really," said Lexy, lessening the weight of the stone.

"That's not the point," said Megan. "Tim's never been without a girlfriend for as long as this since I've known him, which is years, so he must still be feeling cut up about Stacey. Valentine's Day is the perfect time for him to realise that there are plenty more fish in the sea."

"Oh."

"Is that all you're going to say?" My daughter regarded me curiously.

I snapped into a more alert frame of mind. It had thrown me to think about Tim and another girl. I knew that our fling would run its course sooner or later. But what woman with fire in her veins would willingly want to search for a younger, prettier, firmer, replacement?

"Sorry. Migraine coming on," I pleaded and left them to it.

Megan told me the following day that they had settled on Kelly. I tried not to listen to her description. Five foot nine, size ten, legs to die for, long black hair and blue eyes. I hated her already. I considered my five foot five frame with my mop of dark blonde hair and mixed up coloured eyes, complete with laughter lines. I thought about my breasts which looked at their best pushed up by my bra, or when I was stretched out flat on my back. I cringed at the thought of my stretch marks that I did my best to conceal from his young eyes.

I woke up on Valentine's Day with total recall of the previous year. Andy had brought me a cup of tea in bed. There had been a large and sentimental card, a box of chocolates, flowers waiting for me in the kitchen, and dinner that night at the Wishing Well, a classy restaurant not far from Chipping.

This morning I woke up with Tigger and a sick feeling of jealousy in my stomach that Tim would probably be snogging the gorgeous Kelly tonight and knowing him, screwing her as well. My husband had probably received a sly text from Jason, the contents of which I shuddered to think about.

And then there was a timid knock on my bedroom door.

Clutching Tigger to my chest, I called out. "Come in."

Andy was capable, it appeared, of breaking my heart on many levels. He walked into the bedroom carrying a tray with a mug of tea and a plate of pain au chocolat. I could see there was a card slotted up against the mug and a tiny gift nestling beside it. I didn't know whether to laugh or cry.

"I know this probably looks really stupid," he said, carefully putting the tray down on the bed side table and sitting on the end of the bed. "But I can't stop loving you, Eve. And you have always been my Valentine. I couldn't just ignore today."

A lump formed in my throat. I couldn't stop loving him either. It wasn't the same kind of love, but it was love nevertheless. A very painful kind of love.

"I haven't got you anything," I muttered, trying not to cry as I reached for the card. If it was full of soppy, romantic prose I was going to either throw up, or bawl my eyes out. It was neither. It was a beautifully hand painted card of a fairy sitting in a woodland setting, with a rainbow stretching out before her.

There was no verse inside, just Andy's own handwriting.

'To Eve. With love for you always and the wish that life brings you happiness and new dreams.'

"It's beautiful, thank you."

He seemed relieved that I liked it and handed me the present eagerly. "Here, I think you'll like this as well."

The gift box was small and exquisitely wrapped. There was a printed label on the top, discreetly hidden by swirls of golden ribbon. I didn't take any notice at first, just peeled it off so that I could unwrap it carefully. A tiny fairy figure, sitting on a curled up leaf, stared up at me. She was beautiful and so much more charming than many of the Valentines gifts I had received previously. I was touched. He had obviously gone to some trouble to think of a way to mark the day without being too crass or hypocritical.

"Thank you. She's beautiful."

"She reminds me of you," he said with that boyish smile that had won my heart and now made it ache.

"Thank you," I said again. I looked once more at the card noticing how the fairy on the front of it matched the gift exactly. What a clever idea. I tried to think of the shops in Lancaster and couldn't imagine where he had found such an individual present. "Where did you get it?"

"What? Oh, from a craft fair. "

"A craft fair?" Since when had Andy been interested in going round craft fairs? There were always plenty of them doing the rounds of the villages in the area and sometimes I would pop in for a browse, but whenever I had suggested to Andy that he came with me, he had pulled a face. Not his sort of thing.

"I was at one the other week end." He bumbled with a bit of a blush.

"With Jason? He likes to go to craft fairs?"

"His sister actually. She has a stall. She paints the cards to go with the gifts," he said quietly.

"She's a talented artist," I managed to say, my pleasure in the gift vanishing instantly.

"I'll leave you to have your breakfast," he said, shuffling off the bed in a rather cowed manner that made me want to reach out and hold him and hit him at the same time.

I ate my breakfast slowly, tears trickling down my face, the salty tang an odd combination with the chocolate bread.

CHAPTER SIXTEEN

Aside from trying to function with a mangled heart, I was having a good time at the Lodge these days. Now that I was an owner, as well as a part time member of staff I felt even more at home at the stables. Despite the image of snobbery that can accompany horsey crowds, this lot were a friendly bunch. But it wasn't just the camaraderie that helped to restore the balance in my topsy turvy life, it was the horse himself.

I loved animals of all varieties (apart from I must confess the reptilian kind) and having a horse now gave me something else to take my mind off my messed up life. I was keen to learn even though with Sam on working livery the girls could do most of the jobs.

"Thee'll never know it all," said Seth one morning, a week after depositing Sam with me. He had come to ask Jenny when the farrier would next be doing the rounds. Bracken needed his hooves trimming. I had spotted him, hovering around, looking as though he didn't want to intrude, and I called him over to tell him how I was doing with Sam. "I've bin 'round 'orses all me life, an' I'm still learnin'. But as long as thee's kind, and thee listen's t'orse, thee won't go far wrong."

I was brushing Sam, something I found incredibly soothing to do. Skip was curled up in the stable, munching on a carrot that Sam had dropped. It was a bitterly cold day, the threat of snow in the air, but huddled up with animals and Seth, the stable was a cosy place to be.

Seth asked me how I was finding him to ride. "Has thee taken 'im down road yet?"

"No actually I haven't." It was something Jenny had asked me to do before using him as a hack in her classes. "I suppose he's used to traffic?"

Seth snorted, his wrinkled face creasing deeper as he smiled. "Course 'e is lass. D'ye think I'd give 'im t'thee if 'e weren't? Tack 'im up now an I'll walk thee down t'lane."

"It looks like it might snow?"

"Not today. Tomorrow." Somehow I had more faith in Seth's weather prediction than I did the BBC. So I followed his suggestion and tacked up Sam. We walked out of the Lodge together. It was about ten minutes at a good pace to get to the field and by that time I was more than happy riding Sam on the road. We had been passed by a milk tanker and a motor bike (not Tim's) which didn't bother to slow down as it zoomed past us, and on both occasions Sam never flinched.

"I told thee e'd look after thee. Heart o'gold that one." Seth stopped at the gate to the field. He patted Sam and then smiled at me. He was doing that more often these days and something deep inside me responded whenever I saw the twinkling light in his eyes.

"Just like you," I said with a teasing smile of my own, and laughed when he shooed away the comment.

"Away wi' thee lass, tha's bein' soft."

I left him tending his fire and continued my ride down the lane. I had already spent the morning with Mary in the attic as well as finding time to send out some invoices for Sally, so I was due a little me time. Besides, if what Seth said was true, we would have snow tomorrow and then there would be little chance of riding apart from in the school. I would take Sam into the village, round the duck pond and back to the Lodge.

It was a perfect way to pass half an hour and once I had settled into Sam's pace, confident now that he could cope with the occasional traffic, I found my mind wandering to the tangled state of my heart. I knew that Kelly, the girl Megan had set Tim up with, was 'totally into him' and I realised that sooner rather than later, my crazy affair with the youngster would come to an end. My ego perhaps would be bruised, but not my heart. That, I suspected, was in danger from another quarter.

Thus prompted, I decided to take the long route round and go through the entrance at the back of the estate. Sally had told me that she was keeping Jem in employment until the grounds had been thoroughly tamed. She had come up with the notion of building a cross country course round the estate with the money she could make from our findings in the attic. But as she said, no point in thinking about that until she could actually see what land she had!

He was there.

Wheeling a barrow of horse manure, well-rotted down and perfect for compost. The day became filled with brilliance and light. The anxieties and pain that knotted in my soul melted away under the warmth of his smile. How on earth had I kidded myself that I wouldn't think about him anymore? I might as well try and give up breathing.

He lowered the barrow to the ground and walked over to me, one hand sliding up my thigh, the other reaching to stroke Sam's neck. He had the same effect on my horse I thought as I watched Sam's head droop and heard his soft whinny of appreciation. I bent my head down to kiss him.

No need for words between us. It was the most natural thing in the world to press my lips to his and savour his taste as one hand now crept softly behind my neck to pull me close. Shivers of anticipation ran through me, heating up my blood until it turned my muscles to burning lava and my bones to liquid fire. I was ready to drop off Sam's back and into his arms, urgently needing to feel his skin scorching once more against mine.

It wasn't the same basic lust I felt with Tim. There was desire and passion but overriding all of that, a deep need to lose myself in his embrace until there was no division between his soul and mine. Nothing compared to that need. His hands were on my waist, pulling me gently out of the saddle. Sam stood quiet as lamb as if he too had fallen under Jem's spell.

Shattering that magic, my phone went off in my pocket. I groaned, so tempted to ignore it. I glimpsed a darkening of Jem's eyes as my hesitation wavered. I shut my ears to the phone and leant back towards him.

It rang again.

Twenty years of being a mother is hard to ignore. What if it were Megan or Jake?

"I'm sorry," I said to him, the first words I had spoken so far. "Just let me see who it is." It was Megan. I answered it this second time, aware suddenly that the air had gone chilly and when I looked

139

at Jem there was a brooding expression on his face. My daughter's voice rang shrilly in my ears for a long moment before I could make out what she was saying. I had to get her to slow down and repeat herself, by which time Jem was walking slowly away from me.

I could hardly call after him and I inwardly cursed Megan at the same time that I fought down the panic her words had stirred up.

"Are you hurt?" That was the main thing. Damage to her car could be sorted. My daughter in a wheel chair was not something I cared to think about.

"I'm fine," she said, her voice wobbling, so very unlike her. "But can you come and pick me up?"

Of course I would. Once a mother, always a mother. Afternoon trysts are instantly forgotten when your twenty year old drives her car into a cow shed and ends up in a hedge on the opposite side of the road. She had swerved to avoid a chicken. It wasn't very often that Megan needed me but now was one of those rare moments.

By the time I had re-stabled Sam and driven to the farm which lay about ten minutes away, her car was already being towed out of the hedge by a young man in a tractor. I winced when I saw the damage to both the cow shed on the other side of the road, and the hedge, and pictured the way in which the car must have literally bounced from one to the other. If another vehicle had been coming in the opposite direction, then Megan might not have been so lucky.

"Sorry Mum," she hugged me, a little girl once more.

I held her tight. It had been a long time since she had cuddled up to me like this.

"Were you busy? You didn't answer at first?"

"No love. I wasn't doing anything much." Now that I could see she was perfectly alright, the frustration of what I was missing out on jabbed at me. I had to placate a rather cross looking farmer, console my daughter, and no doubt pay a hefty bill to repair the shed, and instead of this, I could be abandoning myself to the magic of Jem's love-making.

"I couldn't hit the chicken," said Megan with a teary gulp.

I looked at the bird that had cost me an afternoon of passion and a few hundred pounds. Stuff the chicken. Kill it next time!

"No of course you couldn't," I said soothingly. "You go and sit in my car and I'll sort things out here."

I took my frustration out on the farmer who had got it into his head to screw me for a completely new barn. No way. I would pay the damage, but no more than that. I berated him fiercely for letting his livestock roam free upon the highway and muttered darkly about the RSPCA, TB inspectors, and any other animal organisation I could think of, until we came to a mutual agreement.

Then I took some photos of the shed, and of a patch of mud on the road which looked as though it could have contributed to Megan's skid. When I spotted this, I subjected him to one of my hard stares and tapped my foot, mentioning Craig Hawthorne's name as if he was a dear friend of mine. The farmer agreed to half the costs of the repairs. I took one more photo for good measure and shook his hand.

By the time we got back home, it was around three in the afternoon and already going dark, the sky ominous and heavy. Megan was shivering with shock and I pushed all thoughts (well most of them anyway) of Jem to the back of my mind as I molly coddled her in a way she hadn't let me for years. When Andy came home the divide between us was instantly forgotten in shared concern for our daughter and what might have happened.

"It hasn't all been wasted, has it?" He asked me softly as we stood on our driveway, surveying the battered heap that was Megan's car.

I sighed and leant against him, thoughts of Tim and Jem momentarily forgotten. "No. It hasn't been wasted." If I had not married Andy, then I would not have Megan and Jake. As I went to bed that night, saying a thank you to whoever might care to listen, that Megan was unharmed, I knew that I would sleep easy for the first time since New Year's Eve.

I did, and more than that, I slept in late to find the world a white and bedazzling place. Seth had been right. The snow had come and it had announced itself with a fury. Andy had apparently managed to get into his office at Lancaster before the worst of it had come down but Megan, Jake and Mark were out in the back garden, cavorting around as if they were five years old.

"What are you doing?" Stupid question really as they were in the middle of a snow ball fight. Actually Jake was taking pot shots at my gnomes which made me glare at him warningly.

"No college or university," he called back from the bottom of the garden. "Heating's off."

I tutted at how soft the world was becoming these days and then had a horrible thought. Oh my God, Seth! He must have been frozen in that caravan overnight, not to mention Bracken. The snow was easily six inches on the ground and still coming down fast. I made a quick call to Sally and then dressed in my warmest clothes.

"Don't argue with me," I announced to Seth as I arrived at the field to find him layering old blankets over Bracken. "I'm claiming my rights as your landlord and finding you temporary accommodation."

His lips were blue with cold and I could see that Bracken's winter coat was standing on end. I kicked myself sharply up the backside for not thinking of this sooner. Whilst I was tucked up in my nice warm bed, poor Seth had been freezing out here. It was lucky he wasn't dead!

"I'm fine, lass," he wheezed, a hacking cough erupting from his chest.

"No, you're not, and neither is Bracken. He's an old horse. He shouldn't be out in this, not when there's a perfectly good stable waiting for him down the road."

"I'll nay take charity, lass, not even from thee."

"It's not charity," I said quickly. "You can work for his keep. Sally said so." Sally had said nothing of the sort. There was no way she was going to take any payment for sheltering the old horse in weather of this kind but I was sure she could appease Seth's honour somehow.

I think it was a measure of his love for the horse that made Seth turn his back on a lifetime of independence and follow me down the lane. It wasn't easy going and we had to stop every now and then to pick out the snow that was balling up in the horse's hooves. As we walked I told him about Megan's crash.

"Thee must 'ave no fear for that 'un," he said as the Lodge drew close. "Young lass is a survivor. She'll allus be alright."

It was difficult to see his face because of the woollen scarf he had wrapped around him but his eyes were bright and the light in them reassuring when he spoke of my daughter.

"You can see things like that, can't you, Seth?"

142

"Aye, lass. I can."

I had the urge to ask him about Jake for some strange reason but then I realised he had not met my son yet. It had only been Megan who had taken it upon herself to go and say hello. But Seth apparently did not need to have met a person to feel something about them. His next words were as gloomy as the weather.

"Tis thee and thy lad wot needs to take care."

I stumbled in a thick drift of snow, my hand on the frozen gate of the Lodge entrance. "What do you mean Seth? Me and Jake, what's the matter?"

He sniffed the air, as if a hunting dog. "Dark things," he said with a nod. "Thee needs to take care where thee treads, an' I don't just mean t'snow."

Annoyingly, he was unable to satisfy my curiosity any further and would only shake his head when I asked him exactly what he meant. All he could say was that storm clouds were gathering in my life. I could avoid them but only if I acted wisely. Not much chance of that then.

When we got to the Lodge Sally had got a spare stable ready for Bracken. I could see that for all Seth's protestations, he was relieved to have found shelter for his beloved companion. I stood back whilst Sally agreed to let him work on the yard in return for this so that honour was satisfied. Seth then refused the offer of a cup of tea and went straight to help Jenny clear a track for the horses to get across the yard.

I was not so quick to refuse a hot drink. Besides, I wanted to ask Sally something before helping Mary in the attic. We sat at the table in the kitchen, warming our hands around our mugs and I listened to Sally tell me about Richard's travel's so far. Then I managed to get the conversation onto Jem.

"Any chance I could have the number of your gardener?"

"I thought you already had someone who came to do your garden?"

I did. A retired gentleman with the greenest fingers ever, came every couple of weeks or so to give me a hand keeping on top of things.

"He's going into hospital for a while," I lied, crossing my fingers and hoping that I hadn't just jinxed Ted.

"Oh, poor love, is it serious?"

"No. But he won't be able to work for a while and now that spring is on its way," I paused and looked out of the window, "well supposed to be, I wanted to get ahead with some replanting."

"No problem. Here it is." Sally, bless her still used an old fashioned address book. She flicked the page to 'G' and turned it towards me so I could see the number she had written next to 'Gardener'.

"Thanks. Right, I'd best crack on with Mary."

"Yes, you'd best," said Mary herself, pushing open the kitchen door. "It's after eleven, where have you been, Eve, I've been waiting?"

I told her about Seth and Bracken which soothed her somewhat and then snatching up another biscuit from the tin, I linked my arm through hers and turned her around.

"Come on, Mary, off we go."

"Don't use that tone of voice with me. I'm not one of your children!"

We squabbled and argued most of the time we were together but it was done with a growing sense of fondness. Over the last few weeks we had come to know each other well as we worked from one end of Sally's huge attic, to the other. I was fascinated by Mary's stories of living through the blitz and in turn, she listened to some of my escapades as a child in care.

We were working slowly and steadily, trying to organise the paraphernalia in the attic into three main piles. Furnishings and ornaments, clothing and accessories, and books and letters. Then would come the mammoth task of deciding what was 'tat' and what was treasure. I was going to take the tat to the tip and various charity shops, and what was left, we would have appraised by a dealer. The part I was really looking forward to was rooting through the books, diaries and letters that we had now got sorted into neat piles. But we had decided to save this treat until last.

The task for today was to bring down a section of small furnishings that were destined for the rubbish heap. Some stuff was just too moth eaten even for charity. Of course Mary did the bossing and I did the leg work, up and down the narrow flight of stairs countless times. By the time I had finished, I had aching legs and arms, filthy clothes, and a nose full of dust. But it was satisfying and I said good bye to Mary with a sense of achievement.

Seth had already left the yard, having finally been booted off by Jenny.

"Honestly, I had to tell him to go," she said when I asked where he was. "He would have worked all day, I couldn't have that. He must be seventy if he's a day. I told him he could come back tomorrow morning and work until lunchtime. I can't have him doing any more than that there'll be nothing left for the girls to do. He's does their work in half the time."

I smiled at her, pleased that the instructor approved so thoroughly of Seth. Now I had one more task myself for the day. The snow had finally stopped falling but a wind had picked up, making it bitterly cold. There was no way Seth was going to sleep in that caravan tonight. Of course there was an argument. I expected one. But I can be hellish stubborn at times and I was not going to take no for an answer. Twenty minutes after turning up at the field, I had persuaded Seth to pack up a small bag and come with me.

"It's only until it thaws," I said, walking him past a horrified Marcus, husband to Deidre who lived opposite us. He was clearing his path from the snow and his face when I turned into our driveway with Seth was a picture.

"Aye, just 'til it thaws," agreed Seth, and clutching his meagre belongings, stepped into my home.

The snow lasted for a week. Brilliantly clear nights meant freezing temperatures which bound the snow on the ground and kept Seth with us for that time. He had refused to sleep on the sofa bed in the kid's lounge, preferring he said, to kip on the floor in the utility room amongst the wellies and washing piles.

"'Tis nearer 't'outside," he argued with a fierce glint in his eye which told me that although he had surrendered sufficient to sleep in a house, he was going to win this argument.

I conceded the point gracefully and informed the rest of my family that we would have a temporary lodger in the utility room for the time being and please could they make sure that they did not deposit their dirty laundry on top of him. I insisted though, that he was going to share our meals with us and use the rest of the house as much as he liked.

Megan promptly began to interrogate him about the Romany way of life and Jake just quietly handed Seth a sleeping bag that he said he had no more use of. I saw Seth's eyes light up as his gnarled fingers handled the top of the range all weather sleeping bag.

"I'll just use it whilst I'm 'ere, till t'snow thaws," he said to Jake with a nod.

"No. Keep it," said Jake and added casually. "I've got another one anyway."

I watched, with amusement, how my son and the old man entertained each other over the next few days. The university had sorted their heating out which meant that Megan and Mark were back attending lectures but further problems had developed with the plumbing at Jake's college so his lessons were still cancelled. Seth would accompany me to the Lodge in the mornings to work for Bracken's keep, whilst I helped Mary and Sally, and then in the afternoons he was drawn into the snug comfort of Jake's lounge.

It was the music that pulled him in.

After lunch on the first day, Jake had begun to play on one of his guitars. I loved to listen to him when he played solo. It was different to how he would play with Tim and Mark. He had the ability to move me to tears sometimes with his music and I would wonder where he got that talent from. I could sing, carry a tune in my head, but I had no skill with instruments of any sort. As the haunting tones drifted through the house, Seth pricked up his ears like Skip hearing the word walk.

"'Tis Jake, playin'?" He was finishing a cup of filter coffee I had brewed for him, savouring every drop with an appreciation most people reserved for the finest of wines.

"What? Oh yes. He's good isn't he?" I answered absently. I had tried to ring Jem three times since Megan's crash had interrupted us. The first two attempts had gone to an answer phone and I had received no reply. The third time it had been picked up by a strange voice, most definitely not Jem, who had told me I must have the wrong number. When I phoned Sally to check, she assured me she had given the correct details. I tried once more and after another failed attempt to reach Jem, I decided to leave it until I actually saw him again.

"Would 'e mind if I went to listen?"

"What? Oh, no of course not. Go right on in. He probably won't even notice you. He's like that at times."

Seth finished his coffee with a slurp of satisfaction and rinsed his cup carefully at the sink. He viewed the dishwasher as a though it were a machine of the devil and refused to use it. Then he went to join Jake, but not before disappearing into the utility room for a moment and rooting something out of his bag.

A short while later, I heard the beautiful notes of a whistle accompanying Jake's guitar playing. I forgot all about trying to phone Jem and went to listen. They played together in perfect harmony, Seth picking up the tune from Jake with no need for words or paper. There was a warm smile on my son's face and a sparkle in his eyes that matched that in the old man's.

It was a lovely moment to witness and later on I saw it as the beginnings of the calm before the storm. Five days later another crack appeared in the surface of my family life. Only small at first it seemed, but it was to go much deeper, although none of us realised it just then.

I was mucking out Sam and cursing the snow which made this task ten times harder, when my phone went off. Despite wearing thermal gloves, my fingers were like ice and clumsy as I pressed the keypad to answer it. I frowned as I recognised the number.

"Hello?"

"Mrs. Armstrong?"

"Yes."

"It's Mark Hughes here, Jake's tutor. I am ringing to check that your son is okay? He has not been in college since we had to close because of the heating and he is not replying to my emails, or phone calls."

"Oh."

"He is alright?"

"Yes, well, I mean he has been a bit off colour," I said hastily, covering for my son with a mother's instinct. "Touch of flu you know, and I'm sorry, I should have called you myself."

"Well yes you should really. You are aware of the college's policies on attendance? We are not one of the best colleges in the country for no good reason Mrs. Armstrong. We set very high standards here and it has to be said that your son is not meeting those standards at the moment. I was disappointed to say the least that I had no response to my letters requesting a meeting regarding Jake's recent performances in his modular exams."

My hackles rose. All at once I was back at school being told I wasn't good enough. Any anger I might feel towards Jake for covering up something like this, disappeared in the face of the tutor's patronising tone. I replied something to the effect that we had been in the middle of a family crisis recently, elderly relatives dying like flies, that kind of thing and promised him I would be in touch soon. Then I dialled Jake's number and swore when it went immediately to answer phone.

I was edgy for the rest of the morning and even Mary didn't attempt to provoke me. Instead, when I told her that I was worried what Jake was playing at, she suggested I started to rummage through the large mountain of books and letters we had put to one side.

"It's far too cold up in the attic for anything else," she said patting my arm. "Why don't we bring down the boxes of books into the library and sit in front of a nice warm fire? You're looking a little peaky, if you don't mind me saying so."

Consideration from Mary was rare, but as I listened to her chest wheezing a little, I agreed that perhaps spending the morning in a freezing cold, draughty attic was not such a good idea for her either. It took me three treks up and down the four flights of stairs to the attic to fetch the boxes, by which time I was red in the face and no longer in need of a fire to warm me up, but it did prove to be a pleasant way of spending the next couple of hours whilst distracting myself from my son's problems.

Sally came in to join us at one point, bearing a tray loaded down with hot chocolate and a plateful of goodies from Mabel's bakery.

"Here we go, ladies, I thought we deserved a little treat for all our hard work."

Mary looked at her archly. "Our hard work?"

148

"Yes, well, I've just been on the phone to the dealer and he told me that he is going to put the collection of paintings in his next auction and he's set a reserve price for guess how much?"

"I've no idea," I looked blankly at Mary.

"Fifty thousand," she said sharply.

"How did you guess that?" Sally asked in surprise.

"I told you I had an eye for this kind of thing."

"Fifty grand!" I spluttered. "For a handful of paintings? Bloody Nora."

"Yes. So that's my cross country course built, and there's still the furnishings, and clothes to sell, not to mention all these lovely books. In fact, never mind the hot chocolate, I think a large sherry's in order, don't you?"

Indeed we did. Knowing I had a headache waiting for me at home, I accepted the glass of sherry gratefully.

"Cheers," said Sally. "And here's to you Mary, I would never have thought of this without you, so well done. I'm very grateful." Obviously the thought of a much longed for cross country course had gone a long way to softening her views towards the old lady. "And I hadn't forgotten that I promised you and Eve a share either. Should be plenty for a nice cruise maybe?"

I think that was the first time I saw Mary actually smile at Sally. "A cruise would do nicely," she said. "And maybe Eve could come with me to keep me out of trouble?"

"Why not," I clinked my glass against hers.

Sally stayed with us for a while and then we continued to plough through the mountain of ancient literature. Mary was more interested with the housekeeping materials, like recipe books and invoices, all so carefully kept and ordered. For me, it was the personal letters and diaries that caught my eye.

"Where on earth are you going to start with that lot?" Mary's cheeks were now rosy pink from the warmth of the fire and the sherry. "It'll take you weeks to read through them."

I looked at the contents of the boxes. Mary's box was much smaller. Mine were overflowing. I grinned at her.

"I don't know. It's like a lucky dip isn't it. I shall put my hand in blind and see what I find." I closed my eyes and reached into the nearest box. Then I drew my hand back quickly. No. That was the wrong box. Eyes open now, I reached deep into the other one, pushing aside bundles of letters and hard backed note books until I found what I was looking for.

I went cold.

What was I looking for? How did I know that there was something in there waiting to be found?

"Are you alright? You've gone awfully pale."

I didn't answer her. My mind was focused on sifting through the contents of the box. My fingers rifled through papers and books until they tightened around a slim, leather bound volume. I drew it out of the box, a tingling sensation running through me. I had to have this book.

"What have you got there?" Mary leant in towards me. She was looking at me rather oddly.

"I'm not sure," I answered breathlessly. "I think it's a diary." I opened the front cover. "It is. 'The journal of Melody Farthing, beginning on the first day of the year of our Lord eighteen eleven'."

"You seemed in a blether to find it." Mary's clever brown eyes held a question that I could not answer.

"I know. I can't explain it, Mary. It was as though it needed me to find it, to read it."

Mary shuddered. "Ooh I don't like that sort of thing, spooky supernatural goings on. It was bad enough at that cottage. There were floorboards creaking, beams juddering, horrible bangs and an awful crying at times. I couldn't bear it."

"I thought you said it was the damp you didn't like?"

"Yes well. I thought it would sound daft if I said anything else, but believe me my girl, there is something not right about that cottage."

I smiled at her. There was definitely something magical about the cottage. I knew that. And it wanted me there, I also was certain of that fact. I thought of the girl I had seen in the mirror and looked at the book I held in my hand. I knew without a shadow of a doubt that it belonged to her. Melody Farthing was the girl I had seen in the cottage, and she wanted me to read her diary.

"Well this is just a book so there can't be anything wrong with this can there? And just think, Mary it's two hundred years old. How often do you get the chance to read what life was like for someone two centuries ago?"

"Mm. Rather you than me," she said, peering at the words on the first page. "That writing is tiny, beautiful, I must say, but it would give me a headache to try and read through all that."

I must admit, the script was so small and elaborately flowing, I did think I might need a magnifying glass to read it properly.

"I'll take it home with me." It felt important that I should read Melody's diary in private somehow. I put the diary in my bag and told Mary that I was going home. "I really need to see what Jake's been up to with college. He told me the heating was still off and it isn't like him to lie."

"Alright my dear, you go and sort your son out. I've got plenty to keep me occupied here. I'll see you tomorrow. Oh and if you could pop into the travel agents for me, that would be kind. I've a mind to look at cruises." She waved me off with a smile that would have been unimaginable a few short weeks ago.

As I walked back to Cooper's Fold with Seth, I told him about the diary I had found. I was sure that he would understand that something magical was going on at the cottage.

"I know she's the girl I have seen in the mirror, Seth, which makes her a ghost, of course, but a friendly one. You do believe in ghosts don't you?"

"Aye lass. Seen a few in m'time."

"I never thought I would," I said as I helped him through the gate which opened into the fields. The roads were now at that treacherously icy state which meant it was easier cutting across the back way, even though there was a good covering of snow thick on the ground. We passed by the copse of trees with the sacred oak where I had met Isabella. I thought of her now and the way she had touched me. I was sure she had passed some kind of magic onto me and I said so to Seth.

"'Appen she did lass, 'appen she did." He then linked his arm through mine and gave it a squeeze, a rare gesture of affection. I placed my hand over his, and we walked like that the rest of the way, reminiscent, I thought of Lucy and her Mr. Tumnus, tip toeing through Narnia.

Thoughts of snow covered fantasy lands were swept from my mind when I confronted Jake about his performance (or rather lack of it) at college. I ventured into his music den with a couple of hot chocolates for us as an indication that I was not actually cross with him. He was deep into his guitar playing and I had to nudge him with my toe to get him to look up. He saw the two mugs, looked at my face, and the penny must have dropped.

"Oh."

"Why didn't you tell me you were having problems at college?" I shifted some CDs that were lying over the sofa and sat down. "I've had Mark Hughes on the phone today. I told him you had flu."

"Thanks."

"Well I'm not going to continue to lie for you. What's going on?"

"I just don't want to do it anymore." He shrugged. "I hate it, the studying, attending lessons, doing homework, revising for exams," he declared passionately. "And whilst I'm doing that I can't do my music."

I smiled at him. He was so much my son. "Well no one's forcing you to do it, although your chances in life will be much better later on if you do have qualifications to fall back on."

"You haven't got any, well none that really count."

"Yes but I married your Dad. I haven't really needed any." I winced as I said this. How utterly feeble was that.

"Well Seth hasn't got any either, he never even went to school."

"True. But as much as I like Seth, in fact I would have to say I have grown fond of him, the Romany way of life is not exactly a career path."

"But I don't want a career. I just want to play music."

And all I had wanted to do was sing in a band which I had done until I had got married. I could totally understand where he was coming from. In my case though, I had received a very intermittent schooling, and showed no talent for anything else. Jake had not only inherited my passion for music but he was also a gifted mathematician. It had been Andy's suggestion that he should pursue this not only at A level, but also onto a degree.

"Maths can open all sorts of doors," he had said to Jake when at the age of sixteen he had wanted to give up education altogether. He had said it again and again, until Jake had finally agreed to continue at college.

"I thought you were happy," I said to him now. "I thought you liked college."

He grinned and flashed that dimple at me. "Oh I do. Just not the work. I've been having a great time. Loads of friends and all that. But the pressure's really on now, Mum, and it's doing my head in." The grin faded. "What if I'm not as bright as they keep saying I am? What if I fail? Dad's got his heart set on me going to university but I'm not sure I can hack it. I hate exams, being tested, really hate it!"

"Jake, listen to me. No one is going to force you to go to university if you really don't want to go. But, I have to be honest, it would seem daft not to finish your A levels when you have only a few months to go." I held up my hand when he started to protest. "No listen to me. I am not suggesting that you slog it out to get A stars but I do suggest that you try and make the most of the time you have left. Sit the exams and then we can think what happens next when we you've done that."

His body sagged as if he was releasing a bundle of tension. "You really don't mind if I don't go to university?"

"No. But try and at least finish what you've started, I always think that's a good idea. And if you want to devote a couple of years to your music and you've got A levels in the bag, then you can go at a later date if you change your mind. Who knows what the future holds, Jake, for any of us? Just take one day at a time and let the rest happen."

He hugged me then. "Thanks Mum, I can always rely on you. You never let me down."

If only.

CHAPTER SEVENTEEN

"Now it 'tisn't that I'm not grateful," said Seth, as he rolled up his sleeping bag and stuffed his small collection of belongings into his duffel bag, "but we did agree, 'twas only til thaw."

I yawned at him across the breakfast table. I had been up until past midnight last night, reading Melody Farthing's diary. It was fascinating, although very difficult to read and I was actually toying with buying a magnifying glass, although I had no idea where from. When I had finally put the diary down, I had fallen into a dream filled sleep.

Jem had been there and so was I, only I was dressed as Melody Farthing would have been. We made love with a desperate passion as though it was our last time together. And then we were disturbed. Someone had found us out! In the dream I was horrified to see Jake staring down at me on the bed, only now it was Tim who was entangled with my body. I had woken with a start, heart jumping and body still pulsing with desire.

My first thought was, thank God it was only a dream. My second thought was I hadn't had sex now in a couple of weeks. Odd when you think about it. I had been celibate for just over ten years and if not exactly content to live like a nun, I had adapted to the lack of passion. Now though, I had a burning need within me to feel that sense of abandonment that you can only get in the arms of a lover. It was as though having stepped into the light once more, I could not face the darkness again.

I idled with my breakfast, thoughts of Tim and Jem bouncing back and forth in my mind like a ping pong ball. Did I really care which one? Was I that much of a slut?

No and yes.

The trouble was I had seen nothing of either of them recently. Jem was unobtainable by phone and Tim hadn't been round since

154

Valentine's Day. The only glimpse I had had of him was that time on his motor bike with Kelly. If he was happy with his new girlfriend, then it really would be beyond the pale for me to get in the way of that.

I sat there drumming my fingers on the table, letting my muesli go soggy and earning a reproachful look from Seth. I had quickly learnt that he hated any kind of waste. So much so that I slid the bowl over to him, mushy as it was.

"I'm really not hungry this morning."

Seth was happy to finish the soggy mess, taking his time as he always did. I was going to miss his quiet presence in our house. I found him comforting somehow and Jake had adopted him as a sort of honorary grandparent, which no doubt would have horrified his actual grandparents. As for me, never having a real father figure in my life, it was easy to start to view Seth in that light. He was kind, gentle, caring, everything I would have wanted my own father to be. I sometimes wondered if he had any children of his own, but I didn't like to pry.

Later that day, when we had both finished our jobs at the Lodge, we walked back to his van. Now that the snow had melted and in contrast a warm sun was shining, he had no reason to stay with us anymore. Bracken had been happy to follow us back to the field, his head lowered to graze as soon as he set foot back on grass. I noticed a crop of snowdrops, bravely peeking up at me, and realised with relief that spring was around the corner. Did that mean that Seth would be off on his travels?

I didn't want him to go. I stayed with him as he settled back into his van and shared a pot of tea, all the while trying to ask him how long he was staying, but struggling to find the words in case he took them the wrong way and thought I wanted him to leave. In the end it was he who broached the subject.

"Thee will tell me, lass, if thee needs me to move on?" Swirly blue-green and brown eyes looked deep into mine. He had sensed of course what was on my mind.

"No. I mean, I don't want you to go, Seth. I really like you being here."

"That's good. My travelling' days are over." He nodded over towards Bracken. "'T'owd fellow 'asn't got long now. I'd like 'im to

155

'ave 'is last days in a place like this. Plenty o'grass an' no pulling t'cart. 'E's earned a rest."

I wobbled inside to think of the old horse dying on him. "You stay as long as you want, Seth. I said that before." I finished my tea and paused before asking. "What will you do when...?" But coward that I was, I couldn't say it.

"When 'e's gone?" Seth pursed his lips. "My folk'll take me wi' them. They'll be passin' this way soon enough. Easter time."

That was in the middle of April. I would have a good six weeks then of his company left. I reached over and patted his hand.

"Well you just sit tight and enjoy being here until then. I shall look forward to meeting your family, Seth, if they're all as nice as you."

His face creased into a deep smile. "Oh they are lass, right enough."

I left him then and meandered slowly back to Cooper's Fold. The house was empty, just me and Skip. I felt a gloomy cloud descend upon me. I hated being in this limbo land. I was living a lie and it rankled with me. I made myself another cup of tea and my eyes caught sight of the calendar on the wall. I had forgotten to turn it over. It was the second of March. Crikey, how had we got there so soon?

Flicking through the pages, I searched until I found the date of Jake's last exam. 22nd June. I had the best part of four months to get through before I could come clean to the world about the state of my marriage. Four months! I had only managed two so far and it felt like it was choking me. Biting down every time anyone asked how I was, chirping out that I was fine, when really I wanted to yell at them all that I wasn't.

It was alright for Andy. He was going around quite happy with his double life. I wondered morosely if that was because he was a Gemini. Split personality and all that. He certainly seemed capable of leading a hidden life, which I suppose in a way I was, but the difference between us was that he could cope with it, and I couldn't.

I sent a text to Tim. I know I shouldn't have. Loneliness is a cruel mistress. It makes liars and meddlers of us all.

'Hi. Just wondering if you could keep an eye on Jake for me at college? He's been a bit down recently.'

Innocent enough. But in the back of my mind I was secretly hoping that it might result in something a shade more devilish. I was full up with tea and poured the rest of my drink down the sink. It was turning into a lovely afternoon and I gave myself a mental kick up the backside to do something and stop brooding. A spot of gardening should do the trick. The cold weather had decimated the rockery at the front of the house and it was badly in need of replanting. First though it needed a good digging over.

Now I hate weeding, fiddling about in the soil trying to get all the bits of roots out. But attacking the ground with a hefty fork and brutalising the earth, I actually found was quite good therapy. It was one way to burn off some calories and frustration at the same time. I had been at it for about three quarters of an hour when I heard that lovely sound of a motor bike turning into Cooper's Fold. I dropped the fork, took my gloves off and raked my fingers through my hair.

I was grimy with soil, slightly sweaty, and flushed from the effort. All of which seemed to appeal to Tim as he took off his helmet and gave me the benefit of that dirty grin.

"You look good," his wicked dark eyes travelled from the top of my tousled hair to the tips of my boots and back up again, lingering in places that made me tingle. He was sitting astride his bike, jeans pulled tight against him. I returned the favour and let my eyes fall to where his groin was displayed across the seat and back to his face.

"So do you."

"I got your text. Is Jake okay? He hasn't said anything."

I liked him for that. We were eyeballing each other like two dogs about to mate, yet he could still think of his friend.

"Yeah. He's just a little off track at the moment. So how are you? How's Kelly?"

He smiled a little crookedly. "She's nice."

"Nice? You make that sound like a fault."

"No, I didn't mean it that way. She's nice, but she isn't you."

Oh yes! Victory to the older woman! I suppressed the mountain of smugness for fear of looking too happy.

"But we can't carry on forever, Tim, you know that," I said softly as I moved a little nearer the bike and he swung his legs over it. "Kelly is right for you, she's your age."

157

"I know, but that's the thing." He was looking at me with a hungry expression that sent liquid fire straight to my groin. "She is my age. And you are..."

I trailed a finger down his chest, unzipping his leather jacket as I did so, eyes on his, my lips parted and tongue moistening them.

"In need of a shower," I suggested on impulse.

He swallowed and checked his watch. "Jake said he was going for a catch up lesson, we should have time."

I hadn't even thought about that. I checked my watch. Megan and Mark would not be home for at least an hour.

"We've time," I said, grabbing him by the hand and leading him into the house. My hands were all over him as soon as we were in the porch and out of sight of any prying eyes. I locked my mouth onto his as I slid his jacket off his shoulders and let it drop to the floor. Only a couple of weeks, but I'd missed him. Missed the sex. A tiny part of my mind pushed in a picture of Jem but then Tim's hands went wandering and I concentrated on the here and now.

"I've missed you, Eve," he groaned, as he pulled up my sweater, tossed it onto the floor in the hallway, and reached behind to unclasp my bra. My legs collided with the bookcase that was home to the house phone and an ornamental lamp. I leant back against it, arching my back to thrust my breasts out for Tim.

He snaked kisses down from my neck to first one nipple and then the other, biting in a way that was painful and erotic at the same time. It was the youthful greed that made everything so intense with him. As his mouth devoured my breasts, I tugged at his own top, needing to feel the smooth skin, stretched taught over his muscles. When the urgent tugging and pulling became too much for me to bear, I drove my fingers into his thick curly hair and moved his head up so that I could kiss him once more.

We stayed tight like that for a long time, upper bodies bare, flesh against flesh, my breasts crushed and moulding to the hard planes of his chest, soft skin aroused further by the brush of the hairs that trailed downwards to the waistband of his jeans. Our hips were so close there was only the fabric between us, one of his thighs, pushing between mine, hard and insistent. Hands roamed over skin, nails scratching, feather light touches teasing, and then gripping hard into the denim that separated us.

It was an erotic torture, half naked, half clothed. It prolonged the agony and delayed the ecstasy as we writhed against the bookcase, knocking the lamp and the phone onto the floor, until I finally broke away from him.

"Upstairs, now," I panted, knowing that if I didn't make a move, we would be doing it right there on the floor, which I had no problem with, but the thought of getting Tim in the shower, smooth with oil, was too much to resist.

I lead the way with legs that were shaking, my jeans and briefs damp against my skin, through my bedroom and into the en-suite bathroom. We had a large step in shower cubicle, easily big enough for two, which had never been occupied as it was about to be. I slammed the jets on full power and peeled off my jeans and knickers, kicking them away from me in a tangled pile. Then I helped Tim free himself from his own jeans and taking hold of his hand once more, stepped into the cubicle, and slid the door to.

The only thing between us now was the steamy water that added to the sensations as we moulded together, as close as limpets. He was ready for me, pressing hard against my thighs, but I wanted more from what could be our last time together. I reached for a bottle of baby oil and with the water trailing down his body, smeared every inch of him with it, until he was slick and smooth as a seal.

He held on tight to the hand rails as his body quivered under my touch, my hands and mouth ruthlessly squeezing every last drop of desire from him, bring to a point where his need was going to hurt.

"My turn," he said hoarsely, and who was I to refuse? The tormentor became the tormented as now I had to brace myself from falling over as he went to work with the oil, and his hands and mouth. When he had finished we were sliding together in a desperate knot of urgency that had us nearly crashing to the floor.

I banged my hand against the shower switch, stopping the water, and half pulled him, half fell with him out of the cubicle and onto the bathroom floor. Wet and slick with oil, our bodies finally joined together as he parted my thighs and drove in deep.

It was going to be quick, and it was going to be hard, there could be no other way after the foreplay we had just indulged in. I lifted my hips up to meet him, wrapped my legs around his waist and held on tight for the ride. He took me with such a pace that I thought I was going to explode, building up an orgasm so wild and intense I was screaming before it even began.

Incoherent words were tumbling from his lips, coarse, filthy words which I knew he would never use with Kelly. But then I was a whore, was I not? A dirty, sexy, bitch. At that moment, yes. And who was I to say otherwise as I let him pummel and use my body with all the energy he had in him. I answered his words with moans of pleasure and taunts that I needed more until the end, when it came, was crazy and violent.

We made so much noise, that neither of us heard the front door shutting, or the anxious shouts from downstairs, or the footsteps racing up to the bedroom.

If time could freeze, then it did so then.

Over Tim's panting body, my eyes collided with those of my son's.

Jake.

He stood, motionless in horror, his face a ghastly grey in colour. "Mum! Jesus Christ Mum, are you alright? Get off her you bastard!" His hands dragged brutally at the back of Tim's head.

"Shit! Jake!" Tim cried out as he was pulled from me. I curled up into a ball and scrambled for a towel to cover my nakedness and my shame.

"Tim! Fucking hell it's you!" Jake staggered back, releasing his hold on his friend.

Tim reached for his jeans, ignoring his boxers and shot into them as fast as he could. I didn't blame him. I had never wanted to get my clothes on so quickly. Of course my top and bra were downstairs so I made do with wrapping the towel around my body sarong like, over my jeans.

"I can explain, mate," said Tim to a shell shocked Jake who was looking from his friend to me with utter horror on his face. More than horror. Disbelief and disgust.

"I thought you were being attacked, Mum," cried Jake hoarsely, tears welling up in his eyes, no longer quite an innocent shade of blue. "I saw the lamp knocked onto the floor and hear the noises from upstairs. I thought someone had broken in and when I heard...I thought you were being raped for God's sake! But I'd seen Tim's bike so I knew he was here, I didn't get it, he wouldn't do something like that, it had to be someone else. I was scared for you..."

"Oh Jake, I'm so sorry, I never meant for you to find out," I took a step towards him, and he equalled the distance, moving back. Tim so far had edged slyly around the bed and was approaching the door.

Jake was breathing hard, as though he had suddenly become asthmatic. "He wasn't raping you was he?"

Would it have been better if he had, I wondered in that twisted moment when everything turned on its axis? Should I say that? And save myself the love of my son? Or could I at least hold onto some sense of morality and be truthful now.

"Fucking hell Jake, what do you take me for?" burst out Tim, perhaps not wisely. "As if I'd rape anyone! She wanted it, it was her idea!"

I shot him a look. Yes I had suggested the shower, but he had made the first move back in January. We were both to blame. But as I saw the despair in my son's eyes as he witnessed the betrayal of his friend, I thought I could rise to one small step of honour.

"He's right, Jake, don't blame him," I could barely meet his gaze. "It was me, I seduced him."

"When?"

"Just after New Year."

"Jesus Christ you were snogging him in the driveway, was that when it started, right in front of us all?"

I couldn't lie. I nodded, unable to frame the words though.

Jake held his hand to his mouth as though he was about to throw up. He took a steadying breath as though mentally piecing it all together.

"So this has been going on since then?"

"We were going to stop," said Tim apologetically. "This was sort of our last time, I'm with Kelly now."

"What so you thought you'd have one last goodbye fuck with my Mum?" Jake lunged at him. Tim staggered back through the door and across the landing. He put a hand out to grab hold of the banister rail. Jake gave him another hard shove and he lost his balance teetering precariously at the top of the stairs.

"Jake, don't!" I cried out suddenly, frightened at what he was about to do.

"You dirty, fucking, bastard!" He spat at Tim through gritted teeth as his right arm came back for a punch. "You could have said no! You didn't have to screw my Mum and make her into a filthy fucking whore! I heard what you called her!" His fist came slamming forwards and connected with Tim's jaw.

It had enough impact to send him tumbling down the stairs.

I screamed. "No! Tim! Jesus, Jake, what have you done?"

"What have I done?" He yelled back at me, rage turning his face unrecognisable, "What have you done? He was right. You are a dirty, fucking, whore!"

As he screamed into my face, I heard the thuds as Tim toppled down the stairs. He cried out in pain and there was a sickening snap of bone as he landed in the hallway knocking his head for good measure on the book case.

"Tim, are you alright?" I cried out to him, leaning over the banister, terrified that he might have broken his neck.

"Is he alright?" Jake snarled, "He fucking won't be when I've finished with him." He caught hold of the post at the end of the banister and swinging round on it, launched down the stairs. Tim was getting to his feet, holding his left wrist to his side, the shock of pain and discovery draining the colour from his face. His dark eyes were stark against his the whiteness of his skin and there was none of the cocky humour about him now.

"Jake, please," he said, staggering slightly against the bookcase, "you're my mate!"

"Yeah, and mates don't fuck each other's Mums, no matter how much of a slut they are!" He jumped down the bottom two steps and launched at Tim once more. He managed to side step him enough to dodge the blow but it was obvious that Tim was shaky from a broken wrist and a banged head.

I flung myself down the stairs after them, before my son could hurt his friend further. I had never seen Jake display such a fury, but then nothing had ever given him need. A memory came back to me in a flash. Me and my foster brother. I was thirteen, he was fifteen. He thought he was going to have some fun at my expense. Adult fun. My rage then in defending myself had ended up with him in hospital and me with record of violence. I saw the same terrifying temper suddenly unleashed in my son and was desperate to stop it.

"Jake, please don't," I begged him as he brought his arm back for another punch."You'll regret it."

His arm went wild and the side of my face took the brunt of the blow, knocking me back against the stair rail.

"No, he'll fucking regret it!"

Tim by now had recovered enough to get to the porch. "I'm sorry, Jake, I really am!" He cried out to his friend, as he rushed to get out of the house.

How, I wondered, was he going to ride his bike with a broken wrist, and possible concussion? He wasn't safe!

"Tim, wait, you can't ride like that!" God, I couldn't have an accident on my conscience as well. "Jake, leave him!" I screamed at my son who was hell bent on going after him. I caught up with them in the drive way where they began to grapple with each other, Tim defensively, Jake out for blood. There was plenty of it, as Tim's nose went with a crunch and Jake's fists continued to pound. I took another blow myself as I squeezed in between them and I felt my bottom lip burst from the impact.

I was screaming at him to stop and all the time he was yelling back at me, abusing me with words that were sharper than any knife or dagger. And in the middle of it, Tim, who was trying to placate his friend and defend himself at the same time. I could see no way of calming Jake down, but in the end I didn't have to.

Maybe for once, I should have been grateful to my nosy neighbours. God knows where it all would have ended if Deidre had not called the police.

I watched in shame and relief as Craig Hawthorne, dark and official grabbed my son by the back of his sweatshirt and hauled him bodily off Tim. For an instant Jake tensed his body, and then when he saw who it was, went limp like a broken toy.

Tim was curled up on the floor, nursing his broken bones, a dazed look in his eyes. I was clutching my towel to my breasts, blood oozing from my lip and my cheek where Jake had caught me, swelling nicely. And Jake was now crying like a child, squatting on the floor, his head in his hands. What a picture of domestic bliss.

Viewing it all from across the road were Deirdre and her friends.

Taking in all the sordid details in one arctic glance, was Craig Hawthorne.

163

"I think we had better take this inside, don't you?"

I helped Tim to his feet and watched with a dreadful sickness in my stomach, as Craig put a hand on Jake's shoulder to lift him back up.

"Come on, son. Time for a chat." His voice was in that moment, kinder than I had ever heard it.

I followed them in, bracing myself for the apocalyptic fall out that was heading my way.

CHAPTER EIGHTEEN

On the way through the hall Tim bent down to scoop up his sweatshirt. He struggled to put it on with a wrist that was clearly broken and possibly a couple of ribs as well. My shame deepened as Craig picked up my discarded bra and sweater.

"You might want to finish dressing yourself."

God was it possible for him to put anymore ice in his voice? Silently, I took them from him and disappeared into the downstairs bathroom where I surveyed my reflection in horror.

Wild, damp hair tangled around a face that was scarlet with the aftermath of passion, lips bruised by Tim's kisses and from my son's fist. My left cheek bore the marks of another bruise, and my eyes were like saucers, shock and fear blazing from the depths. I pulled my clothes back on and splashed cold water over my face. I had to steady myself for a moment, hands braced on the sink as an urge to vomit rose from my belly. I fought it down and walked with shaking legs through to the kitchen.

Craig, so easily in control, had sat Tim and Jake either side of the large pine table. He had quickly found where everything was and had put a cup of coffee in front of them both, loaded no doubt with plenty of sugar. Both boys, and at that moment they looked like boys, were in a state of shock. I could imagine that Tim was suffering from the crash back down to earth that our discovery had brought. But as for Jake, God only knew what was passing through his mind.

I flinched from the look he gave me as I walked back into the room.

"Jake," I began unsteadily, but Craig stopped me.

"I was called to this address by Mrs. Brown from number two, as she reported sounds of a domestic disturbance."

Oh could I possibly sink under the floor and hide from the scathing tone of that voice? It flayed the skin off my back and then

165

ground rock salt deep within. All my defences had deserted me and I could only sit down, before my legs betrayed me completely. No flippant words to my rescue now.

He continued. "And clearly there has been such, which has resulted in bodily harm to this young man here." He looked at Tim and I saw that although there was a hint of reproof in his face, the full impact of the blame was going to land at my door. "By the looks of you, a broken wrist, nose, and a few ribs maybe. You've taken quite a battering."

Those frightening eyes moved to my son who sat there with a blank look on his face, shoulders huddled up, chest hidden away. A boy wanting to hide from a ghastly horror.

"I deserved it," said Tim across the void of the table. "I would have done the same." His voice was younger than it had been such a very short time ago. It was hard to reconcile this image of him with the man who had fucked me so hard and so well.

What the hell had I done? Nausea rose again and I swallowed hard against it.

"It still counts as assault." Craig's voice gentled to Jake. "You do realise that, don't you? If Tim wants to press charges, then I am going to have to arrest you." From his manner, I got the feeling that if he had been Jake, there would have been a battering of equal proportions. But the law was the law.

Jake shrugged. "Like it matters." It was the first time he had spoken since coming into the house and I cringed at the dull, flat tone of his voice.

I had shattered him.

"Jake it does matter," I croaked, aching to take his hand, but knowing he would hit it away. I looked at Tim and pleaded with him. "Don't do that to him as well, Tim."

Tim looked surprised. "As if I would? Jake, I'm so sorry mate, we shouldn't have done it. It was wrong, I know."

Jake stabbed an angry finger at me. "She shouldn't have done it! You're twice his age, you're my Mum, for fuck's sake! It's disgusting." And then another thought must have catapulted into his brain, one we hadn't even considered yet. "Oh my God, what's Dad going to say when he finds out? How could you do that to him?

166

You'll break his heart, you fucking whore!" He banged the table so hard that both coffees spilt.

"Okay, Jake, calm down," said Craig putting a restful hand on his shoulder, just as Megan and Mark hurtled through the door.

"Mum, Jake, thank God you're alright, I saw the car outside, and thought one of you was hurt? Bloody hell, what's happened to your face and Tim's?" She tossed her bunch of keys on the counter, dropped her bag on the floor and faced us all, anxious enquiry in her eyes.

Mark, used to domestic chaos in his own home, wisely stayed in the background, leaning against the counter with watchful eyes.

Jake blurted it all out. In gory, sordid detail, that had me wanting to cover my ears.

"I beat the crap out of him and *she* got in the way, because I found him screwing her, banging away at her on the bathroom floor for Christ's sakes, like a pair of bloody animals, dirty fucking bastard and our Mum, like a whore for fuck's sake!" He turned his tear filled gaze to his sister who was going white before my eyes, "and they've been doing it since New Year!"

Megan began to shake. Mark moved as if to go towards her, but Craig got there first.

"Why don't you sit down? I know it's a shock."

"A shock?" She allowed herself to be moved by him, he had that kind of influence. But she didn't sit down, not yet. First she came to me and stood looking down at me. "Is it true?"

"Yes."

I wasn't prepared for the slap. Her hand came down with full force and fury across my cheek, the side not already bruised. It brought tears to my eyes and not just because of the pain.

"Megan," I tried to speak but she cut me off.

"You bitch! How could you? How could you do that to Dad? What kind of mother does that? I hate you!" She screeched full volume and then began to cry as Craig drew her quietly away and nodded at Mark to look after her.

She was right. What kind of mother does that?

I didn't dare lift my eyes up. I couldn't meet the condemnation or blame in any of them, including Tim who I realised by now would be spinning it all around to save his friendship. I was the older woman who had seduced him. I should have known better. He had been led astray. And what eighteen year old wouldn't? I could just imagine the way he would tell it at college when it got out. Oh bugger bloody bollocks! I hadn't thought about that! What would Megan and Jake suffer?

There was I, gamely going along with the stupidity of keeping their father's sexuality a secret in order not to disrupt their lives and all the time I had been brewing this stupendous calamity. Nice one, Eve! Could I have been anymore stupid, anymore selfish?

The silence which hung like a death knoll over the room was broken by Craig once more.

"We need to clear this up," he said firmly, but not without sympathy, to Jake at least. "Are charges going to be pressed?"

Megan screeched. "Charges, what charges?"

"Your brother assaulted Tim."

"Yes but, of course he would. Tim how could you?" It was as though she had only just thought about his part in it then. "It's sick, she's our Mum! You're our friend. Used to be our friend!" She scowled at him with confusion dark on her face.

"Megan, please don't look at me like that," he said. "I'm really, really sorry. To both of you."

"And Dad?" She said her voice still high and angry. "You've been a guest in our house and you've cheated with his wife!"

I raised my head wearily. "I take the blame Megan, Jake, for all of it. I was stupid and selfish and I am so sorry. If I could turn the clock back I would."

"Well you can't can you? So you can just fucking well shut up, 'cos I don't ever want to listen to a word from your dirty lying mouth again!" Jake pushed up from the table and whirled around like a hurricane with no direction to go in. He was steadied again by Craig who seemed to have a magic touch all of a sudden.

"Sit down. We aren't finished."

The fight out of him, Jake sat. "So what happens now then? Do I get carted off to the nick? That'll help my college work, Mum, nice one!"

Craig looked at Tim who shook his head. "Please don't charge him. It isn't his fault. I would have done the same."

A long, heavy pause and then Craig said briskly. "Well in that case, I had better get you down to the hospital. That wrist needs looking at and you might need x- rays for your ribs." He then turned to face Jake and Megan. "Can I trust you two to keep things calm for the time being? I don't want to be called out to this address again."

Mark stepped forward, a steady, quiet influence. "Don't worry. I'll look after them both."

"See that you do. Right, young man, hospital." He ushered Tim out of the kitchen. His eyes were on the floor and his body held none of his usual swagger. At the door, he turned back to look at Jake, and then Megan.

"I really am sorry." To me, he said nothing.

The clock was the only sound that broke the leaden silence of the room. It was as though someone had put a spell on us, and no one could move, or say anything. I sat there, like a prisoner in my own home, a guilty criminal about to be interrogated and judged by three stony faced accusers. Even Mark had a sour look to his eye that told me he held me mostly to blame. His loyalty was to Megan and she was suffering.

I had caused that suffering.

I had done what no mother should do.

I had destroyed the trust and faith my children had in me.

It was an unrecoverable situation and the agony of that knowledge had not even begun to penetrate the density of my mind. I knew that when it did, the pain would be so much more than Andy's betrayal. And this was a wound I had inflicted upon myself. Daring to cast a glance under my eyelashes at my daughter, comforting my son, big sister hugging little brother, I would willingly have cut my right arm off with a rusty knife, rather than have caused them this pain.

But the damage was done and the shock that echoed round the room like the aftermath of an earthquake was as though there had been a death in the family. I suppose in a way there had been. A death of trust and innocence. Two things which once lost can never be retrieved.

Was there anything I could do?

I tried to speak but found that words stuck like barbed wire in my throat. I made a futile gesture with my hands, imploring them both to

169

turn and look at me. They did so and I wished they had not. To have hatred blazing out of your children's eyes, a burning condemnation for what you have done is to suffer beyond imagination. They were my world these two young people and I had just delivered a nuclear explosion to them.

"Don't even try and defend it, Mum." Megan of course was the one who could hold it together. "It's too gross for words! I can't even think about it." She waved her hands angrily in the air. "God knows how we're going to tell Dad! How could you do that to him?" She demanded once more.

"Because she's a whore," said Jake dully. "I heard Tim call her that and he's right. My mother is a whore."

I couldn't argue with him either. I was. I could be nothing else.

Megan put her hands back onto Jake's shoulders. "He was Jake's best friend, Mum. Did that not even make you stop and think? No. I mean, what were you actually thinking? What on earth made you do it? It's not as though Dad has ever cheated on you. How could you be so cruel? And with Tim of all people! In our home, Mum, in our home!"

I sat there like a fossil encased in stone, not moving, barely even breathing. Eyes lowered now so that not even the faintest shadow of bitterness could betray the secret I still kept. I would honour that secret, even now.

"Our home," echoed Jake in a twisted voice. "But not yours, Mum. Not anymore. You have to go. Now, before Dad gets home."

The stone crumbled a fraction and I could speak. "You want me to leave?"

"You aren't staying here." Jake's blue eyes had grown old and cold. No longer full of youth and mischief. "This is Dad's house. He built it, he paid for it."

"And this is how you repay him." Megan's voice was scalpel sharp. "We want you gone, Mum, like Jake says, before Dad gets back. It'll be hard enough for him to find out, but better we tell him than he has to hear it from you. God knows what the village is going to make of it. Did you think about that whilst you were screwing Tim? Did you think how Dad would suffer?"

I shook my head dumbly. "I'll pack a bag." I stood up with difficulty, my legs had been stripped of bone and muscle and jelly inserted in their place.

"Don't take too long," said Jake, drawing away from me as I went past him, as though he could not even bear to be within touching distance.

I crawled up the stairs like an invalid, hanging onto the banister rail for dear life. How was I going to survive this? Like a robot, I shoved some clothes into a bag, my toothbrush and some toiletries. That was all I could think of. Standing in the bathroom, my memory gave me full playback on the scene that had wrecked my family life. I lurched to the toilet and threw up. Harsh, bitter, bile as poisonous as the seeds of destruction my own actions had sown.

Ten minutes later, I was downstairs. They were waiting for me, Jake and Megan. Mark was nowhere to be seen and I guessed that my daughter had asked him to leave this to them. I was being evicted from my home by the two people who meant more to me than my life itself.

"I'm sorry," I said, forcing myself to meet their eyes.

Jake shrugged. "Doesn't mean anything, Mum. It's just a word. If you were sorry, you wouldn't have done it in the first place."

"We'll look after Dad," said Megan, holding open the front door. "Don't call round whilst we're here. We don't want to see you again."

Jesus, how had I bred such condemnatory children? Was there after all, a dash of their paternal grandparents polluting their genes? It looked like it. Praying that this was just the effects of the initial shock, I lugged my bag over to my car. Tim's bike was still in the drive way, a cruel reminder that would need to be removed later. I hoped Jake would not take out more fury upon it. He could not afford to add vandalism to his growing list of concerns with Craig.

I nearly ran over Deidre who was still hovering around her front driveway, an eager look of curiosity on her face. Maybe I should have thanked her for calling Craig. At least she had stopped Jake from beating his friend to a total pulp. But I didn't. I saw her begin to walk over the road towards our driveway but heard the loud slamming of the door. I could hardly see as I turned out of Cooper's Fold, tears streaming down my face, burning like acid.

It was virtually dark when I reached Sally's. The stable girls had all finished for the day and the curtains were drawn in Jenny's flat, which occupied part of the first floor of the Lodge. I hoped that Mary would be ensconced in her room with either the television on, or a good book to keep her occupied. I couldn't cope with her sharpness right now.

"Eve, what are you doing here?" Sally opened the door, dressed in a hugely fluffy pink dressing gown, checked pyjamas peeking out from beneath and spotted slippers on her feet. "Are you alright?" She had a large glass of what I guessed would be gin and tonic in her hand but even a total drunk would have spotted something amiss. I looked like I had been in a train crash. And she said so as she spotted my overnight bag.

"Come on in, love. We'll get you a drink and you can tell me all about it."

"Oh, Sally," I sobbed as I fell into her arms. "I've made such a mess of things."

"There, there, it can't be all that bad, surely."

"It's worse!" I declared passionately and in complete ignorance of just how bad it was going to get.

CHAPTER NINETEEN

Sally of course was behind me all the way. Once she had got over her initial shock. That first evening when I had arrived at the Lodge, she had poured me a large drink and then extracted all the gory details. Barring of course the reason I had gone off the rails in the first place. I was still sticking to the story that Andy and I were having problems, but then didn't every marriage. There was no way I was going to divulge his secret, even if it would take some of the heat from me. I saw that as the only way I could possibly claw back some measure of respect from Megan and Jake at a later stage.

"You've been screwing Tim?" Sally's eyes could not have widened any further. We were sat either side of a cosy fire in her sitting room, the bottle of gin on the table between us and a box of tissues that I was rapidly shredding.

"Since New Year," I sniffed and then knocked back half a glass full of gin.

"Tim? As in Tim Metcalf, tall, dark haired lad who plays in Jake's group and rides the motor bike?"

"One and the same."

"Jake's best friend."

"Not anymore. I've ruined that."

Sally reached for the gin bottle. "Bloody hell girl, that's some misdemeanour!" She topped up my glass and clinked hers against it. "Down the hatch, my love, you're going to need it." Leaning back into the depths of her armchair, she cradled her glass to her ample bosom and looked across at me. I could see that a myriad of thoughts and questions were whizzing through her brain by the way her face kept changing expression and her mouth opened and closed as though about to speak.

I kept knocking back the gin, in need of an anaesthetic and too full of self- horror to want to talk. Sally, though, finally got to the point where she could not resist.

"And Jake caught you actually doing it?"

"Yep."

"Where? How?"

I told her, sparing myself no shame. "We were making that much noise he thought I was being attacked."

"Oh my God, how awful!" She visibly cringed. "I couldn't begin to imagine what it must have been like to see Jake there. I would have died if that had been Gary." She referred to her son, who was a few years older than Jake and living away from home.

"Yes but you would never be as stupid as to screw your son's best friend would you?"

"God I couldn't!" She shuddered at the thought.

"See, my kids are right, I'm just a total whore."

"No, I mean, I couldn't because I'd be too embarrassed to let anyone that young see my flabby bits. It's alright for you, you're still in good shape, and Tim obviously thought so, otherwise he wouldn't have done it, would he?"

The gin was slowly working. "True," I conceded with a crooked smile.

Sally then smiled herself. "So go on then, what was he like?"

"That would be telling," I answered with some tiny shred of dignity remaining.

"Spoil sport. I've forgotten what sex is like, it's that long since Richard and I did it. I'm not sure I can last another nine months until he gets back from his trip."

I nearly snorted then. Nine months. Try going a decade without it then you might see how desperate you get. But I managed to keep a grip on my tongue.

"Was he good?" She persisted with a wicked gleam in her eye.

I finished my third glass of gin and thought about this. Was he good? Had it been good? Sex in the kitchen, at Badgers Brock, the garden shed, his sister's house, any time, any place, any opportunity. Fast, urgent, fumbling with clothes, hot, wild, sex. Yes. It had been good. Had it been worth it? Hell no. Nothing could have been worth the wreckage I had caused.

I gave Sally the answer she wanted to hear. "Yeah. It was good. But it was the worst thing I have ever done in my life and I'm going to pay for it, Sally in the worst possible way."

"They'll come round," she said, as I began to sob uncontrollably. "It'll blow over."

In the anonymity of a large town or city, it may well have done. But not in Maypoleton where everyone knew everyone else's business. Gossip like this was food and drink to the villagers. I had never wanted to be famous, and I had never courted attention, but my behaviour had earned me the sort of notoriety that refuses to die down easily.

Everyone had an opinion on the matter.

The girls at the stable yard were divided. Some thought I was the bees knees for still having 'what it takes' at forty plus. Others were of the same mind as my children that I was a disgusting creature to be pitied and looked down upon. I soon learnt which camp they fell into. Jenny gave me a hearty slap on the back and said nothing at all for which I was grateful.

Seth was also guarded about the whole affair, not saying much. "The storm has broken, lass, but there's still a dark cloud hanging over thee. Be careful now where thee treads." Really helpful! Still, at least he wasn't looking at me with horror in his eyes. More like concern, especially when he asked me how Jake and Megan had reacted. He looked upset when I told him what they had said but nodded and commented that they were young and inclined to hasty decisions. "They'll come round, lass," he comforted me with a gentle touch of his hand. "Blood is thicker 'n water. You'll see."

"I don't know, Seth, I think I've lost them forever." And then I started howling, unable to bear the agony of it all. It was the first time that Seth held me. In the quiet of Sam's stable, the old man put his arms around me and his touch was so kind I cried like a baby, all the emotion I had held in, pouring out like a river of grief.

"There, there, lass," He said gruffly, and when I pulled away, I had the suspicion he had tears in his own eyes, but mine were too blurry to see properly. "Would thee like me to call round an' see them? Check they're alright?"

"Would you?" I wiped my eyes. "I daren't go, not yet anyway, and Jake really likes you."

Mary, however, was not as accepting as Seth. When she had found out what I was doing staying at the Lodge and the reason why, she had shut down from me. It was as though all the hours we had shared in the attic had been wiped out. I thought we had begun to think of each other as friends, but obviously not.

"How could you do such a thing?" She faced me primly in the library as I turned up to carry on with sorting out the paper work that was still mountainous. "I can't even look at you, Eve, without feeling a sense of..."

"Disgust?"

"Yes," she said bluntly. "One just doesn't do that sort of thing, Eve. Not decent people anyway. Bad enough that you should break your marriage vows, but entertain the attentions of a man young enough to be your son, and in such a public manner, it borders on the unspeakable."

"I'll leave you to finish this by yourself then, shall I?" I didn't blame her.

"Yes I think that would be the best." She dismissed me with a sniff and a curt, "close the door on your way out."

I did, respecting her decision. What I had done was unforgiveable by people my age and younger, for someone of her generation I had stepped completely beyond the pale of civilised behaviour.

And then of course there was my husband. I had nearly forgotten about him!

I was by myself, digging over the muck heap, a task that few volunteered for, but which suited my mood on this occasion. A car drew up into the yard, parking with a squeal of the brakes that told me it wasn't a regular client. They usually drove slower, thinking of the horses. I turned, about to blast the driver with a mouthful and then nearly dropped my fork into the pile of shit when I realised it was Andy's car.

As crazy as this may appear, I hadn't even thought of what his reaction might be. Jake and Megan were all that really mattered. After all, I told myself as I climbed down from the muck heap he was already cheating on me and had been doing so for some time.

I soon found out that there was a difference. Apparently it was okay for him to be a closet gay, and screw a gorgeous therapist on the side, and it was acceptable for him to deceive the rest of the world, including his own children, because he had not made the one basic fundamental error that I had.

He had not been found out!

The eleventh commandment.

Thou shall not get caught!

Well I had, so that made me the biggest sinner of them all. Plus, I kind of got the idea that somehow my wickedness, and the outrageous way it had been discovered, absolved him of any guilt or blame.

Don't you just love the workings of a male mind!

So I stood there, covered in shit and straw, and listened to my husband mouth off at me.

"I think a quick divorce would be best, don't you?" He said, after a torrent of what was coming to be familiar, "How could I? What had had been thinking of?" Blah, blah, blah.

I gawped at him. Was this the same husband who had begged me to stay quiet and keep things exactly as they had been? The same guy who expected me to carry on living in the same house with him, whilst he sloped off to shag Jason whenever he felt like it?

"But I thought…"

"Yes, but that's all changed now, hasn't it." He regarded me icily. "I didn't expect you to do something like this? I suppose he was your way of getting back at me?"

Just then, Anna, one of the girls not in my team, as it were, wheeled a barrow round to the muck heap. Her face was alight with sly curiosity.

"Leave it there," I snapped at her.

She continued to trundle past me, casting a sympathetic glance at Andy which he duly noted with a smile that incensed me.

"Put the fucking barrow down and push off before I stick this fork up your arse!" I growled, brandishing my tool with intent.

She obeyed and scuttled off to no doubt slander me further. Let her. I knew she was not one of Jenny's best girls and right now I was in the mood for a fight. Andy was not impressed.

"For God's sake, Eve, listen to yourself! What have you turned into?"

"What have I turned into?" I gawped some more. The cheek of it.

He continued, disregarding my sceptical gaze with remarkable aplomb. "I can see why you did it," he said, stepping up close so there was no possibility of anyone hearing. "You picked the candidate most likely to cause me the greatest hurt. Someone young, close to home, but you never stopped to think about Jake in any of this did you?"

No I hadn't. I had nothing to defend myself with, so I was left with no alternative but to attack. "And I suppose you did when you first screwed Jason! Did you think of any of us or were you so desperate to fuck another man? How easy was it, my darling husband, to blank us all out when your cock was rammed up his arse?"

He hit me then. The gentle man I had known and loved transformed into a thing of rage. A hard crack against the side of the face that his son had caught previously. I would take a blow from Jake or Megan, but not from him.

I launched myself at him, fists pummelling at his chest and face. A dark fury was upon me and I was yelling at him, cursing him for being a devious, lying, cheating, filthy fucking bastard. I had already kicked him hard in the shins and was raising my leg to connect with his groin when he used his strength and size to overcome me. Another right hander landed on my jaw this time and it was enough to send me staggering backwards.

I fell into the arms of Seth who held me up as I caught my breath.

"Easy, lass." The voice that could quiet any horse, worked on me.

I went limp and stared in horror at Andy who was sporting a cut lip and a look of equally horrified proportions in his own eyes. He cradled the knuckles of the hand he had hit me with, as if they belonged to someone else.

Finally he spoke. "You'll be hearing from my solicitor. And Eve, if you think about disclosing our other matter, consider the damage you have already done to Jake and Megan. You really don't want to alienate them even more do you?"

A subtle threat. Keep my mouth closed about his little secret otherwise he would make matters worse for me.

I nodded, too angry and shaken at what my anger had wrought, to argue.

I spent the next few days being molly coddled by Sally as though I had suffered a bereavement. Well I had in a way. As well as my marriage I had lost the love and respect of my children. A hundred times a day I thought about phoning Jake, desperate to hear the sound of his voice.

I worried about Megan too, but in a different way. Megan had not seen when Jake had. Megan had not been betrayed by her best friend as well as her mother. And Megan was a survivor, I knew that. She would put her own needs before anyone else's making sure that her hurt and resentment would not be bottled up quietly. It was Jake who would carry the scars of this the deepest.

By Monday of the following week, five days after the explosion, I knew that it was already cutting in. I had another phone call from Mark Hughes, Jake's form tutor.

"His attendance has been somewhat sketchy again, Mrs. Armstrong."

I'll bet it had! More guilt to weigh upon my shoulders.

"There was a bit of an upset at home last week, Mr. Hughes," I began to say, hoping without hope that he would be in too lofty a position to have heard the gossip. Apparently not. I heard the sucking in of breath and the acidic tone of distaste in his voice.

"Yes, a matter concerning Tim Metcalf, also one of our students, has been brought to our attention, Mrs. Armstrong."

Our attention? Had the whole staff room discussed it? Probably. I cringed on the other end of the phone as the acid continued to drip.

"Fortunately that individual appears to be able to cope with the events, although I have to say he has found it hard working with a broken wrist! Your son, on the other hand, is dangerously close to being permanently removed from the college. There was a matter of the fight in the classroom on Friday afternoon."

My head began to pound. I could think of nothing to say.

"Mrs. Armstrong? You are aware of the fight?"

"Er, no. I am not living at home presently. I haven't spoken to my son since, well..."

I swear he tutted at me. His disgust was no longer hidden but poured down the phone. "I can't say I am surprised. Perhaps then, I should cross you off my list of parents and continue all further communications with his father instead?"

179

"I think you had better do that," I agreed, hating the thought, hating the way I was being spoken to, hating that I had brought it on myself, hating the fact most that Jake was suffering. Hating myself full stop.

That afternoon I had to go into the village. I had lost all track of the days and had realised at lunch time that I had missed the birthday of my oldest friend, Molly Jones from Birtwistle House, one of the nicer care homes I had attended. We had always kept in touch and sent each other cards and small gifts on our birthdays. This year I had completely forgotten it.

"Would you like me to go into the village and get something for you?" Sally suggested lightly. We had taken to having our lunch in the office, away from the others, only Jenny bobbing in for a brew.

I looked at her sharply. "It can't be that bad, surely?"

Sally and Jenny exchanged a glance. "Some of the gossip has got pretty nasty," said Jenny with her characteristic bluntness. "Sarah Forshawe was complaining at the weekend that you shouldn't be allowed to work around children anymore."

I nearly choked on my sandwich. "What? I'm not a paedophile! Tim is eighteen for heaven's sakes."

"Yes I know. But some of the villagers with sons that age think you are a harmful influence. And she's one of them. So is Bryony Adams."

"She's my friend," I spluttered to Jenny.

"I know," said the instructor calmly. "But it was her I heard Sarah Forshawe talking to on the phone whilst she was here. She told her that she had better keep Ricky out of your way."

"As if I'd fuck him!" I exploded, throwing the rest of my sandwich onto the table. "Jumped up little arse." I was stung by what looked like the betrayal of my friend. And then I thought again of Jake. "Bloody hell, everything's such a mess."

"So shall I pop into Maypoleton and get your friend a present for you?"

"Bless you," I said to Sally who was looking at me with concern. "I can handle a few old sour pusses."

"What about nipping into Lancaster instead?" Jenny suggested, also clearly concerned for my well- being.

"Look," I said, getting up and putting my discarded lunch into the bin, "I've had worse thrown at me, believe me. Besides, I particularly want to get Molly something from 'Just for you'. She's been collecting those butterfly ornaments for a while now, and I want to add to her collection."

But unbelievably, the little gift shop, where I had spent a fortune over the years, paying over the odds with a mind to help promote local businesses, was closed when I got there. Or rather, Judy, the owner, told me waspishly, that she was taking her lunch break.

"I'll only be a moment," I said, spotting immediately what I wanted to buy for Molly. "I know what I want and you don't have to gift wrap it for me. Just one of those butterflies, please, the lilac one."

"I said I'm shutting for lunch," repeated Judy, taking hold of my arm and leading me to the door.

"You never shut for lunch." I pulled my arm back, angrily. "You don't want to serve me do you?"

Judy Morgan looked at me through her thick framed black glasses. "Can you blame me? You're the talk of the village. I don't want to lose custom by selling to you." She actually dared to give me a little shove out through the door. A shove! How dare she? In another lifetime I would have flattened her for such an offense. As it was, I thought that brawling in the street would not be advisable given my current status.

I was muttering to myself as I stomped back across the village green, when there came a loud and angry shout from the other side of the duck pond.

"There she is, the little bitch!"

That would be me then. I looked up to wonder who was making such a clear accusation and wished I hadn't.

"Oh fuck!" I muttered under my breath, suddenly regretting my insistence that I came into the village. Shelly Metcalf, Tim's mother was standing with a group of other mums as they fed the ducks. Shelly was minding her daughter's child by the look of things but she was quick enough to leave the pram in the care of another lady, as she ran round the pond in my direction.

I should have run. I was fitter than her by a long way. She was huffing and puffing after a mere ten yards. I could go ten K no problem. But I don't run from confrontations.

Because I am an idiot!

I should have run. I really should have run.

"You dirty little whore!" Burst out Shelly as her hand came out to slap me across the face. Instinctively my hands itched to belt her back but I had just about enough sense to know not to. She ranted and raved at me whilst the other mums came close, obviously enjoying the afternoons entertainment. Credit to Shelly, she managed to keep most of her language clean for the sake of the children but even so, I got a very clear picture of what she thought of me. It wasn't pretty.

"You should be strung up for what you've done to my Tim," she finished with, hands on hips. "An innocent lad, that's what he was until you got your hands on him."

I know I shouldn't have laughed. Tim had never been innocent in the whole affair. And it was more of a snort really, not a full blown ha, ha, ha! Nevertheless, it was enough to incense Shelly further.

"Ooh you wicked little bitch! You should be locked up!"

"Why don't we?" The suggestion came from one of her friends. "Put her in the stocks for a while, that'll teach her."

Yes there was a set of ancient stocks on the village green. No lock of course, so I wasn't too worried. Until one of them suggested using their daughter's skipping rope to tie through the hand holds.

"Fuck off," I said to them as they nodded in agreement and started to walk away. But a clout on the back of my head, I think from Shelly's bag made me, stagger. Before I knew it, my legs had been grabbed and I was being manhandled by half a dozen of Maypoleton's finest Mums and Toddler group, with a couple of the WI brigade thrown in for good measure.

Oh there was much hilarity as they shoved my arms and legs through the holes, much sniggering and giggling as they looped little Lily's skipping rope effectively through so that they could tie it in place. Even greater amusement when they threw slimy bits of pond weed at me which stuck in my hair and slithered down my face. Much joy to be had all round.

They had their fun and then it started to rain. The buggers left me there as even the ducks took shelter. I must have been sitting there a good couple of hours, as the rain lashed down. I told myself that eventually someone would come. Then when they didn't, I told myself it was because the rain was now that hard that no one would be able to see me, a dark lonely figure, hunched over the stocks.

Finally, I realised that no one wanted to help me. My friends, those I could rely on, anyway, were all at the yard. I watched gloomily as Bryony's four by four went by in a hurry, water splashing from the kerbside. Had she seen? Had she turned away?

Then when I couldn't possibly have felt more uncomfortable, I realised I wanted to wee. You know how it is. When you can't go, you desperately need to. It's all you can think about. I tried all manner of distraction techniques, but in the end it was no use. After an agony of holding it in it, I felt the humiliating trickle become a breaking dam of liquid, hot against the cold wetness of my sodden clothes.

Well there you go. I hadn't pissed myself since I was a child! At least, I thought miserably, the rain might wash away some of the urine. I think it must have done, because there was quite a muddy puddle forming around my bottom by the time I was eventually rescued.

I did have an ally in Maypoleton it seemed.

Struggling to keep her umbrella the right way in the heavy wind, Mabel from the bakery headed in my direction. At the same time, I saw the police car draw up and park close by.

"Oh bless you, Eve, how long have you been there?" Mabel tutted as she approached. "I've been in Lancaster visiting my sister, I've just got back and I heard what had happened. Bunch of narrow minded harpies. They're only jealous, pet, you mark my words. Not one of them could keep a fellow's interest, let alone a strapping young thing like Tim. Now then, let's sort out these knots shall we?"

But by then, Craig Hawthorne strode across and with a murmur of thanks to Mabel and a suggestion that she get back inside the warmth of her bakery, he took over. Wordlessly, he untied the knots that held the stocks in place, tossing the skipping rope to the ground when he had done so. It landed with a splash in one of the puddles. I was too frozen to move and my legs had gone dead on me. I think I heard him swear quietly, but I might have been mistaken. He bent down and put his hands under my armpits to lift me up. My teeth were chattering in earnest now and I wondered if I would ever be warm again.

"Did you come by car?"

I shook my head, water dripping from the ends of my hair like a dog after a bath. "I walked."

"I'll take you then."

His car was parked not far from Judy's shop. I wondered if she was watching as I shuffled back in her direction. Craig opened the boot of the car and took out a blanket, the type you see when people are in accidents, baking foil kind of thing.

"Here, you look frozen." He wrapped me up like a turkey and then propelled me to the passenger side of his car.

"I wet myself," I blurted out for some stupid reason. Was my brain frozen as well? I wished my chattering teeth would bite my tongue off.

To his credit, he didn't flinch, but helped me into the car. At least the foil wrap would stop me leaking onto his upholstery. The short drive to the Lodge lasted an eternity. He didn't speak, he didn't look at me. I could have been invisible. He delivered me back into the care of Sally and Jenny with an advisory note that perhaps I should stay away from the village for the time being.

Then to put the icing on the cake, Anna came into the office with a gloating message that one of Sally's best clients had told her that unless I was off the yard, she would be cancelling her lessons. I stood there, dripping muddy green water on to the floor, a shivering, silver foiled wreck of a woman with pond weed in her hair and snot dripping from her nose, and wondered if there was possibly a hole I could bury myself in.

CHAPTER TWENTY

There was no hole but there was the cottage.

It was Sally who suggested it when I remarked that maybe I should find somewhere out of Maypoleton to stay for a while. Like Australia!

"The last thing I want to do is make trouble for you," I said, having soaked in a hot bath and warmed myself up on the inside with a large glass of Richard's best malt whisky. He wouldn't miss it, Sally assured me as she joined me in a drink. We were in danger of becoming a couple of lushes, I thought, as the level on the bottle went steadily down.

"Don't be silly," she said, although there was clearly some room for concern. She did have a business to run after all and I knew very well just how determined some of the folk in Maypoleton could be. "Look, why don't you move into the cottage for a while? Hardly anyone even knows it exists. Sam's on working livery so you don't even have to worry about doing his jobs and everyone can think that you've gone away for a while."

"God it sounds like I'm a criminal in hiding," I said, morosely. And then I brightened at what she had just suggested. Stay at the cottage. Instantly my spirits lifted. I had not seen or heard anything from Jem since that magical afternoon. Maybe now that spring was on its way, he would be back working on the estate? I thought it prudent not to mention him though to Sally at this point in time, considering what a pickle I had got myself in over Tim.

Sally giggled. "It does rather. You did look a sight I have to say when Craig brought you home."

I scowled at her, as she began to laugh even more. "Oh, Eve, fancy getting locked into the stocks, it could only happen to you, and I can't believe you told Craig you'd wet yourself! Have you no shame, girl?"

"Apparently not."

"Never mind. I'm sure he's seen and heard worse, and it was awfully good of him to bring you back here."

I grunted incoherently.

"Oh don't be like that. I think he's really nice."

I snarled a little.

"He is. And ever so attractive, very masculine. I'd love to see him out of uniform, in fact, I'd love to see him without any clothes at all," said Sally with a speculative glint in her eye.

"Why don't you go and telephone Richard?" I suggested, not wanting to think about Craig Hawthorne, with, or without his clothes. All he represented to me was the worst of my shame. When I thought of the times we had crossed paths, all I wanted to do was to cringe with embarrassment and today had been no better!

Sally's idea of hiding out at the cottage was a good one though, and the following morning, we put the plan into action. We loaded my overnight bag and the two cases that Andy had delivered into the boot of Sally's car and then we drove out of one entrance of the Lodge, down the road for a minute and into the back entrance, via a locked gate which had not been opened in years.

"I suppose I should get this access sorted out," said Sally as we had to abandon the car a few yards into the grounds, due to the appalling state of the track. "I'm thinking we could start the cross country course from this point. It would be great to have it for this summer but I don't think I'll get the money through from the auctions in time. I can at least get the groundwork started. Would you mind if I got the gardener in, whilst you are down here?"

Would I mind? I shook my head innocently.

"Did you manage to get hold of him by the way? I thought you said you had got the number down wrong?"

"No, but it doesn't matter now anyway."

"Are you sure you're going to be alright here by yourself?" Sally asked once we had manhandled the cases into the cottage.

"I'll be fine," I said, feeling the love of the cottage straight away. I was home. "I shall just hibernate here and wait for everything to blow over. Are you sure you can cope without me helping you at the Lodge?"

"Don't worry about that," said Sally airily.

186

"But you can't carry on paying me," I said with a frown creasing my brow, "I won't be doing any work."

"No, I suppose not. Will you be alright for money? I mean, Andy won't just cut you off will he?"

It was something I was going to have to check. I assured Sally that things would be fine, and shooed her off. I wanted to be alone. As soon as I shut the door behind her, I felt an enormous sense of... Well something I couldn't really put my finger on. I think there was a large part of relief in the mix of emotions. I knew that here I really could hide from the world and believe me, after yesterday I had no wish to see anyone right now, unless of course it was Jake or Megan.

I sighed and began the simple task of lighting a fire. No point in brooding. What was done was done. All I could possibly hope for was that in time, my children's feelings towards me would mellow and I would maybe get a chance to explain.

The only angle where I could try and redeem myself would be to continue to guard Andy's secret until he chose to disclose it himself. To reveal the truth to Megan and Jake now, would only make me look more bitter and twisted in their eyes and there was a chance they would not believe it anyway, thinking I was only saying it to make myself look better.

Mulling this over, I began to unpack my cases. They were too large to get up the narrow staircase so I had to carry up my belongings bit by bit. Andy had literally emptied the contents of my drawers and wardrobe in one go and shoved things in any old how. I mean what was the point in packing my swim suit and flip flops for God's sake? Did he expect me to be sunbathing in March? Or maybe he was hinting I should book myself on a flight somewhere far away. On a one way ticket!

The tops of my face creams had not been tightened properly and had leaked out over my underwear, and my best silk shirt, my only silk shirt, was crumpled up underneath my walking boots. The contents of my bedside drawer had been thrown in on top of everything, nail polishes, thankfully screwed up tightly, manicure set, pain killers, bits and pieces of casual jewellery, hair brushes, scrunches, a book mark that Megan had made in primary school and a photo frame decorated by Jake at the same time, both of which reduced me to tears.

I hung my clothes, those that didn't need washing, into the wardrobe, feeling very odd as I did so. It felt so very wrong that I was doing this. I should be at home with my family. I should have a husband who loved me and children who thought the same. And yet this felt so very right. I should be here. I should be hanging my clothes up in this old wooden cupboard and I should be carefully placing my hairbrush on the dressing table, arranging my face creams just so, and sitting on the stool to check my reflection in the mirror.

A youthful reflection with artfully coiled blonde hair and cornflower blue eyes, merry dimples dancing in rosy cheeks.

"Hello, Melody," I said softly, addressing the ghost who had come to keep me company. "It is you, isn't it? I've got your book, your diary. You do want me to read it don't you?" And then I realised that it was not amongst the belongings that Andy had packed up for me.

I heard the sing song laughter, so full of joy and love, it made the cottage come alive around me as though the stones and wood were living, breathing objects. I laughed with her, it was impossible not to. And then I froze as her face changed and a look of horror came over her. Her pink cheeks paled to ivory and her eyes darkened to indigo as her mouth widened to let loose a terrible drawn out cry.

"No!"

I heard it as sure as I had heard the laughter and when I did, the cottage grew cold and dark in echo of her feelings.

"What happened, Melody?" I reached for the glass with tentative fingers, but of course she had gone.

I felt lonely without her presence, as though a part of me was missing. I was frustrated that I did not have her diary with me. I would have liked to have curled up on the bed and spend the rest of the day reading it. After all I had no more pressing matters to occupy my time.

Or so I thought. I had barely finished unpacking when I heard my mobile ringing from downstairs. I ignored it the first time. My phone had been very lively over the last few days but I had quickly realised that anyone calling me was either about to slag me off for my 'disgustingly, inappropriate, shameful, lewd, shocking behaviour,' (mostly Andy's friends making it clear where their loyalties lay) or probing for juicy gossip whilst pretending to be supportive. So I let the phone ring again and again, until it finally irritated me so much that I felt compelled to see who wanted to speak to me so desperately.

Five missed calls, all the same number. Not one that I recognised off the top of my head and it wasn't keyed into my list of contacts so there was no name showing. Could it possibly be Jem? Had he somehow got hold of my messages and was now using another phone to call me?

I could not ignore this chance and I returned the call.

"Eve at last, I've been trying to get you all morning! Look my girl, I've been hearing some wild stories about you, I think we need to get together and soon!"

"Ellie! Hello. I didn't recognise the number?"

"Works phone. Now then, I had an email from bloody Barty Briggins first thing this morning, advising me that Andy was filing for divorce and he wants it sorting like yesterday. What the hell's going on, girl?"

I had to smile. Ellie Mason sounded as though she had been brought up in the home counties and rode to hounds at the weekend, yet I knew she had been born and bred only a few miles from here. I had met her years ago when I had been singing in the band. She had been the girlfriend of the guitarist at the time, but unlike the rest of us, had an academic brain and was going to use it. Whilst we went off touring she concentrated on her law degree. Her relationship with Bradley hadn't lasted, but our friendship had.

We didn't see each other often, maybe just once or twice a year, but our children's birthdays were always noted and presents exchanged. Ellie now ran her own practice in Lancaster, raking in a small fortune whilst her fabulous husband, a chef by profession, gamely stayed at home to look after their children, who were younger than mine by a long way. I had had no need to ever use her professional services and I was somewhat startled now to hear that she had been contacted so abruptly.

"Oh it's that awful Barty," she said when I commented as such. "He thinks he's a Rottweiler in this business, but let me tell you, darling, he's a mere poodle compared to me. When I sink my teeth

189

into a case there's only one possible outcome and that's total annihilation!"

"Okay," I said slowly, trying to take it all in. "So Andy has obviously given this Barty bloke your details to act on my behalf?"

"Correct. We need to get together, what are you doing for lunch?"

"Today?"

"Yes darling girl, today, strike whilst the iron's hot you know."

"Well nothing."

"You are now. Tiggi's at one alright?"

I checked my watch. It was eleven now. Plenty of time to get to the restaurant in Lancaster. I agreed, feeling a little bemused by the whole idea, but trusting Ellie to look after my interests. I couldn't believe Andy had acted so hastily, after everything we had talked about regarding his own 'misdemeanour'!

I always enjoyed my catch ups with Ellie which were usually chock full of amusing tales of what our various offspring were doing and a mutual light hearted moan about our husbands. But I had never seen her in work mode and it was scary.

Tall, dark and thin, with a buzzing energy about her, Ellie commanded attention where ever she went. The waiters always jumped to attention at the merest lift of an eyebrow and we were never kept waiting for our food. We ordered quickly, me because I was starving and Ellie because she knew the menu off by heart, and then it was down to brass tacks.

"Adultery my girl, with an eighteen year old, sounds like fun! I want all the details, and don't spare my blushes I haven't had sex in weeks. Maribelle is having night terrors at the moment and is insisting she sleeps in our bed, it's a total nightmare, so go ahead and make me jealous."

A group of businessmen at a nearby table turned their heads in our direction. Ellie was oblivious to their interest but I could feel the heat scorching my cheeks as I caught the speculative gaze of one of them, a portly man with thinning hair and fleshy lips. I scowled at him and moved places around the table so that my back was towards him. Creep!

Falteringly, I began my tale, only I didn't tell her about Andy. For a while she was simply fascinated by the ins and outs of what sex with a randy teenager had been like and how we had managed to fit it in to our busy lives without getting caught, at least for a while. She was genuinely sympathetic when I described the explosive scene in our house when Jake found out.

"God that's terrible, girl, you must be feeling shattered by it all," she reached out a perfectly manicured hand, with a diamond almost too large to be real on one finger, and squeezed my own with its chewed up nails and lack of polish. She tilted her head and regarded me out of sherry coloured eyes, made huge with false lashes. "Bit of a boob to pick Jake's best friend, but apart from that I don't blame you. I mean who wouldn't want to get down and dirty with someone like that. You say he had a six pack? God, I'd love to get my hands on a six pack! I bet he had a really tight arse as well didn't he?" She licked her lips and did a superlative job of ignoring the waiter's blushes as he cleared away our plates and asked us what we wanted for dessert. I think he was frightened that Ellie might have asked for him, she sounded that hungry for young male flesh.

Then she grew serious and tapped a long nail on the table. "Right, well that's the fun bit out of the way, now tell me the real reason you cheated on Andy. I know you were not simply bored. You set too much store by your family, Eve, to risk it all for a quick screw. Something must have pushed you over the edge."

Her eyes were now like those of a snake's, hypnotic and deadly. I began to see why she was so successful. She lured you in with charm and laughter and when you were off guard, she struck. She was also one of those few people who are content with someone else's silence. She would simply wait until I told her.

I had finished my dessert, and was clinking the spoon against the empty glass, trying to find the words.

"Andy's gay. He told me at New Year that he has a lover called Jason. We haven't had sex in over ten years."

"Well that makes things clearer then." No shock, no drama, just Ellie in work mode. "Depriving you of conjugal rights and mental cruelty, it more than balances out the adultery on your part. Leave it with me."

I pulled a face. "I really don't want Megan and Jake to be hit with that as well. Not now at least."

"No need for them to know dear girl. But if Andy is using Barty Briggins, he's prepared to fight dirty. He's already condoned your kids kicking you out of your home for crying out loud. Do you want to end up alone and penniless?"

No I didn't. My hand strayed to where Andy's bruise had merged with Jake's. Fuck him!

"Okay. As long as it's discreet."

"Would I be anything other? Really darling."

Not surprisingly, I felt rather glum by the time I was negotiating the rough track that made up the back entrance of the Lodge. I was forty two, soon to be divorced, my children hated me, and the villagers thought I was the nearest thing to a witch they had seen in centuries.

And then I saw a slim, auburn haired figure and I forgot everything else.

CHAPTER TWENTY ONE

Yes, yes, yes, I know.

Frying pans and fires.

Would I ever learn?

Probably not.

I was not one for a quiet life. Well, in actual fact I had been for the last twenty years. Motherhood had dampened me down dramatically and nailed me tightly into a box of respectability. The lid was well and truly off now and I had reverted back to type. I was reckless and impulsive with a curiosity for life equal to that of a cat. Ah, but curiosity killed the cat. True enough, and my curiosity was going to have near deadly consequences for me. But I didn't know this at the time. All I could see was a light shining for me in the middle of a black hole of darkness. So I went towards it.

Which you would, if that light was five foot ten, slim but with lovely lean muscles, a warm husky voice, hair the colour of autumn conkers, and bewitching eyes. They held me spellbound the way they lit up and shone like diamonds when they looked into mine. God I would do anything for those eyes smiling upon me.

"I've missed you," he said in greeting, hands in trouser pockets, head tilted to one side.

"I'm sorry I had to cut and run last time. My daughter was in a car crash. She was okay, ran into a cow shed of all things, there was a chicken on the road and she didn't want to hit it. She's like that, Megan, loves animals. I tried to call you," I said, gabbling like an anxious school girl.

Jem gave that quirky smile that lifted his mouth just at the left side. A seductive smile that drew you in and made you want more, teasing and intimate.

"No matter. I knew I'd see you again." He nodded his head to the cottage. "You staying here now?"

"Yes," I replied with a ridiculous grin on my face, totally inappropriate considering the reason why I was there. "Bit of bother at home."

"So it's just you and me then, at last. How it should be."

Like the first time, it all happened so smoothly, dreamlike in its motions. We chatted for a while, then moved inside the cottage as naturally as if we had both lived there a lifetime. I put the kettle on and he drew the curtains and made up the fire. Our talking had stopped, there seemed to be so little need for words. It was enough to look at each other, lock eyes and smile. Share a light touch, a stroke of the hand, a gentle brush of the lips.

And then more was needed. As the fire crackled in the hearth, the heat between us began to grow. I was cradled in his lap on one of the rocking chairs, resting my head against his chest, the tea left to stew and grow cold, and it was no longer enough to feel his body beneath mine, I had to feel him inside me.

He sensed the change immediately and shifted to slide me down onto the hearth rug. Silently we undressed each other, snatching kisses greedily as each piece of flesh was revealed. God he was beautiful, like a marble statue brought to life. I melted into the rug and grew damp with desire, simply by looking at him. How, I wondered in awe, could this man possibly be mine?

How could I deserve to know such pleasure, as his lips and hands brought every inch of my body to life in a way that had me sobbing with ecstasy? Tender kisses over my face, down my neck and into the crook of my collar bone. Skilful hands calloused from work caressed my breasts, moulding their shape into his palms, thumbs rubbing over my nipples until they ached for more. Hungry bites as he sucked hard at the peaks, my hands entangled in his hair as I held him close.

And as his mouth devoured my breasts, one hand supporting his weight, his other hand moved lower. I lifted my hips to rub against him, feline and sensual in my desire, a low throbbing purr of arousal coming from my throat. There was no rush and no fear that I had to hurry him. We had all the time in the world.

My body grew limp and slick as he explored me from top to toe and then turned me over to lie face down on the rug. I felt bereft of his touch for a moment and then he began again, lying on top of my back, his legs pressing down on mine, his hardness falling into the clef of my buttocks. I squealed a little and arched my back against him, hearing the soft wicked laughter and feeling the hot breath in the back of my neck.

"No, no, my love, I shall not do that. Lie still a little more, I am not ready for you yet."

Oh but he was. He was large and hard and I wondered how on earth he could hold himself back as I wriggled against the rug, a squirming mass of desire with my only thought that of release. I dug my fingers into the rug and moaned as he trailed kisses and bites all over my back, his fingers playing into my muscles, tracing their shape and teasing sensations out of them that I had not felt before. He moved lower again, hands and mouth discovering the curves of my bottom and dipping into the dark valley between my thighs until I was begging him, literally begging, him to take me.

If you could kill someone with desire, then that was what he was doing. Oh but what a glorious way to go. His laughter was rich and deep as he rolled me smoothly over, cradling me into his arms and entering me in one easy movement. I had tears rolling down my cheeks as his mouth found mine once more. I lost myself in the motions as his tongue stabbed against mine, a perfect mirror of how he was moving himself hard and deep within me, hips grinding together now with a harshness that contrasted with his gentle foreplay.

I had begged him to take me, and that is what he did. He held my hands above my head, and raised himself up from me, so that he could look down into my eyes. His lips were parted slightly and I could see the tips of his white teeth, sharp against the pinkness of his tongue as his breath grew more ragged. He had locked his thighs outside mine so I could not move my legs to wrap around him. I was his prisoner, immobile beneath him, victim to his passion.

I would have gladly served a life sentence.

All I could do was call his name, over and over and again, and plead with him for more, for harder, deeper, thrusts, to be taken faster and wilder, into the dizzying realms he was leading me. When I finally got there, he commanded me roughly to look at him.

"Open your eyes. Look at me, let me see!"

I did and it was as if he could see my soul, exposed as naked as I was beneath him. As if he was drawing my very essence deep into his own. My body shuddered in time with his and my breath was tortured and harsh. My eyes were bound by his and time stood still in that moment.

He was my love.

He was my life.

He smiled a full, wide, crooked smile.

"I am," he said and eased his body, sated now, down on top of mine where we lay in a coil of sweat soaked limbs, too replete to move.

Dazed, and too happy to wonder how he could possibly read my mind, I lay there in contented abandonment and let sleep drift over me.

It happened every time.

Whether it was morning, noon, or night, Jem's lovemaking was so deeply shattering I could never stay awake afterwards. I felt as though I had some wonderful new drug running through my veins that erased all traces of tension and sent me into this blissful place of soporific euphoria. Whenever I woke he would be gone, but my body was imprinted with such passion and love that I felt the warm afterglow for much longer.

So much so that I never stopped to ask him, why he could not stay?

Of course the thought nudged itself into my mind during the parts of the day when I was by myself. But as soon as he appeared, without warning, or prior arrangement, it was the last thing on my mind. All that mattered was that he was there. He was now. And he loved me.

He used that love to enfold himself around me and within me. I had never felt so cherished, nor, I would think later, would I ever be again. He took the wounds that were deeply imbedded in my heart and one by one healed them. He matched his soul to mine until I felt only half alive when we were parted.

I came to dread the time when I would be by myself and longed for those moments when he was with me, smiling with those magical eyes, murmuring endearments with those sweet lips, and sharing his body with an intoxicating passion that grew more intense each time we made love. Nothing else mattered. And I mean nothing else.

I forgot about Andy. I forgot about Tim. I forgot, heaven forgive me, about Megan and Jake. They were before and he was now. Time slipped by in my love filled cocoon and I had no need of anything to occupy my time or my thoughts. There was Jem. I had no need of anything else. When real life intruded, which of course it did, I was resentful.

"Are you sure you are alright?" Sally asked me one day. I think it was a Wednesday, although it could have been any day really. I had not been out of the cottage for ages, except to wander around the small garden which Jem was cultivating beautifully for me. That had been my only interest and I had started to learn the names of the flowers and shrubs that he had so carefully planted. "You look awfully pale, Eve, are you eating alright?"

I shrugged. "Of course I am. What a daft question. When have you ever known me not to eat?"

"Well I'm worried about you," she said, sitting in Jem's rocking chair. I must have frowned because she looked at me sharply. "There is something the matter, isn't there?"

"No, no, honestly there isn't," I replied quickly, telling myself to snap out of it. She was my best friend, this was her cottage. What was I doing, scowling at her because she was sitting in what I saw as Jem's chair? "I'm just a little tired, that's all. Not been sleeping too well." In fact the opposite was true. I was like sleeping beauty these days, awaking only when my prince arrived to kiss me on the lips.

"I'm not surprised. It has been a hell of a time for you," she said sympathetically. "But at least the gossip seems to be dying down a little in the village."

"Gossip?" I looked at her blankly.

"You and Tim. Good Lord you must be tired if you've forgotten! Anyway, the latest piece of juice is that Chrissy Wentworth is pregnant again. Again, can you believe it? I've lost count of how many she's had and all with a different father. I think this one is number six and there's speculation in the pub that the dad is the new curate of all people, can you imagine that? Well I suppose nothing would shock you, but anyway, if it turns out to be true then all eyes will be on him and you'll be able to come out of hiding."

"Mm," I wondered how long she would be staying. So far Jem had never arrived when there had been anyone else here.

"Anyway, I thought you would want to know. And Sam's doing fine. The children in the ten o clock lesson on Saturday virtually fight over whose turn it is to ride him. You must be missing him but I'm sure it won't be long before you can get back to normal. After all it's been nearly a month now."

Had it really? A month! My brain went from digesting who Sam was, I had all but forgotten I had a horse, to acknowledging the fact that so much time had passed by. It shocked me out of my haze.

"A month! Bloody hell Sally, are we in April?"

"It's the fourth," she said looking at me oddly. "Are you sure you don't need to see a doctor, you do seem very, well, not quite alright, if you don't mind me saying. Maybe you've got that post-traumatic stress disorder thingy, you know, with everything that happened to you."

I laughed then, merry and light hearted. "Oh Sally, I'm fine, honestly I am better than you could possibly realise." I was in love and completely fulfilled for the first time in my life. But that was something I was not ready to share with anyone, even her.

Or Seth for that matter.

It was a busy day in that I had two visitors, one after the other. Sally had left me with a chiding to eat more as she thought I was getting too thin, and then before too long, there was another knock on the door. I sighed, knowing it could not be Jem. He never knocked. I was surprised to see Seth standing on my doorstep, cap in his hand a tentative smile on his face.

"Seth, hello, it's nice to see you." Oddly, it was. I had felt irked by Sally's presence which was wrong of me, but there was something about Seth that always drew me. "Come in, have a cup of tea with me."

He stepped into the cottage and looked around with interest. His unusual eyes were, I knew, looking at far more than the fixtures and fitting. He was seeing beneath the bricks and mortar to what lay hidden. I busied myself in the kitchen preparing a nice pot of tea before cutting some cake from the slab that Sally had thoughtfully bought and carried it through to the sitting room on a tray.

"Are you well, Seth?"

"I am, lass. 'An thee?"

"Oh I'm very well. Enjoying the peace and quiet." I poured the tea and tried to ignore his piercing gaze. "What can I do for you?"

"'Tis about t'field."

"Go on. Is there a problem?"

"Nay, lass. But Easter is comin' up."

"Yes?"

"I've kin passin' through an I wanted t'ask if they can bide wi' me a while?"

He had mentioned this before and I nodded straight away. "Of course you can, Seth, I said so earlier if you recall."

"Aye, that thee did, lass, but I've not sin thee since."

"Well it still stands, Seth. Andy may be divorcing me, but as far as I know the field is still half mine. He hasn't said anything to you has he?" I'd bloody well belt him one if he had.

"Nay, lass."

"Good." Then because his presence had brought to mind those who I had managed to ignore for the last few weeks, including my children, I asked him, "Have you seen anything of Jake or Megan at all?"

"Seen Jake once or twice. Brought his guitar over to play alongside my whistle."

I smiled and felt a twinge of shame that I had so completely pushed my son to the back of my mind. I was the most dreadful mother alive!

"How is he, Seth?"

He didn't say anything but surveyed me calmly with those mixed up coloured eyes and sipped his tea carefully.

"Oh," I said heavily. "Not good then. How can I put it right, Seth? He's my son, and I've lost him. I've lost them both, Megan as well. How can a mother do that, lose her children? It's the worst thing ever."

"Aye lass, to lose a child, 'tis a pain beyond measure." He spoke as though he knew, yet I had never heard him mention any children of his own. "Thee must 'ave faith, lass. Love finds a way in t'end."

"I hope so. In the meantime, Seth, thank you, for looking after him."

He smiled that rare and precious smile. "'Tis no 'ardship to care for Megan and Jake, lass, fret not about that. But 'tis thee who must take care now." He set his mug of tea down and looked deep into my eyes. "Summat powerful lingers in this 'ouse. Thee feels it, I know. Take great care it doesn't feed off you."

I shivered. Feed off me. What a horrible phrase to use. I had no wish to probe further and ask what he meant.

"I'm fine, Seth. In fact I'm happier here than I have ever been." I meant it. Apart that is, from my sadness over Jake and Megan which in all honesty I had blocked out successfully until this morning.

"Aye lass, but 'tis a fine line between t'dark and t'light. Thee must watch thee doesn't get caught twixt t'two."

After he left I wondered what he could possibly mean. And then Jem arrived and Seth and my family were forgotten once more. I spent the afternoon lost in the sensual pleasures of the flesh and soul, abandoning myself to the paradise that only Jem could take me to.

CHAPTER TWENTY TWO

A few days later I was woken by an insistent banging.

"Alright, alright, I'm coming," I grumbled as I slouched my way downstairs. I was sleepy and bleary eyed and in no mood to be so rudely disturbed.

"Eve hurry up!" It was Sally's voice on the other side of the door.

Through the haziness of my mind, I caught the note of urgency in her voice. But still, I could move no quicker than a sleep walker.

"For God's sake what took you? I've been ringing your phone for the last ten minutes. Why aren't you answering? God you're not even dressed yet, are you ill, it's nearly lunchtime? Oh never mind that. Look, its Jake, you have to come with me now!"

I stared at her blankly. "Jake?"

"Christ, Eve, wake up!" She looked tempted to slap me but settled for putting her hands on my shoulders and shaking me gently instead. "Jake is in hospital. It's serious."

That worked.

"What's happened?" Standing in the middle of an icy waterfall would not have shocked me to my senses quicker.

"He took some drugs. He collapsed at college in the middle of an exam. Andy and Megan are with him now. Come on, I'll help you dress," she said as I swayed suddenly.

I couldn't think straight as Sally helped me locate my jeans, sweater, and boots which were strewn over the bedroom floor.

Jake was in hospital.

He had taken drugs.

My baby was in hospital.

He could die.

The journey to the hospital in Lancaster lasted an age and my nails were all but chewed off by the time we had found a parking spot. I would have been lost without Sally's calm presence as we hurried into the main entrance area and spoke to the nurse to find out where my son was.

Then it was down the maze of sterile corridors, each one exactly the same, passing people on their way in for visiting, some looking cheery and a few with glum expressions that spoke of the trauma within their lives. I caught sight of my own face in the reflection on a shiny metal door. The image was distorted but I looked like a ghoul, white faced and wide-eyed with terror.

We came at last to a side room at the end of a busy mixed ward. I had no idea what the other patients were in there for. I didn't see them. I saw nothing apart from Andy and Megan who were looking as awful as I was feeling. The bed in the room was empty and for a moment, a dark, gruesome second, I feared the worst.

"Oh God, tell me he's alright?" My knees buckled and I would have fallen if Sally had not propped me up.

Andy and Megan were inches apart a united front blocking me out.

"We don't know," said Andy in a voice that did not belong to him, but to a stranger. A man I had never met. "They've take him for a brain scan. He had a fit in college and two more since. He's sedated now, but they need to check if there is any danger of more seizures and what damage may have been done."

"Oh God, my beautiful boy!" I couldn't stop the tears from choking up my throat and spilling onto my cheeks.

"It's your fault!" Megan lashed out at me. "He wouldn't have taken it if it wasn't for you! You could have killed him!"

"Ssh. That isn't going to help," Andy pulled her close and stared hard at me over the top of her head. His blazing eyes told me he agreed with her though.

I staggered against Sally, unable to respond.

"What a dreadful thing to say!" Sally was fierce in her defence of me. "How could it be Eve's fault?"

"Because he's hardly been able to concentrate on anything since he realised what a slut we have for a mother," Megan glared at us both, her ferocity far outweighing Sally's. "His grades have gone right down at college and his exams have just started. He didn't want to let Dad down by not getting into university, so he took one of those stupid Whizz tablets. He must have thought that it would help

202

him get through his exam." Her voice was harsh and brittle. "So you see, Mum, it is your fault."

My knees did buckle then and I groped for a chair. Sally stood behind me, hand on my shoulder as I digested what my daughter had said. I could not argue with her apportioning the blame in that way. I could see how, when I had let him down so badly, that he would want to please his father, get the grades he needed to study further. And look where it had brought him.

Hospital.

Seizures.

Risk of brain damage.

I was too numb to think of anything to say. I could only sit there, shaking, as we waited for news. After an agony of time, the door to the private room opened. We all tensed, eyes eager to see Jake but saw instead his grandparents.

Fuck! The last thing I needed right now was Sandra and Steven Armstrong making matters worse. I looked at Andy who dismissed my glance with a tightening of his mouth. He greeted his parents as warmly as he could in the circumstances.

"Thanks for coming straight away."

So he had called them. I suppose they had a right to know. Especially if...No, do not think that Eve. Do not go down that impossibly dark and unforgiving road. He will be alright. He must be alright. Oh please God, whoever wants to listen, let him be alright! My thoughts rambled off wildly and I was deaf to the chatter going on around me, until Sally touched me gently on the shoulder.

"Do you want me to stay? Or shall I go now, seeing that they're here now as well?"

The room was pretty crowded and there was no way of knowing how long we would have to wait. We had been sitting for an hour already.

"You go," I told her. "I can get a taxi back."

"Are you sure? I don't want to leave you if you'd rather I stay."

"You're not family though are you?" Sandra addressed Sally as though she was something I had dragged in with me off the streets. "This is a family matter."

Normally I would have lashed out on Sally's behalf but I was too frozen with fear to act normally. "Thanks, Sally, but I'll be fine. I'll call you as soon as we hear."

"Ok. Take care." She gave me a reassuring smile and left.

As soon as the door was shut, the vitriol began to pour from Sandra's mouth. "What is *she* doing here? Hasn't she done enough damage already? I don't know how you can bear to be in the same room as her, I'm finding it hard enough to even stomach looking at her. How could you do such a thing?"

"You're a dirty, foul, disgusting creature and you should never have married my son. I knew you would be trouble, and look at you! Look at what you've done, you've all but killed your own son, I don't know how you can live with yourself! You should be locked up, you should be..." Her words, which had risen to screaming pitch ended with a dramatic sob as she turned to Andy and cried noisily on his shoulders.

I stared wildly at Megan hoping she would refute her grandmother's words. But she stood immobile, her lips not opening to defend me. The weight of their accusations and the terror that I might lose Jake was making it difficult to breath. I had to get out. I pushed myself up to my feet, legs heavy and sluggish and all but staggered to the door.

"Don't come back," snapped Steven as I passed him. "I don't want to see you in my son's life ever again, or my grandchildren's. If it takes every penny I've got, I'll make sure you suffer for this, Eve."

I pulled open the door and walked straight into the solid black mass that was the muscled chest of Sergeant Craig Hawthorne. The walls were thin. He must have heard everything.

"Sorry," I mumbled up at him, cheeks burning in shame once more.

He moved back a little but didn't step sideways so that I could not pass him. It was both unnerving and comforting at the same time.

"Any news?" He addressed us all equally, his voice level and concerned.

"We're still waiting," said Andy, stiffly.

"And we don't want *her* with us whilst we do!" Sandra screeched venomously. "That wicked little whore doesn't deserve to have a son like Jake, and she certainly doesn't deserve to have my son!"

"I insist she is thrown off the premises!" Steven squared up to Craig which was silly as no one could really do that effectively. He only managed to make himself look small and petty. "You should be arresting her, Officer, as she is mostly to blame for this. If Jake dies, I shall press charges for manslaughter."

The tight knot of emotions that had coiled in my belly since hearing the news suddenly unravelled. I clamped a hand to my mouth and making retching noises, pushed past Craig who sidestepped quickly and went to push open the door to the ladies toilets, which thankfully, were just opposite. With my head down the stainless steel bowl, I had no idea what Craig's response to my father-in-law would be. Neither did I care.

Jake could die.

Jake could die.

Jake could die.

I vomited until there was nothing more to bring up. And then my stomach continued to pull and twist and gripe, as fear induced bile spewed forth. I was shaking all over by the time it stopped. I went to wash my face with cold water and took some deep breaths to steady myself. As I crept into the corridor, like a criminal awaiting execution, I saw that the door to Jake's room was now shut, and Craig was standing guard outside it.

My eyes must have shown despair then because he smiled at me. Actually smiled! There was kindness and reassurance in that smile and I wobbled over to him uncertainly.

"Is he...?"

"He's okay. They brought him back a few minutes ago."

"Oh thank God, thank God," I leant against the door frame, my eyes closed against the tears of relief. "I would never have forgiven myself if...Oh God what a mess I've made of things." I wiped the tears away on the back of my sleeve, and squared my shoulders. "I've got to see him," I said as much to myself as to him. "They can't stop me can they?" My voice held a tremor. My defences were weak, the fight all but gone out of me.

"No," he said. "And for the record, your father-in-law could not have pressed any charges against you. Jake is an adult. He took the drug of his own volition. What may or may not have prompted him to do so does not alter that fact."

"Thank you."

"Would you like me to come in with you? I need to speak to Jake myself, if he can manage it."

I nodded mutely, aware that I was shaking inside.

"Wait here a moment," he held me back from pushing open the door and went through himself. I don't know what he said to them, but a second later, they all trooped out silently. Sandra was still sniffling noisily and Steven was making a fuss of her. Megan just shot me a dirty look that wounded me deeper and Andy completely ignored me.

I didn't care. Not at that moment. Jake was alive. That was all I could think about.

The last time I had seen my son he had been bruised and enraged. Now he was lying in a hospital bed, white and drawn. A nurse was adjusting a drip attached to his wrist. She did this and then made some notes on a chart at the end of his bed, before turning to smile at me.

"How is he?" I croaked, waiting for him to open his eyes.

"Very lucky," she said gently. "The doctor has explained to the others already."

"Mrs Armstrong was taken ill," interjected Craig smoothly, "perhaps you could kindly explain what has happened?" He gave her a smile and I saw that the nurse blushed. So he could charm if he wanted to.

"Of course," she said and then went into a clear, concise report of what Jake had suffered. She concluded by saying, "The brain scan shows there no sign of any damage from the seizures so he should make a full recovery. Just don't let him take whatever drug it was, again. It could have killed him."

"Thank you nurse," I smiled at her more grateful than she could ever know and went to approach the bed.

"He's sedated, but he might be able to talk a little. " Her eyes went to Craig's and again there was a hint of warmth in her cheeks as she spoke to him. "It might be better if you come back later if you need to question him."

Craig thanked her and just stood back whilst I went to stroke the brow of my son.

"Jake, can you hear me?"

His head moved a fraction and his eyelids flickered.

"Jake, it's me, your Mum. Oh Jake, I love you so much, you've got to know that. Get better son." I dropped a kiss on to his brow and gulped back my sobs.

Then, groggy under the influence of the medication, I heard him mumble the words I never thought I would hear again from his lips.

"Love you too."

Of course he was drugged. He would probably deny it when he awoke. Never the less, he had said it. I bit my lip to stop it from wobbling uncontrollably.

"I'll come back tomorrow," said Craig, opening the door for me. "Would you like a lift back home?"

"I can get a taxi," I said, not wanting to be too beholden to him.

"I'm going back to Maypoleton, you might as well save your money."

"This is getting to be a habit," I said five minutes later as he held open the door to his car. And then, perhaps because of the relief I felt over Jake, a stupid sense of giddiness over took me. "At least I've not wet myself this time," I grinned inanely.

I was surprised by his bark of laughter which he quickly suppressed. He said nothing as he negotiated the car park and followed the route to take us back onto the main A6. Then, his policeman's mind back on track, he asked me who I thought Jake might have got the drugs from.

"No idea," I answered, "But I'd like to get my hands on them. I can't believe Jake took it. After everything I've said to him." I stopped myself with a heavy sigh. "But there you go. There's your answer. Why should he put any value on what I've ever said? I destroyed everything he ever believed in? Megan's right, you know. It is my fault. All of it. You must think I'm a terrible mother."

"A little wayward perhaps."

My turn to laugh in surprise. "Wayward? Well that's one way of putting it. You knew didn't you, when you found me at Badger's Brock that I'd been with Tim, well, a man anyway, you didn't know who, but you knew what I'd been doing?"

He kept his eyes on the road, but I saw a tiny muscle at the corner of his mouth flicker. "I knew."

"Did I shock you?" Christ, girl, what are you doing? Stop picking at the scab like this! But I couldn't help myself. I needed to clear the air between us and the only way I could do that was to be open about what I had done.

"I'm not easily shocked."

I paused for a moment. "I'll try harder then."

He did turn his head then, just for a second, but his expression was unreadable. "Don't you ever stop? Your son has nearly killed himself and you're mischief making again!"

"Sorry." I tried to sound suitably chastised, "It's my way of coping. When things get rough, I get either mad or daft. Sometimes both." I continued to chatter stupidly. "I've been pretty well behaved since Megan was born. Quite a role model in fact, you'd be surprised. Went to church with them, brownies, cubs, all that nonsense, on the PTA at school, I didn't quite manage the WI, couldn't get the hang of singing Jerusalem all the time, helped out on school trips, that sort of thing. I even baked cakes for the summer fair, me baking cakes, that was an annual ordeal, let me tell you, well truth be told, they only asked me twice, then they put me on the tombola, thought it was safer. I don't suppose they will ask me to go on any stalls this year. I will probably be banned from turning up. Never mind."

"So what happened?" He slowed the car to pull off the A6 and take the turning to Maypoleton.

"I beg your pardon?"

"Well something must have happened to turn you from a paragon of motherly virtue into..."

"The village slut?" I sent him a crooked glance, daring him to meet my eyes. He did so for a second and heaven help me, I blushed at his gaze. I was the first to look away. That had not happened before.

"I was going to say someone who lived on the edge all of a sudden? Risk taking, reckless behaviour, it smacks of someone who's reacting against something. What happened, Eve?"

I squirmed a little. The confines of the police care were far too intimate. "Nothing," I said, clamping my mouth shut before I could do any more damage. "Nothing at all. Just hormones." Everyone else had believed that, so why not him?

"You're a very good liar, Eve, but you don't fool me." He gave me another quick, penetrating look as he turned into the village. "You're hiding something." Then changing the subject, he asked me where I wanted dropping.

On impulse, I asked him to take me home, to Cooper's Fold. Andy's hostile behaviour at the hospital had brought to mind something that Ellie had been nagging me about. Something I had kept ignoring because of Jem. I knew he would be staying with Jake a while longer, so this was my opportunity.

"I'll be in touch," he said as I got out of the car, "I'll let you know how my enquiries get along. In the meantime, let me know if you hear anything."

"Of course I will. And, thank you." It felt strange to be standing there on the driveway to my home as if I didn't belong there. Maybe I looked a little lost because he stuck his head out of the window and called me back over as I jingled my keys in my hand.

"One more thing, Eve."

"Yes?"

"Look after yourself. You're far too thin. You look like you've not had a proper meal in weeks."

CHAPTER TWENTY THREE

Did I look thin?

I stood in our porch and looked at myself in the full length mirror. I have to say he was right. I looked positively ghastly but then I had received an awful shock. Nevertheless, even allowing for the trauma of thinking my son could die, I didn't look good. My complexion was pale, my eyes had dark shadows underneath and in the light, sunny porch I could see that my clothes were virtually hanging off me.

How had that happened? I hadn't consciously been dieting. I never did. I loved my food. It was a constant source of irritation to Sally that I could devour chocolate on a daily basis and remain a neat but curvy size eight. It must be all that lovemaking with Jem, I thought, with a grin. And then frowned. I must eat more. Jem would soon stop fancying me if I continued to lose weight so drastically. No red blooded male wants to shag a bag of bones.

I could hear Skip barking frantically from the kitchen and scooping up the pile of mail that had gathered under the letter box, I went through to see my dog. It was an ecstatic reunion with hugs and slobbery kisses. I made a huge fuss of him and went to open a tin of dog food, even though he had probably already eaten. In fact, he looked as though he had gained the weight I had lost.

"They're not taking you for walks the same are they, the ratbags." I chattered to him as he gazed up at me adoringly. Standing in the kitchen, with my familiar things around me, it struck me that I had really missed my dog and my home, and yet it was odd how once I was in the cottage I barely gave any of them a thought.

"It's all Jem's fault," I told Skip. "He blinds me with his love, I forget about everything else. But I promise, Skip, as soon as things have settled down a little, I shall make damn sure you come and live with me. I suppose I could sneak you back home with me today, but that wouldn't be fair on Jake if he came home and you weren't here. God knows, Skip, I've done enough to that boy, I can't pinch you off him as well."

I finished fussing over Skip and then kicked my brain into gear. I had a lot to think about and I was horribly aware that over the last month I had let things slide shamelessly. Being with Jem was like being in a dream world, filled with love, laughter, passion and sex that made me oblivious to everything around me. But today had been a wake-up call.

It was time to get realistic about things. I had no idea where Jem lived, or even if he had any family. I didn't for that matter, know if he was married. I knew nothing about him. How could that possibly be? I had been sleeping with him for a month, sharing my body and my bed, not to mention opening up my heart and my soul to him, and I was totally in the dark as to who he really was. I must ask him, properly next time. But forgetting Jem for the moment, there was Andy to sort out.

Ellie had informed me that Andy was claiming a substantially lower financial status than I had been expecting. There was not as much money in the pot as I had thought. And even though she had slung back at Barty Briggins, the cannon load of Andy's hidden sexuality, his slimy lawyer was doing his best to make sure that I received as small a pay off as possible.

Bastard!

So I was going to take this chance to do a little snooping. Andy's accounts were all online and I had been without my lap top for the last month. I dashed upstairs to get it. Whilst I was at it my eyes fell onto my bedside table. Melody Farthing's diary! I snatched that up as well. Then, thinking I might as well be hung for a sheep as well as a lamb, I went into Andy's office, to snoop some more.

I'm not sure quite what I was looking for, other than to maybe get my hands on some of his correspondence from Briggins on the off chance that I might steal a march on the pair of them. As Ellie kept reminding me, all's fair in love and war and we were now at the latter of the two stages.

Andy was meticulously tidy and it was easy to see that there were no letters here from his solicitor. Perhaps they relied on email. Not to be deterred I did a thorough search of his desk, finding an invitation from Bryony to attend a black tie affair. She had scribbled across it that she had a friend she was hoping to introduce to him. Screw you, I thought, tossing the invite aside. I was about to slam the drawer shut and then I realised that something was sticking.

I didn't want Andy to know I had been here so I tugged at the drawer to see why it wouldn't shut properly. Bending my head to look, I saw that there was an envelope, a bundle of them in fact, taped to the top side of the drawer. The edge of one was poking down, stopping the drawer from closing.

Intrigued, I pulled the drawer right out so that I could carefully unpeel the envelopes. There were three in total. All the same. Plain brown, posted locally, addressed to Andy.

I pulled out a single sheet of white paper from the first one.

FIVE THOUSAND POUNDS
WILLIAM TOMLINSONS GRAVE
ELEVEN O' CLOCK SATURDAY

What the bloody hell was all this about? I read it twice over and then ripped open the other envelope, checking the date on the post mark. I had opened them in the wrong order. The first one read like this.

I KNOW YOUR DIRTY SECRET
PAY UP OR I TELL
START COUNTING YOUR MONEY

I read the brief notes again and again until I could be sure they meant what they said. Someone had discovered about Andy and Jason, and was blackmailing him in order to stay quiet about it. I checked the dates on the post marks again. It had been going on since December of last year.

Bloody hell! That meant he had been paying up to keep his secret quiet, even before he had told me. I presumed he had paid up because so far it was still a secret. I don't know what made me angrier. The fact that someone was daring to blackmail him. The fact that he was stupid enough to pay them. Or the fact that he hadn't told me. Either way I was totally pissed off. Twenty thousand pounds since December. No wonder he was claiming poverty to Briggins. Stupid bloody idiot! And then I got even madder. This was half my money as well.

I thought quickly, checking the date of the most recent letter. Whoever this little creep was, he wanted five thousand pounds in a few days. Same time, same place, eleven o'clock, William Tomlinson's grave.

What was I going to do? An image of Craig jumped into my mind. I instantly discounted that idea. Going to the police would mean that everything would come out into the open. Whilst frankly I now didn't give a damn about Andy's feelings, Jake was in too fragile a state to even consider that. I would have to sort this out myself.

Question was, how?

I put everything back in order, having made a copy of the notes including the dates they were sent, and then gathered up my lap top and Melody's diary. I felt regretful about leaving Skip once more, but he would have to wait for now.

"Another time, Skip," I planted a kiss on my dog's nose and then hurried out of the house, my mind spinning in backwards circles.

I was wearing my ordinary boots so I couldn't cut across the fields to the Lodge and headed out of the cul-de-sac to the lane. Across the way I saw Seth running to the gate, his arms waving at me. Of course, he would have heard by now about Jake. I dampened down my impatience at the need to get back and sort out this latest disaster, and gave him a wide smile.

"He's fine. He's going to be alright. They're keeping him in for a couple of days but he won't have any after effects, thank goodness."

Seth hugged me and rambled off a string of words in his Romany tongue. Then he tugged at my arm and said, "Thee must come an' meet t'kin."

It was then that I realised the field was further occupied. I remembered him asking me if his relatives could stay a while. I really did not feel like socialising but there was something about Seth's manner that made me follow him. Next to his old traditional van there was now parked a modern towing van with a pick- up truck and a surprisingly smart looking motor home. There was a row of washing hanging up between two poles and, I suddenly realised, a couple of young children staring up at me. Red haired and green eyed, full of freckles and obviously twins.

"They'm be Micky and Molly, my great nephew and niece," announced Seth, proudly. "And this 'ere is Caitlin, their Ma."

"Hi there." A bonny woman, maybe a few years younger than me, smiled warmly It was obvious where the twins had got their colouring from. "So you must be Eve, Seth's told us all about you. 'Tis grand of you to let him stay here, and us for that matter." Her voice was softly Irish, but not, I thought of Romany origin. "You'll be staying for some supper? You look as though you could do with a square meal."

I found myself settling down by the fire, a mug of tea in my hand and two children around my feet, as Caitlin started chopping vegetables onto a board she steadied on her knees. Her movements were light and quick, as were her words as she spoke. I was lulled into relaxing, despite the whirlwind of emotions the day had wrought, as I listened to her telling me how she had come to be part of Seth's family.

"'Twas love at first sight when I met his nephew Benjy," she said with a sigh and then a giggle. "Or maybe lust, to be perfectly honest, you know how it can be at times?" She titled her head at me. "Aye, I can see that you do. I had a hard time of it at first. My folk were up in arms that I should want to marry a traveller, his folk thought I wasn't good enough for him. There was a real to do. But when his fair packed up to leave our village, I was going with him and that was that!"

"So you left your home to be with him?" I liked the romance of the idea. It was passionate and determined.

"I did. And I've never looked back since. Oh I know I gave up a lot, but then I gained more than I lost. Far more. See, here he comes now. That's my Benjy, the big man, and our eldest two, Shaunie and Bella. You can see they have their father's colouring." Indeed I could. Two good looking youngsters came out of the woods with a man who was drop dead gorgeous in a dark, piratical way. I could understand how Caitlin had fallen for him. There was also another, younger man, more slightly built with colouring of a lighter hue, brown and tawny like a deer.

"That's Jojo, my brother-in-law."

I was greeted as warmly by them as I had been by Caitlin and found that the next couple of hours slipped away far too easily as I shared their supper. Their banter was lively and fast and a lot of it went over my head as they chattered in a mixture of English and Romany, but they treated me as though I was a life- long friend. It was about seven o clock and the spring light was beginning to fade when I finally made a move to go. I still had to walk back to the Lodge

"I'd better be getting back." I said, reluctantly. I could happily have spent the night there, especially as Jojo and Shaunie had struck up on a fiddle and drum. My foot was tapping straight away and I saw a light spark in Benjy's eye.

"You like the music?"

"I do. I used to sing in a band, and now my son plays guitar."

"A family trait then," he said with a broad smile. "Stay a while longer and sing with us?"

"No, really. I have things I must do."

"Problems?"

I nodded, not wanting to be drawn into discussing my catastrophic state of affairs, however likable he may be.

"You can always rely on us, you know," he said, with a serious look on his face now. "You're family after all."

"Family?"

"Sure you are. Anyone who helps one of us is family. You looked after Seth, you took him into your own home, fed him and gave him shelter. Aye, lass, that makes you family."

"Whether you want it or not," added Jojo with a grin. I had quickly learnt he was the joker in the pack, a little like Jake. A lot like Jake in fact or how I imagined my son might be in another few years' time.

"I'm serious, lass," said Benjy as I gathered my things, "If you need help, you only have to ask."

I gave a half laugh. "I'll bear that in mind. Thank you for a lovely evening."

"You let us know how the boy is." Seth asked me as he walked to the gate with me. "Keep in touch, Eve, I've hardly seen you since... you know."

"Since I disgraced myself and wrecked my family," I said for him. "I know. I've become a recluse. I should stop hiding away."

He touched me lightly under my chin and raised my face up to look deep into my eyes. He was frowning when he let me go. "You mind yourself now, lass. The shadows are drawing in around you."

I thought of Jake lying in hospital and the copies of the blackmailer's notes in my pockets. He wasn't wrong there. "Don't worry, Seth, it's nothing I can't handle."

And with that assurance, so blithely given, I trudged down the lane to the Lodge. It was the first time I had called at the house since my 'trip away' and I hoped that Mary would not be around. It still stung me that she had turned her back upon what I had thought had been a growing friendship. I was out of luck. It was Mary herself who opened the kitchen door.

"What do you want?"

"Is Sally about?"

"Obviously not or I wouldn't be opening the door would I?"

"Look, Mary, I know you don't approve of what I did, but I'm paying for it, believe me, now can I see Sally or is she actually out?"

"I'm here," said my friend bustling into the kitchen swathed in a large fluffy bath robe with an alarming bright pink shiny mask on her face. "Pamper night, long overdue. Let me go and wash this muck off and we can talk. Go on through, Eve," she ignored the frosty glances from Mary and bundled me into the hallway. "Help yourself to a drink."

She wasn't long, returning all rosy faced and glowing. "You should do something like that, Eve. You're looking far too pale at the moment."

"So everyone keeps telling me."

"You're not anaemic are you?"

"No. There's nothing wrong with me, apart from a totally fucked up domestic life. But thank God Jake's going to be okay."

Sally shuddered. "I was so relieved when you sent me that text. God it must have been awful for you waiting to find out. How were things at the hospital after I left?"

I groaned and filled her in on my in-laws accusations. "I was actually glad to have Craig there you know. Never thought I would say that, but I was."

"I've always thought he was lovely. I never understood what you had against him."

"Nothing, apart from a guilty conscience." I yawned, suddenly shattered by the long and eventful day. It was only eight o clock in the evening but I was ready to sleep and sleep and sleep. "I'm sorry Sally. I can't keep my eyes open. I'll see myself out. I'll dodge Mary on the way. I was hoping she would have forgiven me by now, but it doesn't seem like it."

"Never mind her. You need to look after yourself. Get eating some more, start holding your head up high again and get back out into the world. What you need, is a new man in your life. One your own age this time, girl." She smiled to soften the jibe. "Leave it with me."

I shook my head and smiled. "No Sally. I really don't need anyone else."

"But you can't stay single forever you know and once the divorce comes through, you'll be free to look."

I tried to stop my mouth from smiling more, but I couldn't. I had no need to look and Sally realised that.

"Oh my God! You've got someone already haven't you? Sit back down, my girl, and give me all the details, I don't care how tired you are, you aren't leaving until I know."

I snook past her to the door, grinning impishly. "You know him already. He's your gardener, the one you hired to clear the grounds."

"Oh? Oh!" She looked at me strangely. "Well," she said slowly. "I suppose that makes a change from Tim. If he makes you happy?"

"Sally I've never been so happy. When I'm with him, I forget everything else. It's like the sun comes out when he walks into the room and the clouds appear when he goes away."

"Well, he's not eighteen, and he's not married, so who am I to comment. I must admit though, Eve, you do have a varied choice in men!"

CHAPTER TWENTY FOUR

I wandered through the grounds from the Lodge to the cottage, enjoying the mildness of the evening air, thoughts full of Jem. I really was going to have to put things on a firmer footing with him. It was all very well locking ourselves away for hours on end, as we greedily devoured each other but we could not continue like this. Most couples had a honeymoon period and we certainly had indulged in ours.

But today's shocks had hit hard. My son was recovering from what could have been a fatal drug dosage and my husband was being blackmailed. Not your average family drama. So in all fairness, I really thought it was time I climbed back into the saddle of reality and faced up to some of my responsibilities.

I would speak with Jem next time I saw him and tell him that I needed to sort things and then move on with the divorce. After all I had no reason to hold back on that now and I wanted to be free to... Oh my God, was I really thinking of marrying Jem? A vision of myself in a long floaty white dress appeared in my mind, which was odd because I had never been the long floaty white dress kind of girl. That's what Jem did to me. Reached inside my soul and brought out another person entirely.

I must have had a goofy smile on my face as I walked up the path to the cottage because I was certainly feeling stupidly mushy inside. Like a teenager again. That what's that Jem did to me. Imagine my shock then, when I opened the cottage door, to find him waiting for me, a look of dark thunder on his face. A different Jem. A brooding, scary looking Jem.

"Where have you been? I've been waiting for you all this time."

"Jem?" My feet were rooted to the floor at the expression on his face. His magical eyes glittered with a fury that frightened me.

"I had to go out. My son is in hospital, Jake, I told you about him." At least I think I had. It was hard to be sure what I had said to Jem and what I had left out. We hardly talked at all come to think about it. We had no need for words.

His body coiled tight like a whip. "You should not go out. Your place is here with me."

"Jem, please, I'm sorry if you were waiting long. I still don't have your phone number. You keep forgetting to give it to me, how silly is that? And then when I went home, I found these letters addressed to Andy."

His face darkened further and the room seemed icy cold. I found the words were tumbling from my lips in a hurry to placate him.

"He's being blackmailed, Jem, and I have to stop it. It's been such a crazy day. I met Seth's family, Benjy and Jojo, and they said that they would help me out if I needed anything, which is kind, don't you think, seeing I only met them today." I was gabbling, something I never did. My torrent of words came to an abrupt end.

"No!" He stormed and reached for me, hands gripping my wrists and pulling me up close. His strength had always surprised me, and now there was a flicker of fear reaching out from the depths of my belly. "You must not be with other folk, I cannot allow it."

"Jem, this is ridiculous! I was speaking to Sally about us. We can't hide away here forever."

"We must, you don't understand!"

Beneath the rage was an anguish that frightened me even more. What on earth was wrong with him?

"Tell me then!" I snatched my hands away, the emotions of the day just too much. I was in no mood for histrionics from the one person I had thought I could let myself be at peace with. "You never talk about yourself, you never say anything, why is that?"

"There is nothing to say, my love. We are meant to be together, now and for always." Some of the darkness had gone out of his eyes and I began to breathe a little easier as he took hold of me once more, this time with that familiar gentleness in his touch that soothed and enticed. His fingers stroked the curves of my face, his eyes probed into mine. I felt the dizzying warm glow begin low in my body, spreading up and outwards. His kiss when it came was long, hungry and hard, a mild rebuke for making him angry.

I groaned and clutched at his chest, my hands reaching around to his back as he tilted me over so that he could deepen the kiss. Was it possible that each time was better than the last? It felt like it. As his tongue searched every crevice of my mouth, his hands began to explore my body with an urgency that told me we would soon be naked and tangled on the floor.

"You are mine," he said with a warning bite at the nape of my neck, "Mine and no other. I have waited too long for you, I will not share you." His hands were already pulling my sweater up my body, but for once, I stopped him.

"No, Jem, listen to me," It was hard to stop him. Like pulling back from the strongest magnetic force or trying to stop oneself being sucked into the centre of a hurricane. I knew that if I didn't break the spell now, all would be lost. I had to stop losing myself in this whirlwind of passion, however hard it was.

"It might be better if I didn't see you for a few days," I struggled to get the words out. I felt as though I was tearing my soul in two and yet all I was really suggesting was that I had a bit more time to myself to deal with my family issues. But as I went on to try and explain this further to Jem, his mood darkened once more.

"They're my family, Jem! He's my son. I must do what I can to help mend what I have broken!" For a little while at least, I had to put Jake first and told him so.

Jem's reaction stunned me. My tender, smiling lover became a storm of dark emotions and actions. The temperature in the cottage dropped to icy cold as his fury unleashed itself upon me. Books were swiped off shelves, the vase of flowers hurled across the room where it smashed against the wall, dripping water onto the carpet. The fire in the grate, which he must have lit, blew out in a second, and a wind seemed to rattle right through the window panes and whip up the curtains that hung over them.

I blinked in terror and disbelief. This was not Jem. This was a monster, out of control. I was not afraid of a good old scrap with anyone, I'd had enough of those in my days at the care home, but I had never faced anyone with such wild energy reverberating from them. Almost, I thought in a daze, as he stalked towards me, almost not human.

And then I stopped thinking as his hands reached for me, eyes blazing into mine, hypnotic and intense. As pathetic as a heroine from an old black and white movie, I was swept up off my feet, held in a vice like grip and carried upstairs to the bedroom. The door slammed shut of its own volition. The bed creaked under our weight as he tossed me down upon the covers.

"Jem, don't, you're frightening me," I gasped as he quickly, savagely, undressed me, his strength so much more than my own, his moves so much faster, unstoppable. There was passion and heat in his eyes and it should have aroused me. But it didn't. It scared the life out of me. He was taking me to a place I had no wish to visit and I struggled against him.

"Do not fight me," he hissed, as he pinned me beneath him, his own body now naked, hard and ready. "You are mine, I shall not share you. I have waited too long."

"Jem don't," I sobbed, hating the way this was turning out. My body was trembling, but with cold and not desire. My skin was covered in goose bumps and my hair was standing on end. "This isn't how it should be!"

"You're right," he said, locking my hands above my head with just one of his own, so strong and agile, making me a prisoner so easily. He kissed me again and I felt the sharpness of his teeth against my lips. His other hand began to stroke my breasts, quick and light, and then dipped lower, down over my belly and between my thighs. He lifted his face to look once more into my eyes and I saw the expression change as his fingers coaxed heat and life into my blood as despite myself I began to move against him, with him, opening myself up to him. A shameless motion I could not control.

His smile melted me more and I was soon begging for him to enter me. But he didn't, he removed his hand, let go of my arms, and then brought both of his hands up to my throat. He propped himself up on his elbows, cradling my neck between his hands, thumbs at the base of the front and his fingers round the back, pressing onto the bones that ran up to my skull. It was disturbingly erotic as he applied a pressure that made me gasp and brought a sardonic smile to his lips.

"Jem."

"Hush, my love." He stopped my words with a kiss, a deep, shattering invasion of my mouth that was in time with his possession of my body. He moved above me, plunging into my depths and drinking from mouth as though from the fountain of life itself. And all the while, his hands around my neck.

Always pressing.

Not too much.

But enough.

Enough to terrify me, as darkness threatened and a roaring dizziness hurtled towards me, even as I heard my moans of tortured pleasure, coming from very far away. His thrusts were more powerful now, harder than they had ever been and I felt as though I were a rag doll, boneless beneath him, limp with dark desire and faint with fear.

I felt his weight collapse upon me, the pressure of his hands ease, the breath come back into my lungs. A softness now, a loving tenderness that moved me to tears. He began his lovemaking all over again. Soothed the bruises at my throat, nuzzled at my breasts, sore from his bites, moved lower to part my thighs and plant kisses on the flesh that had just been battered by his own. His tongue teased where he had just withdrawn from and this time the assault was one of loving devotion.

No less unmerciful. He gave no quarter, his mouth eager to lap up my wetness and create even more, teeth grating slightly, lips brushing gently and tongue ever probing. I cried as I came that time, tears of bewildered ecstasy sliding down my face. Tears which he wiped away with a loving finger, as his mouth moved to cover my lips now and his body came within my own once more.

It didn't stop.

An endless, timeless dance as his hips moved with mine, a perfect partnership this time. His hands were under my bottom, lifting me up to meet the pace he was setting, moulding my flesh deeper and deeper into his own. His mouth never lifted from mine until once more I was breathless and faint.

If you could die from pleasure, then my death came countless times that night. He took me again, and again, with hardly a pause between times. Gently. Savagely. Sensually. Darkly. All those ways and more. Each time I climaxed I felt myself grow weaker and weaker, less able to resist his insistent advances until the night turned into a dizzying abyss of lust and love.

I was groggy when I woke. No surprise there. Dry mouthed and with wobbling legs, I crawled out of bed, finding myself once more alone. I groaned and held my head in my hands. I had done it again! Got completely distracted by his lovemaking to the extent of blotting out everything else. We had resolved nothing!

"You have got to get a grip, girl," I addressed myself in the mirror, but found the image of Melody Farthing staring back at myself instead. She was smiling and it seemed to me that there was a knowing glint in her eye that had not been there before. "I bet you didn't get into such a state over a man did you?" I said to her, and watched as she began to laugh. Only this time, it was not the joyous, carefree laughter I had heard before. It was mocking and sly and for some reason I had shivers running down my spine at the sound. "Oh go away," I snapped and she did so, leaving me to face my own reflection.

"Shit!" I stared hard at the mirror. I looked like hell. My elfin chin was looking so sharp you could cut paper with it and my cheek bones were angular in what had once been a round face. My hair was in need of a good wash, it hung limp around my skull and my skin was pasty and dull. Sally had been right, I was in need of a good pamper session. Then I saw the bruises.

"Bloody hell!" Finger marks were clear around my throat. The memory of Jem's lovemaking came back to me and for once I was not filled with a warm rosy glow. A sense of unease crept into my consciousness and Seth's warnings came back to me, loud and clear. For the first time I had a desire to leave the cottage.

I made up my mind. I would wash my hair, have some breakfast, and then call in at Sally's before ringing the hospital to see Jake. Then I would spend the rest of the day out. I had no idea where, but it suddenly felt claustrophobic in that tiny bedroom. I was on edge as I bathed and dressed and I put it down to the lack of sleep. Jem's passion had been worthy of a marathon and I felt absolutely shattered.

So much so, that I jumped when I heard the thudding footsteps on the stairs.

223

"Jem, is that you?" I rushed to the door, but there was no one there.

And then came the creaking. A heavy, wooden sound. As though the very beam that ran across the ceiling was bowing under some weight. I paused, with my hand on my door, ears straining to make more sense of the sound, eyes struggling to focus on what was taking shape before me. A swinging figure, dark and shadowy, but a man of that there was no doubt. Neck crooked and broken as the head lolled from the noose that was looped around the beam.

"No!" I blinked and the image cleared. "I'm going mad! Too much sex and not enough sleep."

I kept this thought firmly in my head as I went downstairs to make some toast. I opened the bread bin to find half a loaf, disgustingly mouldy. How long had that been like that? Pulling a face, I dropped it into the bin and looked to see if I had another one in the freezer. No such luck. None with the milk either, as that was blatantly past its sell by date. I puzzled over this as I poured the stinking contents of the bottle down the drain.

It should not have been off. It was within the date, just about. Deciding that I would be better off having breakfast at Sally's I fetched my coat and set off across the estate. I no longer cared that the yard staff knew I was staying at the cottage. It was weeks since the fall out over Tim and frankly I didn't give a damn what anyone thought anymore.

Some of the girls still ignored me, or turned their backs but a few at least said hello although even they had a distracted air about them. Jenny caught sight of me and called me over. She looked tired and frazzled, not at all her usual calm self.

"Eve! What a bloody awful few days. Jaspar's got a bad eye infection which might result in him losing it, Pips gone to colic and Bracken died in his sleep. I've just made arrangements for him to be moved from your field. Where have you been? Oh, sorry, I forgot for a moment about Jake, of course you've had other things to worry about. Sorry. It hits you when you see someone like Seth lose an old friend like that and the girls here have been less than useless since we lost Pip, you know he was their favourite."

I stood there like an idiot.

How had all this happened over night? And then I thought of Seth. "He must be devastated," I said sadly.

"I think he knew," replied Jenny. "Said his time was coming. Still, a hell of a thing to lose a horse that age when you've foaled him yourself. And what about Jake? How's he doing?"

"I'm going to see him at the hospital later."

Jenny stared at me. "But he came home Tuesday afternoon, Sally told me. She said she was going to visit, but to be honest we've been run off our feet with Jaspar and Pip I don't think she's had chance. Are you alright?"

I felt the yard begin to spin around me and reached out a hand for Jenny to prop me up. "What day is it Jenny?"

"What day is it?"

I nodded at her, a sick feeling running through my gut.

"Thursday."

"Thursday?"

"Yeah, look, why don't you sit down a second, you look as though you're going to..."

I was and I did. The faint didn't last long and Jenny had caught me in her strong arms before I crashed to the floor. One of the girls had brought me a glass of water and a couple of biscuits that Jenny insisted I ate before I got moving.

"Have you been ill, Eve? You look dreadful."

I couldn't reply for a moment. My head was trying to work it out. It was Thursday. Jake had been rushed into hospital on Monday. What the hell had happened to Tuesday and Wednesday? I had no idea. I began to feel very cold, but managed at least to reassure Jenny that I was ok.

"Had a bit of a bug," I lied. "Not eaten much this last couple of days."

"Thought you'd lost weight. Are you sure you're alright now?"

"I'm fine. I'm really sorry about Pip, and I must go and see Seth first. Tell Sally I'll speak to her later will you?"

I debated whether or not to go back to the cottage and get my car. It was only a short distance down the road to my house and the field, Seth's field as I thought of it now, but I felt horrendous. I wasn't so sure that I was fit to drive either. I decided to risk my wobbly legs. At least if I tumbled into a hedge, I would only harm myself.

I walked out of the yard and down the road, pulling my coat tight around me. It was a lovely April morning that could have passed for a summer's day easily. Yet I couldn't get warm and my hands were like ice as I kept them firmly in my pockets. How had I lost two days? I was aware that over the last month or so time seemed to have slipped through my hands like sand but I had never been quite so blanked out that I couldn't remember a damn thing!

I searched inside my mind until I my head began to ache but the last memory I could get hold of, was of Jem making love to me. I had not imagined that, I thought, conscious of the bruises I had hidden with a scarf. So what the hell had happened in the mean time? I was biting my lip over this quandary when a car virtually drove me into a hedge, the large alloyed wheels churning up mud and splattering my clothes.

"What the bloody hell are you trying to do? Kill me?" I yelled at the driver, before I could even regain my balance to have a good look at them. "Fucking hell, Bryony, have you gone mad?"

It looked as though she had. The usually glossy Bryony was looking rather less than her perfect self. She was still made up to the nines, but there was a harshness about her face that seemed to bring out all the lines she worked so hard to cover up.

"It's all your fault!" She screeched at me from the driver's window. "You've ruined everything!"

"What?" I thought rapidly. Had I been shagging anyone else that I had forgotten about? In my present state of mind, anything seemed possible. Had the last two days been spent in a wild orgy with her husband Carl? Ooh, gross thought!

"Don't tell me you don't know?" She swore when I returned her hostile stare with one of dumb blankness. "Your son has dropped Ricky right in it! He's ruined his chances of going to university now."

Still looking like a goldfish, I shrugged my shoulders which increased her rage.

"Fucking hell, Eve, how can you be so gormless? Jake told the police that my son had given him the drugs, you do remember your son being in hospital don't you?"

Given my memory loss of the last two days that was a fair point, not that she would know that. I found my backbone straightening and my voice was chilled as I replied.

"Ricky is the one pushing drugs round college? Both Maisie and Jake nearly died, he could have killed them!"

"Jake is lying obviously," snarled back Bryony. "My son would never have done something like that."

"Well that's obviously for the police to decide isn't it? Anyway, how is all of this my fault?"

"If you hadn't screwed up your family so badly, Jake would never have needed to try the drugs and he would not have been put in the situation of making a friend a scapegoat to save his own skin. Jake's back at college and my son is under investigation and it's all your fault! You disgust me, Eve, you really do!"

With another mud splattering churning of her tyres, she screeched away.

CHAPTER TWENTY FIVE

As Jake was obviously fit and well enough to be back at college, and I saw no reason for Bryony to lie to me about this, there was no point in me calling in at the house. Unless there had been another note from the blackmailer? It was worth a look. I checked my watch and seeing that it was nearly eleven there would be little chance of anyone being at home. I would check Andy's drawer and then call in to see how Seth was doing. I felt guilty that I had missed the death of his horse entirely.

My feet were not exactly moving fast that morning but they came to a full stop as soon as I turned the corner in to Cooper's Fold. Newly erected at the end of the drive way of Cooper's Barn, number three, Cooper's Fold, was a brightly coloured For Sale sign. I stood there and blinked a couple of times before I was able to make use of my feet once more.

"The bloody bastard!" I said to myself as I walked to the end of my drive. I had it in mind to pull the damn sign down, but after a half- hearted attempt, realised it was well and truly planted into the ground. To continue tugging away would only prove futile and provide more delicious gossip for Deidre across the road, who was already waving to me like an old friend.

"Fuck off, fuck off, fuck off," I said under my breath as she scuttled over before I could shoot up the driveway and into my house. I was fumbling with my keys and thought for a horrible moment that the locks had been changed as well. But it was only the shakiness of my hands letting me down.

"Going to build himself a nice new house on the field," she announced with a similar smile to that of Bryony's. The sort of smile only women can manage when they know another of their sex is in a mess that they could never dream of getting into.

Was he indeed? I could see the beginnings of a long and bloody battle ahead. Bring it the fuck on! My hand itched to ring Ellie and give her the latest info. And then Deidre mentioned Jake and the red haze of rage receded from my vision somewhat. Stay focused, Eve.

"It's nice to see your lad up and about again. Such a shock to hear him using drugs though, never had him down for the type. Now that other lad you know, the one with the motor bike, I could see him being a druggie, you know the one I mean, don't you, Eve?"

Such a sly look on her face that positively demanded I slap it off. If she had been the same age as me I would have done. But even I drew the line at whacking a pensioner. Just!

"Deidre, fuck off." I had the satisfaction of hearing her breath suck in rapidly before I turned the key in the lock and pushed open the door to find Skip loyally waiting to greet me. I fussed over him and then went to check if Andy had received any more notes. He hadn't, which meant that nothing had changed. This coming Saturday he would be depositing five thousand pounds at William Tomlinson's grave for a greedy, interfering blackmailer.

Half of that money was mine. The fury that this thought brought to my mind also lent me clarity. I barked out a wicked laugh. Oh really, it was actually very simple. But I did have to practical. I was five foot five, slight of build and although I was fit and strong, I was certainly going to need some help.

Someone who might enjoy a bit of a scrap. Someone who looked like they could handle themselves and not be too concerned if they were tip toeing the other side of the line, when it came to law and order. Who on earth in Maypoleton could fit the bill? I was hitting a brick wall with the idea when all of a sudden it came to me. He might say no, but it was worth a try. I made another big fuss of Skip and left my house, kicking the for sale sign as I went. I was just crossing the road to the field, when I saw the lorry pulling out of the gateway.

Hell! Poor Seth. I couldn't imagine how awful he would be feeling having his horse carted away. Maybe this was not the time to pester people about my own concerns. But Benjy himself was at the gate, guiding the lorry driver onto the road and keeping an eye out for traffic coming round the sharp bend. He saw me and waved and I reminded myself I must go and speak to Seth anyway.

"I was so sorry to hear about Bracken," I said, as the lorry driver negotiated the turn skilfully. I would have demolished half the hedge by now. "How is Seth taking it?"

Benjy shrugged. "Pretends it don't matter none, but it's ripped 'im up summat hard. 'Es in 'is van if you wants to speak to 'im."

I judged from his tone that it would be best if I didn't. "No," I said, shaking my head. "But please tell him I was asking after him and if there's anything I can do?"

Benjy smiled and his coal dark eyes lit up. "You've already done it lass. Said before, you give 'im your 'ospitality and t'old 'orse chance to end 'is days in a grand old place. What more could you give? 'Tis us wot needs to give summat back now. Fairs fair." He leant on the gate, and regarded me solemnly. I thoroughly understood how Caitlin had fallen for this man and run off with him. Not only was he hugely attractive, he had a warmth about him and a sense of strength that could be relied upon.

Would I be trespassing too far on his generosity in what I was about to ask him? He must have sensed my hesitation because he stepped back from the open gate and put a hand on my arm.

"Come on, lass. Caitlin'll have a pot 'o tea on. Everythin's allus better wi' a pot o'tea."

His wife did indeed have a pot of tea on the go. She asked me if I would rather sit inside their van but warned me that Shaunie and Bella were trying to do some school work and would jump at the chance of being distracted.

"Outside's fine," I said, not wishing to disturb the two teenagers. The twins were playing around the van with an assortment of balls and hoops. I spent a few minutes with them as Caitlin made the tea and then sat on one of the stools, wondering how to begin.

"Spit it out lass," said Benjy with a grin. "I can see you meitherin' over summat."

"I certainly am." I took the hot mug of tea off Caitlin who made a comment about checking on the kids but I asked her to stay and listen. It didn't seem right to be asking her husband to do something without her knowing about it.

"I have a problem that needs fixing."

Benjy grinned some more. "I'm good at fixin' problems." He linked his fingers together and cracked his knuckles. I saw Caitlin send him a look of tolerant affection.

"It would mean bending the law slightly."

His grin deepened.

I looked at Caitlin anxiously. "No, forget it, I shouldn't be asking. I've no right, I'm sorry."

Caitlin was firm when she spoke. "Why don't you tell us what the problem is, Eve, and let us decide what's right and what's wrong."

"Okay. It sounds crazy, but my husband, Andy, is being blackmailed. He hasn't done anything wrong. But someone has found out something about him, which he has always kept secret, and they want money off him for keeping quiet. Andy stupidly has been paying them off. A lot of money. I could go to the police but then everything will come out and Megan and Jake have been through too much recently. Besides, Andy's been treating me like shit and I owe him one as well. I want to get my hands on the money he's given away."

"Fair enough, lass. So what's the plan?" Benjy asked after receiving a brief nod from Caitlin.

"No," she then said, holding up a hand. "Best if I don't know. Can't tell anyone then can I?" She smiled at me briefly and went inside the van.

"I don't want this to cause problems between you?"

"Caitlin understands she has to let me make my own choices," he said. "Besides..."And then he stopped himself and obviously changed what he was going to say. "So, what do you want me t'do?"

I told him what I had in mind and it must have appealed to him because he suddenly burst out laughing and held his hand out to me.

"Aye, lass. You'll do for me." We shook on it then and began to plot. His younger brother Jojo joined us a short while later and said that it wouldn't be a problem and Bessie would help out.

"Bessie?" I wondered if I had missed something here.

Jojo grinned and nodded over to the corner of the field where an old, bright yellow VW camper van was parked up, virtually out of sight behind Benjy's much large, plusher, motor home.

I eyed the VW suspiciously. It had definitely seen better days. "I'm with you on the whole thing, Jojo, but is that thing really up to it?" I had visions of breaking down yards from the church grounds.

"Fret not lass, old Bessie'll see off any competition."

"My little brother has a way wi' t'mechanics," agreed Benjy with an affectionate cuff around Jojo's ears. "Almost as good as 'is way wi' women."

We chatted a while longer until I felt I could no longer reasonably delay my departure. Even though I had only just met Benjy and JoJo, I trusted them completely. I felt safe with them and as I got up to leave, it hit me that I no longer felt safe about anything else.

My pace was slow as I made my way back to the Lodge. I still had not come to terms with how I had managed to lose two days of my life. All morning I had been waiting for the cogs in my brain to start turning and put into motion the events since Monday afternoon. But nothing came to me. I had hidden my bruises with a scarf but I knew I was looking terrible and it was an effort to struggle against the exhaustion that was threatening to claim me.

For the first time since moving in to the cottage, I was reluctant to step back over the threshold. Part of me wanted to climb up the stairs and fall into bed. To go to sleep and never wake up again. To lose myself forever in the oblivion of Jem's lovemaking. To crash over the edge of reality and immerse myself in a fantasy that would never end. I steadied myself against the lintel of the front door, a wave of nausea sweeping over me, chills running over my body.

"Jem?" I called out, anxious suddenly that my lover had let himself in again.

There was no answer and I felt a surge of relief. My legs had gone shaky on me and I needed to sit down. The thoughts swirling round my mind were beginning to frighten me. A tiny, miniscule, fragment of a doubt, needle sharp and piercing my brain with devastating accuracy.

Was I going insane?

Was I imagining Jem?

Was this rosy hued love affair all just a bizarre fantasy, created by my mixed up mind?

I put my hand gingerly to my throat. If that was the case, then how would I have the bruises? Jem had to be real. I pushed up from the chair and went upstairs to the bedroom. I had loved it in here when I first moved in, yet now, all I could see in my mind, was the shadowy figure of a man hanging from a noose, and my lover in a rage with his hands around my neck.

I felt the darkness then and knew that I had to get out. I was too tired to think straight and I couldn't afford to fall asleep here and lose any more time that I could not remember. Acting on impulse, I gathered together a change of clothes and some toiletries and flung them in a bag, then at the last minute picked up Melody Farthing's diary. I still had not got round to reading that and I knew it held the key to what had happened here.

Then, feeling almost guilty as I rushed to get out of the cottage before Jem could appear, I lugged my case out to my car and drove off the estate. I had to keep my wits about me until Saturday night, and I could think of just the person to douse me with a bucket load of reality.

If Ellie was surprised to hear her receptionist telling her that I had arrived in her waiting room, it certainly didn't show on her face as I was ushered into her plush office.

"Eve, I was going to call you, you've saved me the bother. Bloody hell, darling, what have you been doing to yourself since I last saw you? Has Andy been giving you a rough time? You look awful. Sit down, before you fall down." She buzzed through to her receptionist. "Fifi hold my calls for the next half an hour."

"Fifi?" I had to smile.

"I know, ridiculous, but I can't hold it against her, she's a bloody good receptionist." Then she fixed her keen lawyer's eyes on me, leant back in her chair, and tapped a long fingered nail on the beautifully polished wood of her desk. "Now, suppose you tell me what's going on?"

I began in a bit of a muddle. She didn't know about Jake being in hospital, or that Andy had put the house on the market (she scribbled some notes at this point) and she didn't know that I had a lover. Another one. Her serpentine eyes flickered with interest and a smile curved her glossy lips.

"I really should be advising caution here, you know. To gain back some ground in the divorce, you really should be behaving as though you are beyond fault. Then again, I can't help feeling a tad envious.

233

With two children under six, the most I can hope for at the moment with Hugh is a quick kiss and a hug before one of us drops asleep exhausted. Don't spare the details."

"That's the trouble," I said, sounding, even to my ears, rather bewildered. "I don't know a damn thing about him." I explained how we met, that he was Sally's gardener, and that there had been an instant spark which seemed to have the capacity to blind me to everything else. "I'm beginning to wonder if he is even real," I finished and waited for her to laugh at me.

She didn't. Instead she leant forward and asked to see the bruises around my neck. I had told her how frightened I had been of Jem at that moment but how he had swept me away once more with his lovemaking, so much so that when I next woke up it was two days later! Either that or I was losing my memory.

Ellie's immaculately made up face creased into a frown when she saw the marks. "There's no imagining those, honey." She perched her bottom on the edge of the desk and looked down at me. "Look, Eve, he sounds completely gorgeous and I don't blame you for being swept off your feet. Not after what Andy's done. But he also sounds a trifle unstable and you really should know a little more about him. If he won't tell you, then you need to speak to Sally and get his full name and address. Pass them on to me and I'll check up on him for you. I've got friends who can do that easily."

I was impressed. "Wow. You don't think that's a bit underhand?"

"Of course it is, girl. But he's hurt you. He could do worse next time. Promise me you'll take more care of yourself. Don't agree to see him until we know more about him."

"That's the thing," I said. "He just turns up. We never actually make any arrangements." Even as I said it, I realised the oddity of it all. Sitting here in the sanity of Ellie's office, my whirlwind romance with Sally's gardener, who came and went like the mists of Brigadoon, appeared bizarre even by my standards.

The intercom buzzed then and Ellie had to speak to Fifi. When she had finished, she turned back to me and addressed me with the manner of someone used to being obeyed.

"Right, my girl, Hugh's doing the school run now, but he should be home in another ten minutes. Get yourself over to our place. You can have dinner with us and then sleep over. Have a bit of breathing space. You look like you could do with it. In fact, it's nearly the Easter holidays, I'm sure Hugh would love you stay a few days, he goes potty when the kids are at home full time, you could give him a hand?"

I smiled at her. The thought of throwing myself into the hurly burly chaos of her domestic life for a while or so was very appealing. But on Saturday I had a date with a blackmailer, which was something I had not felt appropriate to share with my solicitor.

"I think I'd better get my own home in order first but a night at your place would be great. I was hoping you would suggest that."

Ellie had telephoned ahead and Hugh greeted me with a big warm hug that made me envy my friend the normality of her relationship. He was two or three years older than her, a professional chef who had been happy to swap his role in the hotel kitchens to that of at home as his wife earned far more money than he did. Not many men could cope with that idea and he was one of them. Big in build, big in heart, small in ego. That was Hugh.

Their daughters, Maribelle, aged six, and Phoebe, aged four were two bundles of mischievous fun, with their mother's dark hair and their father's merry blue eyes. I adored them both and was God mother to the pair of them. I didn't seem them often, life just seemed to get in the way, but when I did, it was a joy.

The simple pleasures of chatting to Hugh in the kitchen as he prepared tea for the girls, helping Maribelle with her spellings and Phoebe with her reading, before snuggling onto the sofa to watch television with them, soothed my ragged nervous system. By the time Ellie had come home from the office, just in time for give the girls a quick kiss before bed, I was feeling far more my normal self.

Perhaps being on my own had not been good for me, I thought, as I ate the delicious fish pie that Hugh had prepared. I had had far too much time on my hands this last month to brood and wallow in my own emotions. I talked things over with my friends and they agreed that not working and hiding away was bad for anyone.

"Not surprising you're losing track of reality," said Hugh as he cut me a slice of almond and apple tart. "I feel like that sometimes if I only have the girls to talk to. I have to get out and be with other people. You should start working back at the Lodge again for Sally and if that is going to be a problem with Mary being there, then look for something else."

"You could always retrain," suggested Ellie, looking more relaxed now, but still stylish in a magenta leisure suit that matched her slippers perfectly. "Go and do something else, you're only forty two after all, your children are grown up. You've got a whole chunk of life ahead of you, Eve. Make the most of it. I'll see you get a decent divorce settlement, you won't be penniless. Get out there and start living your life!"

It was valuable advice. My mind was much clearer as I settled down into the comfort of their spare bedroom. The sheets smelt of lavender and the pillows were feather filled. Within seconds I was asleep, cocooned in the cosy haven of a normal domestic home.

CHAPTER TWENTY SIX

I slept so well, I missed the daily rush of everyone getting up for work and school. It was half past ten when my eyes fell onto the clock. I never used to sleep like this, but at least I felt more awake this morning, less like a walk on part for a zombie film. I showered quickly and went downstairs to find Hugh drinking coffee and watching Jeremy Kyle. The lounge smelt of fresh polish and the vacuum cleaner was plugged in at the socket.

He grinned at me, turning the volume down on the television. "Don't tell Ellie. It's my guilty pleasure or one of them at least. I didn't want to start vacuuming in case I woke you. Mind you, the girls made so much noise at breakfast, if you could sleep through that, you could probably sleep through anything. Do you feel better?"

"I do thanks. Best night sleep I've had in a long time." It was true. I slept deeply at the cottage, especially when Jem had been with me. But I would wake there feeling heavy under the grogginess of that slumber. Not refreshed at all. Today I felt much better.

"How about some smoked salmon and eggs for breakfast?" Hugh lifted his feet off the coffee table and jumped up from the sofa.

"That sounds a bit luxurious."

"You're worth it. Ellie's been worried about you, you know." He ushered me into the space age kitchen and settled me onto a bar stool before making me a five star breakfast. He laid the dish in front of me and refilled his coffee cup. "You did look rather dreadful last night. You look better this morning, but I think she's right. You've not been taking care of yourself properly. You're far too thin and pale, Eve. Eat up, it will do you good."

It was so lovely to be looked after for a little while. I had my breakfast and then helped Hugh with the rest of the housework before we both walked down the road to pick up Phoebe from her pre-school. Then it was play time on the swings and back to the house for lunch. In the afternoon, Hugh had to take Phoebe for a dentist's appointment just before he would have to pick Maribelle up from school.

"Why don't you let me do that? That way you won't be rushing," I suggested, wanting to pay back some of his kindness.

"Only if you promise to put your feet up and do nothing for the afternoon," he insisted. "Ellie's got loads of magazines you can browse through."

I thought of Melody Farthing's diary. What better time to sit and read it cover to cover. "Deal," I agreed and helped him persuade Phoebe that going to the dentist really was a good idea. When they had gone, I went upstairs to fetch the diary, made myself a hot chocolate and settled myself down on the comfy sofa in the lounge.

I had to concentrate on reading the elegantly flowing handwriting and the language she used was far more elaborate than that of modern day. My hot chocolate went cold as I became engrossed in the story she was telling me.

At first it seemed little more than a daily account of a young girl living the life of pampered luxury, her father the well-off landowner and squire of the village. Very Jane Austen, I thought, picturing her wearing a sprigged muslin dress and bonnets with ribbons round. There were accounts of what soirees she had been to, and who had said what, and who had worn what. All very innocent and charming. And then it changed. The manner of writing became coy, almost secretive and it was soon clear why.

Melody Farthing had taken a lover, her father's game keeper. It was, by her account, a love affair that was a true meeting of souls. Without him, she could not even breathe nor he without her.

I wondered if this was the truth of the matter, of if this was simply the view point of a naive seventeen year old. As I turned the pages, it became clear that her father, Squire Farthing, had pledged her hand in marriage to the neighbouring landowner.

My stomach churned as I read Melody's description of her betrothed. He was her father's age, if not older by some five years or more, grossly overweight and had buried three wives already, two in childbirth. Melody was to be sold to him like a lamb to the slaughter, all so that Squire Farthing could move up the ladder of Society.

No wonder she had fallen for the charms of the gamekeeper, if she had known that this marriage was on the cards. She wrote with more passion as the diary moved on, her feelings for the game keeper growing stronger by the day, and his in return it would seem. She wrote of running away, making the journey up to Gretna Green in order that their love might be made lawful. She would not, she insisted, marry the odious Sir Andrew Marksberry. She would, she declared, rather be dead.

I felt a shiver at those words and glanced at the clock. I still had half an hour to go and not many more pages of the diary left. I sat up right now, too involved by what I was reading to slouch back lazily.

She did not refer to her lover by name, too frightened that her diary might fall into the wrong hands, and there was no description of him other than he was older than her, but so much younger than her fiancé, with a smile that made the sun come out, and eyes that dazzled her. They had exchanged gifts, upon declaring their own private troth. Not rings because that would be too obvious. He had given her a tiny horse shoe charm to add to a bracelet and she had given him a silver cross which he kept hidden under his shirts. Only she could see it when they made love together.

Another shiver passed through me then. Jem wore a silver cross around his neck. The cold metal of it would lie against the warmth of my skin as our bodies entwined.

It was nothing, I told myself. A lot of people wore crosses.

I carried on reading.

They were discovered. Someone had spied upon them at the cottage. It was the first time she had mentioned where they had had their lover's trysts and it was now clear in my mind why I felt there was something so special about the place. Of course it had happened there! But what had occurred when their love had been found out?

Murder most foul.

Her father and his lackey had strung her lover up. He had hung to his death from the beam that ran across the ceiling in the bedroom. Melody had been forced to watch and then had been told by her father that her lover's body would be tossed into an unmarked grave and she would never know where he lay.

The ink was smeared over these pages, and no wonder. She must have wept herself dry. I had tears of my own trailing down my cheeks as her heartbreak and anguish washed over the centuries and called to me. That laughing girl in the mirror. No wonder she had screamed in horror that time. I had witnessed a moment in history, or at least its echo, trapped within the walls of the room where such a brutal tragedy had taken place.

I thought of the horrible sensations I had felt there from time to time and knew now that I had been offered a glimpse of the past, the chance to see what others had been blind to. It shook me, and for a few minutes I could only sit there as the clock ticked on the wall and take in the enormity of what I had read.

Melody's father was a murderer and the ghost of that soul lingered in the cottage. Not only that, I thought, remembering how my hands had reached so certainly for the diary, hidden away amongst a mountain of other books, Melody and her lover wanted their story to be told. They had lain quiet for two hundred years and for some reason, when I had come along they had reached out to me for help.

Perhaps, it was the fact that I had fallen in love at the very same cottage that linked us? I had met Jem there, as she had met her game keeper. It seemed a reasonable notion, if one can have reasonable notions when considering the idea of ghosts.

There were a couple more pages but I really did not have time. Melody would have to wait a little while longer. I had a six year old to collect from school and the living had to take precedence over the dead. I closed the diary, put it back into my bag and tried to shut out horrific images of a young man hanging slowly to death as his beloved watched.

This was easily done in the lively company of Maribelle and later on Phoebe and Hugh. As a special treat, in honour of it being the last day of school, Hugh suggested that they made Easter egg shaped biscuits before tea which they could then decorate. The girls got stuck into the task and I spent another pleasant hour in their company, covered in flour and icing sugar.

Then it was time to leave this domestic idyll which reminded me so much of how life had been for me over ten years ago now. Where did the time fly? One minute I was a happy, carefree mum, making Christmas cards and cakes with Megan and Jake, and the next I was the talk of the village!

It was a lot to think over as I drove back to Maypoleton. And then there was Melody Farthing. I had not had chance to speak to Ellie to tell her that the cottage was most definitely haunted and now I knew why, as she was still at work when I left. But at least I knew and there was some protection in that.

I was not afraid. I understood now why I had felt the darkness from time to time. Getting away from it for even just a short while had made a difference. I could stand back from everything and see it clearly. Ellie was right. I had been exhausted and worn down from the shock of finding out about Andy and then my own destructive behaviour with Tim. Not to mention Jake landing in hospital. There was nothing wrong with me that a good kick up the arse wouldn't solve.

It was around six when I got back to Maypoleton. I was about to turn off into the Lodge, when I found my hands steering the wheel in the opposite direction. Being with Ellie had done me good in more ways than one. I parked my car in my usual place on the drive, next to Megan's battered heap. Then, telling myself I had every right to be here, I let myself into my home.

There was laughter coming from the kitchen and the unmistakeable smell of pizza and garlic bread. Sure enough as I walked into the kitchen, they were sat around the table, takeaway boxes and wrappers cluttering up the counter top.

Mark and Lexy were with Megan and Jake and they both stood up to leave on seeing me but my daughter told them to sit back down. They did so promptly.

"What do you want?" Megan stood up herself, probably to give herself the advantage. She towered over me, had done since she was thirteen. "If you need to speak to someone about the house, you can go through your solicitor."

"Actually, I've just been with Ellie," I said pleasantly. "The house can't be sold without my signature anyway as the deeds are in joint names, so who ever had the bright idea of putting it on the market was a little premature."

"It was me," said Jake. "I can't stand living here now. Not with what happened."

I looked at my son, grateful to see the colour was back in his face from the last time I had seen him. I chose to ignore his comment and remarked instead that I had heard about Ricky. It was not something they wanted to discuss with me. He had been one of their friends after all, but something bothered me.

"You said when Maisie had to go to hospital, that none of you knew who was selling the drugs? When did you find out it was Ricky?"

"We didn't!" Megan said hotly. "Jake only found out when Ricky approached him. He was talking to him after class one day about how much he was dreading his exams because he couldn't concentrate on anything, and Ricky said that he could get him something to help."

"That simple?" I looked at them all.

"That simple," said Lexy quietly. "And I nearly lost Jake." She put her hand over his possessively.

You nearly lost Jake? What about me? I had hoped that some of the hostility towards me might have faded. I was wrong. I left them to their takeaway, satisfied at least that my son was looking fit and well once more, and went on back to the Lodge.

The stable yard was quiet, just a few of the livery clients making the most of the pleasant evening. I caught a drift of a conversation. At last the focus was not on me, but had fallen instead upon Bryony. How had she let her son become a drug dealer? I smiled.

Jenny was finishing off a lesson with a private client but she called over to me and said she thought I was looking better. Twenty four hours with Ellie's family had done me the world of good and now I was reluctant to go back to the cottage and be alone. Or be with Jem for that matter. I didn't want any distractions before tomorrow night. It was vital I got something right for once.

I went on in to the Lodge to be told by Mary that Sally was in the library having a long telephone call to Richard. Apparently her husband and father in law were now somewhere near the coast of Kenya and both women were worried sick that they might fall prey to the Somalian pirates who had kidnapped a British couple a previous year. I think that stopped Mary being too churlish with me, as her thoughts were focused elsewhere.

I was sorry for the old woman, despite her chilly attitude towards me of late. She was too old to have to fret about a selfish man off on his jollies. I settled myself into the kitchen, knowing that Sally wouldn't mind and waited for the call to finish. It was some twenty minutes later and my friend had obviously been crying.

"Bloody, bloody, stupid idiots! I told them both to get their arses into gear and get the hell out of there before they get kidnapped." She poured herself a huge gin and tonic and looked to see if I wanted one. "I told them that if that happened, they can sodding well forget about any ransom money. They can rot on a desert island before I sell the Lodge! Been in my family for hundreds of years this place! I swear I'd see Richard fed to the sharks before I sell it."

She took a large gulp and then suggested we move into the sitting room where a fire was lit. Although it had been a fairly warm day, this big old house resisted the sun until at least June and even then sometimes it failed to penetrate the thick stone walls. She threw another log onto the fire and then slumped down into one of the worn and comfy chairs, whilst I kicked off my shoes and curled up on the sofa.

I thought I would try and distract her from her worries. "The cottage is definitely haunted," I began. "And I know why now."

She perked up a little. "Ooh, go on. You look better by the way. I haven't seen you in a few days, where have you been?"

"I went to Ellie's. I needed to see her about something and ended up staying. Anyway, I took Melody Farthing's diary with me to read."

"Good grief you mean you still hadn't read it?"

I shrugged. "I kept getting distracted."

She half choked on a mouthful of gin. "Oh yes, I keep forgetting, my delightful gardener. Sorry, do go on," she said when I shot her a look. I couldn't see what was so funny about me sleeping with Jem.

So I told her about Melody's ill-fated love affair and the death that had occurred in the cottage.

"Bloody hell! No wonder it's haunted! How odd though that no one in my family has ever picked up on the fact."

"Squire Farthing was a rich man," I said. "He would have had enough power and influence to keep it quiet. The man servant who helped him was in his pay, and the estate grounds are big enough that a body could easily be buried and no one would know."

"Yes, I understand that. But what I meant was no one has ever suspected the cottage had a ghost. Until you turned up." Her eyes went as round as an owls. "It must be you that's triggered it all off. You must be psychic. Have you ever seen a ghost before?"

"No. But I did meet a funny gypsy woman earlier on in the year. I think I may have mentioned her to you?"

"Oh yes, I remember something about that. She blessed you, you said. Maybe it was a curse instead, if you're starting to see ghosts!" She shuddered. "I wouldn't like it."

"It doesn't frighten me. I think they just want their story to be told." I considered Melody's pain as she had written the awful fact that she would never know where her lover lay. "I think we need to find where the body is buried."

"Yes well, before you go and hire a JCB to dig up my grounds try and get an exact location!"

"Not sure how! Anyway, I'd best be off. "

"Oh don't," she pleaded. "Have another drink. In fact why don't you stay and we can have a girly night? Go on, we can get a take away and put a DVD on. I'll even sit through Gladiator with you," she teased, knowing my crush on Russell Crowe. "Go on, I don't want to be alone tonight, worrying over my stupid husband and damn pirates."

"Of course I'll stay," I said, telling myself that really it was more about helping a friend than shying away from my own demons.

CHAPTER TWENTY SEVEN

Saturday morning Sally and I woke late. We had finished the bottle of gin, watched Gladiator then Pretty Woman (Sally's choice) before falling asleep where we sat in the cosy lounge. Stiff and cold we shambled into the kitchen to find Jenny already on her mid-morning coffee break.

"Jesus, would you look at you two. I was going to ask you, Eve, if you would step in for Lucy for the rest of the day? She's been throwing up all night and Kirsty and Todd are both off on holiday. I've got two birthday parties booked and I could really do with an extra hand? You don't really look up to it though."

I laid my head on the table and groaned dramatically. Birthday parties meant dealing with spoilt kids and their even more demanding parents, matching novice riders to mischievous ponies, and then organising mounted games whilst all the time praying that none of the precious darlings fell off.

But Jenny had been good to me and I owed both her and Sally.

"Of course I will," I promised. "Just let me have a coffee and I'll be right out."

"Good for you," Sally patted me on the shoulder. "I'm going back to bed."

I was still wearing the jeans and hooded sweatshirt from yesterday, which now I had slept in, but there were no prizes for dressing up here, so with the panda eyed look of someone still wearing yesterday's mascara, I went out onto the yard. I tacked up the ponies, found a hat for each child, shortened stirrups, tightened girths, encouraged the riders, scolded the ponies, ran round the school like an idiot, and by the end of the afternoon, was smelly and knackered.

There was one more job to do though. Jenny had finished putting away the last of the school ponies, I had spent some time brushing my Sam, and promised him that I would actually ride him the following morning, and then we both realised that the DIY livery clients had not piled back the muck heap, leaving it to trail down onto the car park.

"Fucking lazy bastards," Jenny swore as she turned the corner on the yard and saw the mess. I had been about to leave. I was desperately in need of a shower and change before my night time activities but I couldn't leave her to dig back the muck herself.

"I'll give you a hand," I said, thinking that another half hours hard work was not going to kill me. I was at that state of physical melt down where the aches and pains were almost becoming pleasurable. It could have been the fact that I had not eaten anything since a snatched slice of toast at eleven and I had spent the afternoon on full pelt, or maybe I was dehydrated from too much alcohol the night before. Or maybe it was something else entirely. Whatever it was, I had a funny turn right in the middle of the manure.

"You okay, Eve?"

Jenny's voice was coming from far away. I felt icy cold and thick headed and for a moment the scenery changed around me. The car park faded and in its place was a kitchen garden, vegetables and herbs outlined in orderly rows, a waft of lavender and thyme on the spring evening breeze. No scent of horse manure, but in its place a more pungent, rotting stench that sickened my stomach. And underlying it all, that horrible, stinging coldness that felt as though it could burn the flesh off my bones.

Jenny's hand was warm and solid on my shoulder.

"Come on, girl you look done in." She helped me down off the muck heap before I could fall face first in its steaming depths. Once at the bottom, I began to feel better. My vision cleared, the car park reappeared and I was no longer frozen stiff. Instead the sweat was rolling down my back like it did when I had been for a long run.

"I think I am," I grinned weakly at her. "I've got soft, Jenny. I need to do more exercise."

"Well, things can get back to normal now," she said. "The gossip has died down over you. Everyone's talking about Ricky instead. You should come back to work for Sally but on the yard instead of in the house with Mary. That'll soon get you fit again. And start riding that horse of yours. The weather's getting better now there's no excuse."

"Yes Jenny," I said meekly. "Are you sure you can finish off yourself?"

"I'd rather do that than have to dig you out as well. You looked as though you were going to topple in head first for a moment." She gave me a long hard look, shrewd Scandinavian eyes assessing me. "You're not pregnant, Eve?"

"Shit! Jenny that's not funny!" I gawped at her in horror, thinking of the irresponsible sex I had had with both Tim and Jem. Then a wheel in my brain started to turn and I remembered that I had had my tubes tied after Jake. I laughed with relief. "No, no of course I can't be. Thank God for that, you had me scared for a moment, Jenny."

"Well you've been worrying me recently," she replied. "You really don't look your normal self. And just then you looked like death. Make sure you have a good tea tonight, you've earned it."

"I will," I said and wandered back to the house to say goodbye to Sally.

She was at the kitchen door, chatting to a sprightly looking gentleman about sixty in age, white haired and wrinkled, but with a lively air about him. I stood back a little as they finished their conversation and nodded at the man as he smiled in turn at me, and walked past.

"What?" I said, as Sally was regarding me with open mouthed curiosity.

"You two no longer at it then?" Her eyes were sparkling with devilish glee.

"At what?"

"You know." She gave me a friendly poke and stepped back to let me into the kitchen. "All that rampant sex that's worn you out so much. Are you and Jeff finished?"

It was my turn to look stupid. I could only stare at her whilst I connected the thought processes together.

"You think I've been having sex with that old man?" My voice rose at least two octaves.

"Well that's Jeff. That's my gardener. You said you'd been shagging my gardener, at it like rabbits since you moved into the cottage."

I laughed. "Don't be daft! That's not him! As if I'd...Oh bloody hell Sally have you seriously been thinking I've been screwing him?" I held my hand over my mouth as I giggled like a school girl. "You mad thing. As if!"

Sally joined in with the laughter, and then perhaps because she had had a long snooze in the afternoon and was more alert than me, she joined up the next dot.

"So who have you been sleeping with? I only have the one gardener."

I stopped laughing. "Are you sure. You don't have two?"

"I think I would know, even with my slap dash estate management. Who exactly have you been seeing at the cottage, Eve?"

I reached for a chair and sat down, legs shaking suddenly. "Jem." I said hoarsely.

"Jem who?"

I shrugged.

"You still don't know anything about him?" Sally was rightly incredulous. It was insane. "Well what does he look like?"

I began to describe him, getting slightly dreamy as I did so, and having to pull myself up sharp as Sally's eyes bored into me.

"Eve, there's no one locally of that description and certainly no one who works on the estate. You need to be careful, girl. He could be a total psycho."

I looked at my hands, trying hard not to think of Jem's tightening around my neck. "He's really nice," I said lamely.

Sally just snorted and then insisted that I stopped seeing him at the cottage, until we knew a little more about him. Like a surname for a start! After our conversation I felt again the reluctance to go back to the cottage, just in case Jem was waiting for me. Too much was spinning round in my head and there were only a few hours to go before meeting up with Andy's blackmailer.

I decided instead to trek onward to the field and meet up with Seth and his family. They would not mind my dirty, scruffy appearance and I persuaded myself there was no point in going to the cottage to get showered and changed if I was going to be grubbing around in the church yard later on.

I had not seen Seth since Bracken had died and was struck by how old the Romany looked now, as if some of the light had gone out of him. Still, he seemed to brighten up when he saw me opening the gate into the field and I heard him calling to Caitlin that there would be one more for supper.

Awkwardly, I gave him a hug and told him I was sorry about his horse. He mumbled something in reply and dabbed at his eyes before excusing himself to tend to the fire. Bella was stirring the pot that hung old fashioned style over the fire and she gave me a friendly smile.

"Da says he's off out wi' you later, but he won't tell us, why. What you up to then?"

It was echoed by Shaunie her brother who appeared carrying a large glass corked bottle, the type you use for home brewing.

"You goin' to tell us, or do we 'ave to get you drunk first?" He held up the bottle. "Uncle Jojo's home brew. You want some?"

"Careful with that, Eve," said Benjy as he walked over from his van. "'Tas been known to send folk daft."

"Well I'm daft already." I grinned, "So maybe it'll have the reverse effect on me." It actually sent me to sleep. I managed to eat the thick broth and home-made bread that Caitlin had made and downed two glasses of the stuff before sliding off my stool and into a deep slumber. When Benjy woke me later on, it had gone completely dark, just the glow of the fire and the stars to light up the night.

"Does Seth know what we're up to?" I asked him, sleepily.

"Aye, lass," said Benjy. "There's nowt I keep from 'im."

"Does he mind?"

"Course he don't," scoffed Jojo. "Why would 'e mind, you're 'is..." But he was stopped by Benjy giving him a sharp nudge.

"Come on lad, get that engine of yours running, we need you to park it in the lay by, remember."

The plan was very simple. We were going to hide in the grave yard and wait for Andy to first of all drop off the money (as he had obviously done previously). Jojo and I were going to wait and see who came to pick it up and grab them on their way out. Then we were going to cross over the fields, via the style in the church yard, and meet up with Benjy.

He was going to be waiting in the field next to the church yard for our signal. If the blackmailer went out via the style, which was right next to the grave so there was a distinct possibility of this, then he would grab him. Sack over the head, rope around the legs. Once we had him, we were going to take him for a ride in Jojo's van, give him a fright, and take back the money. Simple.

And as it turned out, it was.

Just before eleven a figure climbed over the style by the grave and bent to place something near the head stone. Andy, moving furtively and looking around to see if anyone was watching. We were of course, but we were well hidden behind a large ornate memorial. He went back the way he came and then Jojo and I had to wait some more sharing all the while a flask of his home brew which he had tucked inside his jacket. It was chilly now and I was glad of the brew. We were in danger of getting giddy though by the time someone eventually appeared.

There was a wooden gate attached to the style, which had a most helpful squeak as it opened and shut. Jojo poked me and I froze instantly. So our blackmailer was coming in from across the fields was he, rather than via the lane. We heard the crunch of gravel as footsteps moved around William Tomlinson's grave. Andy had weighted the package down with a large stone and it seemed as though the blackmailer had some trouble moving it. A little bit of huffing and puffing which suggested that they were not perhaps all that strong and then a satisfied "Ha!"

Ha! To you, I thought, as we pounced, Jojo from the left, me from the right. No finesse, no useful rugby moves, just a full on scramble, Jojo going for the legs and me tossing the sack over the head. It was one I had taken from the stables and still had remnants of horse shit and straw in it. A nice touch, I thought.

There was a high pitched scream, quickly cut off by Jojo clamping his hand roughly where he guessed the mouth to be and a hissed order.

"Shut the fuck up or I'll cut a finger off for each sound you make!"

I rather think he would too. I kind of liked the idea. There was no need for the knife though as the figure suddenly slumped.

"I think he's fainted," I said with a suppressed giggle. "Not a very brave blackmailer is he?"

Jojo's teeth flashed white in the darkness. He handed me the flask and we shared another drop before signalling to Benjy with an owl's hoot and then a couple of minutes later, he appeared at the style.

"What are you waiting for?"

"He's fainted," said Jojo with a grin, hiding the flask quickly.

Benjy grunted and picked up the figure as easily as if it was a child. Tossing it over his broad shoulders in a fireman's lift, he climbed over the style and started to trek across the field to the gate near the layby. Muffled groans came from the sack and Benjy this time issued a threat of his own, which involved removing slivers of skin from the person's body and stitching them back in different places.

"Ooh I hadn't thought of that," I said with a giggle to Jojo as the figure moaned, or rather whimpered once more and went silent.

Jojo ran ahead to check that the coast was clear and opened up the back of the van. In went the blackmailer and off we went, Benjy kicking Jojo out of the driver's seat having smelt the alcohol on him.

"I told ye, about that," he growled and shot me a look of exasperation as I began to hiccup loudly.

"It was cold," I said apologetically and then began to give him directions to Badgers Brock. Once there, the idea was to rough up our blackmailer until he realised that if he ever tried it again, it would result in a one way trip. We would be bluffing of course about this part. At least I think we would.

Unfortunately, a deer decided to cock it up.

On the narrow one way lane that ran around Badgers Brock country park, we were stopped by a collision between a deer and another driver. The deer of course was dead, but it could be argued that the car was also in a similar state and unfortunately for us was dumped right across the track with no hope of getting past it.

"Bollocks," hissed Benjy. "There's no way I can turn around here, I'll have to reverse all the way back down the fucking hill. Dozy fucking cunt!" He yelled at the driver of the abandoned vehicle who was jabbering about how his dad was going to kill him. Then he started to retrace our path, in a hair raising slide back down the narrow, twisting lane.

Straight into the path of another car. With blue flashing lights on.

"Bugger!"

"Shit!"

"Fucking bollocks!" We swore in unison.

"What the hell are you doing driving like that?" Craig Hawthorne, in uniform and stormy faced flashed a torch into the front of the van.

"Evening, Craig," I tried to form an innocent smile. "We were just out owl spotting, only the road is blocked, there's been an accident, hence the urgent need to reverse. Sorry about that."

Jojo coughed and then coughed some more as muffled noises came from the back of the van.

"I know. Some young idiot's hit a deer. I was the nearest when the call came in. Are you alright?" He looked at Jojo who was now coughing uncontrollably.

"Asthma," butted in Benjy, "And I've just realised he's not got his inhaler, so if you won't mind, officer, we'd best be off."

Jojo began to wheeze effectively and Craig was starting to look convinced. Until the body in the back of the van rolled around sufficiently to crash into the side with such a thump, that the vehicle rocked.

"What the hell have you got in there? Another deer?" Craig turned his flashlight to the back, just as a high pitched voice uttered something with sounded remarkably like, "Help!"

"Right, everyone out, now!"

I couldn't help it. I always get the giggles when I have to be serious. And it wasn't helped by the home brew I had had earlier. But the sight of the body, trussed up in a hessian sack, rolling out of the van and landing with an almighty thud, had me biting my lips. I would have been alright if I hadn't caught sight of Jojo's face but then it was too late and we were both snorting with laughter.

Thankfully, Benjy retained some gravity. "'Tisn't wot it looks like."

"Oh really?" Craig was the master of icy fury. "Looks like kidnap to me." His hands worked quickly at the ropes that were binding the sack in place. "It's alright, you're safe now."

Panting sobs were now emanating from the sacking as it was removed. The warmth of the occupant's body had infused the odour of manure nicely and there was quite a rank smell as it was lifted off.

"Officer, they kidnapped me!" Deidre Brown burst out with a sob, straw and horse shit in her hair.

"You bitch!" I launched towards her, not quite sure in my mind that I was going to hit a pensioner, but seriously tempted, despite the risk of adding assault to my list of crimes. Fortunately, Jojo caught my arm and held me back.

Craig looked from me to her in grimly concealed bewilderment. "Would one of you like to tell me what the hell is going on?"

"She's a kidnapper!" Deidre screeched wildly.

"And she's a blackmailer!" I stabbed a finger in the air above her head.

Craig looked at Benjy and Jojo who in turn nodded at him. He shook his head, an expression of disbelief now on his face and spoke into his radio. "I'm going to need someone else to take over the deer collision. I've got my hands full with something more serious."

"Right, Eve, and whoever you are," he said to Deidre, plainly not recognising her beneath the muck, "in the back of my car now. You two," he spoke to Benjy and Jojo, "follow me to the station and don't even think of taking any detours."

At which point Deidre gave another hysterical screech. "Oh please, Marcus mustn't find out. I'm sorry. It's all my fault." And promptly fell into another faint.

Strangely, my suggestion that I brought her round with a slap was met with a very dark stare.

CHAPTER TWENTY EIGHT

In the end it was Deidre's repeated hysterics that made Craig relent. She came round from her faint, only to start retching at the side of the road.

"Oh please don't take me to the station," she begged between spasms. "Marcus mustn't find out, he'll kill me."

Craig looked torn between wanting to cart us all off to the station, which no doubt would involve stacks of ridiculous paper work and red tape, not to mention a shed load of trouble with the villagers, and wanting to sort this whole sorry mess with as little fuss as possible. I bet he had never had this sort of bother in Manchester.

He moved his car out of the road so that the way was clear for the back-up police, ordered Benjy to do the same, sat the now shivering Deidre on a crumbling stone wall, and then with his laser eyes piercing us all, demanded a full explanation. He added the promise that if there were any more hysterics or threats of violence, from any of us, we would all be spending the night locked up in a cell.

This seemed to stiffen Deidre's backbone and she began speaking. "Oh it was horrible. I thought they were going to kill me. You hear such dreadful things on the news. Women being abducted, and then raped and strangled."

Benjy spat on the ground but turned away when Craig shot him a look.

"I can imagine you were terrified," Craig said to her, soothingly. "Go on."

"I was just taking a stroll, to clear my head, I'd had a migraine you see, and I thought some fresh air would help me sleep. I like going to the church yard to visit my parent's graves at times like this, it comforts me. I can say a few prayers and know that God listens."

"Oh please, I'm going to be sick!"

"Eve, be quiet!"

Deidre carried on. "I was just making my way out of the church yard when the next thing I knew I was being attacked. That smelly sack was thrown over my head and I was being hit again and again, brutally kicked, I shall be covered in bruises tomorrow," she finished on a sob.

"I see," said Craig, grimly, before turning to me.

"Bullshit!" Perhaps not the best response as he continued to look at me as if I had just crawled out from under a stone. "I mean she wasn't kicked and punched. We just threatened her if she made a noise. But we didn't know it was her. We thought it was going to be a man!"

"Oh yes. The blackmailing story. Do go on."

"It's true," I protested. "We only did it to get my money back and to teach him, I mean her, a lesson."

"I've no idea what they are talking about," said Deidre shrilly, clutching her chest as though in pain. "I only went for a walk."

"So what were you doing with this on you when we jumped you then?" Jojo had darted into the van and thrust the package into Craig's hands. "Go on, open it."

He did so, his face remaining inscrutable. "There's a lot of money here."

"Five grand," I told him. "And she's already had twenty!"

"It's nothing to do with me," Deidre maintained her innocence. "I don't know where that money came from, Sergeant. I told you, I only went for a walk." She began to cry again.

"We saw you pick it up!" Jojo was now getting angry.

Craig held up a hand in warning. "Best if we all stay calm."

Benjy stepped in. "She's telling the truth, Eve, I mean. 'Er 'usbands bein' blackmailed and we was tryin' to 'elp 'er catch t'bastard wot's doin' it. Never reckoned on it bein' a woman. All's we was gonna do was put the frighteners on 'em and get t'money back. We'ren't goin' to do 'owt 'else."

Deidre was looking a little panicked. "You can't prove it, and besides, who would you honestly trust to tell the truth? The village slut and a bunch of gypsies, or the captain of the golf club and member of the Women's Institute. Reverend Michael will vouch for me, you'll see!" Her voice rose again.

255

Craig looked exasperated for the first time since I had met him. "Right," he said after giving it some thought. "There's been enough trouble in the village lately, and I've no wish to see more bad blood brewing up."

"Aren't you going to charge them with kidnap and assault?" Deidre interrupted him and I saw the first flash of anger directed at her. Good!

"I'm not going to charge anyone until I have a clearer understanding of the facts! For now, you can all go home. You two in my car," he spoke to both Deidre and myself curtly, "and you lads, clear off for now. I shall be round to speak to you in the morning. Don't think of taking off anywhere, I will track you down."

Benjy nodded at him. Jojo gave me a wink and then they got into the van, turned it round and drove off. I then had the joy of sitting next to Deirdre whilst Craig drove us both back to Cooper's Fold, that den of iniquity, home to harlots and blackmailers!

He escorted Deidre to her door, and told me to go inside and wait.

It was only as I was trudging through to the kitchen, that I realised what a stupendous mess I was now in. Was there any chance of getting through the next half hour without waking up the rest of the household? Could I possibly keep this latest fiasco a secret from them?

Not a hope.

I had left the front door open for Craig, but had not bargained on Skip. He sprang up from his basket in the kitchen, giving his rousing bark to announce that there was someone new in the house. Craig easily quietened my dog, crouching down and making a fuss of him, but by that time a sleepy eyed Megan had wandered through.

"What's, oh my God, what's going on now? Mum, what the hell have you done? Craig, what's going on?"

"Perhaps you can put the kettle on?" Craig suggested, taking a seat at the table with the air of one not about to be hurried.

Megan's lip curled but she did as he said. And then went to get everyone else. Great! I slumped into a chair and rested my head on my hands. Now I was in for it! Five minutes later, Andy, Jake and Mark were all gathered in the kitchen, their curiosity battling with animosity. Aware that I must look a sight, dressed in my clothes from the day before, grubby from stable work and playing hide and seek in the church yard, I could only begin to imagine what they were thinking.

Craig had calmly swatted away their questions and told them that if they wanted to sit in, they were welcome to, but they had to stay quiet whilst he questioned me.

"What in God's name have you done now, Eve?" Andy looked at me as though he no longer knew me.

I chewed on a thumb nail, gazed dumbly at the floor and twirled a strand of hair round a finger. Oh to be anywhere but here right now? I was beginning to think that maybe a stretch in prison would be a good thing. I could hardly get into trouble under lock and key could I? And I would be safe from the torture of having those I loved looking at me like they were now.

Craig broke the silence. "Eve has been involved in a matter of kidnap."

Of course that made them all explode but he shushed them with a look. He really was rather good at that. I quite admired the talent. And then he turned those killer eyes upon me and I shrank as small as I could in my chair.

"Let's start right from the beginning shall we, Eve," he said and with his pen and paper at the ready, waited for me to begin.

My flippancy deserted me. Any chance of deflecting the seriousness of this with humour had long since passed by. I had totally, royally, fucked up. I looked across at Jake, my darling son who still hated me and was now probably going to despise me even more. There was no chance of keeping his father's secret now and I would be the one responsible for blowing it out of the water. Way to go, Eve!

I told it as it was. No short cuts. No embellishments. I found the notes. I wanted to stop it. I asked Benjy and Jojo for help. They said yes. End of.

The silence was quivering round the table when I had finished. But with Craig sitting there, as thundery as Thor, they managed to keep a lid on things. For now.

"You do still have the notes?" Craig asked me when I had finished.

"They're in Andy's drawer. Well it is still my house!" I looked at them all defensively.

The spotlight was turned on Andy, who under Craig's interrogative stare could do no other than go and fetch them.

I heard an intake of breath. I think it was from Jake as his father returned with the letters and slid them across the table to Craig. The bold black print was big enough for everyone to see. It was hard to say if there was any change in Craig's attitude. He read the notes, which didn't take long, and set them to one side. All the time he maintained his quiet, steady demeanour.

"Would you mind telling me, sir, why anyone would want to blackmail you?"

Oh what a relief not to be the focus of that diamond hard stare. Ha, serves you right Andy. I watched my husband as he went scarlet underneath the scrutiny.

"Nothing," he began to say, his eyes flickering over to me and then back to Craig's. "I haven't broken any laws." His voice sounded as though he had been chewing on sandpaper.

"Dirty little secret?" Craig's voice on the other hand was fluid and smooth. He waited for an answer and the silence began to stretch.

It was Megan who broke it.

"Oh this is ridiculous! Dad, tell him there's nothing wrong. As if you've got anything to hide. It's probably just Mum making it all up now to get our attention. She's set out to make you look bad for something so that she can look better herself."

"Jesus, Megan, is that what all that stuff at university teaches you?" The workings of her mind appalled me. Did she really think me capable of that?

She glared at me, defying me to argue with her.

It was Jake though who got his father to speak. He placed his hands flat on the table, a gesture I think of defeat and spoke with a weary tone that was far too old for him.

"Just tell us, Dad. Whatever it is, it can't be as bad as what she did."

She. Not mum. Still she.

"It would help to clear this up," said Craig. "If there has been a serious attempt to blackmail you and your wife has mistakenly tried to protect you, then I can begin to see how the events of tonight have occurred. Believe me, I would far rather sort this out without anyone being dragged to the station and charged. This is a small community. Bad enough we've got one lad on charges of drug dealing, which could have killed two others, Jake included. If I go formal with this, the ripples will be much greater. And I need to know that despite what you say, you have not committed any crimes."

And that was the crux of the matter. He was not going to go until he knew.

Andy shot me a look then of pure malice. "You stupid bitch! You couldn't just leave well alone could you?"

That did it! That was the tinder to the flame that made me explode. After everything I had been through and the fact that my children still hated me, something snapped.

"I couldn't leave well alone? I couldn't leave well alone?" I repeated with a harsh screech. "If you mean I couldn't handle it when you told me you were gay then no, I couldn't. I fucked Tim because of it, because you threw my life on the scrap heap and yes I was damned if I was going to let some shitty blackmailer rob me of money just so you could carry on hiding your secret!"

I pushed away from the table, choking down a sob and went straight for the cupboard that housed the alcohol. Sod them all, I needed a drink. I half-filled a tumbler full of whisky, downed it in one, refilled it and turned to face them, leaning against the counter with a belligerent scowl on my face.

I regretted my outburst as soon as I looked at Jake. He was chalky white. His sister was reaching over to hold his hand. They both were staring at me and their father as though we had just walked in from a horror movie. Two monsters they could not believe they were related to. Now I know what they mean when they say you could have heard a pin drop. It would have fallen like lead into that silence.

"Dad?" Megan had tears in her eyes. Not so much in control now. "What is she saying?"

"She is trying to say that he's queer, gay. Our Dad a homosexual? It's just another filthy lie though isn't it, you bitch!" God it was blistering that inferno of rage that Jake directed at me.

I think even then Andy would have denied it. Had it not been for Craig.

"Well sir?"

259

Andy crumpled and turned a sickly shade of grey, sweat forming on his brow. "It's true. I told Eve on New Year's Eve and asked her to keep it quiet for the time being. His name is Jason."

I pitied my husband then. Jake, our quiet boy, our happy child, the one who always smiled, never moaned, never lost his temper lost it now and it was a thing to behold. He launched at his Dad a mad fury in his eyes.

"Easy now, lad," Craig stepped towards him as he had done on that occasion with Tim.

Jake stood there trembling. "How can you keep something like that from us? How can you lie to us like that? We're your kids we deserve to know the truth!"

"Son, let me explain..."

"Just shut up!" Jake clamped his hands over his ears. A gesture more poignant because of its childishness. "Shut the fuck up! You're as bad as her!" He stabbed a finger at me. "No, actually I'm wrong. At least she screwed someone of the same sex. Your blackmailer was right, it is a dirty little secret, you are a pervert Dad. You make me sick, both of you!"

"Jake!" Megan called after him as he legged it from the room. Doors slammed and the house shook. Not meeting our eyes, Mark got up from the table and went after the pair of them.

"Are you satisfied now, officer?" Andy said to Craig, looking much older suddenly.

Craig collected his papers, along with the blackmail notes. "I'll speak to you again in the morning. I suggest for now you try and find a way to resolve this within yourselves. I'll see myself out. As he was speaking there was the sound of more doors slamming, and Megan's voice in distress. Then she flung the kitchen door open and burst in again, a banshee on the warpath.

"Nice work you two! He's only just come out of hospital, after nearly killing himself, and now you drive him away! God only knows what he'll do! Dad, how could you? How could you?" And then she collapsed into a chair, crying in the way I had not seen her do since she was about three years old.

Andy went to her and I shot to the door. "I have to go after him," I said to Craig. "Please, will you help me?"

He nodded silently and we hurried out of the house and into his car. We had just turned out of Cooper's Fold when Craig's high beam picked up Jake's figure. He was bent over at the road side, just under a street lamp, throwing up into the gutter. Craig stopped the car and went to him. He shook his head at me to stay back whilst he talked to my son.

From across the way, there was movement at the gate to the field. Seth was standing there, a worried look on his face. No doubt his nephews had filled him in. They would perhaps have been waiting for Craig to descend upon them.

Seth walked over to me. "Oh lass, the storm's fairly breaking now in't it."

"Seth, it's such a mess," I leant on the shoulder he offered, grateful for that gesture of support. "I'm so worried about Jake. We've totally screwed him up, me and Andy both. Megan will be alright, she's got Mark, and I know he's got Lexy but he's only just met her really, and he was in hospital, and what if..."

"Shush lass," he stopped my ramblings. "Don't thee fret abut Jake. I'll take care o' t'lad." He went up to Craig who was still talking to Jake. I could see that Jake was listening, whatever he was being told. Then I watched as Seth leant in and said something to him. My son nodded and without looking at me at all, walked across the road to the gate where Benjy was now waiting.

Seth's nephew called to me. "You looked after ours, now we'll look after yours." He opened the gate to let Seth and my son walk through.

"He'll be alright with them, Eve."

I jumped at the sound of Craig's voice so close to me. I hadn't even noticed him moving. "They're good people. They won't let him come to any harm."

I grunted in disgust. "No. It's only his parents who manage to do that."

"Come on, you need to go to bed, you look ready to fall over."

I was not prepared for the gentleness of his tone, nor the manner in which he helped me back into the car for the short drive down the road to the back entrance of the Lodge. His kindness was my undoing. Tears fell down my cheeks and for once I didn't care. I cried all the way and was still sobbing as the car stopped a few minutes later.

"Eve," he said, and there was a note in his voice that made me wipe my tears away so I could look at him properly. In the dim light of the car, I could see the concern on his face. And something else? God knows. I didn't know anything anymore, other than my life was a total fuck up.

"Thank you," I said, snot dribbling down my nose. I wiped it on my sleeve. "For looking after Jake, I mean."

"And who is going to look after you, Eve?" He asked the question almost as if to himself than to me. Then, taking me totally by surprise, he reached across to me and wiped a last stray tear away with a finger. "Take care. I'll be round to speak to you in the morning."

I nodded dumbly and let myself into the cottage. As I climbed the stairs to the bedroom, and crashed asleep fully clothed, I didn't give a single thought to Jem, or to the ghost of Melody Farthing's lover. All I could think about was how between us, Andy and I had shattered our kids and I could see no possible way of repairing the damage.

CHAPTER TWENTY NINE

He came of course.

I should have known he would. I woke in the early pre-dawn hours to find him slipping under the covers with me. His mouth was already pressing against my own, his tongue seeking entrance. That first time I was half asleep still. Dazed and drowsy and then weak willed with lust. I returned his kisses with thoughtless passion, opened myself to him and followed his moves as though I was the puppet and he the master.

I clutched at his head as his mouth suckled eagerly at both breasts, I tangled my fingers through his hair as he parted my thighs with his fingers and worked me up to a frenzy that had me calling his name and begging him to take me, begging him not to make me wait. Of course he did make me wait. He held back his own needs as he used first his hands and then his mouth to bring me to the edge of heaven and beyond, before finally burying deep within me.

A total possession.

He rose above me as his hips worked against mine, elbows propped either side of my face, eyes boring deep into mine, the light glimmering more sharply with every long and powerful thrust. His beautiful mouth curved into a knowing smile as I moaned in pleasure and arched my neck and back, my nerve endings as taut as any bow string.

He laughed as I wrapped my legs around his waist, pulling him in deeper, further. He took ownership of my mouth as my hands roamed the muscled planes of his back, his tongue fighting with mine as my fingers scored scratches into his skin. Sharp teeth pierced the skin on my neck as I began to pant and gasp for breathe. My head rolled from side to side, my mind emptied of all thoughts, only able to feel.

The heat between us made our bodies' slick with sweat and the sheets around us tangled in a damp knot. He took me once and then again and finally a third time, until there was no substance to my bones, no breathe left in my lungs, my blood a molten river of passion coursing out of control from a heart that felt it was going to burst.

I wept against him, so drained of emotion that all I could do was to cling to him like the most fragile of battered boats in the stormiest of seas. He was my rock, my anchor, my harbour. Within his embrace I had come home. No more dangers to be faced, no more pain, no more loss. Just him.

I must have fallen asleep with these dizzying thoughts in my mind, because I knew when I woke next, that I really did not want to open my eyes and face the day. If only I could stay here, in this bed, locked in Jem's arms forever. No more worldly problems. No more dramas. No more worries. No more anything.

Just Jem.

He was all I needed.

"Then stay with me, forever." He spoke as though he could read my thoughts.

I opened my eyes, startled to find him actually in the bed next to me. Usually, when I woke, he was long gone, the sheets cold where he had lain, the pillow empty of his head. Not now. I turned to see him beside me, propped up on one elbow, looking at me with such an expression of love on his face I nearly cried.

"What time is it?" Had I slept through any more days, I wondered, exhausted by his passion.

"Nearly midday," he answered. "I must be going soon but I want you to come with me, this time."

His moonlit eyes drew me into him, and it would have been so easy to lift up my mouth to his and begin once more the dance that took us to paradise. But somewhere in the deep recesses of my mind there was a conscious thought that niggled. Something had happened yesterday. Something important. I could not stay here in this dream like existence with Jem all day. I must get up. There were people to see. About something.

"No my darling," he leant to kiss me, and the cross around his neck dangled against my skin.

It was important that cross. Somehow I knew it, but for the life of me I couldn't make the connection. My thoughts were fuzzy, not quite in order.

"Where did you get this?" I asked him suddenly, preventing him from kissing me.

His eyes darkened, the pupils nearly eclipsing the silver grey irises. "You know where I got it from," he replied and then succeeded in claiming my mouth with his. I surrendered for a while, letting him savour the taste of me as I was content to devour him. Such a greed between us. I wondered if I could ever grow tired of him. His taste, his touch, his scent.

Dimly, from very far away, I thought I heard someone calling my name.

"Jem," I pushed away from him. "There is someone calling." I was sure of it now. I could hear my name being called through the door downstairs.

"Eve, Eve are you in there? It's Craig. I need to talk to you?"

"I've got to go," I said to Jem, struggling to move past his arms. We were both still naked in the bed, and the last thing I wanted was for Craig to come in and find me like this. I could not remember locking the door last night.

"No!" Jem pulled me back and trapped me in one swift move beneath him. His body was hard and tense, muscled straining with a barely concealed fury. The darkness of his eyes terrified me. "You cannot go, you cannot leave me. You must stay with me forever. You love me don't you?"

Despite the fear chilling my blood, I had to say yes. "I love you, Jem."

"Enough to stay with me, never leave me?"

I could not escape that gaze. His eyes bored right to the very deepest part of my soul and scorched it with a heat that must surely leave a branding mark. I was his, I could be no others. Already he had nudged my legs apart and was working that magic. That sensual spell that he wove so cleverly around me, melting the fear, chasing away the doubts, blinding me to everything other than his own overwhelming presence.

"Yes," I moaned, weakly against him, my hands already pulling him closer, my ears refusing to listen to the noise from outside.

"Say you'll come with me?" He kissed me long and hard, drugging my mind with his passion, driving all my wits from my brain as he clasped my hips to his and moulded our flesh together.

"I'll come with you," I murmured, not stopping to wonder where we may be going.

"For now and always, say it, my darling, you need to say it."

Oh God how could I refuse him anything when he made me feel like this? How could I even consider for a second that there could be no more of this? This was all that mattered. This was my life, my existence, my reason for being. This wild, dark, intense love that obliterated all else before it.

"For now and always," I repeated breathlessly as the tension between us mounted.

I scarcely felt his hands slide around my throat as they had done once before. I was too driven by my own desperate need to be sated to protest that his grip was beginning to hurt. I was too far gone in lust and desire to realise that my moans were now anxious gasps for breath. I was falling far too deeply into the wonderful darkness of his passion to pay any attention to the whirlwind that was hurtling around the bedroom, as wild and tempestuous as my lover, as dangerous and destructive. I cared for nothing as I was swept away into that abyss that had been beckoning me ever since I had laid eyes on him.

CHAPTER THIRTY

"Mum?"

"Mum?"

"Mum, wake up, please?"

It was a voice I knew. A voice I loved. But not Jem's. I tried to open my eyes but they weighed heavy upon me. It hurt to swallow and I really had no energy to do anything more than flicker my eyelashes briefly. Let me sleep. I just wanted to sleep. Now and forever. With Jem. In that long, never ending, sleep of death.

I jerked my eyes open, my heart suddenly pounding hard in my chest, lungs on fire with the need to breathe.

"Doctor, doctor, please come, she's awake." Another voice, also one I recognised. My vision was blurry and I could only make out dim shapes. God it was so bright! Where was I? There was a mixed up jumble of mutterings and murmurings, hands touching me, gently probing, shifting things around me, shining a light into my eyes.

I didn't want to listen to any of it but I wanted less to go back into that cold dark place.

Where Jem had taken me.

To death and beyond.

Fear forced my eyes open again and this time they stayed open.

"We thought you were dead." Jake sat at one side of the bed and Megan on the other. It was my son who spoke to me first. "Craig called us. He told us he'd had to get an ambulance and there was a chance you might not make it."

I looked at my son who was holding my hand. It had a drip attached to it and liquid was running into one of my veins. I eyed it curiously and then realised that my son was actually holding my hand. I gave his a little squeeze. It was all I could manage.

"Craig said it looked like you had been strangled." I don't think I have ever heard Megan sound so unsure of anything. Not even when she was a toddler. She looked at me now with a wondering fear in a way I had never seen her look. A way that required a mother's reassurance.

"I'm fine," I said. Or rather tried to say. Where had my voice gone? I couldn't speak.

My eyes must have shown alarm because Jake said quickly, "Don't talk. They said it would hurt for a few days."

They weren't joking, whoever 'they' were. I felt as though I had been gargling with stones. I heard a door opening and a man walked in. I didn't recognise him at first. Without the uniform, Craig looked different. Hard to describe really, but then it was difficult to focus on anything. I smiled weakly at him, still not quite sure where I was and how I had got here.

"They said you were awake." He approached the bed, but shook his head at Jake who offered to let him have his chair. "How are you feeling?"

I just looked at him, pain and confusion making the tears well up in my eyes.

"It's alright," he said quickly. "There's time. You need to rest. Do you two need a lift back to the village?"

"No I drove," said Megan, her words starting to drift over me. I vaguely felt her leaning over me to kiss me, and then caught a waft of the after shave that Jake wore as he did the same. And then I gave into the sleep, but this time it was a slumber that healed.

The next time I woke, it was to find Craig, polished and official looking, in the chair next to my bed. There was an air of patience about him that I had never felt before. Then again, I had never been in such a situation before, whatever that situation actually was. There was so much muddled still in my mind. At least though, I knew where I was. In hospital and Jake and Megan had been to see me. I could remember that much. A smile played on my lips at the thought of this. My children had come to see me.

"Are you feeling better?" I had not noticed before how warm his voice could be. Full of rough grit, yes, but now it made me think of the sound pebbles make when the sea washes over them.

"I think so," I said cautiously and tried to sit up. I felt as weak as a kitten and Craig was quick to help me prop myself up against the pillows. Pathetic, I thought. Like a Victorian miss with a fit of the

268

vapours. This lily livered creature was not me. I shook my head at him. "I'm sorry. I'm not usually like this."

"You've not usually nearly died by strangulation." His words were hammer blows to my heart. I could only stare at him in horror. It had not all been a dream then? The memory of my lover's hands around my throat, the swirling blackness that I had welcomed so eagerly.

"What happened?" How had I ended up here? Where was Jem?

Craig looked at me then in a way that sent lightning bolts of shock to my core. So familiar. Such a deep and penetrating look. So different from all the times he had looked at me with disgust or disdain clouding his eyes, or turning them icy cold. Now they were probing, but with a questioning light that made them burn with fire. What stoked that fire, I wondered?

"What can you remember?" He turned the tables back on me.

I held his gaze for a moment, and then with the flaming betrayal of my blushes, dropped my eyes. "I was with someone."

Dear God, how could I tell him that I had another lover so soon after Tim? How shameless would that make me look? And how much did I care what he thought!

"This Jem," he prompted. "Sally has told us that you were under the impression he was her gardener but that appears not to be the case. She says that you have no idea who he is, what his full name is, or even where he lives?"

It really did look bad. I was such a tramp! "That's right," I whispered, my fingers plucking at the bed clothes. In this cold, sterile environment, stainless steel and bright lights, it all sounded so utterly ludicrous. Christ almighty, if Megan had got herself entangled with a bloke under such terms, I would have throttled her for such stupidity. How naive and dangerous.

"Can you tell me anything about him?"

I shook my head.

"Okay," he said gently. Far too gently, I thought. "You were with this Jem, and then what happened?"

Still unable to look at him, I said as frankly as I could, "We were in bed. I could hear you calling. I wanted to answer, but he wouldn't let me." My cheeks burnt even hotter. "He started to make love to me, and then, everything became blurred, dizzy. I couldn't breathe."

I put my hands to my throat. "I could feel him squeezing the life out of me, but I couldn't stop him. Because I wanted him to." I started to cry silent tears. "He wanted to take me with him, but he didn't say where. He was trying to kill me wasn't he?"

Craig let me have a moment. He breathed in a heavy sigh. Stood up and walked over to the window where he looked out for what seemed like a long time. When he turned back to face me, there was an expression of deep concern and puzzlement on his face.

"You heard me calling?"

"Yes."

"And he was with you then?"

"Yes."

"What have you done with him?" I suddenly thought to ask. Was Jem right now locked up in a police cell? The thought of it ripped my heart in two, despite what he had tried to do.

"That's just it, Eve," said Craig, dropping back into the chair with a heavy sigh. He snapped his notebook shut and shook his head. "There was no one in the room when I found you."

"So he must have left."

"No. I was at the door calling to you, remember. You didn't answer, but the door was unlocked. Your car was there and I presumed you were too. I was worried about you. You had looked so ill the night before. As if something was draining you completely. When I stepped inside the cottage, I heard it. Felt it."

"What?" I cringed to think of him downstairs, listening to our lovemaking.

He shrugged his shoulders. "Eve I'm a policeman. I've spent twenty odd years on the force. I've come up against armed robbers, murderers, rapists, you name it. I came back to Maypoleton after my wife died for a quiet life. Small chance of that with you around." A touch of humour softened his mouth. It made him look quite boyish.

"But all of that doesn't compare with what happened in that cottage three nights ago."

I stared at him. "I've been here that long?"

"The doctors said they couldn't understand it. Aside from the strangulation it was as though all your vital signs were fading away. Anyway, back to the cottage. There was something there, Eve. But no man. No Jem."

"What do you mean, no Jem? Of course he was there he was making love to me." My fear overrode my embarrassment sufficient to make me look right at him.

"No he wasn't. Something was. Something dark, Eve, and powerful. Very powerful." He paused and again I saw a change in him. An uncertainty that was not in his usual manner. "The cottage was angry, Eve." He gave a shame faced laugh as though he expected me to mock him. How could I?

"Go on," I prompted, desperate to know, dreading the outcome.

"It was as though it wanted to stop me from entering. Things flew at me, ornaments, vases, pictures fell off the walls. The ash from the fireplace hit me in my face as though it had been thrown. And from upstairs, I could hear..."

I blushed deeper and covered my face in my hands. I could only guess at what he had heard. I was wrong.

"I heard a storm raging, Eve. Wind howling. It was terrifying. I tried to get up the stairs but something kept pushing me back. Twice I was knocked to the bottom of the stairs. I cracked my head on the banister, got a hell of a lump." He touched it gingerly now. "But I wasn't going to let it stop me."

No, I thought. Not even a demon from hell could stop Craig Hawthorne if he decided he was doing something. Not a demon or whatever it was that I had shared my bed with. I looked at him blankly, as he continued.

"I had to kick the door down, when I finally made it to the top of the stairs, that is. And it stopped. Just like that. As soon as I entered the room, it was over." He looked me straight in the eye. "There was no one there, Eve. Just you. On the bed. So close to death, I thought I was too late. Barely a pulse, Eve. And on your neck, finger prints, as clear as those on my own hands."

I started shivering then. My teeth began to chatter and I huddled up in the blankets, wanting to pull them over my head and to yell at him to go away.

"Eve?"

"He was real," I insisted. "He was there."

"Something was, Eve. And it tried to kill you. Very nearly succeeded." Craig poured me a glass of water and held it out for me.

271

My hands shook as I took a mouthful, wincing slightly as I swallowed.

"Are you telling me, that Jem, my lover, doesn't even exist?"

"I am saying that when I found you in the cottage, which at that time, by your own admission, you were making love with him, there was no one there. And yet, clearly, seconds before I got into the room, someone, or something, had tried to strangle you. Seconds, Eve. That's all it would have been. Any longer than a minute, say, and we wouldn't be having this conversation."

I shut my eyes. Tried to shut out the horror and the pain. Jem was real. Wasn't he? But then which was worse? To have a lover who wants to kill you? Or have a ghost try and do the same?

"Am I going mad?"

"No more than I. I spoke to Seth. Or rather, he came to find me when he heard. He told me things he thought I ought to know."

"Such as?"

"Such as only a fool refuses to believe in spirits and ghosts and the power they can wield. I'm no fool, Eve. I'm a man of logic and order but I'm no fool. I know when I am experiencing something out of my understanding. And just because I don't understand it, that doesn't mean that it isn't real." He paused. "He also told me that he had felt something around you for a long time. A dark cloud that threatened you. He had thought at first it was all the trouble in your family."

Was there now, the smallest hint of sympathy when he looked at me?

He continued. "But now, he realises, it was much worse than that. He went into the cottage after the ambulance had brought you here. He told me that the energy created by whatever, or whoever it was, still lingered, and that you must not go back there. At least, not until it has been laid to rest."

I nodded at him. A glimmer of understanding beginning to creep into my consciousness.

"I think I know who Jem is. Or was, rather," I said, my voice breaking. "Oh dear God, how is it possible? How can I fall in love with a ghost? He was so real! I could touch him, feel him. He loved me! I know he did." And then I thought about it. "No. No, it wasn't me he loved. It was someone else. Someone from a long time ago." I let the craziness of it all wash over me until a sliver of hysteria poked out.

"How typical of me," I snorted back my tears, wild laughter threatening to take over. "I marry someone who's gay, I then do a Mrs. Robinson and tear my family apart, and to top it all off, my final choice of lovers is a ghost who wants to kill me." I did start laughing then, in between sodding great gulping sobs.

Craig just sat there and let me get it out. When I had finished, he passed me a box of tissues and proceeded to collect the sodden ones and tip them in to the bin for me.

Then he asked quietly. "Is there anything I can do for you? Get you?"

I blew out an exhausted sigh. "A bottle of malt would go down great right now. Might as well add alcoholism to my sins of debauchery and lunacy."

"You're not debauched, Eve. And you're not a lunatic either."

"No? Well what am I then?"

"Different." He said with a smile. "You're definitely different." He left me then, alone with my thoughts.

When the doctor said I could go home, I was surprised to find Megan and Jake in the waiting area. I had called Sally to ask her if she could come and pick me up. It was further surprising to see the bunch of flowers that Jake awkwardly held out to me.

"These are for you."

"They're beautiful, thank you."

They exchanged a look. "Sally told us she was going to take you home to her place," said Megan. "But we want you to come home. With us."

I stood there amidst the hustle and bustle of the hospital and wondered if these walls had witnessed many other similar family reunions. Did a brush with death bring people back together again?

"Are you sure?"

"Yeah." It was Jake who answered. "It doesn't mean that I'm cool with what you did. I still hate the thought of it and I don't think you should have done it."

"But we hate the thought of losing you more," interrupted Megan with a sharp look at her brother. "And we can sort of see that you were in a bad place. What with finding out about Dad and everything."

"How is your Dad?" I asked, not wanting to move from this neutral ground until I was a bit more certain of my footing.

"He's...coping," said Megan.

"There's been a lot of shit flying round the village," said Jake. He shoved his hands in his pockets and scuffed his boots on the clean tiles of the floor. "It's been as bad as when everyone found out about you and Tim."

"I'm sorry." I felt tired suddenly. Not ready to face yet more drama and fall out. I went to a row of chairs, and sat on the end one. "You'll never know how sorry I am about the whole damn mess. But there is nothing any of us can do to change your Dad. He is what he is and he's tormented himself long enough without others sticking the boot in as well. It isn't his fault you know. He can't help it."

"We know that," said Megan sitting beside me.

"But he still should have told us," said Jake. "He should have told you. Before I mean, not left it so long."

"I don't want you turning against him. He's your Dad and he loves you to bits."

Jake looked uncomfortable. "How can you stick up for him? He didn't do the same for you."

I pitied them their dilemma. To suddenly be faced with a choice of which parent to stand by and which to potentially alienate. No child should be put in that situation, however young or old.

"Because in a weird way I will always love him. He gave me you two. How can I hate him for that? Besides, some people are just tougher than others." I shrugged my shoulders. "I grew up differently to your Dad, it made me stronger. But that doesn't make him any less a man. Or the fact that he is gay."

There was a pause as they digested this.

Then Jake got fidgety and spoke. "Are you coming home?"

How could I refuse? I sat in the back of Megan's tatty little car, clutching my flowers and wondering what it would feel like to be back in my own home. No question of course about going back to the cottage. I shivered. I still could not grasp the enormity of what had happened there. Fortunately, Sally had done a sterling job of keeping things quiet at that end and only Craig, Seth, and my family actually knew about the strangulation by persons known or unknown, alive, or dead.

Everyone else had been told I had been struck down with an attack of food poisoning. There had been quite enough gossip decided Sally, and Craig, it appeared had agreed with her. I was grateful for that. The thought of facing ghoulish questions from nosy villagers was too much to cope with. Craig had also told me that in light of recent events, he was not going to do anything about the matter of blackmail and kidnapping between Deidre and myself.

He was, he had told me, thinking of Megan and Jake when he made this decision. It would serve no purpose to prosecute either Deidre or me, providing we could both promise to live opposite each other in a civil and responsible manner. I had nodded so hard my head had hurt. Yes, yes, I could promise that. Besides, I had told him, I didn't think I would be living opposite her for much longer anyway.

But when Megan turned her car into Cooper's Fold, I saw that the For Sale sign, outside our barn at number three, was no longer there.

"We're not ready to move," said Megan when she saw me looking. "It's too soon. We need to take stock of things before we can move forward, all of us." Then, when I must have given her a quizzical look, she blushed and added. "I've been having some counselling at university. Talking things through helped. Jake won't though, says it's too dippy."

He grunted. "I don't need to talk to some fancy therapist," he said, unwittingly giving me a picture of Jason in my mind. "I've got Seth to talk to. He's sound."

"He's looked after you then?"

"Yeah," said Jake, going on ahead and unlocking the door, leaving his sister to explain to me that it was Seth who had spoken to them both. Rather a lot it would appear.

"He gave us a right bollocking," said Megan "Told us we should be damn grateful we'd had a Mum to look after us all our lives, doing the best you could for us, even if you had gone off the rails for a bit." She paused. "He reminded us that you hadn't."

She held her arms out to me then to hug me. Careful not to squash my flowers, I revelled in my daughter's embrace, not thinking to wonder how Seth knew I had never known my parents.

Inside, Andy was waiting for me. There was a box of my favourite chocolates on the kitchen table and by the smell of it, a roast chicken in the oven.

"I thought we could eat lunch together."

"It's not Sunday is it?" I had lost track of the days.

"Wednesday," he answered and then went on in response to the raising of my eyebrows, "I took a few days off work."

"Oh?" I stood there in the room that had seen so many dramas played out this year, wondering if this was some cruel trick. The about face my family had done was so swift and full on, it was hard to digest. Nice, but hard. I think I was still too shaken about Jem to really trust in anything at the moment. My whole world had turned into fantasy, why not this set up too.

Andy started to look uncomfortable and I realised I was frozen, holding my flowers, and staring at them all in disbelief.

"We thought we could maybe have a truce?" he said. "I know I handled things badly, I should have understood more the effect everything would have had on you."

Everything. The small matter of his lies. Years of deceit. Months of betrayal. A life changing confession. Yes, he should have been more understanding. But who was I to condemn? I had spent the last few weeks closeted away with a phantom lover who had wanted to kill me.

I took a step forward and then another. And released my flowers into the care of Megan who set about putting them in a vase. I watched, numbly, as Jake opened a bottle of wine and began to pour. It was Megan who made the toast, hesitantly, maybe, but with a look in her eye that told us we all had to respond.

"To new beginnings."

I raised my glass and found that my son could look me in the eye with, if not his old easy love, at least a lessening of the hatred. It would have to be enough for now, I told myself, as I began to tuck into the meal. I was starving I suddenly realised, and ate with an appetite that had been missing for weeks.

I was treated like an invalid the next couple of days, which for the first time in my life, I did not object to. The truth of the matter was, I still felt disgustingly weak and had dizzy moments that sent me leaning on a wall, or finding the nearest chair quickly. It was, Seth told me, the probable after effects of an intense supernatural experience.

He came to visit me the next day, bringing not flowers, or chocolates, but Melody Farthing's diary.

"You need to finish t'story lass. 'Tis wot's all abut. This Jem and his sweat'art need to lie together again. Need to be at peace."

I could understand that. We were sitting in the conservatory, me with a rug over me, despite the warmth that came through the glass, and Seth with his shirt sleeves rolled up to the elbows and his top couple of buttons undone. Caitlin had sent a bottle of homemade elderberry cordial and we were enjoying a glass as we sat in companionable silence. I was grateful for that silence. To just be with someone who understood without the need for questions or probing looks.

Megan and Jake had been very good. They had not pestered. But I could see they were holding back and would pounce upon me as soon as I had got my strength back. I couldn't blame them. Once they had got over the shock that I had nearly died, there was a certain amount of glamour and excitement to be had at the thought that a ghost had nearly taken me 'over to his side'.

I held my hands out for the diary, almost reluctant to take it. When I had first started reading it, all it had been was a story. A glimpse into someone else's life. Now it was so much more. How could I bear to read the words of the woman who had loved Jem before me? How could I absorb her pain as she grieved for her love, whilst all the time I was grieving for my own?

You see that was the really cruel twist.

Whether Jem had been real or not, alive or a ghost from the past, I had fallen in love with him. I had been ready to give him complete possession of my soul, to the extent that I had welcomed him taking me through that thinnest of veils, the curtain that separated life and death. He was the other half of my soul.

I would hear what Melody had to say, but not just yet. I wanted a little time to keep some small part of Jem to myself. And over the next couple of days, as I regained my strength, I spent most of my time, gazing into nothing, and letting my mind slowly say goodbye to a love that was impossible. A love that had never really existed. A love that I would reach out to again, given half the chance.

I think Seth alone realised how deep the wound had gone, because it was he who insisted eventually that I got dressed and came with him to the Lodge. It was evening and the yard was quiet. He had spoken to Sally and asked that we be left alone. Sally, bless her had been consumed with a ridiculous notion of guilt that I had almost come to a 'hideous end' as she put it, at the hands of her ancestor's lover.

We were all convinced by now that Jem could be none other than Melody Farthing's game keeper. It all fitted really and if I had paid enough attention, I would have picked up on the references to his description sooner. But then love is blind, and none blinder than a love that is paranormal.

"How will we find him?" I asked Seth as with some trepidation I set foot on the yard. It had been a beautiful mid-April day. Easter Sunday in fact. The sun was just setting through the trees, the sky pinky gold with the promise of another bright day tomorrow.

"We open our eyes, lass. Look t'what others cannot see. Take my 'and, lass. Stronger connection w'i two'o us."

And when he clasped his hand in mine, I didn't need to question any more that Seth had the ability to find where a ghost lay. There was an energy that seemed to crackle between us. I gave him a searching stare, which made him smile. Then we began. We walked for hours that night. In slow, thoughtful paces, beginning in the grounds immediately around the cottage and then radiating outwards.

We didn't talk. Just felt. It was new to me this acceptance of a gift and in between thinking about Jem, my mind wandered to the old Romany woman I had met at the beginning of the year. She had warned me then, soon after blessing me with this gift. Had she seen the darkness that threatened to take me? Of course she had. What had been her words? Be careful where I trod? Well I was being very careful now, and although I could feel Jem very strongly around the cottage, it was clear to both Seth and I that he was not buried nearby.

Such patience, I thought, as Seth steadfastly refused to be beaten.

"We'll find 'im lass, nay fret." We were in the middle of the grounds now, close to where Sally wanted to build the cross country course and I was beginning to despair. Seth paused for a moment and told me to take a deep breath.

"Shut thine eyes, lass."

I did so.

"Open your eyes from within," he said, placing his hands over my face so I wouldn't be tempted to look. "Let yourself feel everything you felt for Jem. Don't be afraid, now, 'e cannot hurt you wi' me 'ere, I shall not let 'im. Concentrate on the love you felt for 'im. Let it guide thee."

He had such a soothing voice, it was so easy to listen to him and do as he bid me. And then I pushed past the wall of fear that had been blocking my senses and reached back to the love that had captured my soul. Opened myself to it.

And saw Jem right in front of me.

Eyes smiling, face full of love, he held out his hand and I took it.

I walked with him, felt his arm around my waist as he guided my steps.

The longest journey ever and one I did not want to end.

But it did.

He came to a halt, and placed his lips upon my brow, his dazzling silver grey eyes melting my heart once more and branding my soul with his eternal love. I felt the softness of his breath as his mouth came close to my ears.

"Forgive me."

"I forgive you," I whispered back and opened my eyes reluctant to face a world where I would never see his face again. That I knew had been my last sighting of him.

"'E's 'ere, lass, thee found 'im." Satisfaction was clear in Seth's voice as he released my hand from his.

I looked around and gasped. "Oh my word, did we walk all the way here?" Across the estate from where we had been standing, to the far end of the yard, through the car park, up to the muck heap of all places. "Oh my God, that time when I was here with Jenny, after I had been seeing Jem. I felt horrible, like I was going to faint. He's here isn't he?"

Seth nodded. "Aye lass, reckon so. Never liked being around 'ere and now I know why. Poor soul is buried there, and now 'e can get laid to rest." He put an arm around my shoulders. "Well done, Eve. I'm right proud of thee, lass."

I looked at him in surprise. What on earth had I done to make him proud of him? He looked as though he was about to say something else, but then changed his mind and said promptly that we needed to speak to Sally.

279

CHAPTER THIRTY ONE

We could do nothing for a day or so. The farmer who regularly cleared the muck heap was happy to shift that pile on the Easter Monday but what then required breaking up was the concrete beneath, and according to Sally, the cobbled surface that lay under that. In Melody Farthing's time, the muck heap had been used as the place where rubbish was left to rot down and then used for compost. I supposed it had been an added insult, intended by Melody's father, that he should bury his daughter's lover in such a spot.

It was impossible to keep such a thing quiet in the village. For one thing, the girls on the yard needed to know that the muck heap was out of action once it had been emptied. At the mention of a body being buried there, even if it was two hundred years ago, speculation began to fly from the stables to the pub, around the shops, through the golf club and Women's Institute until there wasn't a soul left in Maypoleton who had not heard about it. Once more I was a cause celebre.

Consequently, on the Wednesday morning after the bank holiday, there was quite a small crowd that had drawn up at the Lodge to nosy in on the proceedings. Not that Craig Hawthorne was having any of it. Used to dealing with mobs and gangs in Manchester, he had no trouble shooing everyone away, including a persistent reporter who wanted a story for the Maypoleton Mail.

"Thank you," I said to Craig. "Although I'm sure you have better things to be doing with your time than playing door man for us."

He gave me neutral look. "If there's a body, there's a report to be filled in. Whether its two hundred years old or two days."

Of course, I hadn't thought of that.

"Are the digger's ready?" he asked Sally who had appeared beside me.

"They are," she said. "Eve outlined an area for them to start digging earlier on."

Craig looked at me.

"I've been here a while," I explained. I had not been able to sleep a wink the night before and at the crack of dawn had gone to the yard. The stable girls had not even arrived for work yet, nor any of the livery clients. There was only Jenny around and she let me wander over the site unheeded. In the early morning light, I had opened myself once more to that sixth sense that was still so new to me.

It didn't take long. When my body went icy cold and started to shake, and an urge to be sick overcame me, I knew I was standing directly over Jem's body. I had no need to mark the spot. I would find it easily enough again.

So now, with Craig keeping the yard staff and any incomers out of the way, and Seth and Sally beside me, along with Megan and Jake, I gave the nod to Steve, the man in charge of the digger. It took a while for the thick layer of concrete to be broken up and enough of the rubble shifted to expose the cobbled surface beneath.

Then it was matter of sledge hammers and pickaxes. Jake tossed aside his hoody and went to help, enjoying, I think, the male banter that was going on between the men. Craig stood on the side lines but every now and then I was conscious of his gaze settling upon me. I knew he still found it difficult to come to terms with this whole 'haunting' business, even though he had experienced it first-hand. Sally was doing her best to conceal her excitement and her enthusiasm for the task was rubbing off on Megan. I caught them whispering together about other ghost stories they had come across. Jenny, good old, sceptical Jenny was watching with an interest that had more to do with placing a bet with Sally that there would be no body.

As for me, I could only stand there like block of ice, not daring to feel any emotion for fear that I would lose control completely. Seth knew. He stood by my side like a guard dog, protective and loving at the same time. I think I felt closer to him at that moment than I had with another person for a long time. A real person, I mean. Not a ghost.

281

At last the old stone cobbles had been moved away, the black earth exposed. Time to dig now.

Steve, the man Sally had hired, looked at me, shovel in hand. "You sure this is the spot, love?"

I nodded. "Be careful," I said suddenly. "It's only a shallow grave."

He gave me an odd look and then sunk the edge of the shovel into the ground. I was already freezing cold, but I watched as everyone else shivered. A blast of icy cold air had lowered the temperature making it feel more like winter. I saw Steve's hand pause on the shovel. He had sweat on his brow.

"Here, let me." Craig surprised me then by stepping forward and taking the shovel from Steve's grasp. He had taken off his jacket and in shirt sleeves continued to dig where Steve had outlined the grave.

It didn't take long. It was, as I had predicted, a shallow grave. Craig had only been working for about five or ten minutes when he cast the shovel aside and crouched down next to the hole. He began to clear some of the soil away with his hands. There was a gentleness and a respect in his movements that made me want to cry.

And then the smooth ivory. Two eye sockets quickly followed by a nasal cavity and a grinning mouth. Craig's hands still for a second. He raised his eyes to meet mine. I couldn't return his gaze properly. I had to wipe away the film of tears. Then I nodded at him to carry on.

Steve and his colleague stepped back as I walked nearer. I noticed that the younger man had taken his cap off. I heard Jenny swear quietly and then Sally's satisfied comment that she was fifty quid better off. Megan and Jake were now standing side by side, focusing on me as I knelt down by Craig. It was my hands that uncovered the rest of him. Bit by bit, uncaring that the soil became embedded under my nails, and that my fingers were so cold they hurt to move, I uncovered my love.

Around his neck was the silver cross.

I lifted it carefully from the bones and soil, my hands shaking and my body ready to fall into the grave with him. I would have done too, had Craig not gently caught me and pulled me to my feet. Then I was in Seth's arms and holding the necklace tight in my hand, I leant against the old man and wept my heart out.

The rest of the day passed in a drunken haze. Megan drove me back to Seth's field where Caitlin took over. She tucked me up in Seth's van and poured me a glass, a very large glass of Jojo's home brew. I gulped it down as I poured out my grief and horror, crying against her shoulder, before finishing another couple of glasses. Then, cocooned in multiple layers of blankets, I slept.

Two days after discovering Jem's skeleton, Sally and Mary came to visit me at home. I had been tempted to stay sheltered in the easy warmth of Seth's family, but as I told him, I had to work at rebuilding my own. Andy had gone to work but not before making sure I was okay. I know the thought of anything supernatural terrified him and he seemed a little in awe that I could be so deeply involved in something like this.

Equally, Megan and Jake did not quite know what to make of it all. I had shown them another aspect to their mother that they had no prior conception of. Maybe this was no bad thing. Perhaps having a mother who consorted with ghosts, in some way atoned for having a mother who consorted too closely with friends their own age? I had certainly acquired another status in the village now, as the number of my visitors proved. Most of them, I turned away.

But Mabel from the bakery, I welcomed into my home eagerly and not just because of the chocolate brownies she brought. I spent a cosy half hour with her whilst she steadfastly refused to ask me anything at all about Jem and instead regaled me with colourful tales of her own spooky experiences. She left me with a smile on my face and an invitation to join her and a group of close friends one evening.

"Don't worry, dear, there's only me and one other from the village, the rest come from around and about. You might find you have a lot in common with us."

"How many are there of you?" I asked her with a twinkle in my eye.

"Twelve for now," she replied with an answering glimmer. "You would make thirteen, and then we'll be full up."

Great! I was being invited to join a coven. Shortly after Mabel left, there was a knock on the door, and I went to find Sally and Mary standing there.

"Mary would like to say something to you," Sally greeted me with a beaming smile and a hand behind her mother-in-law's back to push her forward.

It was a sniffy apology but at least it was being offered. "I'm sorry for being so hard on you. Things were different in my day." Then she thrust a tin into my hands. "I've baked you a cake."

It seemed I was soon going to put back the weight I had lost. I invited them in and made coffee and in the cosiness of my lounge, a fire going to ward off the chills I still felt, I told them the rest of Melody's story. It wasn't pretty.

After her father had murdered Jem, he had ordered her to marry the Squire as soon as possible, but Melody had spoilt those plans by declaring openly that she was expecting a child. Confinement in the cottage followed with only her old nanny to keep her company. It was a difficult birth and the nanny begged Melody's father to get the doctor but he refused.

He had raged at his daughter as she lay in the agonies of childbirth, cursing her for bringing shame on him and shouting that he hoped she died and the brat along with her. No bastard son of a gamekeeper was going to grow up on Farthing land. He would see to that. And then he had left her. Melody had not died. At least not straight away. She clung on with enough strength to see her son born.

And then in desperate fear of what her father would do enlisted her nanny's help. Before her father could take her son, the nanny did. He was put into the loving care of a woman in the village who had also just given birth to a child who had not survived its first night. The infants were swapped and when Melody's father came to see her take her last breath, bleeding to death in the bed she had lain with Jem, he was satisfied that what he thought was his daughter's bastard was also dead.

I had cried when I read the last entrance. The words were shaky as Melody had obviously struggled to write. But she had been determined that an account would be made somewhere, of what had happened. The faithful nanny had then hidden the book to be found one day two hundred years later.

Sally was in floods herself when I finished retelling the story and even Mary looked suspiciously damp eyed.

"Bloody hell, Eve, what a story. Poor Melody and poor Jem. No wonder they wanted the truth to be told. But what a long time to wait." She wiped her eyes with a tissue and gave her nose a blow.

"I wonder what happened to the child." Mary said quietly.

I said nothing. I had my own enquiries to make first. For now though, I wanted to sort out what was going to happen to Jem. We all agreed that he had to be buried with Melody and Sally promised me she would badger Reverend Michael to get it arranged as soon as possible. I shook my head. It was my responsibility. I would do that. Besides, I needed to ask him if there were any old parish records still in his keeping.

It turned out there were, and the following day, having persuaded him to bury Jem alongside Melody Farthing, he allowed me to look at the old records. He wasn't altogether happy about having me in the church, or looking at what he deemed his property, but the mention of a donation to the church roof funds soon made him forget my behaviour earlier in the year.

There was no reason to delay the burial and the following Sunday, after the morning service, Jem was finally laid to rest. It had taken us a while to actually locate Melody's grave, as it was separate from the family crypt. It was a lonely spot in the far end of the church yard, neglected and over grown. I had cleared away the weeds and moss and had ordered a new head stone to be erected in place of the original one which only bore Melody's name and her dates. Now everyone would be able to see where she lay and who she had loved.

To be fair to Reverend Michael, I didn't like the man, but he served Jem well. The small ceremony, attended by only those I considered part of the story, was dignified and meaningful. I dropped a single yellow rose onto the coffin as it was lowered carefully into place and as I did so, I heard that girlish laughter ringing in my ears.

"Be happy now," I whispered to them both and walked away from the others, needing to be alone.

It was a strange kind of grief to experience.

How do you cope with the pain that you have lost someone you have fallen in love with? How do you come to terms with the knowledge that this person was a ghost? How is it possible to wish that they had taken you with them? Over to the other side. To death and beyond.

You see, that was what I faced. A lifetime now without Jem, when I could be lying with him for eternity. I suppose it was justifiable that the shock of it all led to a deep slump in my mood over the next couple of weeks. Despite the fact that Megan and Jake were beginning to show signs of acceptance over everything their father and I had done, I felt removed from them. Detached.

I went through the motions. Got back into the household routine. Listened to Andy tentatively talking about how we could move on. Went to the Lodge. Helped Sally. Rode my horse. Walked my dog. But I wasn't really there. It was a shadow in my place. My soul, I felt, had trespassed into another land and did not want to return.

I attended Seth's birthday party, along with others from the village, who had now got to know the old man and no longer saw him as a threat. My gift was a wooden carved horse which reminded me of Bracken. I put care and thought into the card I made myself for him. I stood next to Caitlin as ladles of hot pot and home-made red cabbage were served out. I watched Jake and Megan chatting to Shaunie and Bella, together with Lexy and Mark and a few other youngsters from the village.

I tapped my feet as the fiddles played, and Jake joined in with his guitar. I danced in the warm evening air with Benjy and Jojo and even Andy come to mention it. I probably laughed too, as everyone else was having so much fun. And a tiny part of my brain registered that Craig Hawthorne, looking younger and more handsome in jeans and a light grey sweater, had a smile that was every bit as warm the evening sun.

But I wasn't part of it. Not anymore. I had left them all behind and only my body was there. It felt as though I was watching myself from outside and I had no idea if I was ever going to be able to reconnect my mind with my physical presence. And to be truthful, I really didn't care.

So much so, that when Andy's parents came round to visit one day and he told them about Jason, I didn't even feel satisfaction at watching their faces contort with horror, shame, and dread. It should have made me laugh. It should have been payback for all the sanctimonious crap I had had to swallow from them over the years. It meant nothing.

I just simply didn't feel anything, because there was nothing left to feel.

And then one morning, sometime after the May bank holiday, which had seen the local children dancing round the ancient pole that had given the village its name, something happened which roused me out of my stupor.

Another shock. But this time, the sweet far outweighed the bitter.

I was sitting in the back garden with Skip at my feet, thinking that I really must get round to doing something about it. But not today. Maybe tomorrow. A sudden urge to rip out the sensible shrubs and replace them with whimsical roses tugged at me. And with it a dreadful pain that was too much to bear. An image of Jem snapping a rose off its stem and handing it to me.

No. I could not plant roses. Could I ever bear to smell one again?

I drew my feet up beneath me and sat huddled like this on the bench, arms around my folded knees, head tucked in, tortoise like. Not even the gentle nudging of Skip's cold, wet nose was enough to shake off my despondency.

And then I heard him barking. A welcome to someone coming into the garden from around the side of the house. I stifled a groan. Go away! Leave me in peace!

"Ay, lass. Thee must put it be'ind thee." Seth's voice held pain as though he too could not bear to see me suffering. The bench creaked as his weight joined mine.

Only for him would I raise my head and pretend to smile. But as I opened my eyes I saw Benjy and Jojo standing there as well. Okay, so I could manage a smile for them as well.

"That's better," Benjy smiled back and sat on an upturned plant pot, his long legs sticking out untidily. Jojo perched on the end of a small section of stone wall, a serious expression on his usually impish face.

"What's wrong?" Of course something must be the matter for nothing these days ever seemed to be right. "Are you leaving?" I suddenly knew that must be the case. Benjy and Jojo had only supposed to be visiting for a couple of weeks in April and now we were into May. Seth would be going too. My heart sank further and I shoved my head back into my tortoise posture.

287

His hand gently stroked my hair. "Benjy and Jojo have to move on, lass, they'm travellers. Rest o' their kin is away o'er in Scotland. 'Tis time for 'em to join 'em."

"And you're going with them," I said to him, lifting my head up once more. I was teary eyed and snotty nosed by now, but that didn't matter. "I shall miss you Seth. You've become a true friend. You all have."

There was a long silence then. A shuffling of feet from Jojo, a fiddling of the thumbs from Seth and finally a frustrated grunt from Benjy.

"Oh man, are ye not goin' to just tell 'er. Ye came all this way, waited so long. Will ye not just spit it out, or do we 'ave to do it for thee?"

"What?" I sat up a little straighter. What more did I need to face? What more horror lurked around the corner for me? I looked at Seth and saw an expression on his face that terrified me, for reflected in his own eyes, was fear. What did the old man have to so afraid of?

"Is it to do with Jem?"

"Nay, nay, lass." He covered my hand with his. It was shaking. "Thing is." Another heavy silence that lasted until Jojo burst from the pressure.

"He's your Da."

Seth hissed between his teeth but his eyes met and held mine. Eyes, I realised stupidly, which were so like mine. A swirly mix of blue, green, and brown, as though God had been unable to decide which colour to settle on.

"You're my Da." It seemed right to use the term that Jojo had. I said it again. "You're my Da."

"Aye, lass."

"I've never had a Da." I said stupidly.

"Is it too late for thee to 'ave one now?" His voice broke and his dark wrinkled face streamed with tears. His bottom lip trembled as he waited for my reply.

"It could never be too late," I clutched at him and in reaching out to my father a small part of me began to climb out of the pit into which I had fallen.

CHAPTER THIRTY TWO

Perhaps it was the similarities in my own story that sparked the connection with Jem and Melody. Or maybe simply that my heart had been broken and I was reaching out for love of any kind. But as Seth put forward the missing pieces of the jigsaw puzzle, I could only wonder at the cruel games that were often played upon us.

His voice, shaky at first, Seth took me back to a time when he was younger. A fine strapping man of twenty eight, looking much like Benjy did now, only with different eyes. He would have been dashingly handsome, I thought, enough to make any girl lose their heart, especially with his kind nature. He was that rarest of species, a true gentle man.

And my mother, well, listening to the love in his voice, she was nothing short of an angel walking on this earth. A dainty slip of a thing, fine-boned and fair-haired with the voice that could rival bird song. Only eighteen, the vicar's daughter and never been kissed. Protected and sheltered all her life, she was forbidden to go to the fair as it travelled through her small village, a long way from here, in Devon.

It was the first time my mother, Faith was her name, had disobeyed her father. She had gone to the fair with friends, and had met Seth. Did I believe in love at first sight, he asked me? Who should know better than I the force with which that thunderbolt can hit you? Oh yes, I told my father with a squeeze of his hand. I believed in almost anything now.

Seth had wanted to do things properly. Asked her father for permission to marry her. Was refused. He was thrown off their property with a threat of the police if he ever came back. Faith's Mother had given him a letter from her, saying that she had changed her mind it had all been a mistake. Of course the letter had not been written by Faith at all, but he only found that out much later.

His face had gone dark and grim and I was hesitant to ask for more. But I had no need to probe. The stopper had been pulled from the bottle and Seth could not now hold back. He carried on, a heavy bitterness in his voice and I ached for him, hearing the regret that he had been too trusting of those who had played him false, and not trusting enough of the girl who had won his heart.

She had been pregnant of course. Her mother, terrified of what her husband would do, had sent her away to her aunt to keep the whole thing hushed up. It was my great aunt who delivered me and left me on the hospital steps, at dusk, hence my name. And it was my aunt who years later paid the post mistress in the village where Seth and Faith had met, to pass on a letter, should the fair ever pass that way again.

It was a letter written by a dying young woman. Cancer took my mother. She was only in her twenties. Two years passed before Seth received the letter, along with one from my Great Aunt Beatrice. She helped him then, to track me down at the home of the adoptive parents I had been settled with. Watched me playing in a garden with other children. I would have been around five years old. I looked happy. Well cared for.

And that was exactly what the authorities had told him when he had tried, with Beatrice's help, to claim me. It would be unfair, the social services had said, to uproot me now. Besides, surely he could see that I would have a much better chance in life where I was?

I could well imagine the opposition he had faced.

"Broke m'eart all 'o'er again it did, leavin' you," said Seth hoarsely. He was looking out into the distant land of memories, and the pain was clearly etched on his face. "But I 'ad to do right by thee. You were 'appy." He turned to me suddenly. "Tell me you were 'appy, child?"

How could I break his heart once more? How could I tell him that not much longer after he had seen me that I was moved from those adoptive parents who turned out to have a drug problem? There on after, traumatised from the separation, I never settled again with anyone else. Moved from home to home, courting trouble, kicking back against authority.

I leant towards him and kissed his cheek. "I was happy."

We sat for a while, hand in hand, alone as Benjy and Jojo had quietly left us to it, and then I asked him how he had found me this year.

"'Twas my mam's doin', your granmam o'course. Isabella."

"Isabella?"

"Aye. She came to visit thee. Met wi' thee by th'owd oak tree."

The gypsy woman who had blessed me. Given me the gift I realised now, of connecting with spirits. She was my grandmother!

"But where is she...?" I had to stop myself suddenly.

Seth looked wistful. "'Avn't thee guessed child. Mam was already walkin' the spirit road when thee met. She died just afore New Year. Knew it was comin'. Said it t'were time for me to find thee once more. Said thee would 'ave need o' me."

"Well she was right," I sighed heavily, thinking of the last few months. "But how did you know where to look for me?

He grinned for the first time. "Easy lass. Mam's gift were powerful strong. Second sight, tarot cards, crystal ball and runes. Only one village wi' an ancient May Pole in it. Only one Eve in Maypoleton. Only one lass wi' funny coloured eyes. Just like mine. And 'ers," he added softly.

All my life I had thought my eyes were odd. Not at all pretty. Neither one damn colour or another. Now I knew they were eyes that could see beyond this life and into the next. Eyes inherited, along with that gift, from my grandmother and my father.

We spent the rest of the day talking, moving into the house when the air grew chilly late afternoon. I was cutting up some bread to eat with cheese and ham when Megan, Mark and Jake arrived back from university and college and had persuaded Seth to stay and eat a little with me. The fractures in my home were still too deep and wide for family meals these days. One step at a time.

But seeing Seth in the kitchen drew them all in.

What, I wondered, would they make of this latest bombshell?

It turned out to be a blessing. I saw a smile on Jake's face for the first time since, well you know.

"So," he said slowly, sitting down beside Seth and messily hacking off a slice of bread, "my Dad is gay, my Mum is a ghost hunter, and my Granddad is a Romany. I suppose in a weird, wibbly wobbly, kind of way, that's quite cool." And then he went on to tell me that even if he did manage to scrape together high enough grades to get to university, he was not going.

"I've decided that as you and Dad have both gone off the wall this year, I don't see why I should stick at doing something I hate, just to make you happy. So I'm going to do something with music instead. Don't know what, but I'll think of something. I'll do my exams, but don't expect much 'cos I really haven't been arsed about college recently." He shrugged and challenged me with his eyes.

I could only smile at him warmly. "I think that's a good idea, son."

Megan then commented that she was thinking of writing to Jeremy Kyle. "Honestly, Mum, I reckon they could do a two hour long special on us." She then smiled at Seth. "Welcome to the family. Are you sure you want to be a part of it?"

"Never been surer o'anythin'."

CHAPTER THIRTY THREE

Benjy, Jojo and Caitlin moved on. Summer was on its way and they had other family to reconnect with and fairs to bring to life. Seth stayed, his old caravan now a permanent feature in the field which Andy had promised me he would not build upon. Not just yet a while anyway. He had a healing touch on us all, did Seth, and over the next few weeks, wounds began to close.

Jake sat his exams but was looking ahead to a different future with more of his old sunny attitude. Megan acted as a mediator between her father and me, even going so far as to suggest that we all met Jason.

As she put it, "If we are going to have a dysfunctional family, we might as well go the whole hog." I had to admire her bravery in inviting her Dad's lover round one evening. I had to admire her courage as she handled the introductions with the diplomacy and aplomb of a woman far older than her years.

Andy and I got our heads together, without interference from Barty Briggins, or help from Ellie, and worked out a reasonable split of the family assets. He was going to move to Lancaster with Jason where they would buy a larger apartment, one big enough for Megan and Jake to stay over whenever they wanted. A small portion was going to be for Megan and Jake to help them rent a property for the next few years. It was time, they both declared, to be independent and besides, neither of them wanted to make a decision as to which parent they lived with.

And for me, a small cottage in Maypoleton. There would be me, and Seth and Skip of course. It would be enough. It would be more than enough.

But Seth argued with me one morning with a twinkle in his eye. "Nay lass, there's more for thee in store yet."

I groaned and shook my head. "No, Seth, don't say that, please don't. I've had quite enough excitement thank you very much."

He continued to grin at me, shaking his head, but refusing to say any more.

I was determined though. No more drama for me. There was, however, one last tiny thread of Jem and Melody's story that needed stitching up. I had put it off for a while, needing to let some of the pain diminish before I could make what I saw as the last good bye.

But one warm and mellow evening as the longest day approached and Maypoleton was awash with summer blooms, fragrant and heady, I decided it was time. I took the velvet pouch from my dressing table and set off for a walk. It was far too nice a night to take the car and it gave me chance to think a little as I went down the lane to the centre of the village.

I knew by now where he lived. I also knew, courtesy of Mabel, that his wife of eighteen years had died from pneumonia after a lifetime of battling MS. I knew that he had turned down more than one promotion in order to care for his wife, and that when she had died, he had returned to the place of his birth, a village where his ageing mother still lived.

I knew all this, and I also knew that I was strangely apprehensive about seeing him again. It had been weeks come to think of it. In fact not since Jem's burial. Of course I had seen him around the village, it would have been impossible not to. But we had not spoken. What on earth could we have said?

I could only blush in deepest embarrassment at the thought of how he had found me, naked on the bed, flushed and damp from Jem's lovemaking, nearly dead at his hands. And totally, utterly alone. No lover in sight, just a tormented ghost that wanted to be alone no longer.

No, it wasn't really something you could talk about easily. And certainly not with him. Not after finding me with my knickers around my ankles at Badgers Brock, wet and half naked from my shower with Tim, and then in cahoots with Benjy and Jojo as we kidnapped Deidre. Small wonder then that I felt the need to dress demurely for once in a dress, a cotton affair with tiny coloured flowers printed on it that could not possibly say slut or maniac.

He lived on Cobbler's Row, a delightful higgledy-piggedly collection of houses in a narrow cul-de-sac, three on either side. His number, I had been told, was six. Hoping this was correct I dithered for a few moments on the pavement and then pressed the bell. There was music playing in the background which was lowered in volume as I stepped back to wait.

"Oh hello?" He looked surprised to see me there. "Is everything alright?"

He was not in uniform, which stupidly I had not expected. In snug fitting jeans and a crisp blue t-shirt which stretched across his well-muscled chest, he looked far too, well, just far too! Not fair, I thought grumpily. I could cope better with him all cool and official. Not standing there looking one hundred percent masculine and very, very tempting.

I snapped at him. "Can I come in?"

"I suppose you'd better," he said with a quirk of his eyebrows.

The cottage was, unsurprisingly, immaculate. Warmly decorated in terracotta with splashes of blue and yellow, it spoke of a personality much richer than the facade he presented. Shelves lined with books which were obviously well read and not just for show, made it clear that he was a man of many interests. Walking, sightseeing, navy battles, food, history. The photos on the mantel piece told me that he kept his wife in his mind even though she was no longer here.

I am very nosy, I know, but I blushed when I realised he was regarding me with some amusement.

"Do I pass? Your inspection, I mean?"

"Sorry." I stood there, a little unsure of myself. Actually, a lot unsure of myself. Quite a novelty.

"I take it you haven't come round just to check up on how I live?" Deeper amusement this time and I think some of it was down to my uncertainty.

I glared at him again which only provoked a wider smile. Damn it he was laughing at me! I opened my mouth to say something sharp and shut it quickly. He was looking at me in such a way I couldn't speak. How could I not have seen it before?

The faintest of resemblances. Diluted over generations, but there all the same. It was in the chestnut brown hair, his darker but still ruddy in the sunlight, and the grey eyes, not quite silver, more stormy, but still with that hint of fire in them. How could I ever have thought his eyes were cold? They were just the opposite.

In fact they were burning into me now with a heat that was making me feel really peculiar. The last time I had felt like this, had been with Jem. But he hadn't been real. He had been a ghost. A phantom from the past who had bewitched me.

Maybe I was being bewitched again?

Yes, that had to be it. I was under another kind of spell, because in normal circumstances I would not be looking at Craig Hawthorne and wanting him to rip my clothes off. So I did the only sensible thing I could in the circumstances.

I slapped myself across the face. Hard!

"Ow!"

"Are you quite alright?"

"I'm fine!" I snapped. "I just came to give you this." I reached into my pocket and brought out the silver cross which I had wrapped up in tissue paper. "It belonged to Jem. You should have it."

He clearly thought I had gone mad.

"Look, can I sit down?" I asked feeling my legs going wobbly on me.

"Of course, I'm sorry, I should have said."

I sank into a cosy sofa and began to tell him the whole story which finished with telling him what I had found out in the parish records.

"You are a direct descendant of them. Melody Farthing and Jem, whoever he was, were your ancestors."

"Wow, that's some story."

"Tell me about it. Anyway," I said, standing up and holding out the cross to him. "You should have it."

His hands closed over the silver necklace. He looked at it closely for a moment and then shook his head.

"No. It should be yours. Turn around, Eve."

I stared at him dumbly, and let him place his hands on my shoulder to turn my back to him. He looped the chain around my neck, brushing aside some of my hair to do so. I shivered as his fingers touched my skin. And then stopped breathing as I felt his lips press against the back of my neck.

Only for a second and then his hands pulled me around to face him. I had no time to speak as his mouth came down to kiss me. Short and hard at first and then perhaps encouraged by my shocked gasp of pleasure, long and lingering.

God he was good at this.

I kissed him back with all the passion I had felt for Jem but this time it was real. The only dizziness I felt was that of love, not dark magic.

"Wow," was all I could say when he finally eased up the assault on my mouth. His kisses had been sure and thorough, a foretaste of what was to come. I was having trouble standing up and I revelled in his solid warmth. Then, just to check he was real, and not some ghostly apparition, I thumped him on the chest.

"What was that for?"

"Just checking you're real."

He kissed me again then, his strong hands roaming over my body, heat burning through the thin cotton dress. When his hands slid down the thin straps along with those of my bra and cupped my breasts, I moaned out loud.

"Does that feel real?" He asked as he bent his head to bite at my nipples, one by one.

"I'm not sure," I licked my lips as I looked at him under hooded eyes. "You might be a phantom, a figment of my imagination."

"In that case, I'd better make sure you know the difference," and with a smile that held the barest hint of Jem he scooped me up and carried me upstairs, ducking his head under the low beamed ceiling of the cottage.

Hours later, exhausted and satisfied beyond measure, I laid my head on his chest and listened to his heart beating.

"Well?" He asked, trailing his fingers lazily now down my limp, boneless body.

"Oh yes," I murmured happily. "Now I know the difference. Now I know."

Printed in Great Britain
by Amazon